T

Dark Inheritance

Dark Inheritance

CAROLA SALISBURY

DOUBLEDAY & COMPANY, INC.
Garden City, New York

All of the characters in this book are fictitious, and any resemblance to actual persons, living or dead, is purely coincidental.

To Larry

Chapter 1

My life was changed on a spring night in 1845, a few days before my twenty-first birthday.

I knew something was the matter with Father; I had known since the previous day. To begin with, he had been drinking heavily, as he always did when his left arm troubled him—that phantom arm that had been amputated by a ship's surgeon aboard an East Indiaman twenty years before. At the times of the wet southwesterly gales, he would complain that the lost hand and arm were plaguing him with rheumatism. That morning, he had risen early and was taking spirits at a table in the corner of the tap-room before it was fully light. By the time our potman Jesse opened the door to the first of the customers at eight, he was sunk in a surly silence. To each newcomer's greeting, he responded with a grunt—or with nothing. It was plain to see that the men did not like it: if there had been another tavern in Pennan Haven, I think we would have starved long before.

I could bring myself to pity Father, for I believed him to be a good man at heart. The loss of his arm had ruined his life, because he was a seaman, first and last. When we left Plymouth and came to Pennan Haven, after Mama passed away, and he took over the Frigate, a small ale and cider house in the narrow street above the quay, he bought himself a fifteen-foot lobster boat. Ten years later, it still stood on the jetty, freshly painted every season and cared for as a woman will care for her only child—but never used. Even in the lightest weather, no one-armed man, however strong, can handle a boat in the great undertow off Ramas Head, where the lobsters teem.

I knew he still grieved for Mama, and I was little comfort to him. Cruelly enough, the money that he had dutifully spent on having me educated far above my station as the daughter of a discharged seaman-turned-publican had only served to draw us further apart. Father, like all our neighbours, could neither read nor write; the notion that a mere girl walked freely in a strange world that would forever be barred him—that she held the key to the incomprehensible—made him feel diminished as a man. I once made the mistake of attempting to teach him to read, but it was a disaster: my patience ran out and I scolded him for being so slow to understand. He never tried again.

In recent years, his drinking and the surliness that accompanied it had become more frequent. On this particular day, I decided to take him to task. I brought his midday meal to the table and sat down before him.

"Eat up," I said brightly.

He pushed the plate aside. "I want none of it. I'm not hungry."

"Father. What's the matter?" I asked.

"Matter? What should be the matter?" His eyes were bloodshot and angry, and there was something else in their expression—a slyness—that filled me with great unease.

I thought I saw the reason for his present condition . . .

"Father. It's Luke Pendry, isn't it? He's been at you again."

"Still your tongue, girl!" His eyes flashed sidelong, searching to see if I had been overheard. There were two fishermen at the other side of the room and they were deep in conversation with Jesse the potman.

"Then it is Luke!" I persisted. "Oh, Father, why can't you shake off that man's influence before it's too late; before he drags you to ruin with himself and the others? Before . . ."

Reaching out, he seized hold of my arm so tightly that I cried out with pain.

"Will you be silent, damn you?" he shouted.

Angry and frightened, now, I shook off his grasp and got to my feet, aware that the men at the other side of the room had fallen quiet and were staring at us in awe.

"I won't be sworn at, Father," I said, as evenly as I was able. "And I'll not be manhandled by you or anyone! I'm going out."

"You can go to the devil!" he cried. And, as I turned, he swept his hand across the table, sending the plate of food spinning across the room, to strike the far wall and shatter, spilling a streak of gravy and broken food down the whitewash.

I did not look back at him, but, pausing only to pick up my shawl, went past the regarding eyes of Jesse and the two fishermen, and out into the street.

Our house was in a higgledy-piggledy terrace of similar habitations, all stone-built, with slate roofs and front windows that faced the houses opposite, which were so close that one could lean out from a top window and touch hands with someone at a window across the street. In contrast, the windows at the back gave a view of the tiny harbour and the blue-grey Atlantic Ocean that never stopped till America.

Wrapping the shawl about my shoulders, I stepped down the steep, cobbled street to the harbour. My mind was racing, and my heart heavy with dread.

The fisher-folk of Pennan Haven are a close-knit group; clannish and suspicious of outsiders, like all Cornishmen. Father—though Cornish himself—was born in far-off Falmouth, which might just as well have been the Outer Hebrides for all the help it was in winning their friendship. The key to our acceptance had been . . . Luke Pendry.

When we came to the Haven, Luke had been a man in his middle twenties. Tall and brawny, with dark, Cornish good looks, he was already the acknowledged ringleader of the fishermen. He also organised and led a band of smugglers.

Fishing the treacherous Cornish coast is a dangerous trade that brings lean profits, and in the previous century the smuggling game had put food into many a family pot from Looe Bay to Lands End. The game was not what it had been, thanks to the energy of the Revenue Officers, and to the savage sentences of imprisonment and transportation that awaited the offenders; but it still existed in isolated pockets along the coast. It thrived in Pennan Haven—and the cellars of our humble ale-and-cider house were used to store hogshead casks full of far richer beverages, upon which not a penny of duty was destined to be paid.

Father played no active role in the game; it was Luke Pendry and his picked companions who took their boats out, on the appointed nights, and met the waiting Frenchmen offshore, in the concealing darkness; but he was a conspirator and the guardian of the contraband. One day, I knew with a dreadful certainty, Joe

Button, landlord of the Frigate, would stand in the dock with Luke and the others—and be sentenced along with them.

* * *

Years before, I had decided that, with one possible exception (and more of *him* later), Luke Pendry was the most detestable male that I had ever come across. I hated the hold that he had over Father. I hated, also, the way he had come to look at me now that I was no longer a gawky schoolgirl. The only time I had ever seen Father show anger towards Luke was an occasion when the latter had put his arm round my shoulders—I must have been about fifteen then—and laughingly announced that Father was saving me for him, till I was old enough to be wed. I thought Father would strike him down, but Luke was cunning enough to see that he had gone too far, and he joshed Father into accepting that he had only been joking.

The memory of that incident came back to me when I reached the quay. The tide was in, and half a dozen boats were bobbing at their moorings. Instinctively, my eyes searched for Luke's craft, and I gave a guilty start when his voice rang out across the water:

"Hello, Susannah! Looking for me, were you?"

He was baiting hooks in the stern of his boat, and he waved to me, a mocking smile on his thick, sensuous lips.

I shook my head.

"Want to come out with me today, Susannah? I'll bring you back before dark, never fear!"

This sally was greeted by a chorus of rough laughter from the men in the other boats. I felt a hot flush rise to my cheeks and despised myself for it. Turning on my heel, I set off up the lane that led inland to Pennan village—and their laughter followed me.

I walked quickly, and the lane grew steeper. I was quite out of breath by the time I came abreast of the church and the rectory, so I paused and looked back and down. Below me were the roofs of the haven, nestling under the high shoulder of the great headland. A fishing boat was shaping course out of the harbour, trailing a mackerel wake, its brown sail shaking as it met the wind beyond the arm of the breakwater.

Tonight, I told myself, Luke Pendry and his companions would be putting out for their rendezvous. Of course, there was no moon tonight and concealment would be perfect. I would wake in the dark hours, to hear the casks being rolled up the cobbled street

4

and into our cellar below. The plans had been made, like as not, the previous night—which was why Father had started to drink heavily. For Father was a frightened man. Like me, he sensed that their luck could not hold forever; that sooner or later—perhaps that very night—a patrolling Revenue cutter would come out of the darkness. Lanterns would pick out the scene. There would be a scuffle. Fists and cudgels would be used—perhaps, even, firearms and sharp steel. At the end of it, every house in the Haven would be searched. They would find the hoard of contraband spirits in our cellar, and it would be Botany Bay for the landlord.

I shuddered, and resumed my walk, puzzling my mind for a way out.

There was no way out. Father was too deeply involved with Luke ever to extricate himself. The younger man had the whip-hand, for proof of the other's guilt lay in the mute testimony of the huge hogsheads of spirit with which our cellar was forever stocked. Let Father try to break faith with Luke, and he would be denounced to the Revenue Officers and left to take the whole of the blame.

Useless to think of getting rid of the evidence. A one-armed man and a girl cannot move hogsheads—and not a soul in Pennan Haven would help, Luke Pendry would see to that.

The sun grew hotter, and I let my shawl trail in my hand. The village was behind me and I was ascending the sloping valley that led to Landeric. I could hear the far-off sound of a running stream, and the drone of bees was everywhere; though, for all that, a great stillness seemed to hang over all.

The lane petered out into a grass track. I skirted a screen of high rhododendrons—and it was all before me. . . .

The glassy surface of a small lake. On the far bank, an ivy-covered doll's house of a temple. Beyond all that, an ascending sweep of parkland, lined each side with noble trees that cast bands of deep blue shadow, where deer cropped in and out of the spring sunlight and the shade. Above it all, high against the skyline at the head of the long glade, the many-windowed front of a great white house, with six tall columns at its porch.

Landeric . . .

As always, the wonder of it made my eyes mist with unbidden tears. Landeric had always had the power to do this to me, from the very first time. I remembered it well: an evening in autumn, shortly after we came to live in the Haven; Father and I walking,

5

hand-in-hand up the selfsame path from the village, in all the languorous warmth and breathless stillness. We had stood in this same spot, and I had told him that the great white house and its breathtaking surroundings must be fairyland. He had laughed at that, and gave it as his opinion that the people who lived up there were of flesh and blood, just the same as we.

Flesh and blood they may have been; but no other human beings of my limited experience ever looked and walked and talked quite like the lordly and insufferable Dewaines.

* * *

The Reverend Mr. Cyrus Mawhinney, rector of Pennan, who had attended to my elementary education, told me that the family name had originally been spelled De Vaine and that they were descended from one of the Norman adventurers who came over with William the Conquerer. After Hastings battle, William parcelled out England to his supporters, giving to De Vaine the long valley called Landeric, from the top of the escarpment, where the present mansion now stands, down to the Haven. For seven long centuries, then, the Norman Dewaines had lorded it over the native Cornish of the valley—and in seven centuries, they had never unbent one inch.

The present master of Landeric was Sir Tristan Dewaine, whom I knew only from afar as a tall, heavily-whiskered man with a booming voice and a scarlet hunting coat that went well with his high complexion. Sir Tristan was a widower with a certain reputation that was always discussed with sniggers and arch looks by the customers in our tap-room. Our potman Jesse had it from an aunt of his who had been in service up at the big house that the master of Landeric was "a four-bottle man with an eye for the ladies." On his son and heir, I was able to testify at first-hand aquaintance. Likewise his equally insufferable daughters.

The Dewaines never seemed to descend to the stature of ordinary folk; but always stared down their very straight noses from the high backs of thoroughbred horses; so that, in my childhood imaginings, they always seemed to be part-human, part-horse, like the mythical Centaurs. In this guise, they stalked the land that was theirs by ancient right. The winding notes of the horn told us that the Dewaine staghounds were out in the valley and that it was best not to wander far abroad, for fear of spoiling the scent or getting in the way. The clatter of their horses' hooves on the cobbled streets of the Haven warned the people to bring their small children indoors, lest they be run down. For a proud and ancient people, the local inhabitants bore the alien Dewaines' arrogant ways with a remarkable degree of acceptance; in all my days, I never heard it even suggested that things should ever be arranged any differently. Because I was educated and had widened my horizons—in books, at any rate—beyond the confines of the Haven, I regarded the Dewaines and all they stood for as a challenge to me as a person. Two years previously, I had had occasion to face up to that challenge.

It was on a day of a stag-hunt, when a fine buck had been driven to make its last stand in the very waters of the harbour. I can see him yet: defiant to the last; his fine, antlered head lunging and stabbing at the surrounding hounds, while the Dewaines and their friends curvetted their horses in the shallows, blowing their horns and holloaing for blood.

There was blood in plenty. When they had dragged ashore the slaughtered buck, I saw Mark Dewaine dismount and, having touched the dripping carcass, draw two scarlet lines across his youngest sister's brow with his daubed fingertips.

"Now you are blooded, my dear Hester," he said loudly, and all the huntsmen blew a fanfare in salute.

Hester Dewaine would have been about six years of age at that time. I shall never forget her unformed young face as it was then: wide-eyed and slack-lipped with emotion, with the bloody marks standing out against her pallor.

Later, they clattered to the door of the Frigate and called for stirrup cups. Father's hand trembled with anxiety as he snatched a freshly opened bottle of his best Madeira from Jesse and poured out four glasses.

"Take this tray and serve Mr. Mark and the young ladies, Susannah," he said. "I'll attend Sir Tristan and the other gentlemen."

I remember it all so well: Mark Dewaine, tall and soldierly in the saddle—for he was an officer in the Blues; Alicia and Jessica, the two eldest of his sisters; the newly-blooded Hester. The girls all haughty as peahens.

I took a deep breath, and . . .

"Four glasses of best Madeira at twopence-farthing a glass," I said firmly. "That will be ninepence. Cash."

Mark Dewaine's hand wavered. From under the visor of his

hunting cap, his green eyes narrowed with a sudden puzzlement. But only for a moment.

"One of the whippers-in will pay you," he said coldly. And his hand reached out again, with assurance.

My nerve nearly failed me; but I fixed my mind on the memory of the dying buck and the hounds dragging him down.

"*You* will pay me," I said flatly. "No money—no stirrup cup!"

He flushed with anger. For a moment, I thought he was going to strike me across the face with his whip.

"This is ridiculous!" he grated. "Have you gone out of your mind, girl? Where's the damned landlord? Where's that fellow Button?"

"Insolent creature!" snapped the older sister, Alicia. "Hasn't someone taught her how to behave?"

Oh, yes, I know well enough how I *should* behave, I thought. The stirrup-cup's an offering to the lordly creature on the horse; a libation for the godly ones. *You* don't soil your fingers with money, that's for the common people. One of the hunt servants will toss a handful on the ground as he rides off—if he remembers. That's the way it *should* be. But, for the sake of that beautiful creature you've just hounded to a shameful death, *this* time's going to be different. . . .

"First the money," I said defiantly. "Then the Madeira!"

"She's mad!" snapped Alicia Dewaine.

From the corner of my eye, I saw Father come running.

"What's amiss, Susannah? Why aren't you serving the ladies and gentleman?" he cried.

"There seems to be some question of payment, Button," said Mark Dewaine icily.

"Payment? . . . *payment?*" Father stared at me as if he was seeing me for the first time ever. "You're old enough to know the difference 'twixt right and wrong, Susannah. 'Tis a terrible thing, to demand money off a gentleman!"

That was the end of my small token protest against the lordly Dewaines. It seemed to gain me more kicks than ha'pence in the long run, as well as in the short. I achieved nothing, but to win for myself the scorn of Mark Dewaine and his sisters. I occasionally saw the former riding past when he was home on leave from his regiment, and it seemed to me that he always recognised me—and smiled contemptuously at the recollection.

Which was why I always made Mark Dewaine the one possible

exception when I declared Luke Pendry to be the most detestable male I had ever come across.

* * *

I could think of no solution to Father's problem, and even the magic of Landeric could not lift the weight of gloom from my mind. When the afternoon shadows had spread themselves right across the long glade, I retraced my steps back to the Haven. The harbour was empty of boats: no sign of Luke Pendry. Father was asleep in the tap-room, his head in his arms and slumped across the table. I decided I could face no more of him that day, so I went up to my room and opened the little window that let out to a view across the sea. I stood there for a long while, watching the gulls circling lazily in the sunshine of the dying afternoon. Then, feeling drowsy, I lay myself down on top of the counterpane and was soon fast asleep. It was dark when a tapping on the door woke me up.

"Miss Susannah . . . Miss Susannah, are you there?" It was Jesse.

I got to my feet and opened the door to the potman. He carried a lantern.

"What is it, Jesse—what ails you?" I demanded.

I have not yet thought to mention that Jesse—one of the dearest and kindest men that you could ever meet—was a dwarf. This is because his big heart had always seemed, to me, to more than compensate for his diminutive stature, so that I often forget his affliction. On the day, ten years before, when Father and I arrived at the tavern, with all our personal possessions and household traps piled high on a hired wagon, Jesse greeted us at the door with a one-eyed tabby cat in his arms. We inherited dwarf and cat with the business. In the years between, the cat died; but Jesse remained, to serve us faithfully with his great heart and his willing, puny strength.

"It's your father, Miss Susannah." Jesse was clearly upset about something; he was swaying from side to side and gesticulating with his misshapen little arms. "He's gone out, miss. God help me, I didn't have the courage to stop him."

"Gone out? Gone out where, Jesse?" I demanded.

"Out into the night, Miss Susannah—with Luke and the others!"

A gust of wind rattled the window frame, and a sudden flurry of rain lashed against the panes. I crossed and looked out. There was no moon, but I could just make out the darker bulk of the breakwater and the tell-tale light patch at the foot of the entrance, where the sea foamed.

"There's a storm brewing!" I cried. "Why has Luke made Father go out with him on a night like this? What use could he possibly be out there?"

"'Tisn't smuggling they're at, miss," whispered Jesse hoarsely. "Not tonight 'tisn't. The boats be still at their moorings."

I stared at him, puzzled. A strange dread was closing in on me. I sensed peril ahead and all around—with me weaponless and vulnerable.

"But you said they'd gone out, Jesse. And you still haven't told me *where* they've gone!"

"Miss Susannah! I . . ." The dwarf buried his huge face in his stubby hands. His misshapen body shook with heart-rending sobs. "I should have tried to stop the master . . . Heaven help me for what I've done!"

"Jesse! Tell me!" I put my arm around the little form, and he clung to me, crying bitterly. "For pity's sake, tell me what's going on tonight between my father and Luke Pendry! Please, Jesse!"

Another onslaught of wind set the windows rattling again, and roared in the chimney. Jesse lifted his uncomely, tear-streaked face and gazed up at me with all the misery of his afflicted life written upon his expression.

"I—I overheard it all tonight, Miss Susannah," he said brokenly. "I were in the cellar, and the cellar door were ajar, when Luke did come in and shake the master and tell him it was time to be off. Then he went through their plans for the night—twice over, to make sure that the master had taken them in, him being befuddled with the drink, like."

"Plans?" I cried. "For Heaven's sake, out with it, Jesse! What are my father and Luke Pendry about, tonight? What business are they on?"

Jesse's face was pale in the lantern-light. "Miss—God forgive us all—they've gone . . . *wrecking!*"

"Wrecking?" I recoiled in horror. "Oh, no, Jesse! NO!"

If smuggling was the centuries-old tradition of the Cornish coast, the evil crime of wrecking had long been its curse and abomination. I had thought—it was generally assumed—that the vile practice had perished with the dawning of our new age of civilisation, that such barbarity was a thing of the dark ages. Of course, I knew in my heart—everyone knew—that a civilisation which can support the slaughter of innocent animals in the name of sport and the hanging of children in the name of Law, remains a breeding ground for every other form of vileness.

And now, it seemed, I was being asked to believe that Father was one of those hellish ghouls!

"It can't be true, Jesse!" I cried. "You must have misheard them! They were planning a meeting with a French boat offshore!"

"Would that I heard wrong, miss," said the dwarf. "But 'twas as plain as your words are to me. There be a lugger coasting with a cargo of tobacco from Bristol, heading for Falmouth, but like to put in here, tonight, in the Haven, if a storm blows up. Luke had wind of this from a travelling tinker, who did some business aboard the lugger when she put in further down the coast yesterday. . . ."

Yesterday! It all fitted of a piece. The evil plan took its first form yesterday. It was then that Luke Pendry must have told my father that he might be required for a wrecking foray tonight!

And now, the weather had played into their hands. A night of storm and no moon . . .

Jesse was still babbling of what he had heard: "I swear to you that the master wanted no part of it, miss. But Luke did threaten him with ruin, if he didn't join in. They'll be needing the cellars to store the casks of tobacco. . . ."

It was true. I knew it now. Gradually, Luke Pendry had snared Father further and further into his lawless activities, till there was no way out for him; nothing he could do but wade deeper and deeper into the mire. But—wrecking!—the deliberate and premeditated abandonment of the unwritten laws of common humanity, and carried out by men who themselves earned their hard livelihood by trafficking on the bosom of the treacherous and implacable sea!

"Where are they, Jesse?" I cried. "How are they planning to do this dreadful thing?"

"Why, up on Ramas Head," he replied. "When they do sight the lugger's lights, Luke and the master will put up a lantern by the cliff edge. The others will put up another at the water's edge below. They on the lugger will take them to be the leading lights for Haven—not being able to see the true ones, because Ramas Head will be in the way. They'll turn towards the lights . . ."

"And steer straight for the great rocks at the bottom of the cliff!" I supplied. "Jesse! We've got to stop them—no matter what!"

"I'm with you, Miss Susannah!" he cried. "Curse me, for not having raised a hand against them earlier. But I was afeared, miss. Being what I am . . ." he bowed his head.

I snatched up my shawl and threw it over my shoulders. Then I took him by the hand.

"We'll face them together, Jesse," I said, with more confidence than I felt. "My father, at least, can't be so far gone in vileness that he won't listen to an appeal to his humanity. Let's hope we won't be too late!"

The faithful dwarf and I left the house together: out into the darkness and the driving rain; down the slippery cobblestones to the harbour. Not a soul was about save the two of us; all the houses were blank-faced, closed and shuttered against the gathering storm. Behind every ground-floor window where a muffled light showed thinly was gathered a fisherman's family, tight and snug against the hostile night. In how many of those warm rooms, I wondered, were wife and children awaiting a breadwinner who was, even now, doing the Devil's work up on Ramas Head? The very thought appalled me, I who had always had such a great regard for the proud and steadfast folk of the Haven.

The wind's full keenness met us when we came out of the shelter of the terraced street and on to the quay. The boats were bobbing like corks at their moorings. Incoming waves were already spending themselves over the top of the breakwater; before long, a man would move along there at peril of his life. I tried to picture what it would soon be like among the great, fang-shaped rocks at the foot of Ramas Head. And I shuddered, as if a stranger had walked over my destined grave.

At my order, Jesse had left the lantern behind, so as not to announce our approach to the cliff top. Hand-in-hand, still, we ran swiftly up the flight of steps behind the houses lining the harbour wall; raced through a boat yard stinking of wet tar and rotting bait; ducked under a fence, and set off up a steep, slanting path that led round the seaward face of Ramas to its summit.

We ascended quickly. In no time at all, the houses of the Haven were reduced to dark rooftops, and we were looking directly down upon the bobbing boats. The only lights to be seen, now, were the two leading lights—one at the arm of the breakwater, the other on the far heights of the valley—that gave sailors safe guidance into the small harbour. These were the lights that the wreckers were planning to counterfeit, for the destruction of their prey.

When the path grew even steeper, I relinquished Jesse's small hand. His poor legs soon left him far behind me. To my left, now, the path fell away to a sheer drop into the wave-lashed rocks outside the breakwater—but I felt no fear. I knew the path from the early days of my childhood in Pennan Haven, as I knew every nook and cranny of the coastline and beach from headland to headland; having scrabbled barefoot over the rocks for mussels and for gulls' eggs, and searched the rock pools for young crabs. Here, among the rain-drenched gorse that soaked my skirts, I had once come upon an adder and her young. They hid among her sleek coils, and she defied me to approach. I had not been able to bring myself to harm them, though I carried a long stick, as Father instructed me.

From the far side of Ramas, also, I had often looked down on to the men tending their lobster pots close inshore, where the spent breakers rebounded from the cliff face and pitched the little boats about like bits of chaff. The men's skill was a marvel to watch: one man to handle the oars and keep the craft stemming the steep swell, while his mate hauled in the pots, hand over hand. They all wore the heavy thigh-length seaboots that would certainly carry them straight to the bottom, with no hope of rescue, if an incautious move toppled them over the side. Hardly a man in Pennan Haven knew how to swim, for how would they learn? They all held the sea in mixed awe and detestation, seasoned with deep respect. To them, the sea was a capricious source of livelihood and not a playground.

"Miss Susannah! Miss Susannah, wait for me! Don't go any further without me!" Jesse was calling, and he seemed far away and below. I ignored his entreaties, not wanting to involve the poor, frail creature any further than I could help. I had few fears from my father—or so I told myself—but there was no knowing how Luke Pendry would respond to any interference in his murderous plans.

Moments later, I reached the top of the path and felt the full force of the westerly gale sweeping the crest of the Head. I paused there, reaching out a hand to steady myself against an outcrop of rock, my eyes trying to probe the darkness ahead. I could just make out the darker curve of the cliff top. Beyond all that was the sea where, even now, the doomed lugger could be making her way, under shortened sail, with every pair of eyes aboard her straining the blackness for the leading lights of Pennan Haven and the boon of a safe anchorage for the night of storm. There was no sign of anyone on the cliff top. No Father. No Luke Pendry.

Then, in the bright glare of a boat's lantern suddenly unshrouded, I saw both of them not twenty paces distance from me. The straighter, slighter figure of Luke Pendry was nearest to the light. It was he who had just taken away a piece of sailcloth that had been shielding the lantern; the effect, seen from out at sea, would have been like that of a light suddenly coming into view round a headland.

Father was just beyond him, near the cliff edge and looking out to sea. I watched, breathless and irresolute, my heart pounding, as Luke Pendry cupped his hands round his mouth and called down over the edge to their companions among the rocks below.

"Hoy there, Abel! Do you hear me, Ned?" he cried above the noise of the wind. "Do you spot her out there yet, hey?"

There was an answering shout from below.

"Keep looking!" cried Luke.

"I see her!" shouted Father. And he pointed out into the blackness offshore. Straining my eyes, I just made out a pinpoint of white, winking and bobbing in the distant swell; moments later, a red light appeared beneath it.

"They're keeping well offshore," cried Luke. "They'll have our leading lights in view by now, but they'll not turn in till they have 'em both in line. The wind's just right for 'em to bring her thundering in on a broad reach. By glory! I thank my Maker that I'll not be aboard her when she strikes!"

Father made no reply. I steeled myself for action. It was now or never, if I was to save the unsuspecting men out there!

"She's turning!" cried Father.

I felt my heart falter in its beat. Quite clearly, I saw the lugger's masthead light playing upon her flapping sail, as she went about. The red light moved, and then a green light blossomed on the left of it.

"She's heading straight in!" shouted Luke. "She's ours, lads! She's ours!"

A gust of wind caught at my wet hair as I raced forward, blinding me for a few moments. When I saw clearly again, the lantern was close in front of me, and I stretched out my hands for it.

Luke Pendry saw me first. He caught me roughly round the waist and dragged me to him. I screamed.

" 'Tis that confounded wildcat daughter of yours!" shouted my captor.

"Susannah!" Father's voice was raised in a wail of despair. His face closed with mine, wild-eyed in the lantern's light, slack-lipped with guilt and terror. "Oh no, Susannah! Not you!"

"You can't do this awful thing!" I cried. "Douse the light, for pity's sake!"

Luke Pendry swore a foul oath and struck me across the mouth, so that I felt the warm blood flow across my lips. I cried out with pain and tried to rake his face with my fingernails, but he released my waist and took me by both wrists.

"Leave her be!" cried Father.

"By God, I'll break both her arms first!" shouted my captor.

I felt the shock of Father's weight as he threw himself on Luke Pendry and struck at him. Luke released me, and I stumbled sideways, caught my heel in the hem of my skirt and fell heavily.

Rolling over and struggling to rise, I saw the two men locked together, grappling and kicking, in the shifting light of the lantern, with the gale tearing at their hair and coat-tails.

The lantern!

As I found my footing and set off towards it, I cast a swift look out to sea. The lugger's lights were terribly close now. I saw her straining sails, and could even make out the dark shapes of the men on her heeling decks. Surely, any instant now, they must realise their danger!

I knocked the lantern to the ground. The wick flared up and then died. We were alone in the wind and the darkness on the high cliff top of Ramas Head, the two struggling men and I.

It was then that the chilling cry clamoured upon my ears: the last utterance of a man in mortal dread. I think it came from Luke Pendry.

Turning, suddenly horrified to my soul, I was just in time to see them topple over the cliff edge—still locked in each other's grip. When I got to the edge, I was joined by Jesse. The dwarf's trembling hand clutched at my arm.

"Don't go too close, Miss Susannah!" he cried brokenly. "There's nothing we can do for them now—nothing!"

I thought I could see movement down among the rocks below. The other lantern was still burning, but even as I gazed, it flickered and went out. All I could see then was the phosphorescent whiteness of the breakers among the jagged rocks.

There was a shout from close offshore. The men in the lugger, having lost both lights, were suddenly aware of their peril. More shouts—and then, with flapping sails and a flurry of foam, the tubby vessel turned sharply into the wind, hung for nerve-racking moments in the trough of a mighty comber—and then presented her stern to Ramas Head. They had missed the outer rocks with only feet to spare, and were soon vanishing into the darkness from which they had come.

Father . . . my thoughts returned to him.

Jesse and I found a way down there; stepping from one sharp-edged cleft to another, slithering in the scree. There was a narrow strip of sand at the bottom that was covered, ankle-deep, at the far-flung limit of every wave. It was on this beach that the other men had set up the second light. It would also have been their task to deal with such of the lugger's crew who had managed to make their way ashore: those poor wretches who had escaped being beaten and broken among the cruel rocks would have been cudgelled to death in the shallows—and by fellow-seamen. The wreckers' code is implacable: dead men tell no tales!

There was no sign of the remainder of the gang; with the retreat of the lugger, they had made themselves scarce by way of another path along the cliff side. Had they also taken Father and Luke Pendry?

Jesse and I began to search; wading in the pools and scrabbling over the limpet-covered rocks in the profound darkness that was lightened only by the luminous waves that crashed, house-high, just beyond the shoreline.

It was I who found Luke Pendry. The man who had led my father to his final ruin was lying, face downwards, in a pool. The limbs were hideously broken and hung at all angles. He was quite beyond human aid. I breathed a silent prayer for his departed spirit and went on with my heart-breaking search.

"Here he be!" cried Jesse from the bottom of the cliff further on. " 'Tis the master. And he be alive!"

Alive! My heart leapt. If, by some miracle, Father had escaped that terrible drop, how different would be our life together in the future, with no Luke Pendry to blight us both. I was building dreams in the air as I splashed towards where the dwarf figure was hunched over the dark shape by the cliff wall: dreams of a new understanding between us, forged in pain and terror.

Though it was dark, one look at Father's crumpled form was enough to tell me that my dreams were in vain. There seemed so little left of the sturdy man who had once carried me on his shoulder, all of a languid autumn afternoon, up the valley to Landeric.

Only the eyes seemed alive: wide and staring at me from out of the broken face.

"Su . . . Susannah, lass . . ."

I dropped to my knees beside him; pillowed the ruined head in my arms.

"Father! Please . . ." I could not bring myself to frame the words: "please don't die and leave me alone in the world!"

His mouth worked convulsively. I realised that he was trying to speak, and bent my head closer, the better to hear him above the crash of the surf and the roar of the mounting gale.

He seemed to utter a single word, but it was stifled at birth by a hoarse rattle in his throat.

"What is it, Father?" I pleaded. "What are you trying to say to me? Can I help you? Is it about the terrible thing you nearly did tonight? Be at peace about that. You saved those men at the last moment; but for you, they would all be dead now. And, in saving them, you saved yourself. . . ."

I bowed my cheek against his. Still, he struggled to speak, but the movements of his lips were growing weaker. His hand scrabbled for mine, the fingers kneading my palm, as if to spell out the thought that was crowding all of his fading mind.

Another chilling rattle deep in the throat; then he spoke one word, quite clearly:

"*Landeric!*"

And yet again:

"*Landeric!*"

It was while I was staring down into his closing eyes, bemused, that he whispered: "Forgive me, Susannah." Then his head slumped in my arms and he was gone.

We left the two of them where they lay—for we did not have

the combined strength to carry them—and climbed the cliff-side path, to fetch some men from Pennan Haven.

* * *

My remembrances of the days immediately following Father's terrible end are vague in shape and substance. Some of the events, however, are clearly etched in my mind. I shall never forget the funeral, when the men carried the two coffins into the tiny seamen's chapel above the harbour. The bearers were all in their Sunday best of rusty blue serge, and their heavy boots rang hollowly on the stone slabs. I knew them all to be members of the smuggling gang that Luke Pendry had led; and it was a matter of particular horror to me that two of those who carried Father's coffin—Abel Trennan and Ned Hannock—were the men who had lit the light at the water's edge, to whom Luke had called down on that awful night.

The gale, which had raged without ceasing for three days and nights, roared about the ancient chapel and provided an uneasy background to the rector's quavering voice as he spoke of the tragedy that had befallen our small community; of the two brave toilers of the sea who had met their ends while going about their hazardous work.

I wanted to scream out the truth of it—but the thought of Father's eleventh-hour repentance kept me silent. Let the dead keep what rags of honour they could. The people of Pennan Haven had banded together in a conspiracy—who was I to cry out that Father and Luke Pendry had not been drowned while tending lobster pots under Ramas Head; that Luke's boat, which had been found stove-in near the scene of the tragedy, had been towed there by his former accomplices?

All the evidence had been swept away. The tell-tale hogsheads of spirit were taken from our cellar. It must have been Jesse who admitted the men; I heard the heavy casks being rolled away in the dead of night, and I pulled the sheets over my head. The secret was kept. It was as if Luke Pendry's smuggling and wrecking activities had never existed. The close-knit community of the Haven drew a tight curtain across its sins.

No enquiries were ever made. If the lugger's skipper ever reported the incident of the disappearing lights, I never heard tell of it. It is to be supposed that he and his crew never suspected that wreckers had been at work to bring about their destruction.

The weeks dragged past. My twenty-first birthday came and

went, and summer bloomed and faded. I lived in a limbo of grey emptiness, not knowing or caring what to do with myself and my life. Jesse ran the Frigate single-handed, giving me the meagre takings at the end of every day and consulting me only when it was necessary to buy in more stock. I spent most of my time in the little parlour behind the tap-room, with its bow window overlooking the sea wall, where I read or sewed in an aimless and desultory frame of mind, till one day melted imperceptibly into the next and are lost to my recollection.

And yet . . . and yet . . .

Every so often—and I remember it well—I seemed to hear Father's dying words again, and was puzzled.

"Landeric . . . Landeric . . ."

Why, I asked myself, had it seemed so important to him to squander his last, agonising efforts upon uttering that name?

* * *

It was in the autumn that I took stock of myself and awoke from my limbo. It was Jesse who brought me to it. One day, he came into the parlour and told me that the Frigate was no longer paying its way and that I should do best to buy in no further supplies, but to remain open only till all the existing stock of cider and ale was drunk and then close the doors for good.

"But what will *you* do, Jesse?" I asked him.

"Farmer Polowen 'ave promised to see me all right," replied the dwarf. "My dad did work for him all his life and he always said there'd be work and a bed for me if 't'ever came to it. But what about you, Miss Susannah? 'Tis you I'm worried for. What will *you* do? You—a young lady with a fine education. 'Twouldn't be right for you to be working with the fishwives on the quay or lifting tatties for Farmer Polowen."

"It may come to it, Jesse," I replied ruefully. "For, though Father saw to it that I could read and write, it took all his lifetime's savings. I've no fortune to enable me to live like a lady. It's work or starve for Susannah Button!"

This was perfectly true. Father had kept no account books; his business transactions had revolved round a small supply of ready money that went in and out of a battered tin cash box, which he had always kept at the top of his old sea chest under his bed. At the time of his death, there was an amount of a little over ten sovereigns in the cash box—now there were five only. Five sovereigns and the value of the stock in hand were all my capital—and it would not last me for long. As I have said, that was the day I woke up from my lethargy and took hold of myself.

When Jesse left me that day, I turned to the back of the book I had been reading, and there on the end papers I made a list of my accomplishments and the possibilities open to me. I still have the volume, and the pencilled notes I made, all that time ago, in my twenty-first year, still have the power to scare me, when I think of the slenderness of my few qualifications—and how I might so easily have taken a different path from the one I did.

> Susannah Button [I wrote], aged 21 years 6 mths. Learned elementary Scripture, Reading & Writing from the Rev. Mr. Mawhinney. Afterwards at the Misses Hunnables' Academy for Young Ladies, St. Errol (Cert. of Competence in Religious Instruction, English, French, Needlework, Drawing, Dancing & Arithmetic).
> Possible opportunities for employment:
> School teacher (Where? the Misses Hunnable have now closed down).
> Lady's companion (Where? No great houses in the St. Errol district—unless you count Landeric!).
> Librarian? Housekeeper? Book-keeper? Governess? (Where? Same argument applies).
> Conclusions: No schools in the district & no great houses (other than Landeric), which means I shall have to leave Pennan. (To where? Truro? Plymouth? Or even—London?)

Further down the page is still to be seen the one word, written in big capital letters and underlined three times:

LANDERIC!

I remember so well, how I stared down at the thing I had written, with a tingling sensation at the back of my neck and every pore of my skin puckering with gooseflesh at my audacity. The very idea: that I should presume to think that I could ever find the sort of employment I was seeking—at Landeric!

Looking up from the page, I met my own shocked reflection in the mirror on the wall opposite, saw myself as I was then: oval-faced, with a commonplace nose, dark chestnut hair, unremarkable mouth—and hazel eyes that were surely far too bold and forthright for my own good.

I smiled at myself. And why not? I thought. What had I to fear from Landeric and the mighty Dewaines? The whole world was at my feet. Slender though the capital at my disposal was, it was sufficient to take me to Truro, Plymouth, or even London; but it would surely be an absurdity to go to the trouble of plucking up my roots and setting them down elsewhere—without first exploring the only possibility on my own doorstep.

I would beard the Dewaines in their own den: present my credentials and let them know that I—Susannah Button—was willing to accept suitable employment in their household.

If Mark Dewaine and his sisters, or Sir Tristan himself, chose still to bear a grudge against me for something I had done two years before, let them. They could not eat me; only send me packing from their door.

The decision having been made, there was no point in further delay. I would go up to the big house that very afternoon.

In this way do the human heart and mind, when they have persuaded their owner into a seemingly impossible course of action, drive that person pell-mell into the fray.

Buoyed up by the heady excitement of my own daring, I attended to my toilette: redressed my hair in a modest and practical chignon, and put on my best dress of grey wool trimmed with bright red braid. This I crowned with a new straw bonnet with a ribbon and trimmings to match the braid.

I took a long, last look at my reflection in the mirror, then, not entirely disapproving of what I saw, I put in my reticule the Certificate of Competence that I had gained from the Misses Hunnables' Academy for Young Ladies and set forth.

It was a hot afternoon, hung all over with the heady scent of the harvest, and I was glad to accept a ride on an empty haycart as far as Pennan village; I sat on the tailboard of the cart, swinging my feet in delight. The long weeks of unaccustomed limbo were over and I was back in the world again. The world, let it be said, seemed very sweet to my untried and untutored gaze that memorable afternoon.

The carter put me down beyond the church. Instead of continuing up the lane (which would have brought me only to the edge of the lake and what had, thus far, been my closest view of the great house on the edge of the escarpment), I turned and walked straight into the forbidden gateway of Landeric; between the tall, granite gateposts overtopped by carved lions bearing the Dewaine arms between their paws; past the twin gatehouses and up the steeply-ascending carriage drive. No one challenged me from the gatehouses; their ears would have been attuned only to the sound of hooves and wheels; not that it would have worried me one jot if someone had come out and demanded my business. I had the answer at the tip of my tongue: "Miss Susannah Button, presenting her credentials to Sir Tristan."

The carriage drive ran in a curving path up one side of the valley, in an avenue of tall trees that shut out the view of the great house. Not till I reached the top of the escarpment and saw the drive curving sharply ahead of me did I become aware of habitation. Then, through the thinning of the trees, I saw the first hints of gleaming white stonework and the dazzling blue of the sky reflected from countless window-panes.

A little further on and Landeric was laid out before me in all its glory of terraces and colonnades; with broad, curving sweeps of steps that began at the columned porch of the central block and swept down, tier by tier, through water gardens where tall fountains played skywards and cypresses stood like sentinels. I had never seen the vast building at such close quarters; the remote whiteness that it assumed at a distance was warmed by a gentle patina of pale golden lichen. Despite its overwhelming size and complexity, it was a curiously *friendly* place, like some huge, beloved doll's house. I stopped and gazed, enrapt.

"Upon my word! Not another Dewaine come to plague me!"

I gave a start at the sound of the voice close at hand. Turning, I saw the speaker standing in the shade of a plane tree. He was tall and fair, dressed in a pale lemon-coloured suit of some silky material, a large and floppy neckcloth, and a broad-brimmed straw hat. He was quite youngish—about twenty-eight or nine was my first impression—and incredibly handsome. And knows it, too, I told myself.

"Or are you merely a visitor, like myself?" he said.

I found my tongue. "A visitor," I said.

He was a painter. There was a table set beside him which was covered with tubes, bottles, rags and vases full of a multitude of brushes. His picture was on a large easel and looked the size of a barn door. I was consumed with curiosity to see it, but the back of the canvas was turned towards me.

"Come and have a look," he said. "No need to sidle round in an underhand manner. Would you care for some champagne? No? As you will."

There was a large green bottle in a silver vessel at his feet. He took it out and filled a tall glass with the sparkling wine, till it frothed over the rim.

"A toast to you," he said. "And to this confounded picture, which will never be finished in my lifetime, the way things are progressing."

"It's beautiful!" I cried.

"Such sincerity cannot be counterfeited," he declared. "You have done more for my *amour propre* than a learned dissertation on my painterly gifts by the President of the Royal Academy himself."

It was a picture of Landeric, just as it looked from where we stood, with all its subtleties of light and shade, which he had heightened by setting a mass of tumbled clouds in the background. The very walls looked solid, and the grassy lawns so deliciously cool that you could imagine yourself kicking off your shoes, to run barefoot across them.

"Really beautiful," I repeated. "I think it's . . ."

I turned to him. He was looking reflectively at me over the rim of his glass. Something in his glance made me falter, and I felt my skin pucker with gooseflesh and the colour mount to my cheeks.

"I entirely agree," he said, smiling. He had disconcertingly pale blue eyes and a quirkish, lop-sided smile that lifted one corner of his lips.

To cover my confusion, I turned back to the painting. There was a large area in the foreground—it represented the sweep of lawn immediately in front of where we were standing—that had an incomplete look; there were thin brush marks that appeared to represent the outlines of figures.

"What are you going to put here?" I asked.

"There, for my sins, I have to paint the entire Dewaine family now extant," he replied. "For this reason, I expect to be engaged on this commission when I am a very old gentleman in a Bath chair. The Dewaines, as you may or may not know, my dear young lady, are seldom to be found."

He picked up a sketch-book from the table and opened it to show me.

"I presume you are acquainted with this gentleman?" he said.

I nodded. It was a drawing of Mark Dewaine. He looked older and sterner than when I had last seen him. The artist had represented him in undress uniform of short patrol jacket and striped overalls, lounging up against a chimney-piece, gazing out at the observer. Despite the informality of the pose, there was no mistaking the Dewaine arrogance; the calm assumption of superiority that always had the power to make my hackles rise.

"It's very like him," I commented.

"I'm glad to hear it," he said. "I drew it last week, in his quarters at Knightsbridge Barracks. He was a very bad and very impatient model. The sisters, however, were most cooperative. . . ."

I registered, with satisfaction, that Mark Dewaine was in London and that if anyone showed me from the door of Landeric that afternoon at least it would not be he.

Alicia and Jessica Dewaine looked out at me from the next page. They wore identical walking costumes, bonnets and muffs. The elder sisters had both grown extremely beautiful. I wondered if young Hester had ever forgotten that moment when her brother wiped the smear of warm blood on her brow.

"I had to travel to Paris to make that drawing," said my companion. "They are at finishing school there. But you must know that. Indeed, that's probably the connection—you are a school friend of the Misses Dewaine." He took off his hat, revealing a smooth sweep of butter-coloured hair. "It really is most remiss of me not to have introduced myself before now. I'm Durward de Lacey, at your service, Miss . . ."

I gave him my hand, the way I had been taught by the Misses Hunnable. "Susannah Button," I said.

"A visitor at Landeric," he supplied. "Staying at the house."

"Not quite," I replied. "I've simply walked up here, from Pennan Haven, to look for employment."

He gave me a surprised glance. His brow furrowed slightly giving him the air of a man who enjoyed delivering witticisms more than receiving them. Then he smiled knowingly.

"Miss Button, you are having me on," he declared. "You're a lady if I ever saw one. Come now, admit it."

Angered, I lifted my chin. "By your apparent standards of a lady, I am afraid you are mistaken, Mr. de Lacey," I replied coldly. "My father was a common seaman turned publican, who provided me with the superficial advantages of an education he did not himself enjoy. I'm sorry to have deceived you, sir. Good day."

"But, I say . . ." he began.

"Good day, Mr. de Lacey," I repeated, turning on my heel and setting off across the grass to a flight of steps leading towards the nearest wing of the great building.

His voice came after me.

"I drink to you, Miss Button!" he cried. "And I would wish you good luck, but with your tremendous style you'll scarcely need such a thing as luck!"

I smiled to myself. All in all, I had quite enjoyed my encounter with the fascinating Mr. Durward de Lacey. And I wondered if our paths would ever cross again.

* * *

A lesson that I learned immediately after parting from Mr. de Lacey was that it is almost impossible to announce one's arrival at a great house such as Landeric, if one comes uninvited.

Landeric has a central block and two wings, each of which is joined to the main part of the mansion by curving galleries. The flight of steps brought me to the grand entrance of the right-hand wing: a huge double door reached by another flight of steps flanked by statues of nymphs. There was no bell and no knocker. I drummed my knuckles on the dark oak of the door, but produced no more sound than if I had tapped it with a feather. There seemed no alternative but to try the handle, which I did. It turned as smoothly as a watch key, the great door slid open on well-oiled hinges, and I stepped into the forbidden fairyland of Landeric with the scent of waxed woodwork and potpourri at my nostrils.

I found myself standing in what appeared to be a music gallery, for there was a pianoforte in the middle of the vast open space of tiled floor, and great organ pipes rose above a vaulted loft at the far end. There were some folding chairs stacked along one wall, but no other furniture or pictures. My skirt rustled loudly and my heels set up such a racket on the tiles that I tiptoed with my hem lifted most of the way towards a promising-looking door opposite. It opened to the touch, and I was looking down a long corridor that curved out of sight and was obviously the connection with the main part of the mansion. The corridor was lined with pictures on one side; the other was windowed and looked out across the descending slopes of the parkland as far as the ornamental lake with its toy temple. There being no other way of declaring my presence save to find somebody, I closed the door quietly behind me and continued on my journey of exploration. I had by this time frankly accepted that the longer I could proceed and the more I could see of the inside of Landeric before I was challenged, the better.

I tiptoed on, past a long line of portraits, most of which seemed to be of long-gone Dewaines, in their powdered wigs and feathered hats. Without exception, they held their heads high and looked out from their gilt frames with the total assurance of their wealth and their Norman blood. How furious they made me—and how I envied them in my secret heart, for all the things I should never possess.

The corridor ended with a heavily ornamented and gilded archway that let straight into a columned chamber of such magnificence that I stopped and caught my breath with awe. Its wide sweep of floor was patterned with a carpet of coloured marble, and the shafts of the tall columns rose, ceiling high, and veined in exquisite shades of pinks, blues and greens. I wandered out across the oval-shaped floor, till I was standing on a rosette that marked its centre, and gazed up at the painted ceiling. High above a sprawling mass of painted gods and goddesses swirled across a pagan sky in chariots drawn by winged horses, and cherubs blew silver trumpets for joy.

I was overcome with a sense of almost total disbelief that such a setting could have existed so close at hand to our narrow little house in the Haven without my having been aware of it. But, of course, this was the fairyland of my childhood imaginings. This was Landeric as I had always dreamed it might be.

And this, surely, was a ballroom. In the century past, the tinkling notes of a court minuet had sounded the nights away under those regarding gods and goddesses, while the lordly Dewaines and their powdered and painted friends trod the delicate measure, hand-to-hand, advancing and retreating, under the dazzling candelabra. I could see it all so clearly.

The music of my imagining changed to a valse; I gathered up the edge of my skirt as I had been taught by the Misses Hunnable and, laying my hand in that of my partner—who was a handsome lancer in a red tunic that matched the trimming of my dress—I slowly began to circle the floor, turning the while, faster and faster as the music increased in tempo. My gallant never took his eyes from mine, nor I from his. Three times, we toured the entire room, till my cheeks were glowing with excitement and I wanted it never to stop. . . .

("'Pon my word, Miss Button, ma'am, you valse like a dream."
"I am in good hands, Captain."
"You are engaged for every dance this evening, of course?"
"Of course."

"A pity. I rejoin my regiment at midnight."

"Every dance till midnight shall be yours. . . .")

My swirling skirts caught the edge of a spindly-legged side table. With a cry of alarm, I reached out my hands to advert disaster, but it was no use. A green Chinese vase toppled to the floor, and smashed to shards that skittered away across the smooth floor. My horrified gaze followed the pieces—till my eyes met those of two people who were regarding me (and how *long* had they been regarding me?) from an archway at the far end of the room: a man in hunting scarlet and a young girl.

"Bravo!" cried the former. "As elegant an exhibition of the terpsichorean art as I have witnessed for a long time." He clapped his hands. "Join me in applause, Hester dear," he added. "This room has scarcely seen the like in your lifetime."

It was the master of Landeric himself and his youngest daughter!

Faltering some kind of excuse, I rushed forward and stooped to pick up the pieces, but Sir Tristan would have none of it. With the toe of his Hessian boot, he disdainfully kicked them to the corner of the room. Then he advanced towards me with his hands extended.

"Ma'am, I believe I have the honour of the next valse," he said. "Hester, my dear, in lieu of musical accompaniment, I should be obliged if you would clap your hands in three-four time, since, as you know, I am extraordinarily erratic with my tempi." He took my unresisting fingers and placed his right hand at my waist. "Shall we begin, ma'am?"

"*One*-two-three, *one*-two-three, *one*-two-three," chanted Hester Dewaine, clapping in time. And we set off along the greatest length of the room, with the gods and goddesses and all the cherubs looking down at me: little orphan Susannah Button, dancing with Sir Tristan Dewaine, Fourth Baronet, in the ballroom of his great house.

True, my present partner fell short of my imaginary lancer in many physical particulars. For one thing, he was old enough to be my father. The veins of his bucolic face were crazed and broken, and the front of his yellow waistcoat swelled grandly. For all that, the watchful green eyes under the grizzled eyebrows were clear and merry, and his teeth were even and white as those of a man in his prime. Nor did he lack for energy; but guided me to turn faster and faster, till I was panting for breath.

27

He brought us to an end in the middle of the ballroom, on the marble rosette, and kissed my hand with practised gallantry, eyes twinkling down at me appraisingly.

"A singular pleasure, ma'am," he said. "You must give me more lessons. But to whom do I owe the honour of . . . ?"

"She's the innkeeper's daughter from down at the Haven," piped Hester Dewaine flatly. "She was once most terribly rude to Mark, and he didn't like it at all."

I felt the colour mount to my cheeks and could have wished for the floor to open up and swallow me from their concerted gaze. But Sir Tristan laughed.

"Did you, now?" he said. "Well, there are many things in this life that my estimable son and heir will have to learn to like by the time he's my age. What is your name, my dear young lady?"

"Susannah Button," I blurted.

"Address me as Sir Tristan," he said mildly. "You have a very pretty name—which is fitting." He took my chin between his finger and thumb. "Charming. Charming. And to what do we owe the pleasure of this visit, Susannah Button?"

I took a deep breath. "I came to look for employment, Sir Tristan," I declared.

"Did you now?" retorted the baronet. "But one has heard news of your father's tragic end—for which I offer my condolences. Surely this sad circumstance leaves you with your hands full at the inn?"

I explained how the business was failing. He nodded sympathetically.

"Well, then, something must be done for you. I will send you to Mrs. Horabin, the housekeeper, who will wish to find you a place somewhere below stairs." He smiled with the air of a man who had ordered everything to his satisfaction.

I paused for a moment, then: "I'm sorry, Sir Tristan, but I had hoped for something better than a place as a serving maid."

He raised an eyebrow. "Had you, now?"

"I've been educated."

"Educated!" He seemed to examine the word—and decide it could scarcely have any real connection with me.

"I can read and write," I said. "And I am also proficient in Religious Instruction, Needlework, Drawing, Arithmetic and French." I fumbled in my reticule. "Here is my Certificate of Competence from . . ."

He waved it aside.

"Pouvez-vous avoir une conversation intelligente en français?"
"Oui, monsieur. Je le puis."

The grizzled eyebrow rose even higher.

" 'Pon my word!" he exclaimed. "Young lady, I do believe that you may have been sent here by the hand of providence itself. I really do." He eyed me from head to foot, drawing back his head, so as to regard me down the side of his very straight Dewaine nose (and uncomfortably recalling his son to my mind!). "And you say that you are competent in general subjects. Do you have any musical accomplishment—the pianoforte, for instance?"

"No, Sir Tristan," I replied. "I don't play an instrument, but I sang a little at school."

"She knows how to valse," interjected young Hester, who had been a silent witness to my interrogation. "Better than Alicia, Jessica or any of their friends. I'll have her, if she'll teach me to valse like that." With those words, the girl sat down on a sofa and eyed her father stubbornly.

I looked towards Sir Tristan, confused.

"I should explain," said the baronet, with a cold glance at his daughter, "that there are certain impediments to this little chit's continued education. Despite threats and bribery, she refuses to go to boarding school. . . ."

"I'm not leaving my darling Caprice, and that's final," declared Hester.

"Don't interrupt me, miss!" snapped her father. "She refuses to be parted from her favourite pony. One is left with the alternative of employing a governess. To date, Miss Discord, here, has caused the removal of three perfectly adequate governesses in as many months."

Hester made a face. "All of them were old and ugly," she said. "But Miss Button is tolerably pretty. And if she will teach me to valse better than Alicia and Jessica, I'll put up with her."

I stared tremulously at Sir Tristan, a great hope rising in my heart. A governess at Landeric—this was the sort of post that I had hoped for, but never really expected to be offered. If, indeed, it was to be offered . . .

"Will twenty-five pounds per annum suit you, Susannah Button?" he demanded. "Paid in advance. And if you fall out with us, or we with you, you retain the advance. How does that strike you, eh?"

I swallowed hard, my head spinning with the glory and splendour of it. "I think that is very generous, Sir Tristan," I replied.

"And I should be most happy to accept the post and only hope that I am adequate for the task."

"Hurrah!" cried Hester. "Can we have a dancing lesson now?"

"There will be no further activity," said her father, taking out from his waistcoat pocket an enormous turnip watch. "It is past three o'clock and I have much to attend to. Be so good as to ring the bell, Hester."

A bell cord summoned a young footman in full livery of knee breeches and wig, who gave me a quick speculative glance as he attended himself to his master's instructions, which were to ask Mrs. Horabin to attend in the marble drawing room.

The housekeeper of Landeric was a plump woman of some sixty years, dressed in black bombazine with a white lace cap and a chatelaine loaded with a formidable battery of keys.

"Mrs. Horabin," said Sir Tristan. "This is Miss Button, who will be commencing as governess to Miss Hester as soon as conveniently possible. She will occupy the room next to the nursery, take her meals with Miss Hester and with the family on the occasions when Miss Hester dines downstairs." He turned to me. "A conveyance will be sent down to the Haven to pick up your traps. Will tomorrow be too soon?"

"I shall be ready to come tomorrow, Sir Tristan," I replied.

"Capital!" declared Sir Tristan. "I never thought to hope that the business of a replacement governess would be settled so smartly on this very day. I look forward to seeing you tomorrow, Miss Button. Good day to you. Mrs. Horabin will show you out." He strode from the room with Hester at his heels; my pupil-to-be turned by the archway and flashed me a mischievous smile.

"The first lesson will be a lesson in the valse," she said.

I decided, there and then, that Hester was going to prove something of a handful.

Mrs. Horabin led me through a corridor to a door at the front of the house and held no conversation save to bid me good day. For my part, I was too excited to think of anything but my timely good fortune in getting employment—and with twenty-five whole pounds in advance.

I went back to the Haven by the same way that I had come. I had hoped to see Mr. Durward de Lacey again but the artist was gone and his picture with him; nothing remained but the table cluttered with squeezed-out paint tubes and the empty bottle of champagne lying by.

Chapter 2

The settling of my slender affairs at the Frigate was soon accomplished. Jesse agreed to stay on there for a few weeks till the stock was disposed of. The house, like all the others in the Haven, belonged to the Landeric estate and was rented for a few shillings a year. It was doubtful if the inn would ever find another tenant-landlord.

I packed my belongings—my few costumes, a couple of books, and a trinket box containing some cheap pieces of jewellery that had belonged to Mama—in a wicker hamper. The portable furniture of the house amounted only to two beds, a table, some chairs and a cased clock: these I gave to Jesse, who lived with his widowed mother a few doors up the street. I could not bring myself to sort through Father's gear in his old sea chest, let alone dispose of it—so the chest went with my wicker hamper, in the governess cart that was sent down from the great house to fetch me.

Jesse and his mother waved me off, and on the way through Pennan village I was hailed by the rector, who waved to the driver to stop. The Reverend Mr. Mawhinney was a pouch-eyed man with a twice-around neckcloth and gaiters, who had always seemed as old as Methuselah to me. Though he had played his part diligently in my elementary education, I had never learned to like him. He always contrived to give others the impression that he had taught me out of charitable kindness, though I knew well that

Father had paid him for his pains. In later years, when experience had taught me understanding and compassion, I had come to appreciate Mr. Mawhinney's position as the younger son of a local landed family, condemned by the laws and customs of primogeniture to a poor living in a tiny parish like Pennan. I had learned to pity the way he clung to his few rags of pride: to the pieces of good furniture and pictures that various members of his family had bequeathed him; and to the fact that he had attended Harrow School at the same time as his patron, Sir Tristan Dewaine.

He had heard about my new employment at the great house and was full of good wishes for my success and happiness. With voice trembling with emotion, he declared that it was with pride that he consigned his dear ex-pupil to the care of the Dewaines. A very satisfactory solution to my affairs, he added. I kissed his cheek and we went on our way.

I was brought to a side door of the main block of Landeric, where a shirt-sleeved manservant and a little under-housemaid were waiting for me and my gear. The girl—she could not have been more than thirteen—dropped a curtsy and gave me a large-eyed look. Would Miss please follow her to her room?

I followed her up a back staircase, to a broad corridor that ran along the rear part of the mansion. She opened the door to a large and airy room that was panelled in white-painted wood. There was a brass bed with a high and comfortable-looking mattress and a counterpane of pink candlewick. A simple chair and desk, a dressing-table, wardrobe, an armchair and a small sofa completed the furnishings. Compared with my frugal bedroom at the Frigate, it was luxury indeed; and from a large window, I could look out over the back lawns to the countryside beyond the escarpment, with the rugged moorlands of central Cornwall and the blue of distant hills.

The manservant brought my luggage, and I directed him to put Father's chest in a corner of the room, where it could serve as a spare table top. Then the little housemaid curtsied again and told me that the master wished me to accompany Miss Hester to family luncheon in the dining room at one-thirty o'clock. I should find Miss Hester in the nursery next door, she said.

Alone, I caught my reflection in the dressing-table mirror. My cheeks were flushed with excitement and it was scarcely surprising. I was about to take luncheon with a fourth baronet and his daughter. Come to think of it, I was about to take the very first luncheon of my life—unless one counted the frugal midday meals at the Misses Hunnables' Academy, which were graced with that superior title. The poor people of the Haven, Father and I included, sat down to only one main meal a day—and that we ate at noon and called "dinner."

I had no watch, but discovered, when looking out the window, that I had a clear view of a stable block to the rear of the mansion, which had a clock tower surmounted by a weathervane in the shape of a rearing house. It was twelve-forty. I was wearing my best grey that I had worn on my first visit to Landeric, and there seemed no point in changing. Not that I had anything better to put on: new clothes would have to wait till I had received my twenty-five pounds advance from Sir Tristan.

To occupy my time, I took out my costumes and hung them in the wardrobe, and put my linens in the drawers underneath. My trinket box, I laid on the dressing table. It was while I was doing this that my eye caught a strange irregularity on the surface of the counterpane of my bed: as if something had been left underneath in the making, something like a slipper or a hairbrush, perhaps.

I crossed over to investigate the object; turned back the counterpane, but whatever the foreign body, it had been made into the bed. I hesitated for a moment, thinking it a pity to disturb the smoothly-laid sheets and blankets, and that it could wait till I retired that night. Then it occurred to me that the maid who had made up the bed might well be at her wit's end to know what she had done with the thing—whatever it was.

I drew back the sheets. Next instant I was recoiling in shocked horror. I drew in a choking breath, and let it out in a scream that should have been heard right through the great house.

The thing that lay in the middle of my bed, upon the bottom sheet, and formerly sandwiched between it and the top sheet, was a large and very dead rat. By its posture, it had clearly been killed in a break-back trap of the kind that we used to use in the cellar of the Frigate; a small amount of blood had issued from the creature's open mouth and had stained the stark-white sheet.

My first impulse was to run out into the corridor and communicate my horror to those who must surely come running in response to my scream; but I had not taken into account the stout walls and doors of the mansion, nor the great distances that separated the different parts of the establishment. The only person likely to have heard me was Hester in the next-door nursery—and she had not come running. I had a notion why. . . .

I have a detestation of rats that Father had fed with lurid stories of the creatures' foul depredations on shipboard, and it was with a total revulsion that—after first opening the lower part of the window—I took the tip of the thing's tail beween finger and thumb and dropped it down into the shrubbery below. I then washed my hand, pouring the water in a generous libation over my defiled fingers.

So, you have played your disgusting little welcoming prank, my young lady, I thought. You may have heard my scream, and I'm sure it will have given you plenty of amusement. But you shall not have the satisfaction of seeing me upset! Whereupon, I smoothed my hair and went out to collect my pupil for lunch.

Hester was waiting for me at the head of the staircase which lay immediately opposite the door of the nursery. Her face was devoid of all guile.

"Hello, Miss Button," she said. "Is everything all right? I thought I heard you call out."

"Hello, Hester," I replied sweetly. "How nice of you to be so concerned for me. I assure you it was nothing. Shall we go down to luncheon?"

I marvelled at my composure and thought I saw a look of disappointment cross the girl's face. I was still congratulating myself when we reached the open double doors of Landeric's sumptuous dining room; but there my marvellous composure received a rude check.

There was a tall figure in a tweed suit lolling by the window at the far end of the room. His back was to us, but he turned round at the sound of our footsteps.

Mark Dewaine had come home!

* * *

The memory of that, my first formal meal at Landeric, will remain engraved upon my memory for as long as I live.

There were four of us: Sir Tristan, Mark, Hester and myself. We sat at one end of a vastly long table; Sir Tristan at the head, with Hester at his right and his son at his left. I sat next to my pupil and nearly opposite Mark. I recall every detail. I even remember the food: there were cold joints of beef, pork and ham on cut; a dish of cold poultry; a hot meat hash; and hot rump steaks and mutton chops under silver covers; as well as cheeses and fruit. I never saw so much food, in any one place and at any one time, in all my life. We were waited on by no less than five servants: a butler, a footman and three housemaids, the men in full livery, the women in starched aprons and coifs; and all in a chamber the size of the ballroom—or bigger—with a painted and gilded ceiling and massive crystal candelabra over our heads. I was too overcome to have any appetite, but accepted a small helping of cold beef from the first dish that one of the maids offered me and ate it slowly, with my eyes lowered to hide my nervousness.

I was recoiling from the shock of the unexpected encounter with Mark Dewaine, who had greeted me with a curt nod in answer to the curtsy I had given him: no word of welcome, no reference to our previous meeting—nothing. You would have thought that I was a piece of furniture. On reflection, I realised that this was precisely how the Mark Dewaines of this world saw the likes of me: portable furniture, provided for the convenience of the rich and high-born. Mere chattel.

While I addressed myself quietly to my cold beef, he held forth in answer to his young sister's eager enquiries about life in London. This he did in a bored and disinterested manner, with constant glances towards his father at the head of the table. As well he might; I myself could not keep myself from stealing the occasional, covert peep at my employer.

Sir Tristan presented a very different appearance from the jolly, bucolic gentleman who had playfully valsed with me for his daughter's amusement in his marble ballroom the previous day. He was wearing a dark coat whose facings were rust-coloured with spilt snuff, while his neckcloth was half-untied and hanging in loose ends that trailed in his food. And he was, to my eyes, very much under the influence of drink. His plate was piled high with various meats, which he forked into his mouth in large quantities, washing it down with deep sups of red wine. He had not spoken since coming to table, but his eyes were darting from side to side, bright and angry, like those of a savage dog. It seemed to me that it only needed someone to utter a word out of place and he would explode into fury.

I was correct in my guess. And we did not have long to wait. Hester had just put a question to her brother, when Sir Tristan thumped the table with the palm of his hand.

"Strawson! Where are you?"

"Here, Sir Tristan," cried the butler, from over by the sideboard.

"Come over and stand by me, you scoundrel!" bellowed the baronet.

The butler did as he was bidden. He was a short, stoutish man and a trickle of sweat was running down the side of his face from under his powdered wig. He looked to be in mortal terror of his master, and I did not blame him.

Sir Tristan poured a half glass of wine from the decanter by his elbow and held it out to the unhappy Strawson.

"Taste that, man," he grated. "And then have the bare-faced effrontery to inform me that it's the Chateau Duclos 'thirty-five!"

"Su-Sir Tristan . . ." faltered the poor wretch.

"Father . . ." interposed Mark Dewaine, but his father silenced him with a savage glance, then returned to his victim.

"Drink—*dog!*" he ordered.

The butler's hand trembled so badly that he could scarcely bring the glass to his lips, and he choked on a mouthful. The baronet sat back in his chair and eyed him watchfully.

"Well?" he demanded. "Name the claret and its vintage, Master Butler. You are in charge of my cellars, purchase my wines, keep them in condition and know the whereabouts of every last bottle. Name the wine that you've just tasted."

"It—it is the Chateau Duclos—the 'thirty-five," stammered Strawson.

"Liar!" shouted his master. "You're robbing me wholesale, like all your kind. Taking bribes from the wine-merchants. Filling my cellars with their confounded red ink and calling it vintage claret. You're all in the conspiracy, the whole rabble of you." His angry eyes swept towards the other servants—the footman and the three maids—who stood watching him, wide-eyed and white-faced with fear.

One of the maids was extremely fine-looking: tall and fair, with the complexion of a milkmaid. Sir Tristan pointed to her.

"You—Annie," he said. "Come here!"

The young woman obeyed. The baronet poured himself another glass of the despised wine and tossed it down in one draught, then refilled his glass. His eyes never left the maid.

"Are you in this conspiracy against me, Annie?" he demanded.

"No, Sir Tristan," she replied in a soft Cornish burr.

"Not plotting to cheat me, like Strawson here?"

"No, Sir Tristan," she whispered. I could see tears starting in the corners of her soft blue eyes and I wanted to cry out, to stop him from tormenting the poor creature.

"How old are you, Annie?" he asked.

"Twenty, Sir Tristan."

"Twenty. And how long have you worked for me, Annie?"

"Since I was sixteen, Sir Tristan."

"Since you were sixteen." He took another swallow of wine and hooked one leg over the arm of his chair. The savage anger had gone, and now he seemed to be enjoying himself, to be revelling in his cruel baiting of the young woman. "And what would you do, Annie, if I discharged you—threw you out without a character reference?"

"I—I don't know, Sir Tristan." She was unashamedly crying now, wiping at the tears with the napkin she carried, and her slender shoulders were racked with sobs.

"Don't you know, Annie?" he smiled at her. "Then I will tell you. If I were to decide that you are part of this conspiracy against me, and discharged you without a character reference, you would never get further employment. You would be reduced to the streets, to beggary, to theft. The former would turn you into a raddled hag by the time you're thirty; the latter would likely bring you to the gallows, where a hempen rope would choke the life from that pretty neck!"

There was a scraping of a chair, as Mark Dewaine leapt to his feet.

"Father!" he cried. "I must protest. This is . . ."

"Be quiet, sir!" shouted the baronet. "I am the master here, and I will let it be known. I am being conspired against. Cheated. But I will have my way. Oh, yes, by God. I will have my way!"

With this last, cryptic utterance, he rose unsteadily from his chair, roughly brushing aside Strawson's hand when the butler tried to assist him. We all stared as he staggered across the wide sweep of floor and out through the double doors. There was a long silence in the dining room, till the footfalls of Landeric's master had faded away.

Mark Dewaine sat down heavily.

"I should like some pudding," he said in a clear, cool voice.

The servants were stirred into sudden activity by his demand. Strawson himself presented bowls of fruit trifle and lemon cream for the young master's choice, and he took the trifle. Annie spooned clotted cream on to his plate. She was still crying.

"I hate Papa when he gets this bee in his bonnet about being conspired against," said Hester petulantly.

After a while, her brother said: "The Royal Family are at Osborne. On Thursday last, I commanded the escort that accompanied Her Majesty to the railway station."

"How splendid," replied Hester. "Did you see the baby prince? What's he like?"

"An average, ordinary sort of baby. I'm told that Her Majesty and the Prince call him 'Affie.'"

Hester laughed. "Those nicknames! And you told me they call Princess Alice 'Fat Alice,' or 'Fatima' for short. I don't think that's very complimentary, do you, Miss Button?"

This, the first remark that had been addressed to me throughout that astonishing meal, made me start.

"Er . . . no," I replied weakly.

Mark Dewaine turned his head slowly to face me. His gaze was as blank and bland as the still surface of the ornamental lake at the bottom of the park. And when he spoke to me, it was as if he was addressing a dumb animal.

"When luncheon's over, I should be grateful for a few words alone with Miss Button," he said distantly.

* * *

There was a slight wind from the sea, and it brought the tang of salt and the unforgettable scents of the shore. Gulls were wheeling overhead, and a row of them were perched around the edge of one of the ornamental fountains beneath the terrace on which Mark Dewaine and I were walking. Neither of us had said a word since we stepped out of the long windows of the dining room that opened out on to the balustraded terrace fronting the main, central block of the mansion.

We reached the far end and turned together. It was then that he spoke:

"Forgive my asking," he said. "But do you have any finances? I promise you that there's a perfectly good reason for my intrusion into your private affairs."

"I've a few pounds," I replied. "When the stock of my father's business is all sold, I suppose there will be about ten or twelve pounds in all." I looked at him questioningly, but his face told me nothing.

He stopped and looked straight at me. He had his father's eyes: the deep, sea-green Dewaine eyes—but they never strayed, as Sir Tristan's always strayed.

"I am willing to finance your journey to any place of your choice," he said, "and supplement your capital in order to give you . . . let us say . . . six months in which to settle yourself in suitable employment. The condition being that you leave Landeric immediately. Today."

I shook my head in disbelief; searched his face, but could find nothing but the blank wall of his cold contempt.

"Why?" I asked. "Why is it so important for you to get rid of me?"

"There are—valid reasons," he replied.

I could have laughed at him. "Surely not because I was once rude to you in front of your sisters?" I said. "You wouldn't go to the trouble and expense just for *that*. You'd just have your father dismiss me."

"Rude to me?" He looked puzzled for a moment—genuinely puzzled. Then his brow cleared and he almost smiled. "Oh, *that!* I promise you that your small demonstration of disapproval on that occasion has no connection with my present offer."

"But you don't want me here?"

He shook his head. "It is vital that you leave Landeric," he said.

"But you won't tell me why?"

"It isn't necessary that you should know the reasons. You must accept my assurances that the reasons are sound."

I could feel my fury rising against the insufferable arrogance of this man. Who did he think he was?—to be able to order the comings and goings of mere mortals like me, as if we were sheep. Of one thing I was determined, though: he was not going to make me lose my temper—that satisfaction, at least, would be denied him.

"No reasons—no departure!" I said sharply.

His green eyes flared with anger. I am sure that, if there had been a carriage and horses ready at that moment, Mark Dewaine would have picked me up and bundled me inside, whipped up the horses and driven me off to the nearest railway station.

"Is that your last word?" he grated.

"Yes, Mr. Dewaine," I replied coolly. "Your father, Sir Tristan, employed me as governess to Miss Hester at the sum of twenty-five pounds per annum in advance (which sum, I may add, I have not yet received). He is entitled to dismiss me; you, with the greatest respect, Mr. Dewaine, are not. Thank you for your offer of money, but it just doesn't fit the case. I have a good place here and don't need to look elsewhere."

He was silent for a few moments, and then:

"This is a very unhappy house, Miss Button," he said. "We are a disunited family. There are undercurrents of ill-will at which I cannot even begin to hint. My father . . ." he checked himself and looked away.

Despite myself, I felt a pang of sympathy for him at that moment. The memory of Sir Tristan's drunken outburst at the luncheon table was rankling with him. For a man of his overweening pride, it would be a torment to see his own father go to pieces in front of the servant classes. And was I not, also, a member of the servant classes?

"Sir Tristan has been agreeable to me," I said. "Very agreeable indeed. I have no complaints whatsoever. And I shall not give up my position. Will that be all, Mr. Dewaine?"

He nodded briefly and turned his back to me. When I left him, he was standing with his hands resting on the balustrade of the terrace, looking out across the fountains and the ornamental cypress trees, down the long valley—to heaven knows what secret thoughts.

* * *

I received my wages that same afternoon: Mr. Pendower, Sir Tristan's estate bailiff, called at the nursery to see me, gave me the money in cash and had me sign a receipt. This set the seal on my rejection of Mark Dewaine's offer. Sir Tristan had generously designated the advance of wages as non-returnable under any circumstances; I was determined, on my part, to honour my side of the contract.

It was obvious—I had witnessed it with my own eyes—that my employer was given to outbursts of ugly temper when he had been drinking heavily. It was no concern of mine. Men are strange creatures, I told myself, and given to strange ways. Father had sought consolation in drink, but had not been utterly destroyed by it at the end.

Though I could not condone Sir Tristan's treatment of Strawson and the maid Annie, I had no way of knowing if there was not a seed of justification for it. Perhaps the butler *was* robbing his master. Perhaps all the lesser servants were well aware of it and kept their silence.

I wanted very much to keep my position as governess at Landeric—the fairytale palace of my childhood imaginings. And I was more than willing to make allowances.

For this reason, also, I decided to say nothing to Hester about the dead rat that surely she—and if not she, then who else?—had put in my bed. We had tea together in the light and airy nursery that she still occupied, with its relics of childhoods long past: the rocking horse that had first been ridden by Mark, so Hester told me; the dolls that had been passed down to her from her older sisters Alicia and Jessica.

Alicia and Jessica were expected home any day, she informed me. It appeared that the coming Saturday was the anniversary of the death of their mama, who had passed away when Hester was only a babe; and it was a family custom to foregather and pay honour to her memory in the private chapel of the great house, in whose crypt she had been interred, in the company of departed Dewaines since time immemorial. The news that I would soon be meeting the older sisters filled me with some dread. What reaction would I receive from them, I wondered; what memories did they retain of that incident on the Haven quayside two years before?

Bowing to my pupil's entreaties, we spent most of the remainder of the day in practising the finer points of the valse. I then began to teach her the schottische, which had been very popular with the girls of the Misses Hunnables' Academy. Hester had a good sense of rhythm and moved daintily; I was able to assure her that she would speedily shine in the ballroom.

In the evening, we dined together in the nursery: a delicious meal of fricasseed fowl, followed by a gooseberry trifle and clotted cream. We were served by the maid Annie, whose eyes betrayed the fact that she had probably spent the greater part of the afternoon in tears. I spoke to her amiably, but received no kind of response save polite monosyllables and lowered glance. If Hester had any embarrassment about the way her father had humiliated Annie that day, she never showed it, but prattled on about the comings and goings of life at Landeric. I pricked up my ears when she mentioned Mr. Durward de Lacey. The painter, it seemed, had decamped with his picture, having spent a month working on it in and about the mansion. Hester had liked him very much, she told me; I could not but echo her judgment.

My young charge went to bed at eight-thirty, and I sat in the armchair in my room, reading a story book that I had found in the nursery library, but the tales of elves and fairies, of knights and dragons failed to charm; and when the light faded, I decided to wash and retire. It had been a long and trying day, but I doubted if the many and varied impressions that teemed in my mind would long keep me from sleep.

There remained the problem of the soiled bedsheet. I could not bring myself to lie upon the spot that was dabbled with the rusty brown of dried blood; so I took off the sheet and settled myself down on the under-blanket.

I had scarcely closed my eyes when a resounding crash echoed up the corridor outside. It was followed by a cry—a man's cry—of anger or fear, or both. I was out of my bed in a trice and, slipping on my *peignoir*, I opened my door and peered out. The corridor and the great staircase beyond were bathed in bright moonlight. There was no sight or sound of anyone.

I looked into the nursery. Hester was fast asleep, her dark, unbraided hair spread out across her pillow, a guileless softness to her lips. I quietly shut the door.

The windows at the top of the staircase gave a view along the terrace, where the moonlight cast heavy shadows. Walking in and out of these shadows, deep in animated conversation and gesturing to each other, were Mark Dewaine and his father. When they came to a wrought-iron seat some distance along the terrace, the older man slumped down on to the seat, legs sprawled out before him, hands in pockets, regarding his son with a truculent tilt to his head.

I could not hear a word of what passed between them. It was hardly like eavesdropping; more like being the fascinated spectator at a shadow show. Mark Dewaine seemed to be pleading with his father; making sweeping gestures with his hands and sometimes ticking off points on his fingers. The latter gave his son a poor hearing; constantly interrupted him and pointed a scornful finger as he denounced Mark's arguments. Finally, the son seemed to be goaded into a remark that brought his father lurching unsteadily to his feet. To my alarm, Sir Tristan took hold of the facings of his son's black evening coat and shouted something into his countenance. Mark bore the assault and tirade with surprising dignity and forbearance; only when his father had finished shouting, did he take the other's wrists and detach himself from his grasp. He then made his reply—and what he said seemed completely to take the fire and fury out of Sir Tristan: he sagged back on to the seat and stared up at his son in slack-mouthed dismay.

It was then that conscience won over curiosity and I realised that I had intruded on their privacy for too long. Turning, I went back to my room. The last I saw of them, Sir Tristan was still regarding Mark, and Mark was returning his father's gaze, arms folded; silent, implacable.

Contrary to my expectations, sleep was long in coming to me that night. The quarrel between my employer and his son gave me cause for plenty of speculation. It could scarcely not be connected, in some way, with the offer that Mark had made to me after luncheon. Not that I had the temerity to think, for one moment, that my name had even been mentioned during the encounter I had witnessed; but what I had seen was all of a piece with the things that Mark had said to me. In the stillness of my moonlit room, the words seemed to come back. . . .

"This is a very unhappy house . . . we are a disunited family . . . undercurrents of ill-will at which I cannot even begin to hint . . . My father . . ."

It was all very puzzling. But one thing was quite clear in my mind: as I had resolved to myself that afternoon, I was not going to let Dewaine family quarrels, nor Sir Tristan's conduct during that luncheon, frighten me away from Landeric.

It seemed almost as if it was written in the stars that I should come to Landeric. Perhaps that was why Father had spoken the name with almost his last breath.

I clung to his thought for a while, and in doing so, I must have drifted away into sleep.

* * *

The morning brought a light, drenching rain: the sort that was very familiar to a dweller on that part of the coast, when mist shrouded the dark head of Ramas and the sails of the lobster boats were hidden from sight so that you could only hear the men calling to each other as they tended their pots. From the landing window outside my room, I looked down on to the scene of the midnight encounter that I had witnessed; the terrace was deserted and gleaming wet with rain. The long glade ended just beyond the formal garden; beyond that, I just could see a trio of deer moving like ghosts among the rain-mist. Shuddering, I pulled my shawl more tightly about my shoulders and went to look for Hester.

My pupil was already up; her hair was being plaited by one of the maids, and she was demanding breakfast. We ate together at the table by the nursery window: coffee and delicious new-baked rolls. Despite her pleas for beginning the day with yet another dancing lesson, I insisted on starting with Arithmetic. She made a moue, but accepted it with a fair grace—and I soon discovered the reason: Arithmetic was, literally, child's play to Hester; she could add, divide and subtract in her head more speedily and accurately than I; a considerable embarrassment. I privately determined to consult my old schoolbooks and prepare myself to introduce her to the more advanced branches of Mathematics. Meanwhile, with some relief, I smoothly brought the lesson to a close and announced that we would now do History.

It was at that moment that a maid tapped on the door and announced that the Misses Alicia and Jessica were approaching up the drive.

"School's over for the morning," said my pupil firmly, rising. "Come, Miss Button. Let's go and see what sort of frills and furbelows they're wearing in Paris this season." She took my hand and we went down the staircase together.

Hester may not have noticed it—if she did, she made no comment—but one of the long mirrors set into the panelled wall at the foot of the stair was cracked right across, as if something had been thrown at it from a distance. This, I decided, must account for the crash in the night that preceded the angry conversation on the terrace. But which of them, I wondered, had thrown the chair or whatever?

The speculation faded from my mind, as we walked out under the great columned portico of Landeric. Sir Tristan and his son were ahead of us and descending the steps to the carriage drive, where a coach and four was slowing to a halt. Much clattering of hooves, jingle of head harness, and two footmen leapt down to open the emblazoned door and lower the mounting-step.

Alicia Dewaine, the elder sister, was the first to alight. She carried her eighteen years with the special assurance that only breeding, wealth and an expensive education can give. She was dressed in figured orange silk, with a bonnet to match. At the very sight of her, I felt every tiniest patch of careful darning and mending on my best gray screaming out for inspection. She took her father's hand and kissed him on both cheeks.

"Did you have an agreeable crossing, my dear?" The baronet had regained his warm, bucolic front; the angry dog of yesterday might never have been.

"Smooth as a lake, Papa," she replied. "Hello, Mark. You've grown, Hester." Alicia's green-eyed gaze flickered over their shoulders, encountered me, treated me to a quick search—and dismissed me.

Jessica stepped down. At sixteen, she seemed slight and immature compared with her elder sister. She was in a floral-patterned costume braided with green, that was a mite too old-looking for one of her girlishness. She exchanged greetings with her relations, but seemed not to notice me.

"And this is our dear, dear friend Amelie," cried Alicia. "Amelie, *ma chère,* may I present our papa and brother Mark. Amelie de Quatrefois."

She was a little older than Alicia; a complete woman who bore herself like a duchess. She posed for an instant on the step of the carriage and let her amused, blue-eyed gaze sweep over us.

Amelie de Quatrefois' skin was transparent like porcelain, and her hair was silver-gold. Her costume made those of the Dewaine sisters look entirely commonplace, and left me feeling like one of the slatternly women who gut fish on the quayside of Pennan Haven. She wore a gown of white silk, with a contrasting bonnet of black, trimmed with black lace, and she carried—like the sceptre of the Queen herself—a black silk umbrella fringed with white.

Sir Tristan stepped forward and gave her a hand down. I caught a sight of Mark Dewaine's profile and was intrigued to notice that he was staring intently at the new arrival, mouth slightly parted. As I watched, he passed the tip of his tongue across his lips—as if they had gone suddenly dry. Next moment, his back was to me and bent over the French girl's hand.

"*Mademoiselle,*" he murmured huskily. "*Je suis enchanté de faire votre connaissance.*"

To say that Amelie de Quatrefois treated him to a coquettish look would be to put too crude an interpretation on her manner; her style was far removed from anything so obvious as coquetry. For a brief moment, when he raised his lips from her hand, she forsook her expression of slightly amused boredom and gave him a sudden look of surprise—a flaring of her blue eyes and a momentary parting of the lips—that must surely have made Mark Dewaine realise that he had immediately created a very favourable impression upon the young Frenchwoman.

My view of the pair was obscured by Sir Tristan, who turned and gestured towards the house.

"You young ladies must be weary after your long journey," he said. "Might I suggest that you will wish to retire to your rooms till luncheon. You can give us all your news at luncheon."

"A capital idea," said Alicia.

It was then that Sir Tristan noticed me for the first time.

"Very remiss of me," he said, giving me a kindly smile that swept away any lingering doubts I may have had about my decision to stay on at Landeric. "This is Miss Button, who has just taken over the duties of governess to Hester."

Alicia and Jessica gave me the briefest of nods as they swept past. The French girl's acknowledgement was warmer, but entirely impersonal: the sort of vaguely indulgent glance—instantly put on and as quickly taken off—she might have given to a small dog (not her own) that had just performed its party trick of sitting up to beg for scraps.

Mark Dewaine did not even look at me. At least, I think not—for I did not look at him.

* * *

Hester took luncheon with the family, but I was spared the embarrassment of having to accompany her on that occasion—and for a reason that was to play no small part in my future life at Landeric.

Shortly before midday, while I was sitting in my room and dipping into Euclid, in preparation for introducing my pupil to the mysteries of Geometry, a knock came to my door. It was Strawson. The butler was in a plain, tailed suit and minus his powdered wig —revealing himself to be almost bald. Respectfully, he asked if I would accompany him to Mrs. Horabin, who had had some kind of collapse. The physician had been sent for from St. Errol, but it would be some time before he arrived. In the meantime he was dreadfully aworried about Mrs. Horabin's looks, he said.

I went with him readily enough. On our way through the long corridors to the west wing, where the housekeeper's apartment was situated, he explained that Mrs. Horabin was given to these at-

tacks, being dropsical and subject to weakness of the heart. I was
flattered to have been summoned to help; but sincerely hoped that
I should not be called upon to give any medical aid to the poor
woman. I had twice seen someone bled, but it was not an operation that I would have been happy to perform, no matter how
grave the emergency.

The housekeeper's apartment comprised a sewing room, a small
parlour, and a bedroom. Strawson delicately left me at the door of
the latter. There was a young housemaid sitting by the sick
woman's bedside; she got up and curtsied to me. Mrs. Horabin was
asleep or unconscious, and her face white and swollen. I felt her
brow: it was damp and feverish. It was then I noticed that the
bedside table, the window-sill nearby, and even the floor by the
bed, were all strewn with account books, wads of what appeared to
be tradesmen's bills tied up with string, receipts and the like.

My toe kicked against an account book and I picked it up. In a
shaky copperplate hand, I had my first introduction to the practical running of the fairytale castle of my childhood imaginings:

Quarter ending March, 1845:—

	£	s	d
Coal—seven tons —	10	10	0
Dry goods —	6	15	6¾
Linens, etc. —	1	10	0
Cook's a/c (victuals) —	98	15	4
Sundries —		10	6
Total:	£118	11	5d

I was absently wondering at the large amount of money involved in what was only one department of the mansion, farms,
and estates that comprised Landeric, when a tap on the door announced the arrival of the physician from St. Errol. He was a
small, birdlike man with spiky hair that stood up like a sweep's
brush round a bald dome; who took one look at the patient and
produced from his bag a lancet and basin. Bidding me to hold the
basin, he proceeded to tie a piece of tape around the left arm of
the unconscious woman, just above the elbow. Almost immediately, I saw the branches of bluish veins stand out below the bend
of the elbow. The watching housemaid gave a squeal of horror—
instantly suppressed by a sharp glance from me—as the little physician then thrust the tip of his lancet into a vein, made a gently
curving incision and brought it out, leaving a half-inch, lengthwise

cut along the vein, from which the bright blood cleanly issued into the basin that I was holding.

When he had satisfied himself that sufficient blood had been taken away my companion unfastened the tape and laid the ball of his thumb firmly over the incision till the bleeding had finished. Finally, he placed a lint pad over the wound and bound it tightly with a roll of linen—pronouncing that the operation was a success and that the patient would speedily recover. Indeed, even as he was packing away his instruments, Mrs. Horabin's eyes flickered open and regarded me with puzzlement. I hastened to assure her that all was well with her.

When we were alone, she confided in me, tears in her eyes, that recurring illness was making her work suffer—here she made a gesture towards the unkept accounts that littered her room—and that she feared for her position. I had heard enough of conditions in the great world beyond Landeric's valley to know that the loss of employment, at her age, could only lead to the workhouse or starvation. Offering what comfort I was able, I left her.

Strawson was waiting for me in the parlour beyond. From his manner, it was plain that he was on good terms with Mrs. Horabin (by no means a commonplace situation between higher servants) and he, too, was worried about her work. Things were in a turmoil in the kitchen, he told me. Bills were not being paid, nor provisions ordered in. Furthermore, the estate bailiff had declared that Landeric must be the only great house in Cornwall which was being dunned by tradesmen. If it reaches the ears of Sir Tristan, he added, the entire staff would likely be dismissed.

It was then that I had *my idea.* . . .

I asked him to have a word with Mrs. Horabin and, if she was agreeable, to send the outstanding bills and uncompleted account books to my room, and I would attempt to sort them out as best I could. Strawson was hugely delighted with my suggestion. Mrs. Horabin would be most grateful for my help, he told me, and he would bring round the accounts himself that very day.

Leaving the west wing by a side door, I took advantage of a pleasant break in the rain by walking along the terrace towards the central block.

It was while passing a line of windows immediately above the dining room that I became aware of being watched. Glancing up, I saw Mark Dewaine and the two older sisters gazing down at me. Their faces were devoid of all expression, but Mark's lips were moving. I knew, without any room for argument, that I was the subject of his remarks: that he was probably telling them of the offer he had made me—and of how I had thrown it back in his face.

I continued on my way, but the sense of being watched only grew more acute: I could feel their concerted eyes, like fingers probing at my back, and my scalp crawled with a strange fear. Mercifully, the feeling had passed off by the time I reached my room, where I consigned my school Euclid textbook back to the bottom of my trunk.

"I won't be needing *you* for the time being, my dear sir," I said wryly.

Since I had missed luncheon, a maid brought me a collation of cold meats and a mixed salad. When she had cleared it away, I asked her to inform Miss Hester that I should be pleased to see her for afternoon school in the nursery at two-thirty o'clock.

Hester greeted me with a request that was half-way to a demand:

"May we have dancing all the afternoon?"

I shook my head. "I've revised the time-table completely," I said gently. "Dancing lessons will be a moveable feast, depending on your attention to and progress in your academic subjects. If all goes well, the second period of this afternoon will be dancing. The first period . . ." here I took a deep breath . . . "will be arithmetic."

"But we had arithmetic this morning!" cried my pupil. "And I can do adding, multiplying and subtracting in my head, better than you can!" She raised her chin, her lower lip stuck out defiantly and she looked at me down her straight, Dewaine nose—very like her brother.

"There's nothing like reinforcing success," I said smoothly. "Practice makes perfect, my dear."

Strawson had brought round a thick wad of bills and account books while I was having my collation; I laid them on the school desk.

"What's all that?" demanded Hester with the deepest suspicion.

"Practical arithmetic," I replied, sitting down. "You can start by adding up the totals of those bills, one pile at a time, calling out the amounts, for me to enter in this book. It's all very good practice for you, Hester." And when I saw her chin go up again, I added sweetly: "How would you like to spend the second period learning . . . the polka?"

* * *

"Oh, no! This is really going too far!"

My bonnet—my only bonnet, the new straw with the red ribbon and trimmings—lay in the corner of my bedroom with the ribbon ripped off and a deep dent in the crown. I saw it as soon as I came in after taking a stroll in the grounds that evening after supper in the nursery.

I picked it up. The dent—which was of a size to have been put there by something like the heel of a shoe—had cracked the straw, and it still showed after I had straightened it back into some sort of shape.

How could that dreadful child do this to me? I asked myself.

The afternoon had gone surprisingly well. With Hester's help, I had managed to clear up two months' arrears of housekeeping accounts for Mrs. Horabin. The child had not seemed to find it too tedious or difficult—at least, she had not complained. The polka lesson that followed, surely, should have removed any lingering resentment she might have felt about the extra arithmetic.

But, apparently not . . .

First the dead rat in my bed, and now—this!

I swept out of the room, carrying my violated bonnet, and into the nursery. A young housemaid was tidying up the room; she met my furious gaze and informed me, with some alarm, that Miss Hester had gone down to the stables to say good night to her pony.

My resolve—which was to corner the young minx in the quiet of the stables and give her a severe dressing-down—suffered a rude check on my way there.

At the foot of the stairs, a door opened, and I came face-to-face with Alicia and Jessica Dewaine and their beautiful French friend. They wore dinner gowns and had obviously just left the menfolk at table. I backed away against the wall to let them pass and instinctively tried to make myself look as small as possible.

Alicia paused close by me. She eyed me reflectively, tapping her chin with her folded fan. Her green, Dewaine eyes looked very hard.

"I believe we have met on a previous occasion, Miss Button," she said coldly. "And, to tell you the truth, I am surprised to find you here in Landeric."

"Alicia . . ." faltered Jessica, glancing nervously from her sister to Mademoiselle de Quatrefois, then back to her sister. "Don't you think? I mean . . ."

"Take Amelie along to the drawing room," retorted Alicia sharply. It was obvious who was the dominating character of the pair. "I will join you later."

With many an anxious backward glance, Jessica did as she was told. Not till their footsteps had faded away down the long, curving corridor did Alicia Dewaine turn her gaze back to me. When she did, it was not merely to register the distaste and contempt that a highly-bred lady might feel for an erring peasant; the hatred in her green eyes was the hatred of one woman for another—just that. The impact struck me with near-physical force.

Her next remark was oblique; it took me by surprise.

"I see you are carrying your bonnet, Miss Button," she said. And now the look of hatred had vanished from her face and she was all bland and honeyed. "Don't tell me that you regularly go out in the air bareheaded."

"This evening I went for a walk in the park without my bonnet," I admitted, puzzled.

"A thing you do regularly?" she persisted.

I nodded.

"I thought so," she declared. "It shows." She reached out and touched my cheek with her forefinger, tentatively, as one touches a toad. "Your skin is quite red and rough from exposure to the sun's rays."

Her own cheeks were as pale and limpid as the flowers of a tulip tree. I felt myself flush hotly with embarrassment—and despised myself for it.

"And your hands are a disaster," she said. "Show them to me."

Hesitantly, reluctantly, I did as I was ordered: held out my hands, palms upward, like some child undergoing inspection for cleanliness at table. Alicia Dewaine clicked her tongue in disfavour. Then she held out her own. Even allowing for the stain of ink that still remained from my afternoon's labour of book-keeping, the comparison was—or so it seemed to me—like that between the hands of a china doll and the paws of a Barbary ape. I swiftly withdrew mine and hid them behind me.

"Why are you tormenting me, Miss Dewaine?" I breathed.

Her eyebrows shot up and the green eyes regarded me with feigned surprise.

"Tormenting you, Miss Button?" she repeated. "Now, why did you say that, I wonder?" She smiled, but there was no humour in those eyes. "Can you not see that I am only trying to help you—to point out some of your—er—deficiencies? I should like to help you. Insofar as it would be possible to help you, that is. Your figure is a trifle—how shall I put it?—*full-blown*, and I doubt if even the most rigorous of tight lacing will ever correct that. But something might be done about your complexion. I shall tell my maid to give you some unguent. Glycerine is very good. So is a little whiting paste."

In an agony of humiliation, I could only hang my head before her contempt: and she two years my junior, but armed with the assurance that her position and upbringing gave her.

"Thank you, Miss Dewaine," was all I could bring myself to murmur.

"Not at all. It is a pleasure," she replied. "Good evening, Miss Button. And don't forget to wear your bonnet at all times out of doors."

With this, she turned and left me, down the corridor, the way her sister and friend had gone. I remained where I was; leaning back against the wall; not fighting back the tears of humiliation any more, but letting them well out from the misery in my heart.

Forgotten, the incident of my defaced bonnet and my plan to confront Hester; I trailed back up the stairs to my room and locked myself in.

My reflection stared at me from the mirror on the dressing table: a face with red-rimmed and swollen eyes, one I scarcely recognised as my own. I sat down at the dressing table and took stock of my appearance. Alicia Dewaine was right: I was ugly. Twenty summers of exposure to the sun of the West Country had indelibly discoloured my skin, and no amount of bonnet-wearing was going to bring a feminine pallor to my disgustingly rosy cheeks. I looked down at my hands. Peasant hands, large-boned, sunburnt and—horrible phrase—capable-looking. And my figure: large-boned, too, and far too solidly-fleshed.

A genteel young lady's education had not turned Susannah Button, daughter of a common sailor-turned-publican, into a lady. A peasant I was, and a peasant I would remain: that was the hard lesson I had come to learn in fairytale Landeric.

Miserably, I prepared myself for bed. When my lamp was out, and I lay looking up at the dark ceiling, I seemed to see their faces looking down at me: Mark and Alicia Dewaine.

What had they got against me?

Why had Mark made such a determined effort to get rid of me? Why had Alicia taken so much trouble to hurt and humiliate me? Why should I—a humble governess, lowly-born—be singled out for such attentions from the lordly Dewaines?

I sought for consolations: remember how Sir Tristan had been kind to me; how, despite her unpleasant practical pranks, Hester seemed quite content to have me as her teacher.

Then I remembered the artist, Durward de Lacey. He, at least, had briefly mistaken me for a lady and had treated me in a gratifyingly complimentary manner. I clung to this thought till sleep took me away.

* * *

The next day was Saturday. I woke early and went to the window. The dawn sun was causing a mist to rise from the back lawns; and through the mist I saw a long line of men advancing with brooms, which they swung in time to their stride, sweeping the paths and terraces to face the new day. There must have been twenty men, under the command of a foreman-gardener, who controlled their advancing and their turning by tapping his stick upon the granite flagstones.

As the line drew closer, I saw that every man's left arm was tied with a black mourning band—and it was then I remembered it was the anniversary of Lady Dewaine's death, and that, as Hester had told me, the family and servants would be attending the memorial service in the chapel. Last night's incident had driven it from my mind. I had intended to see to my mourning costume before retiring; and I was thankful that the glance out of my window had provided me with a timely reminder.

I had not had the money to buy complete mourning for Father, but had made shift—as was the custom among the womenfolk of the Haven—with a black shawl and black trimmings for my bonnet. Delving into the bottom of my hamper, I took them out and set to work, sewing the broad mourning ribbon in such a way as to cover most of the damage caused by the dent.

The chapel bell began to toll immediately after breakfast, and I left the nursery with Hester, who had not betrayed her guilt by so much as a glance at my bonnet. She looked demure and doll-like in full mourning, with black lace mittens and sable fur trimmings. I had chosen the most sombre costume from my slender wardrobe: a plain dress of dark brown, from which I had removed its white collars and cuffs, to fit the occasion. And my black shawl was pinned with a jet brooch from Mama's trinket box.

The family was already assembling on the terrace. The elder sisters were heavily veiled, as was Mademoiselle de Quatrefois, who stood with them. Sir Tristan and Mark were in frock coats, with their tall hats heavily swathed in mourning crepe. The two men gravely raised their hats at our approach. Because of her veil, I had no way of telling the expression on Alicia Dewaine's face, but I saw her glance sharply towards me.

Sir Tristan took out his watch and consulted it.

"I think we will take our places in the chapel," he said. "You will wish to lead the way, Mark, and I will bring up the rear, after the ladies."

Accordingly, we moved slowly in this order along the terrace, towards the chapel, which stood beyond the west wing: a tall, many-windowed building in the same style as the mansion, with a portico over the door and a dome surmounted by a cross at its eastern end.

The door was flanked by menservants, who bowed deeply as we approached. I saw Strawson's bald head and, beyond that, the candlelit gloom of the interior. Mark Dewaine led the way through the door and down the aisle, between crowded pews, where the servants and workers of the Landeric estate were bobbing to their feet at the arrival of the family who employed them and ordered their lives. I was aware of scores of watching eyes as I walked with Hester at my side, following Mark's broad back, till he paused by the open door of a high-walled pew and motioned us to enter it. We womenfolk took our places in this pew, under a great stone carving of the Dewaine arms supported by two lions. There was a profound silence. Mark remained at the still-open door. Presently, with slow tread, Sir Tristan walked down the aisle alone: the master of Landeric come in all his pomp and power, to mourn his departed wife. He took his seat in the front row of the family pew; Mark Dewaine nodded towards the organ loft—and the reedy notes of a pipe organ brought us to our feet for the opening hymn and the entrance of the Reverend Mr. Mawhinney attended by a group of surpliced urchins from Pennan church, barefoot like all the children of the village and Haven, carrying long candles.

I have little recollection of the service, save that Mark read from the tremendous twenty-first chapter of the Revelation of St. John in a firm and sonorous voice, and the candlelight seemed to soften his face as I had never seen it before.

> "And God shall wipe away all tears
> from their eyes; and there shall
> be no more death . . ."

My thoughts returned to Mama, as I remembered her. She was a white-faced doll with scarlet touches at the cheekbones, like the doll that Father had given me (he bought it at a fair in Penryn, and I have it with me still), with staring eyes, who looked up at me from the pillow and held out a thin hand to touch me on the forehead. This was in a house in Plymouth, where she and father had married after he quit the sea-service of the East India Company. At that time, she was dying—and some trick of memory tells me that I instinctively knew it, child though I was. She never came to Pennan Haven. There was grief, an empty house; and then Father and I were jogging westwards under a lowering sky, with all our household traps and personal belongings piled high on a hired wagon. A few days after our arrival, he took me for a walk and I saw Landeric for the first time.

Landeric . . . the Dewaines . . .

My attention wandered to the plaques and carved busts and statuary that lined the long walls of the chapel: last resting places of the lordly masters of the valley. The nearest inscription bore a date, and I clearly recall that I had decided it must be seventeen fifty-three, or perhaps fifty-eight.

"Fire!—There's fire at the big house!"

The shouted interruption came from the open door of the chapel. It silenced the Reverend Mr. Mawhinney, echoed and re-echoed from the marbled walls all round in a clamour of terrible sound.

We were all on our feet and looking round. Mark Dewaine slammed open the pew door and ran for the door, closely followed by a group of the men.

"Hurry there, lads! Bring out the fire-engine!"

"Get ladders!"

"Where's the outbreak, then?"

The chapel bell was tolling a fast, frantic alarm when we crowded out into the sunshine and looked towards the main block of the mansion, beyond the noble curve of the connecting gallery. A smudge of black smoke hung over the slated peak of its roof, sullen against the azure blue of the sky.

"It's at the back of the building!" cried someone.

"One of the back bedrooms!" confirmed another.

A sudden dread clutched at my heart. . . .

"It's the room next the nursery!"

My room!

With a rattle of iron-shod wheels, the men were dragging a heavy fire-engine from the direction of the stables. I watched, as they uncoiled a leather hose and bore down on the pump handle, two a side. A long jet of water played against the white walls of the great house. By the time the rest of us reached the spot, the jet was being directed through the open window of my room, out of which the black smoke still poured in rolling clouds.

Heads appeared at the nursery windows and at the window on the other side of mine.

"How is it up there?" cried one of the men at the pump.

"We can't get inside the room for the smoke," came the response, "but you're gaining on it, lads!"

A spare water-cart was brought up, drawn by a fat pony. The water was immediately transferred into the fire-engine. The men continued to labour at the pump handles; the thin jet poured ceaselessly into my window. I shuddered to think that it might not, after all, be sufficient to extinguish the flames; that Landeric might be completely burnt to an empty shell.

"How could it have started?" cried Hester, who was at my elbow. "Surely you didn't leave a candle burning, Miss Button."

I shook my head. A heavy sense of foreboding was oppressing me. My throat was dry and I could scarcely control a trembling of my nether lip. I knew, beyond all doubt, that something terrible was about to happen to me.

A cheer went up from the watchers, as the smoke thinned and a man stuck his head out of the window of my room and waved to us below.

"Stop pumping!" he shouted. "We can manage the rest of it with the water we have in the house."

"What caused the outbreak?" A stern, clear voice at my elbow. I turned to see Mark Dewaine had put the question.

The man's head was withdrawn. A few moments later (agonising moments for me), he reappeared. In his hand was a candlestick—my candlestick—which he held up for inspection. My heart gave a lurch.

A murmur went up from the watching crowd. I sensed their eyes probing me like knives.

"Are you saying it started by a candle?" shouted Mark Dewaine.

"Found the candlestick lying on the floor by the window here, master!" came the reply. "The rug were all burnt to ash!"

"That can't be! It couldn't have happened like that!"

A strange, strangled voice uttered the denial. With a sudden shock of horror, I realised it was mine. Everyone was staring at me in hostile disbelief. I felt cornered. Trapped.

"Why could it not, Miss Button?" asked Mark Dewaine quietly. His eyes searched mine expressionlessly.

"The candlestick was on my bedside table when I left the room," I protested.

"Lit?" he demanded.

I shook my head wildly. "No!" I cried. "It hadn't been lit since last night. When I woke up this morning, it was almost broad daylight."

"What nonsense! The creature's lying!" Alicia Dewaine lifted back her veil and glared at me malevolently.

"It's true!" I protested. I turned my appeal to Mark, searching for a spark of sympathy and understanding in his impassive countenance. "It may be that I could have moved the candlestick to the table by the window. I could done that without thinking, but . . ."

"She has a convenient memory," said Alicia tartly. "Remembers only what's to her advantage."

Mark gestured his sister to silence.

"But you're sure you didn't light the candle at all this morning?" he demanded.

"I'm positive of that," I said. "It was nearly daylight when I got up and drew back the shutters. There was no need for a candle."

"We will go upstairs and inspect the scene of the mishap," he said grimly.

Evidence of the fire was apparent as soon as we set foot over the threshold of the mansion: water was still pouring down the marbled staircase, and a line of housemaids were advancing across the hall, sweeping a veritable tide before them. We passed men with empty buckets coming down the stairs.

The once-white panelling of my room was blackened with soot, particularly by the window, where the smouldering remains of the sofa stood on the charred rags of what had once been a rug. There was a small table by the window also, lying on its side. The man with whom Mark had had the shouted exchange was there, candlestick in hand. He laid it down beside the table.

"That be where it were, master," he said to Mark. "'Twas almost the first thing we did notice when the smoke had cleared somewhat." His statement brought a chorus of agreement from the other men with him. Mark crossed over to the window and seemed to measure with his eye the distance from it to the table.

"Did you leave the window open when you went out this morning, Miss Button?" he asked.

I thought for a moment, to make sure. I sensed Alicia's eyes on me and I did not want to blunder into an unwitting falsehood.

"I left it slightly open," I said. "Yes, I remember slightly raising the lower sash, to allow some fresh air into the room while I was out."

Mark nodded. "Your bed has not been made," he said, "because all the housemaids would have been on their way to chapel at the time when they would normally be attending to the bedrooms. So we will take it that it must have been you, indeed, who transferred the candlestick over here, without thinking. . . ." This brought a sniff from his sister. He glanced at her, then went on: "We are now left with the possibility that a sudden gust of wind from the partly-open window overturned this rather spindly-legged table and the candlestick with it."

"But—I told you—the candle wasn't lit!" I cried.

"And sufficient wind to overturn the table would also have blown out the candle!" cried Alicia. "In which case there would have been no fire. Mark! I don't know what you're trying to get at. It's perfectly obvious that this creature started the fire, out of carelessness or stupidity. It's also obvious that she isn't going to confess. And quite how she did it is not of the remotest interest."

"I didn't do it! I swear I didn't!" I pleaded.

"You did!" said Alicia Dewaine flatly. "And you could have burnt down Landeric!"

I appealed to Mark: "Mr. Dewaine, it wasn't me. . . ."

His eyes suddenly flared wide. "Then who did?" he demanded.

I saw danger ahead—a new danger.

"Miss Button! Are you suggesting the fire was started by someone else?" he persisted.

Over his shoulder, I saw Hester staring at me. As I met her gaze, she avoided my eyes and became absorbed in tracing her fingertip against the sooted panelling. My mind went back to the ruined bonnet, the small horror in my bed. . . .

"Her silence implies that she does," grated Alicia.

"Be quiet, Alicia!" snapped her brother. "Miss Button, will you answer me?"

I looked around me. There was no escape. They hemmed me in: Mark and Alicia; beyond them, Jessica and the French girl; the silent regarding estate workers; Hester, still drawing white lines in the soot with her finger.

"Well, Miss Button?"

Suddenly a new voice: "Well, what a confounded mess. Thank God, it's no worse." Sir Tristan stomped into the room, prodding at panelling with his cane. "If this woodwork had caught fire, the whole place would have been in flames by now, and no steam-driven pump nearer than St. Errol. Why are you all standing around like an Irish parliament, eh?" He looked from one to the other of us, and settled his gaze on me. "What are you crying for, miss?"

"Sir Tristan, the fire. I . . ." I could get no further.

"Papa," said Alicia. "Papa, this sly creature is trying to avoid the blame for nearly burning Landeric to the ground by throwing the blame on someone else, for upsetting the candlestick that started it all."

"No!" I cried. "I wasn't blaming anyone." I appealed to the baronet: "Sir Tristan, I swear that I wasn't blaming anyone. I'm perfectly willing to accept the blame."

"Of course, of course," he replied soothingly. He came towards me and pulled a large black mourning handkerchief out of his tail pocket. "Dry your eyes and blow your nose, young lady. No one's attaching the slightest blame." He stared hard round at his family. "No one will *wish* to attach any blame to you for this accident. Candles are frequently overturned. I blame myself for the paucity of counter-fire arrangements in Landeric, and I shall order Pendower to purchase a steam-driven pump at once. But no blame is attached to you, Susannah Button. None at all."

I dabbed my eyes. "Thank you, Sir Tristan," I murmured gratefully.

"There, there. The matter is closed." He patted my shoulder.

"Do we resume the memorial service, Father?" asked Mark in a chill voice.

"The ceremony had reached a virtual conclusion, when we were interrupted," replied his father. "We will let it rest there. I will see you all at dinner. You will attend dinner with Hester, Miss Button."

59

Alicia gave a quick intake of breath and, turning on her heel, swept out of the room, followed by her middle sister and Amelie de Quatrefois. Mark remained. His face was white with a pent-up fury that he scarcely troubled to conceal.

"I should like a few words with you, Father," he said. "Alone."

"Certainly, m'boy," said Sir Tristan carelessly. "Come down to the library and we'll have a glass of Madeira. It's been a most fatiguing morning. Good day to you, Miss Button."

They went out together, leaving me with Hester and the desolation of my room. As far as I could judge, none of my belongings were damaged, though soot hung over all and everything would have to be washed. It could have been so much worse. I shuddered at the thought of it. Then my eye caught Hester: she was watching me from over by the window. I felt a sudden surge of anger and determination.

"Hester," I said. "I think the time has come for you and me to have a straight talk."

"A talk?" she asked in seeming innocence. "A talk about what, Miss Button?"

"I am speaking of a candle that overturned," I said. "Not of its own free will, but because someone—some person unknown—deliberately overturned it. Following on that, I will touch upon a bonnet—this bonnet—that suffered damage from that someone—that person unknown. Does all this strike a chord of memory in your mind, Hester?"

Her young and unformed face remained guileless and puzzled. I had a slack feeling of despair. Perhaps, after all, I had made a terrible mistake about her. There seemed no way of turning back; better to forge ahead. I waited for a few moments till she replied:

"I don't know what you mean, Miss Button. I really don't."

I swallowed hard. It seemed to me that I would soon be reduced to explanations and abject apologies.

But this was not to be. . . .

"After the candle and the bonnet, Hester," I persisted, "there is the matter of the dead rat in my bed."

I saw my shaft speed straight to its mark and strike truly home. Her face paled; her green eyes flared wide.

"Miss Bu-Button," she stammered. "I—I can explain about the rat. You see . . ."

I was filled with an unworthy sense of triumph that I had beaten through the child's defences and reached the truth.

"Explain away, Hester," I cried. "Begin with the rat, by all means. When you've done that, proceed with the other matters."

Tears started in her eyes. "Yes, I did put the rat in your bed," she wailed. "One of the footmen had just taken it from a trap, and I brought it upstairs in a bucket. I—I thought it was rather funny at the time. But . . ." She choked.

"But what, Hester?" I asked.

"But I didn't harm your bonnet, Miss Button! Nor did I set fire to your room. You must believe this. You must! I wouldn't dream of doing such dreadful things. The rat—well, that was just a rather horrid joke. Oh! I wish I hadn't done it!"

She burst into a flood of wild sobs and, brushing past me, she ran out of the room; leaving me standing there, trying to digest a hard and unpalatable fact that had just been presented to me.

If Hester had not been responsible for damaging my hat and setting fire to the room (and the manner of her confession convinced me she had not), then there was someone else in Landeric whose actions were directed by more than thoughtless childish mischief.

Someone—not a child, but a grown-up person—was attacking me with a purposeful intent to *destroy!*

* * *

Two footmen arrived then, to carry my belongings to a spare room where, they told me, I was to be lodged while my own room was cleaned and redecorated.

I went with them to a pleasant front chamber on the floor above, with a view down the glade of parkland that also included the glint of green-blue sea beyond Ramas Head. The men put my hamper and Father's sea chest in a small dressing room, bowed to me, and departed.

It was then I realised that I had left my reticule behind in the pew in the chapel. The shock of the fire alarm had driven it clean from my mind. No matter—I would go and fetch it immediately.

The hot sun was causing clouds of vapour to rise from the pools of water that still lay on the steps and the terrace. No one was about. A heavy silence hung over all. I crossed to the chapel door and opened it, stepping into the candlelit gloom. My footsteps sounded unnaturally loud in the empty vault of marble: instinctively, I went on tiptoe.

The reticule was where I had left it, of course. I took it up and advanced to the monument whose inscription I had been trying to decipher before the alarm was raised.

It was an elaborately-carved marble catafalque, set in an arched alcove. Above it, the marble bust of a man in an eighteenth-century wig gazed down at me, disdainfully, in the Dewaine manner. Sir Cedric, I decided, must have been the second baronet, probably Sir Tristan's grandfather. The next monument was a simple oval-shaped medallion of black slate, with the profile of a lady carved upon it in low relief. There was an inscription under:

Anne Harriet Mainwaring Dewaine
Beloved wife of Sir Tristan Dewaine, Bt.
Departed this life November 8th, 1837

This was she for whom the memorial service—so rudely terminated—had been held that morning: Sir Tristan's wife and the mother of his son and three daughters. Hester was eight, so Lady Dewaine had died when she was only an infant, perhaps she even perished in bearing her.

The dead Dewaines were all about me. They were even beneath my feet. Looking down, I saw that nearly every flagstone in the aisle was inscribed with the names and the dates of the departed. Some were plain: the last resting-places of future Dewaines; masters and mistresses of Landeric as yet unborn.

It was while contemplating upon this that I saw, or thought I saw, a movement from the corner of my eye. I quickly glanced up, and as I did so, it seemed to me that a pale flash of a face was looking in through one of the semi-opaque windows—and was almost immediately withdrawn. I felt my scalp prickle with alarm. Somebody was spying on me. Was it the someone who had twice already vented his—or her—spite against me in acts of destructiveness?

Something brushed against the window. It was the branch of a tree; I could see its pale leaves trembling in a slight breeze. Blessedly relieved, I smiled at my terror and retraced my steps to the chapel door.

But suddenly, unaccountably, I shuddered. Someone, I told myself, must be walking over my grave.

* * *

On inspection, I found all my costumes had been marked by the smoke and soot, so my dark brown day dress would have to serve for dinner. No matter: the humble governess would not be expected to shine in the company of the magnificent Dewaines. I washed out the detachable collar and cuffs that I had removed for the memorial service and asked one of the maids to iron them for me. With the addition of a brooch of pale blue glass from Mother's trinket box, they would have to serve for the formal occasion.

A quarter of an hour before dinner, there was a timid tap at my door. It was Hester, come to escort me down. The child was in a contrite and sorrowing frame of mind; she looked at me, large-eyed, like a puppy who seeks assurance that its shortcomings will be overlooked. I smiled at her and took her hand, commenting brightly on how nice she looked in her short dress of figured blue velvet—as indeed she did. Neither of us made any mention of what had taken place between us in the smoke-blackened bedroom; but, on the way down the staircase, I caught our reflection in a mirror, and saw my pupil giving me a look of relief and gratitude.

Strawson had announced to the company that dinner was on the table; they were filing out of the corridor leading from the drawing room, and we attached ourselves to the tail-end, behind the two older sisters. Strawson met my eyes at the dining room door, where he was stationed, in full court dress and powdered wig. We exchanged a brief, conspiratorial smile, and I wondered how Mrs. Horabin had found my account-keeping.

Hester guided me to my place at table, which was next to her and about half-way from each end. Sir Tristan was at the head, flanked by Amelie de Quatrefois and his eldest daughter. Mark Dewaine was placed at the other end from his father, with the Reverend Mr. Mawhinney and a lady guest next to him. There was one other guest: a youngish man whom I took to be the lady's husband. No one thought to introduce the mere governess to the newcomers, but the rector acknowledged me with a brief bow before he sat down.

The men were in evening black, with mourning crepe armbands; the women were not décolletée and in sombre colours—with the exception of Amelie de Quatrefois, who was wearing a creation of pale lemon silk that stopped only just short of scandal. Sir Tristan leaned sideways to address her; but from the way her blue eyes were sliding watchfully along the table towards Mark Dewaine, she would obviously have preferred a different table-placing.

The Reverend Mr. Mawhinney intoned grace, coupled with a

discreet and tasteful allusion to the departed Lady whose memory we were mourning that day. I could scarcely keep my wondering eyes from the table, with its burden of silverware, floral decorations and sumptuous desserts. Strawson had taken his stand behind and to the left of Sir Tristan's chair, ready, at his master's signal, to remove the covers and set his small army of footmen and maids about their tasks of serving the diners. And behind the vast array of foodstuffs already on view on the sideboards more rich and exotic dishes awaited in the vast, distant kitchens. For, as I was quickly to learn, the Dewaines dined like lords—and in the manner known as *à la Russe*, that is to say with courses carved and served from the sideboards, to suit the requirements of each individual guest, by a team of highly trained servants.

There was a menu card by my place, made out in what I recognised as Mrs. Horabin's shaky copperplate. I still have the card among my early souvenirs of Landeric.

Julienne Soup   *Vermicelli Soup*

*   *   *

Turbot and Lobster Sauce   *Red Mullet and Italian Sauce*
Stewed Eels   *Crimped Cod and Oyster Sauce*
Soles à la Normandie   *Perch—Water Souchy*

*   *   *

Filets de Poulets aux Coucombres   *Roast Haunch of Venison*
Mutton Cutlets and Sauce Piquante   *Braised Beef*
Lobster Rissoles   *Oyster Patties*
Pigeon Pie   *Larded Sweetbreads*
Roast Beef   *Chicken Cutlets*
Roast Saddle of Mutton   *Tongue*
Ham and Peas   *Boiled Turkey and Celery Sauce*

*   *   *

Capon   *Roast Ducks*   *Hare*
Green Peas à la Francaise   *Salad*   *Tomatas [sic]*
Marrow Pudding   *Charlotte Russe*   *Punch Jelly*
Damson Tart   *Neapolitan Cakes*   *Pastry*
Iced Pudding

*   *   *

Dessert and Ices

I hardly looked up from my soup during the first course, but while the plates were being cleared, Sir Tristan caught my eye and smiled encouragingly. His face was heavily flushed and he constantly replenished his glass from a decanter of sherry at his elbow; but he seemed in a cheerful and buoyant mood, and it seemed unlikely—considering the guests—that there would be a repetition of the kind of scene I had witnessed at that memorable luncheon, or so I told myself.

Neither Mark nor Alicia looked my way, but Jessica, who was sitting opposite me, surprised me by gently enquiring if much harm had come to my belongings as a result of the fire. I was able to tell her that they had only been slightly soiled. She nodded and shyly looked away. I noticed that the exchange won her a severe glance from her older sister.

It must have been fully an hour and a half later, during the third course, before anyone addressed me again. This time it was the rector, requiring to know how my pupil was progressing. I murmured a few complimentary remarks about Hester's satisfactoriness in work and conduct—and I was pleased to notice that the young miss had the grace to blush and half-choke on her oyster patty. This set Mr. Mawhinney reminiscing to his neighbour, Jessica, of how he had added to the many calls upon his time and charity by attending to the rudiments of my education; but I dismissed the rector's mumbled and hazy recollections, for I had suddenly become aware of a slight but tangible air of tension—like the first broodings of a coming storm—that was being set up between one end of the table and the other; between father and son.

Sir Tristan, who must have partaken of at least half the dishes on the menu, and who was now well down his second decanter of claret wine, had kept up a lively and accurate conversation with his neighbour in her own tongue. Amelie de Quatrefois, whether driven by boredom or from the effects of champagne, was lightly flirting with the baronet; patting her silvery-gold chignon and fluttering the long lashes of her brilliant blue eyes. Every so often—in the middle of telling her an anecdote or stating some opinion—Sir Tristan would interject, in a louder voice, some such remark as: "At least, that is what my fine son tells me," or "If you do not believe me, you must ask that clever son of mine." The interjections were clearly intended for the ears of Mark himself. As soon as I realised that, I was able to observe their effect.

The heir of Landeric was slumped in his seat, white-faced and smouldering-eyed with pent-up fury; making no attempt to converse with the lady on his left—a Mrs. Penbury—and totally ignoring the rector on his right. Every time a footman proffered him a dish, he waved it brusquely aside. A portion of meat lay on the plate in front of him, toyed with but untasted. He held a wine glass in his hand, slowly revolving the deep-red liquid in a whirlpool. And his eyes—those angry, brooding eyes—never left the face of the older man at the far end of the table.

Nor, of course, was I the only one present to notice it. The servants were very swift on the uptake—as servants always are—and muttered to each other uneasily at the sideboards, casting anxious glances back to their master and his son. Alicia had stopped listening to the man at her side, Mr. Penbury, so that his conversation dribbled to a halt and he, too, realised that something was amiss and joined Alicia in eyeing the causes of the rapidly-mounting atmosphere of unease.

Soon, there were only two voices at the table: the bumbling tones of the Reverend Mawhinney and Sir Tristan's deep growl. In the end, the atmosphere even penetrated the self-absorbed mind of the old cleric, and his reminiscences faded into silence. Sir Tristan, now that he held everyone's attention, slipped smoothly from French to English in mid-sentence.

"And Paris has much to commend it, Mam'selle," he declared, "but London is a gentleman's city—as my gallant son will confirm."

All eyes moved to Mark Dewaine, who drew a deep breath and seemed about to make some retort. He was forestalled by Mrs. Penbury, who showed more courage than was implied by her timid looks, and made an attempt to engage him in a conversation.

"Gentleman's city or not, Mr. Dewaine," she said, "London has much that commends it to ladies. Regent Street, with its arcading, is most convenient when shopping in inclement weather. But I have read that there is a move afoot, on the part of the shopkeepers, to have the arcading removed."

"I have heard something of the sort, madam," replied Mark uninterestedly.

"I hope nothing will come of it," declared Mrs. Penbury. "Don't you agree?"

"My son's military duties leave him little time for speculating upon matters architectural," interposed Sir Tristan heavily. "I doubt if the calls of the Brigade permit him to go traipsing down Regent Street, be the weather inclement or otherwise."

"Oh," said Mrs. Penbury, dismayed. And again: "Oh."

"My father," began Mark savagely, "my father knows very well that the military duties with the Household Brigade do not occupy its officers for more than a few brief hours a week."

"You must be such a comfort to Her Majesty," breathed Mrs. Penbury. "Such pretty uniforms."

"My son," sneered the baronet, "can scarcely speak with authority on the duties, arduous or otherwise, of the Brigade, since he is so seldom to be seen in London."

"I can never remember," faltered Mrs. Penbury, "whether it's the Life Guards or your regiment, Mr. Dewaine, who wear the scarlet tunics. Nor who wear the blue ones, for that matter."

Sir Tristan refilled his glass and drained it in one draught.

"In fact," cried Mark, "the application of a little arithmetic will establish that, far from exceeding the six months' furlough per year to which I am entitled, I have spent more than my allotted time in London."

Mrs. Penbury opened her mouth to make another comment, but a savage side-glance from Mark Dewaine slew the words on her lips.

Sir Tristan thumped the table top with the flat of his hand, so that the glassware and cutlery jangled. Mademoiselle de Quatrefois gave a shrill scream of alarm and brought her hands to her throat.

"Damn your eyes, sir!" he shouted down the table to his son. "When are we going to see the back of you? Answer me that!"

Mark Dewaine seemed to relax. Carefully placing his glass upon the table, he folded his hands in his lap and eyed his father with a blank and contemptuous stare.

"Answer me, sir!" repeated Sir Tristan in a voice of thunder. "Your commission in the Blues cost me twelve hundred pounds. When am I next to see some return for my money, hey?"

"If you mean, when am I returning to Knightsbridge Barracks," replied Mark, "the answer is—not for some time yet."

Again, Sir Tristan smote the table. I thought Mademoiselle de Quatrefois would faint with terror, and discovered that my own hands were trembling.

"By heaven, I'll write to your colonel and request that he order your return, sir!" shouted the irate baronet, whose eyes were now staring from his head and whose face was purple with choler.

"Then I shall resign my commission," responded his son, without a moment's hesitation.

"You will—you will do—*what?*"

Sir Tristan struggled to his feet, supporting the weight of his body with his hands on the table. A choking sound came from his livid lips and he raised his left hand to his throat, as if to loosen his neckcloth. In the act of doing so, his whole body overbalanced forwards and sideways, so that he fell towards his eldest daughter. Alicia, screaming, made an attempt to save him, but was herself borne down by his weight. Sir Tristan's right hand clutched convulsively at the table-cloth, taking it with him, together with a tangle of napery, glassware, crockery, broken food and spilled wine.

We leapt to our feet and crowded round, as the sobbing Alicia was helped to her feet. Strawson knelt by his master and laid his bewigged head against the other's chest. He gave a nod of relief and signalled to two of the footmen, who came forward and picked up the unconscious baronet between them.

In the hubbub of horrified comment that followed Sir Tristan's departure from the great dining room, I looked for Mark Dewaine and was surprised to see that he, of all of us, had remained in his place at table. He sat there, eyes closed, the bunched fist of one hand pressed against his agonised brow.

* * *

Hester was, naturally, greatly upset about her father. I took her up to bed and stayed with her, comforting her as best I could; till one of the footmen came with the news that the physician from St. Errol had been, had bled Sir Tristan and pronounced him to be out of immediate danger. After that, the child fell asleep from sheer dog-weariness. I left her, snuffing the candles and quietly closing the door. Next, I went along to the west wing and gently tapped upon Mrs. Horabin's door. The housekeeper was awake and looking much better. She was pathetically grateful for our help with her accounts, which were now in very presentable shape, she told me. I made her a pot of tea and shared it with her. It would have been about ten-thirty o'clock when I bade her good night and went back to my own room in the central wing.

No sooner had I entered the door and closed it behind me, than I sensed that something was wrong.

The shutters were open, and a patch of moonlight under the window provided the only illumination. The candlestick, I knew, was on the bedside table. I could just make it out in the gloom.

And the candle had just recently been extinguished—I could smell the tang of its dying smoke.

Someone had been in the room not many moments before!

It was while I was coming to grips with this fact that I saw a scattering of objects on the floor, near the edge of the patch of moonlight.

"Oh, no!" I cried aloud.

My mama's trinket box—a cheap thing of lacquered wood, but greatly treasured by me—had been trampled and broken underfoot, and her few, pathetic pieces of paste jewellery that represented the sole personal luxuries of her hard-working life had been similarly scattered and stamped upon.

My enemy—my secret enemy—had struck yet again.

He, or she, had come into that room quite recently and perpetrated yet another act of senseless destruction against me. The thing had been done very recently. The smell of candle smoke was only just fading. He, or she, may even have heard my footsteps on the stair outside and hastily snuffed the candle and fled at my approach.

Or . . .

Could still be hiding in the room!

I strained my eyes against the darkness at the far end of the room, beyond the bed, where a cluster of darker objects marked the positions of a chair, a sofa, a dressing table, something else.
. . .

"Who's there?" I cried.

The shape moved before I could collect my wits; reached the door, flung it open and was outside in the passage before my mind directed me to follow. But follow I soon did, with righteous fury lending me speed and resolution. I gained the corridor, in time to see the form of the moonlight intruder flitting up a steep flight of stairs leading to the upper floor.

"Stop!" I shouted. And raced in pursuit.

At the top of the stairs, I paused and listened. I could clearly hear my quarry's running footfalls—muffled, as if barefoot or in stockings—retreating along the dark corridor to my left. What was more, the sound of the intruder's laboured breathing also reached me clearly. A change of rhythm in the footfalls—and they were ascending another flight of steps.

A door opened in front of me, and Strawson appeared, carrying a candle. He was in nightgown and tasselled cap. He gaped in alarm to see me.

"Why, 'tis Miss Button!" cried the butler. "I did hear the shout. What ails you, miss?"

No time for laboured explanations: calling to Strawson to follow, I set off down the corridor as fast as I could run. He came more slowly, but his candle's light threw a giant shadow of myself before me as I climbed the steep flight of steps at the end of the corridor.

Again, I paused when I reached the top. Somewhere far off, I thought I heard the swiftly-padding feet—but then there was silence. I waited till Strawson had nearly reached me, then I moved forward again, but more slowly, pausing from time to time to listen.

The corridor was narrow and twisted. Sometimes it was only a wooden bridge spanning a dark vault of open space. The ceiling was low, hung with cobwebs and none too clean. I realised that we must be high up under the great steep roof of the mansion, where no daylight ever came. What was more, the place was a labyrinth: at every turn, corridors branched off into new, secret places of darkness. I stopped, stared about me in despair. My quarry had given me the slip.

"What's the matter, miss?" Strawson had managed to catch up with me at last.

"I found someone in my room," I explained. "I didn't see who it was, but some of my possessions had been deliberately destroyed."

The butler clicked his tongue in wonder and dismay. "Why, 'tis a terrible thing to have happened, Miss Button," he declared.

"We'll never find the culprit now," I said.

"We haven't given up yet, miss," he said stoutly. "Follow after me, do, and mind your head on the low ceiling."

Yet another narrow and ricketty stair brought us to a corridor which, by the shape of the ceiling, must have been directly under the very ridge of the roof itself. Narrow doors were dotted along this corridor, and it was upon the first of these that Strawson hammered with his fist.

"Open up!" he cried. "Open up, and mind you look sharp about it!"

From beyond the door there came a sudden muttering of surprised voices, a few bumps and bangs—and then the door was opened by a sleepy-eyed girl in a non-too-clean nightdress and hair in plaits.

70

"Mister Strawson, sir!" she gasped. "What be amiss, sir?"

"Stand aside!" And the butler elbowed his way past her. I followed.

By the light of my companion's candle, I picked out at least a dozen white, frightened faces regarding us from a line of pallets laid along the floor of a narrow room half the size of mine. There was not a breath of air in the windowless chamber, and I choked on the odour of unwashed bodies. Hanging along one wall were a dozen kitchenmaid's frocks and aprons belonging to the occupants of that human pig-stye.

This—under the same roof and all of a piece with the marbled splendour of the great apartments below—was where some of Landeric's small army of servants lived and had their being.

"Are you all here?" demanded Strawson.

A chorus of affirmation greeted his question. Notwithstanding, he counted the pallets and then counted heads.

"Has anyone been out into the corridors since you retired?"

"No, Mister Strawson, sir."

"Did you hear anyone go past. Just now. A few moments ago, like?"

Wide-eyed stares and the shaking of heads.

"Be you all telling me the truth?"

Nods.

Strawson motioned me to precede him out of the door, which he closed behind us.

"We'll keep trying, Miss Button," he said grimly. "Some wretch may not have found his or her way back into a rightful bed this night."

I measured the wrongs that had been done to me, and they suddenly seemed of less consequence than before. My mind returned to the pale, frightened faces beyond that door.

"Perhaps—it's scarcely worth bothering," I faltered.

"Oh, yes, miss!" he retorted, appalled. "The miscreant must be searched out and punished. Why, miss, I'll not rest easy in bed again till we have the scoundrel safely under lock and key in St. Errol gaol. Why, if we let this night's evil work pass unpunished, where's it all going to end? We'll all finish up by having our throats cut in our sleep! This way, miss."

So we proceeded down the corridor, with Strawson knocking on doors and demanding entrance. Some doors he merely opened without a knock: these were the rooms where menservants slept;

in these cases, he indicated with great delicacy that I should remain outside.

We reached the end of the corridor without finding a trace of our quarry, or of anyone who admitted to having heard footfalls in the night.

"The door at the end's only a cupboard," said Strawson. "We'll make sure our fellow isn't hiding in there, then we'll try the rooms along the next corridor. It may be a long search yet, Miss Button."

He opened the door of the cupboard, the walls of which were black with soot and hung with cobwebs.

We both cried out together at what we saw.

There was a woman suspended by the neck from a rope tied to one of the low beams. Slender, bare feet barely cleared the dusty floor. The pendent body was still in death, but slowly swaying and revolving on the rope. When it turned into the candlelight, I saw a livid countenance part-hid by a cascade of unbound hair the colour of ripe corn.

My moonlight intruder—my secret enemy—had been Annie, the beautiful blond housemaid who had served at table.

Chapter 3

All that following morning, I heard the comings and goings on the carriage drive below my window, but I kept the shutters closed. The maid who brought my morning tea told me that Miss Hester was still sleeping. The girl had obviously been weeping, so I did not press her for any more news. I sat till nearly midday, trying to read a book, but only succeeding in continuously re-reading the first page without taking in a jot of the sense; the clamour of my thoughts shut out all concentration. Shortly before noon, a footman delivered the message to me that Mr. Mark presented his compliments and would Miss Button be so good as to join him in the library?

Mark Dewaine was standing by one of the tall windows when I entered the huge, book-lined chamber. The white-painted mouldings of the window alcove intensified the light and made his face look pale. He was wearing a black riding coat and long boots.

He turned and said: "Good morning, Miss Button."

I curtsied.

"Please sit down," he said. "I should tell you that my father departed for Bath this morning. On medical advice. We have a town house in Bath, where he will stay for a protracted cure, taking the waters daily. I do not think we shall see him back in Landeric before next summer."

"I'm very sorry, Mr. Dewaine. Sir Tristan was very kind to me. I hope he makes a speedy recovery."

"Thank you, Miss Button."

He crossed over to the great fireplace and kicked at a log that sullenly burned there. His back was still turned to me when he spoke again.

"Would you care for some refreshment?"

"No, thank you," I replied.

"A glass of sherry? Madeira?"

"Thank you, no."

There was a long and awkward silence between us, measured out by the heavy ticking of a long-cased clock in a far corner of the room. I looked across at the back of his dark-maned head set squarely on his broad shoulders, and thought how strange it was that, in all my life, I had never known such a sense of isolation from another living person as that which I always experienced in the company of Mark Dewaine. In the old days, I had detested him for what I had imagined to be his lordly contempt; closer acquaintance had told me that to feel contempt for me was far beneath his dignity; for him, I simply did not exist as a person, in the sense that he and his family were persons.

Presently, he cleared his throat, and said: "Concerning the events of last night . . ."

"Yes?" I said.

He turned to face me, but his eyes were blankly expressionless.

"The police have been informed. They came this morning. The inspector collected a statement of evidence from Strawson, and seemed quite satisfied when it was suggested that you shouldn't be distressed any further."

"I see." What, I asked myself, was he trying to tell me?

"The matter will be treated with the greatest discretion," he said. "Strawson made no mention of the fact that the girl had been to your room."

"You mean—you told him to keep quiet about that?" I asked incredulously.

An angry shadow passed across his brow. "Strawson needed no instructions!" he snapped. "As a faithful retainer of this family, he is as concerned as I, or the rest of us, that no breath of—unpleasantness should be bruited around the duchy."

"A girl hanged herself last night," I retorted. "That was unpleasantness enough, surely."

He flushed and pursed his lips. Then, seeming to take control of himself with some effort, he said: "The unhappy woman committed suicide for reasons of her own; reasons that don't concern the outside world. The police are quite satisfied. We are all satisfied. That is the sum of it, Miss Button. That is the end of the affair."

"Oh, no, it is not, Mr. Dewaine!" I cried. "With respect, it is far from the end of it!" I faced him across the room, breathing heavily with the force of my emotion.

"What else?" he asked in a faraway voice.

I took a deep breath and said: "Before I came to Landeric, I had never before set eyes on the girl who killed herself last night. She may have seen me around the district, but not to my knowledge. Yet on two occasions, she made deliberate and destructive acts against me. . . ."

"The fire in your room," he said. "Yes, she was responsible for that."

"You *knew?*" I cried. "You knew when you were questioning me?"

"I knew when I had *finished* questioning you," he replied.

I felt helpless, bemused. There seemed no end to the veils of mystery surrounding the strange link between the dead girl and me. So even Mark Dewaine knew about it; had known about it before I had. What else did he know?

"Why?" I asked him. "Why did she do it?"

"Do you really want to know?"

"Yes."

"It will distress you, Miss Button. Better let the matter die here."

"Mr. Dewaine," I said wearily, "last night I was very angry to find that someone had wantonly broken a few cheap but very treasured souvenirs of my mother. On the impulse of that anger, I raised a hue and cry against the intruder and hounded her into a corner from which, in her opinion, she had no escape but to kill herself. I am not angry any more, Mr. Dewaine—only full of guilt that, but for my actions last night, Annie would still be alive. Nothing you are likely to reveal to me could possibly distress me more than that."

He nodded briefly and gave a sigh of resignation. "Very well," he said. "I take your point. You will obviously have to know the whole story. Are you quite sure you won't take a drink?"

I shook my head.

"Then, with your leave, I will," he said. And he poured himself a stiff measure of spirit into a rummer. I watched him half drain the glass. Somewhere across the lawns, a peacock gave out with its haunting cry. The clock ticked on.

"Well, Mr. Dewaine?" I prompted.

"I will not insult you, Miss Button," he said, "by trying to secure your promise that what I shall tell you must remain a secret between us. . . ."

"You have that promise," I interjected. "In advance and unconditionally."

He nodded gravely. "You have to know, to make any sense of this rotten business, that the young woman in question was, has been, my father's—concubine, I suppose that's the term in common parlance—for the last two years!"

He drained the remainder of his glass. I lowered my eyes to look at my hands, folded and trembling, upon my lap.

He went on: "It is not my place to make moral judgments upon my father's behaviour. I simply state the fact. It is known to me, to my older sisters, and to most of the servants, I should imagine—but, so far as I can guess, to no one outside the walls of Landeric. My father is not overly discreet, but he is . . . careful."

"I still don't see how this concerns me, Mr. . . ." I began.

"Wait!" He interrupted me. "I am now coming to the part of the story that is going to cause you distress. The young woman in question directed her destructive spite against you, Miss Button, because she was of the opinion that you had been brought here, not only as my youngest sister's governess, but to supplant her—Annie—in my father's favours."

"Wha-a-a-t?" I cried, rising to my feet, feeling the blood flee from my cheeks and my heart begin a wild hammering. "How can you say such a thing of me, sir? You must know it couldn't be true."

He shrugged. "She believed it to be true, Miss Button," he said.

"But—why? How could she?" I demanded.

"On evidence," he said.

"What evidence?"

"She had been told as much. Quite unequivocally, I should imagine."

"By whom?"

He paused, and then: "By my father. You have seen my father in certain of his . . . moods. When the spirit moves him, he has a very direct approach to people. Oh, yes, I should think that he did not mince matters with the young woman. You saw him deal with her at luncheon."

I sank weakly back into the chair, confused and frightened.

"I can't believe it," I said. "He was so kind to me. We valsed together and made Hester laugh. He was like a kindly uncle."

"My father can be very kind when he chooses," said Mark Dewaine dryly. "He was inordinately kind to the young woman in question for all of two years!"

Somewhere outside the confusion in my mind, a clear, hard-edged thought was fighting for recognition. I reached out for it and it burst upon me with a lantern-brightness. I stared up at Mark Dewaine.

"Now I know why you offered me money to go away and leave Landeric on that first day," I cried. "You also believed that terrible lie. You wanted me out of the way because you thought I had come to bring more scandal upon Landeric and the Dewaines."

He raised a hand of protest. "Miss Button, I assure you . . ."

But I was angry now. I saw it all too clearly. And I was determined that he was not going to sweep anything under the carpet.

"Why did you offer me that money, Mr. Dewaine? Why did you share that girl's belief about me?"

"For the same reason," he replied. "My father informed me of his future intentions regarding you. I decided, there and then, that the arrangement was—totally unsuitable."

"*Totally unsuitable!*" I could have struck him across his face at that moment.

"I'm sorry," he said, lowering his glance.

I could feel that my lower lip was beginning to tremble. At any moment, I should break down and make a fool of myself before this man. There was not much time: I had to say what must be said before my emotions choked the words in my throat.

"Totally unsuitable!" I repeated bitterly. "I know very well what you meant by that, Mr. Dewaine. For a higher servant—a person of some education, but a servant, nevertheless—to aspire to the position of—what was your word? concubine—would be a social disaster. Such a person can assert what she might consider to be her rights. She can speak up for herself without fear and confusion. She can write letters. Make all manner of mischief.

"Oh, yes, I can very well understand why you decided that I should leave Landeric immediately. Better that I be bought-off beforehand than be allowed to remain and turn out to be an expensive embarrassment.

"The Annies of this world don't have to be bought off, Mr. Dewaine. They can safely be . . . *discarded!*"

I had said it, and it scarcely mattered, now, that my eyes were so misted with tears that he was only a silhouette against the light of the window beyond; scarcely mattered that my lips were totally beyond my control.

But what was he doing now? Was he looking at me?

The silhouette remained steady. After what seemed a very long time, he said very quietly: "You are quite right, ma'am. I stand rebuked."

Then I saw him bow his head towards me and walk out of the room.

* * *

I left the house by a side door, fearful that I should meet with any of the Dewaine sisters, or that any of the servants would see me in my present state. I had to go somewhere quiet and remote, to escape and to think.

My footsteps carried me, by chance or design I shall never know, to the very spot, under the shading plane tree, where I had met the painter Durward de Lacey—was it only a few days before? My foot touched something in the grass. Stooping, I picked up a twisted and discarded paint tube.

The sun came out from behind a bank of cloud, and all Landeric stood bathed in the noontime glow, warm and curiously friendly, as it had been that first time. The thought that I should have to leave it wrenched at my heart; lying there in the sunlight, it was so easy to forgive the dark warren of slums that lay under its high-pitched roof; fatally tempting to forget the death agonies of that unhappy girl, and the callous wickedness of the owner. Landeric drew me to it with a bond that was all but irresistible. I knew that when I left (and leave I must, and that very day), there would remain a space in my life that would never be filled.

I remained under the plane tree till the middle afternoon, soaking in the loveliness, uncaring of food or drink, till I reckoned that it was time to put together my few things and ask Strawson to arrange a carriage to transport me back to the Haven. Jesse and his mother would accommodate me; tomorrow, or the next day, I would set out to find work.

I met no one on my way to my room, where I was surprised to find a large bowl of autumn flowers on the window-sill. There was a fan of paper tucked into the side of the bowl. Unfolding it, I revealed a brief message, written in careful, schoolgirl's round-hand: Hester's testament of her regard.

Please don't go.

The treacherous tears prickled my eyes once more. I carefully refolded the paper and put it in my reticule. At that moment, there came the sound of horses' hooves in the drive. Peering down, I saw Mark Dewaine riding from the direction of the stables with one of the grooms closely following. He did not look up (I had drawn myself back against the shutters), but cantered on past and down the drive in the direction of Pennan village.

A few moments later, a tap at my door announced a footman bearing a letter on a silver salver. It was from Mark Dewaine. He had filled half a sheet with his dashing, impetuous script.

Dear Miss Button,

I have two hopes. The first is this: that you will find it in your heart to forgive the wrong that has been done to you—not least by myself, in the clumsy and inopportune manner in which I revealed your part—your entirely innocent involvement—in this shameful business.

You took me to task over an infelicitous phrase I used. The rebuke was justified; but you were quite wrong in your interpretation. The phrase "totally unsuitable," as applied to yourself, Miss Button, has an entirely different meaning from the one you seized upon. So much for my first hope.

My second hope is that you will reconsider what will surely (and rightly) be your first reaction to what has happened: to leave Landeric this very day.

It is my sincere wish that you stay, at least for a while, for I know that Hester will miss you greatly. You need have no fear about meeting my father again; as I told you, he will not be returning from Bath before next summer.

This letter is written in some haste, for I have to ride to St. Errol on urgent family business. When I return tonight, I shall hope to find that you have responded favourably to my entreaties.

> I remain, Miss Button,
> Yours sincerely,
> Mark Dewaine

A maid tapped on the door and entered with a pile of my linens that had been freshly laundered after having been soiled in the previous day's fire. Almost without thinking, I asked her to lay them in the chest of drawers—and not pack them in my wicker hamper for departure.

So, without any great strain, I overturned my earlier decision and remained in the fairytale palace of my childhood imaginings. Whether I was more influenced by Mark Dewaine's somewhat effusive epistle, or by Hester's simpler and more direct appeal, I had no way of telling at that time.

* * *

Memory is a house with many doors that open and close of their own accord; and windows that often prove to be nearly opaque, so that they only present a ghostly outline of what lies beyond.

So it is that the events of the months that followed—in the autumn, winter and spring that spanned the years '45 and '46—are patchily recorded in my mind: sometimes springing forth unbidden; sometimes slipping beyond recall: people and happenings of considerable importance becoming as insubstantial as past dreams; and the commonplace taking on a strange importance.

I remember the departure of Alicia, Jessica and Mademoiselle de Quatrefois back to France.

Alicia had not addressed a single word to me since my interrogation on the day of the fire. Her whole attitude remained that of total contempt, and it was not hard to see why: she, at least, was quite convinced that her father's unspeakable plans concerning me had been made with my knowledge and approval—only this could account for the way she had treated me from the very first.

No farewell, then, from the eldest sister; but Jessica made a point of calling at the nursery to say good-bye to Hester and me together. She took my hand and shyly wished me every happiness at Landeric, adding that she looked forward to seeing me again at Christmas. There was something else: somewhere concealed behind her timid, reserved manner was the fact that Jessica seemed to be trying to communicate a secret message to me. The impression was very strong—but I could not account for it.

As for Amelie de Quatrefois, her superior brand of coquetry was, by the time of her departure, being almost constantly directed upon Mark Dewaine. They were often to be seen riding-out together, strolling in the park and the water gardens, feeding the peafowl and the deer. I came to recognise her way of listening to him with her head slightly on one side, lips tremulously parted, and to predict the moment when her slender hand would come up and smooth her side curls. I decided that the French girl's style of attracting men was not so different, after all, from that of the fishermen's daughters down at the Haven. From Hester, I learned that she was the daughter of a count. No doubt a connection of the two families in marriage would be considered a very desirable union. Somehow, for all his many faults, the thought made me feel rather sorry for Mark.

All in all, it was a relief to see their carriage receding down the drive to St. Errol and the railway station. Now there was only Hester and myself. And Mark, of course—a distant and formerly somewhat alarming figure, now become almost human in stature.

Only a few days after the girls had returned to France, the long and balmy autumn gave way to the first chill winds of winter, so that it called for a roaring fire every day in the nursery grate, and Hester and I wore our cloaks and shawls when we went out for our walks. The colder weather, also, had a bad effect upon Mrs. Horabin's infirmity: the old housekeeper was mostly confined to her bed, and I was obliged to take over more and more of her duties. She suffered a severe relapse before Christmas. It was left to Strawson and me—with Hester our indefatigable arithmetician —to order in the vast quantities of provisions and make the arrangements for the festive season's junketings.

Some time before Christmas Hester told me that Mark had formally resigned his army commission. He had been to London only for one short visit before then. I wondered how his father would react to the news. No one ever made a mention of Sir Tristan, but it was accepted that no provision would be made for his return from Bath till the summer. I had decided, of course, that this event would be the signal for my departure from Landeric. Meanwhile, there stretched ahead of me a brief season of delight in my fairyland palace.

I was much relieved when news arrived from Paris that the two elder sisters had accepted an invitation to spend Christmas at the home of Amelie de Quatrefois. Nothing now remained to mar my happiness in Landeric; no sour-faced Alicia to remind me of what I preferred to put right out of my mind.

Christmas at Landeric was a round of balls, dinners and parties. It began with a Tenants and Staff Ball in the great ballroom at which I officiated as hostess in place of Mrs. Horabin (who told me, poor woman, that this would be the first "Tenants and Staff" she had missed since coming to Landeric forty years before, as a housemaid). I opened the ball by dancing a valse with Mr. Pendower, the estate bailiff (who was all at sea), after which the tenants of the outlying Landeric farms and their wives, and the indoor and outdoor staff of the mansion, took the floor and danced the evening away beneath the painted gods and goddesses. Towards the end of the proceedings, Mark Dewaine briefly appeared with Hester, and the two of them gave presents to everyone— money to the staff and boxes of handkerchiefs to the tenants.

The following night, being Christmas Eve, Mark gave a dinner party for the local gentry. The rector and the Penburys were present, together with a dozen Cornish squires and their ladies. Hester and I sat together, as usual. It was an event so totally different from the night of Sir Tristan's collapse as to carry no disturbing overtones of memory. Mark Dewaine was urbane and good-humoured and actually *smiled* at me, though only briefly. Afterwards, we all repaired to the chapel, where the Reverend Mr. Mawhinney conducted a midnight service.

It was on Christmas Morning that I went back to the Haven for the first time; with Hester, in a landau, to help distribute money to every man, woman and child in the valley. This had been the custom since time immemorial, when the lordly Norman De Vaines had first come to Cornwall. It struck me how poor and ill-nourished the people looked, and how different from the way I remembered them when I lived among them. Even little Jesse— who grinned shyly at me from the crowd and touched his forelock as if I, too, had been a Dewaine—seemed no more stunted and toilworn than most. It occurred to me to wonder if the menfolk had resumed their smuggling activities; I much doubted if they would attempt wrecking again. We stayed in the Haven only long enough to distribute half-sovereigns; afterwards I laid a wreath of holly on Father's grave in the little seamen's cemetery above the harbour.

The round of merrymaking, of bell-ringing, carols, present-giving and receiving, of laughter and goodwill, gave way to the new year, and on New Year's Day I started to keep a diary for 1846. The volume itself, handsomely bound in red Morocco, was a present from Hester. It is still with me—another of my souvenirs.

Prompted by my diary, I remember that it was a hard winter in

Cornwall, with gales raging round the coasts, making it impossible for the fishing boats to put out. This, coupled with a drought in the summer that had caused a disastrous harvest, brought terrible hardship to the people of the valley, who would have starved but for the intervention of Mark Dewaine. He ordered Pendower to scour the duchy as far afield as Redruth and Penzance for every bushel of wheat he could lay hands on for cash. This was all distributed free. At that time, I do not recall that we at Landeric, even when dining informally, ever sat down to a choice of less than four meat dishes in the second course. Neither Hester nor her brother seemed to see anything abnormal in this; they were the Dewaines, and the Dewaines were not to be deprived of so much as a crust of bread—not even if all the forces of Nature conspired against them. I am glad to say that I felt ashamed when I thought of those pinched faces down in the village and the Haven.

Presently, the long winter gave way to spring, and the sides of the glade sweeping down to the lake were carpeted with snowdrops and later with daffodils. Landeric seemed to take on a fresh life again, its great bulk glowing warmly in the new sunshine.

Spring brought extra delights. It brought long walks on the moors above the valley and drives along the coast road.

It also brought the St. Errol Fair—and a day that will remain imprinted in every detail, without need of a diary's prompting, till the day I die.

* * *

"Oh, look, Miss Button! Look at the sky. Not a cloud in sight. Without our parasols, we'd all get as brown as gipsies!"

"Or as fisher-folk—like me!" I said, smiling indulgently at Hester.

"I'm sorry," she said. "I didn't mean . . ."

"My dear, I've long since ceased to break my heart about my sun-browned complexion," I assured her, which was true. It seemed another age when her elder sister had been able to reduce me to tears by mercilessly pointing out my defects. The months at Landeric had given me a new assurance, brought a serenity into my life and and character; almost as if some of the splendid solidarity of my surroundings had entered into my heart.

"Here come the carriages," cried Hester, dancing with excitement. "And here's Mark."

We were off to the St. Errol Fair, along with everyone in that part of Cornwall who had the strength to walk or the means to transport himself. Only, being the people from Landeric, we were doing it in grand style—Dewaine style.

For one thing, we were taking along thirty guests and as many servants. That, together with provisions for a picnic, called for a procession of ten carriages and an equal number of wagons. Mrs. Horabin had insisted on sitting up in bed and personally writing out the bill of fare for the picnic, as she had done every year since she became housekeeper. The hampers that were being loaded upon the carts contained—as I knew, for I had seen to their preparation—joints of cold beef both roast and boiled, cold ribs and shoulders of lamb, cold roast fowls and ducks, as well as hams, tongues and various meat and game pies of the largest size, lobsters fresh from the Haven, and salads of every variety; for dessert, we carried bottles of stewed fruits, pastry biscuits, fruit turnovers, cheese cakes, blancmanges and cabinet puddings all in moulds, cheese and butter, as well as ample loaves of bread both tin and household; for beverages, there were quart bottles of ale and cider, ginger beer, soda water and lemonade, sherry wine and claret wine, hocks and champagne.

"Good morning, Hester. A fine day, Miss Button."

Mark Dewaine was travelling with us on horseback. He clattered to a halt beside our carriage and swept off a broad-brimmed straw hat, bowing to us. In some ways, I had grown easier in his company over the course of the months, but there was always a mutual constraint that was not entirely explained away by the fact that we were, to all intents and purposes, master and servant. No —there was still that strange antagonism that I had sensed from the very first, from the time when I had defied him on the day of the stag hunt. If anything, despite the surface improvement in our acquaintance, the tension between us had got worse. Sometimes I caught him eyeing me sidelong, reflectively. And his sudden appearance in a room or meeting him in a corridor or on a staircase had the power to make me uneasy.

But this day, the day of the St. Errol Fair, he seemed determined to make himself specially agreeable; riding beside our carriage as we rolled down the long drive and out along the winding, hedge-hung lanes to the Fair; chatting with his young sister and not entirely excluding me from the conversation.

"Will there be a fortune-teller at the Fair, Mark?" demanded Hester.

"I should think it highly likely, wouldn't you, Miss Button?"

"Yes, indeed," I replied. "Some of the gipsies are said to possess strange powers."

"I shall have my fortune told," declared Hester.

Mark laughed. "And what dread revelations do you hope to have plucked out of your future, Hester?" he asked.

"I should like to know," replied Hester, "how long I am going to live, for a start."

"That would be a terrible thing to learn," replied her brother. "Better to ask the gipsy not to tell you that. Even if she were wrong—which is certain—the knowledge would blight your life. Better to ask her something harmlessly intriguing. Something like: who are you going to marry and how many children will you be blessed with?"

Hester clapped her hands. "Yes, I should like to learn that," she cried. "What about you, Miss Button—what shall you ask?"

"I hardly know," I confessed.

"Surely you'd like to be told the name, or description, of your husband-to-be?" she persisted.

"You assume too much, Hester," interjected her brother. "Perhaps Miss Button is not so hopelessly romantic as you are. Would you say not, Miss Button?"

I felt the colour mount in my cheeks. A glance at his face told me what I had suddenly guessed: he was teasing me.

"I am as romantic as most," I replied tartly. "I think you should ask Mr. Dewaine, Hester, if *he* is going to ask the gipsy fortune-teller to name his future bride."

"It would be a waste of time and money, poor dear," said Hester. "For the lady has already been named."

"Hester!" Mark Dewaine's sudden anger was very evident. "We will talk about something else."

But the girl was not to be put off. Assuming a crabbed and screwed-up facial expression seemingly intended to represent that of an aged gipsy fortune-teller peering into the mists of the future, she intoned: "I have the first letter of your beloved's name. It is . . . let me see . . . her name begins with . . ."

"Hester! Will you be quiet!"

"I see the letter 'A' . . ."

"Will you still your tongue, child!"

"Followed by the letter 'M' . . ."

With a snort of fury, Mark Dewaine wheeled round his horse

and rode off back down the line of carriages following behind us, leaving his young sister giggling mischievously and me thoughtfully digesting the not unsurprising gobbet of news that Hester had dropped into my lap. So my guess that Mark was destined to marry Amelie de Quatrefois had been correct: the matter was already under discussion, but was still a family secret. Perhaps there were impediments: perhaps the lady in question had not herself been told of her glittering prospects. I was still turning this over in my mind when the spire of St. Errol church rose beyond the hedgerows and our coachman whipped up the horses to take the steep hill above the town.

St. Errol Fair is one of the oldest institutions in the duchy, older even than the junketings at Padstow, Helston and elsewhere. That year, as always, it took place on "Old Billy," a rugged, flat-topped hill that dominates the town, and from whose bracken-covered heights one can see the silvery strip of sea lining the horizon from east to west.

Half-way up Old Billy, with the horses flagging badly, we heard the concerted sounds of the fair: the sharp cries of the vendors and the side-show touts, the screech of steam engines' whistles, a brass band playing out of tune, and above it all, like some vast beehive, the hum of countless voices.

We arrived at the Fair. Hester must see everything at once. She took my hand and pulled me towards where the crowds were thickest, down a wide avenue formed by booths and roundabouts.

"Be back for luncheon, Miss Button," cautioned Strawson. "Mr. Dewaine has instructed me to lay luncheon over there . . ." he pointed to a deserted part of the hilltop some distance away from the limits of the Fair "at one-thirty o'clock."

"That gives us plenty of time to go right round the fair and pick out the best things for this afternoon," cried Hester, pulling at my hand. "Come on, Miss Button."

Hester leading, we plunged into the crowd and were instantly pressed in by the laughing, jostling throng; adrift in a sea of tall hats and bonnets.

"I can't see a thing!" wailed Hester from somewhere down below.

"Up on my shoulders," came a voice at my elbow. It was Mark Dewaine. He hoisted his young sister (who was no mean weight) up onto his broad shoulders, so that she sat with her long pantaloons and her pink, buttoned boots dangling over his chest.

"That way, Mark!" pointed Hester. "I can see a dancing bear!"

There was indeed a dancing bear. A big, shaggy creature with doleful looks and a coat like a dusty old kitchen doormat, who loped and shambled to the music of a squeaky violin played by an ancient Italian. I found it distasteful, but the ring of onlookers laughed themselves to tears at the poor thing's antics. Mark Dewaine seemed to agree with my view; he scowled, tossed a coin into the Italian's hat, and we moved on.

There was a troupe of blackamoor minstrels, with banjos and tambourines, singing songs of the American plantations, accompanied by much eye-rolling. We watched their zestful performance while Hester had a ride on the round-about horses. After that, she demanded to be bought a toffee apple on a stick. Mindful of luncheon, I glanced enquiringly at Mark Dewaine, but he hunched his shoulders in resignation and dipped his hand in his pocket.

"Let's look for the fortune-teller now," mumbled Hester through a mouthful of sticky apple. I saw Mark purse his lips with a sudden, angry recollection of the conversation on the journey.

In the event, we chanced to come across a booth where a very thin young gipsy with a long, pale face and a much battered tall hat set atop his raven curls was cutting a paper silhouette of a young girl. A wide-eyed semi-circle of people watched every twist of his bright scissors, and an admiring murmur went up when he had finished. Pasted on a card, and held up beside the sitter's profile, the black cut-out presented an admirable likeness.

"Come now, sir! How about a souvenir of the Fair? Portraits of you and the two lovely young ladies. I'll tell you what—you may have three for the price of two. How's that?"

The speaker was a grey-haired gipsy woman of enormous size, seated at a table in the front of the booth. It was she who collected the money and pasted the finished silhouettes on to cards. Her offer was addressed to Mark Dewaine. Her piercing, dark eyes were regarding him appraisingly.

"Oh, let's have our silhouettes done, Mark!" cried Hester. "Me first!"

Her brother nodded, and she sat down. The young artist began to slash rapidly with his scissors, meanwhile turning the square of black paper this way and that, his eyes flashing between the model and his work. It was soon done, the unmistakable Dewaine nose and all—and very like Hester.

"You next," murmured Mark in my ear, gently urging me forward.

The stout gypsy woman said: "Take off your bonnet, dearie, so that my Tom may do your lovely head to advantage. Ain't that indeed a lovely head, Tom?"

"Indeed it is, Mother," retorted the artist. "Chin up a little, ma'am. Yes, there's real nobility in that face."

I felt myself flush with embarrassment and tried not to see the line of staring faces that turned from me to the contortions of the artist and back again.

Presently, the silhouettist said: "You may now relax, ma'am. I have captured you for posterity. See?" He held up his work. His flattery had led me to expect too much, and I was greatly disappointed. The prim-faced miss with the smoothed-back hair and the tight-lipped looks gave me a jolting reminder of what I was: a commonplace, spinsterish schoolma'am!

"It's very clever," I commented.

"Next, the gentleman," said the artist's mother. And Mark Dewaine took off his hat and sat down.

"I think yours is lovely," whispered Hester, squeezing my hand. "I wish you'd give it to me, to hang in my room."

"It's yours, with pleasure," I said.

The artist caught Mark's likeness marvellously well. The telltale Dewaine nose was there, of course; but also the more subtle detail of the set of his head—arrogant, almost defiant.

"Thank you, my man," said he. "How much?"

"Three copies of each, mounted for framing—that'll be one and six-pence to you, sir," replied the artist. He saw our puzzlement, and, with a wink, he separated the black silhouettes, revealing that he had cleverly cut three time at a time of each sitter.

"What a splendid idea," cried Hester. "Now we'll each have a set."

The artist passed the cuts to his mother, to paste them down on sheets of card, and turned to deal with his next sitter: a merry-faced gentleman with a nose of the proportion and colour that betrayed a lifelong dedication to the bottle; indeed, he joked of it to the watching crowd and advised the artist to provide himself with a large sheet of black paper for his task.

Hester and Mark Dewaine were amused witnesses to this impromptu pantomime, so they were all unaware of what took place between the artist's mother and myself. . . .

It was an incident that I have relived a thousand times in my dreams and in my waking thoughts. It happened very quickly, too quickly for me properly to register at the time; it is only in recollection that it comes back slowly and with great solemnity, like a figure from a stately dance of the olden time, splendidly unhurried.

The woman was pasting down the silhouette of Hester. She tapped my elbow and withdrew my attention from the artist and his model.

"Was you wanting yerself and the gentleman mounted on the same card, dearie?" she asked.

"What?" I stared at her, bemused.

"Like this—see?" She placed my silhouette on a large card, opposite that of Mark Dewaine, both facing inwards, profiles nearly touching. "Ah, what a fine, handsome pair indeed."

I cast a hasty glance round for Mark Dewaine: to my heartfelt relief both he and Hester were still being diverted by the artist and sitter.

"No—please!" I whispered. "On separate mounts."

"There's some as like 'em hanging side by side," she said, busying herself with the paste brush, "and some as like to be mounted together. There's no telling with sweethearts, so I allus ask. There you are, dearie. They'll bring memories of St. Errol Fair when the both of you are old and grey, with grown grandchildren."

I stammered some sort of thanks and made to take the mounted silhouettes from her hand. But her fingers did not release them at once, and those dark, luminous eyes fixed me with a look that was full of an ancient wisdom.

"You will know much unhappiness through him," she said. "And I don't see far enough beyond the veil to be able to tell you how it will all end. But this I tell you, dearie—and I am the seventh child of a seventh child, with the gift of seeing—you will never regret that you have given your love to that man."

Struck to silence, I turned away. Hester ran towards me and took the silhouettes from my hand.

"I shall keep my set all my life," she said, "to remind me of this lovely day."

"Very commendable," said her brother, and the sound of his voice made me start. "I think we must cut short our wanderings for the morning and return to our guests, who will be needing some refreshment. My throat is parched. I hope you reminded

Strawson to provide plenty of ice for the champagne and hock, Miss Button."

* * *

It was ridiculous, I told myself. Absurd. One would think I had been drinking (I had not). Best to put the whole thing completely out of my mind and get on with the task in hand. And the task in hand happened to be helping to supervise the picnic. I followed Strawson on a last-minute tour of inspection of the arrangements. The food had been laid out upon large table-cloths spread on the ground, ready for serving. All seemed in order.

(Where was he? Somewhere over by the carriages, talking to a lady in a white dress and black bonnet—reminding me of the outfit Amelie de Quatrefois had worn on that first occasion. . . .)

Strawson was addressing me. I came to with a start.

"I think, with your approval, Miss Button," he murmured, "that the footmen can commence to pass among the ladies and gentlemen with the menus."

"Er . . . yes," I concurred.

The guests—the younger ones at any rate—were seating themselves on the ground, while the older and more sedate remained in the open carriages, under their parasols. Some of the servants were circulating with trays of beverages. One of them paused by me and my hand strayed towards a glass of lemonade, then—most untypically of me, for I normally have no partiality for wine—I firmly picked up a glass of champagne and raised it to my lips.

(He was still talking to her. Laughing. She's quite young, no more than twenty-six or seven and quite pretty. A daughter of another of the big local houses, perhaps. . . .)

The chill effervescence of the wine played riot with my nose and throat and I doubled up in a paroxysm of coughing. Strawson hurried to my side, all solicitous.

"Be you all right, miss?" he asked.

"Yes," I replied firmly. "And I should like another glass of champagne if you'd be so kind as to summon a footman."

This was speedily done.

"And what would you be fancying for luncheon, miss?" asked the kindly butler. "A few slices of rare-done beef, or a bit of game pie? Find yourself a cosy spot to eat, and I'll serve and bring it over to you myself, along with a nice salad."

"Thank you, no," I replied. "I'm not hungry. In fact, I don't think I can ever remember feeling less hungry in my life." Which was perfectly true.

"Be that so, miss?" said Strawson, eyeing me wonderingly. "Be that so indeed?"

I smiled a secret smile to myself, looking down into the amber fountain within my wine glass. The bubbles prickled my nose again, but this time it was a caressing and pleasurable sensation. I felt strangely elated.

(Where was he now? . . .)

Hester ran up to me. She was holding the hand of a small boy in a sailor suit.

"This is Toby," she said.

I said: "Hello, Toby," and he took off his straw hat very nicely.

"Strawson is having Toby's and my luncheon made up into sandwiches," said Hester. "Can we take and eat them over there, on the rocks?" She pointed to a tumbled heap of boulders at the far end of the hilltop.

I nodded. "Of course."

(It was then that I saw him again. He was raising his hat to the lady in the white dress, bowing and taking his leave of her; it may have been my fancy, but she seemed reluctant to let him go, and continued talking to him, trying to keep him with her. . . .)

"Don't drink too much champagne," cautioned Hester. "It will only make you giggle. It always makes the rector giggle. Come on, Toby. Race you to the rocks."

The Penburys took my attention: called me from their carriage to join them. I went over and said that I was not eating, but would sit with them for a while. I had not seen much of them since the night of Sir Tristan's collapse, and Mrs. Penbury wanted to know the latest news of him, but of course I had none to tell. Not one bit put out, she then launched into a long account of a relation of her own who had been given to sudden seizures, and how this great-uncle had, nevertheless, lived to a fine old age. I sat and gazed at her, nodding when it seemed called upon me to do so and interjecting a word or a mild exclamation at the apposite moments. Mr. Penbury addressed himself stolidly to his piled luncheon plate and bottle of claret. Most of my mind was entirely absent, and with half an eye I was trying to see under the rim of my parasol and round the back of the carriage. There was no sign of Mark.

I was only half-jolted into reality by the thin scream of pain and terror: Mrs. Penbury's mouth stayed open in the middle of a word and I thought for a moment that the sound had come from her.

"It's Hester!" someone shouted. And I saw Mark Dewaine vault over the shafts of a carriage and go haring off towards the rocks, towards the humped figures of Hester and the boy in the sailor suit. Almost before I knew it, I was after him and half-way to the rocks. A group of us arrived there all at once. Hester was crouched on the ground, nursing her right arm and keening to herself. Her eyes were shut close and her face was the colour of parchment. The boy in the sailor suit was crying.

"The adder bit her," said the boy Toby, pointing. "Hester saw something move in the bracken and put her hand inside. It bit her twice, then slid away."

"Twice?" exclaimed Mark. Our eyes met across Hester's head.

"Give me your poor hand, dear," I put my arm round the trembling child, but she only clung more tightly to her right hand and arm.

One of the footmen was questioning the boy. "How big was the adder then, Master Toby?"

"Big one," said Toby. "Long as your arm. Big as I've seen."

" 'Tis bad when they're big," said the footman. "And 'tis a bad time of the year to get bit, in the spring. The poison's very strong this time o' year."

"Will you shut your mouth!" spat Mark savagely. "Hester, you must give me your hand."

Between us, we managed to prise away the grasp of the child's left hand. Her right hand was tightly clenched, and a thin trickle of bright blood lay across the knuckles. Mark took the hand in his, dabbing at the blood with his handkerchief, patiently uncurling the small, slim fingers, till, with a small shock of horror, I saw the wounded palm: two bluish-coloured puncture marks.

"I'm going to die!" cried Hester, and she began to scream hysterically.

"Get a tight band around her upper arm," said one of the young male guests. "Here, take my necktie, Mark. It's important to stop the poison from spreading through the system."

"Thank you, Piers," said Mark. He nodded to me. "Roll up her sleeve, please, Miss Button."

Hester had stopped her cries and had buried her face against her brother's shoulder. He was still holding her wounded hand as I drew up the sleeve. There were sharp intakes of breath, and exclamations of horror and pity all round me—as a second pair of ugly punctures were revealed just above the slender wrist. Toby was right: the adder had struck at her twice.

Mark knotted the necktie above the elbow joint and called for a spoon, which he slipped behind the knot, turning it, to tighten the band. Then, bidding me to keep a firm hold of the spoon, he bowed his dark-maned head over his sister's arm, sucking at first one pair of wounds then the other, and spitting out. His head was so close to me that I could see the tiny, black curls in the nape of his neck, and I had a disquieting impulse to touch him.

"It hurts—so much," sobbed Hester. "Am I going to die? Am I?"

"Healthy folk don't perish of adder-bites, my dear," came the cheerful reply from the young man who had given his necktie: he was about eighteen, golden-haired and dashingly handsome; I recognised him as one of the Trevallion menfolk, big landowners from farther down the coast. "I was bitten when I was a lad, and look at me now."

Hester gave a wan smile—and was immediately sick.

"We'd best get her home," said Mark to me. His face was set and anguished as he stroked his sister's trembling shoulders.

A carriage was brought up, and willing hands lifted Hester tenderly on to one of the seats and covered her with rugs. A groom was already on his way into St. Errol to fetch the physician; another was dispatched to ride after him and divert the physician to Landeric. I crouched on a cushion beside Hester, dabbing her feverish brow and speaking soothingly to her, as the carriage swept down the road from Old Billy and the fair that had suddenly turned into a nightmare.

Mark Dewaine rode alongside us. From time to time I looked up, and our eyes met. He never held my glance for more than a moment, but switched his gaze to the stricken girl beside me.

* * *

A sultry afternoon gave way to a stormy evening. I stood at the top of the great staircase at Landeric and watched the distant lightning playing over the sea beyond Ramas Head; watched it slanting in jagged forks from the indigo sky of the dying day. And the rain streamed down as only West Country folk know it, rebounding knee-high from the flagged terrace, overflowing the gutterings and swamping the ornamental ponds. The last of the sun went down in a narrow strip of sky that was tinged an unhealthy yellow—

abandoning Landeric and all within its walls to the night and the roaring rain.

The physician had left an hour since. Hester was sleeping peacefully: I had just come from looking in at her. In the long hours of unremitting agony and nausea, her robust young body had thrown off the evil effects of the venom—assisted by the application of lunar caustic, the taking of hot brandy-and-water with *sal-volatile*, of mustard and hot water, and an opium pill— and, of course, the sovereign remedy of copious bleeding by the physician's keen lancet. Nor had her recovery—now certain—been by any means a foregone conclusion; in the dark hours of that sultry, threatening afternoon, when the rolling of distant thunder made the casement windows rattle, Mark Dewaine and I had lived with the physician's sombre warning that the bites were both deep and strongly envenomed—of the type, in fact, that give rise to the occasional fatalities among children in the locality.

The crisis came in the late afternoon after a bout of terrible vomiting, induced by the mustard and hot water, had so weakened the young patient that her pulse all but faded to nothing, and I had the thought that she was slipping away from us. In that moment, also, I felt Mark Dewaine's hand upon my shoulder, and looked up to see that he was gazing down at his sister's pale face with an expression of such utter desolation that my heart cried out for him. But the worst was over and Hester presently slipped away into an opium-induced sleep.

"She will be all right, Mr. Dewaine," said the physician.

"Thank heaven!" cried the other.

We left the sick room together. The physician bobbed a little bow to both of us and went off down the stairs. I glanced irresolutely at Mark. He was deep in his own private thoughts and seemed only to remember my presence with an effort.

"Oh, Miss Button," he murmured.

"Mr. Dewaine?"

He passed his hand across his brow. He really did look terribly tired and overwrought. I had known that there was a deep and special bond between him and his youngest sister, but it surprised me that even the terrors of that day could have produced such a profound effect upon a strong and resilient man like Mark.

"As to what happened . . ." he began.

"Yes?"

"I really am most profoundly grateful for your help and support," he said. His firm lips attempted a smile; but it died in the making.

"It was nothing, Mr. Dewaine," I replied. "What I did, any woman would have done, and many better—for I am the worst possible person in such an emergency, because illness and injury distress me so much."

He shook his head. "You did wonders, ma'am," he said, "and I shall always be grateful."

The silence between us hung in the air so that you could have reached out and touched it. Outside, the rain sluiced down, and a distant drumbeat of thunder rolled across the night.

"Er . . . Hester will be all right till morning?" he asked.

"I will sleep on the sofa in the nursery, with her bedroom door open," I assured him.

He nodded. "Good. Then I will say good night, Miss Button."

"Good night, Mr. Dewaine."

Mark went some way down the stairs, then his footsteps slowed. He paused and looked round, up towards me. His brow was furrowed with something that looked like anger, and I felt suddenly afraid.

"There's something else, Miss Button," he said slowly.

My heart gave a treacherous lurch. "Yes, Mr. Dewaine?"

He hesitated, and then he said: "Nothing. No matter now. It isn't important. Not important at all." He looked away and continued on down the stairs. I stood watching him till his tall figure vanished from my sight round the curve of the staircase well, and never drew breath till the last faint sound of his footfalls faded away in the direction of the library.

* * *

I went to my room and prepared myself for bed. Hair unbound and wearing my nightdress and peignoir, I crossed over to my wicker hamper and raised the lid. My Bible lay on top, where I had left it. When I picked it up, the pages fell open at the beginning of the Song of Solomon—and the silhouette of Mark Dewaine.

Susannah, Susannah, I told myself. You are no Cinderella. Put it out of your mind. You came to the fairytale palace—but the handsome prince is not for you. . . .

It was the sunshine, the excitement, the noise of the crowd that affected you. That—and the champagne. Whether the woman

95

was right, or whether she was wrong, makes no real difference. It would be madness for you even to hope. . . .

With a sigh, I closed the Bible and laid it right at the bottom of the hamper. Then I went to the nursery.

Hester was still sleeping soundly. There was a light beading of sweat on the child's brow that I dabbed off with a handkerchief. I closed the bedroom door quietly, leaving a slit through which I would be able to hear her if she woke up and called out.

It was useless to think of sleep. The thrumming of the rain on the landing windows met me as I crept out to the top of the stairs and looked out at the fading day. When the last rays of the sun had gone, I laid my cheek against the cold window-pane and closed my eyes, allowing myself to drift along with my thoughts.

I had seen enough of Mark Dewaine to know that behind the facade of the aristocrat there existed a true gentleness, the sort that only the strong possess. And there was kindness. Here was a man who would not deliberately give hurt to anyone—even to anyone like myself, whom a thousand years of high breeding had taught him to recognise as one of the lower orders. For me, and for my sort, he was able to extend the careful courtesy that was of a piece with the consideration he showed for his horses and his staghounds.

I stood beyond the pale. I—who in a blinding moment of self-knowledge prompted by the strange insight of a fairground gipsy—had been presented with the truth about myself and the heir of the Dewaines, which was this: from the very beginning, from the time when I had defied and challenged him on that far-off day of the stag-hunt, through the living present and through all time ahead, I had loved and would continue to love Mark Dewaine beyond all reason, all sense, all questioning.

And to him I was—nothing.

Chapter 4

When I look back on the weeks that followed the revelation of my feelings for Mark Dewaine, it is like a recollection of youthful innocence seen through the misty sweetness of fond remembrance, as when the rough edges of reality are smoothed away and the everyday world takes on the rose-tinted outlines of perfection.

I suppose I was frequently unhappy. It must have hurt me, often, to be near to Mark and yet so far from him in every possible way; I may have cried myself to sleep on more than one occasion; he almost certainly hurt me many times, through ignorance of my feelings—all these things may have happened; all I can say is that I do not recall any of them.

There is only the remembrance of golden days of the early spring, of scented blossom and laughter in the easeful, lengthening evenings; memories of dear Landeric, warm-walled above the long green cleft of parkland; and always—everywhere—the presence of Mark.

Hester made a quick recovery. She was on her feet within days and riding her pony by the end of a week. Easter came, so I declared a holiday from lessons. Hester and I must have spent long hours walking and driving through the countryside. We probably went out in one of the bigger fishing boats from the Haven. We certainly played bat-and-ball among the fountains and croquet on the lawn. I have forgotten it all.

Things I remember. . . .

Mark joining us for tea on the lawn and my asking him if he did not miss the army life very much; the way he shrugged his shoulders and said that the life of a country gentleman suited his taste very well, but that there would almost certainly be trouble with the Russkies before very long, and he supposed that would have him back in uniform; how that night I dreamed of him being cut down from his charger in battle, and woke with my pillow wet with tears.

The time at luncheon when he read aloud to Hester a letter he had received from Jessica in Paris: my relief that the sisters had no plans for coming home at Easter, my joy that the name of Amelie de Quatrefois was not even mentioned.

The day when, practising archery on the lawn with Hester, he came up and showed me how to draw the bow correctly: when I close my eyes, I can still feel the touch of his hands on mine, his nearness and warmth.

It all came to an end, my rose-tinted springtime, just when I had almost convinced myself that it could last forever.

* * *

Mark had summoned me to the library after breakfast. He rose to his feet without looking up; gestured for me to take a seat and went on reading a letter that lay on the desk before him. I knew without any shadow of doubt that my world was crumbling apart.

"My father is coming back to Landeric," he said.

"Is he?" I replied in a voice that sounded very unlike my own. There seemed nothing else to say.

"You will wish to make other . . . arrangements." It was hardly a question; more a statement of fact.

I nodded. "Yes, Mr. Dewaine."

He looked at me for the first time. As always, there was no expression in his eyes; merely the straight look, head slightly aside and drawn back.

"Quite so. But you don't have any specific plans?"

"No," I replied truthfully. Had I not been living, all these weeks in a cloud-cuckoo land, where nothing has an end and everything is a long languid afternoon of beginnings?

He got up from the desk and walked across the room, passing my chair and moving behind me. When he went out of the scope of my vision, I could sense his eyes on the back of my head.

"You will simply go out into the world and seek for employment?"

"Yes."

"Well then, Miss Button. I will tell you that I have had the presumption to make some arrangements for your future. Please turn round, will you?"

I turned my head obediently, puzzled.

"Now," he said. "Regard that painting on the wall over there, above the fireplace. Do you know what place it represents?"

It was a large canvas that I had noticed on my previous visits to the library: a view down a wide sweep of canal, lined with tall, balconied palaces; the whole surface sprinkled with boats and people.

"Why, it's Venice," I replied. "I've seen it in pictures many times. It must be the most easily-recognisable place in the world."

"Of course," he replied. "You're quite right, Miss Button. The painting is by Canaletto, himself an eighteenth-century Venetian. It is one of several canvases that my grandfather brought back from a tour of Italy. He was particularly enchanted by Venice, so much so that he afterwards purchased a *palazzo* on the Grand Canal which is still in the family. The present resident of the Palazzo Dewaine is my Aunt Marianne Newstead, a widowed lady of delicate health." He crossed over to the desk again and picked up the letter he had been reading when I entered. "This is from my aunt, in reply to an enquiry of mine. She tells me that, as I had guessed, nothing would make her happier than to have the company of a young lady companion."

I stared at him. "You mean . . . *me?*" I breathed.

His eyebrow raised. "Is it so terrifying, Miss Button? Venice is not the end of the world. There is a boat leaving Southampton on Saturday next that will dock in Genoa within the fortnight. I think you will find the sea voyage more agreeable than travelling on the somewhat exiguous French railways and their appalling roads. The coach journey from Genoa to Venice will take you a further couple of days and be most pleasant. You will journey through the Plain of Lombardy: through Piacenza, with its notable sixteenth-century walls; thence to Cremona, remarkable for a very fine cathedral; Brescia will commend itself to you because of the Roman remains, particularly the Capitolium of Vespasian, which is also very fine; thence to Verona—Verona, Miss Button, immortalised by our national poet as the native city of the tragic lovers Romeo and Juliet. Miss Button, I do not appear to have the pleasure of your undivided attention."

I shook my head, bemused. "Oh, you have, Mr. Dewaine. Only, this is all so bewildering. All so—sudden."

He frowned. "Do I understand that you don't wish to do as I am suggesting and accept my aunt's offer, Miss Button?"

How could he know the absurdity of his question? How could he not guess that I would go anywhere, do anything—even, as I then realised, stay and endure the embarrassment of Sir Tristan's presence at Landeric—at one word from him? Surely it must show in my looks. In the way I walked and talked. In my eyes.

"Of course I'll be glad to go and be companion to Mrs. Newstead, Mr. Dewaine," I assured him.

He gave a nod and looked pleased.

"Capital," he said. "Then it's settled. One of the Landeric coaches will take you and your baggage to Southampton. In the meantime, you will need a couple of strong travelling trunks. Oh, and a complete wardrobe suitable for the climate of the Adriatic. That, of course, you can have made when you arrive in Venice, but you must go to a dressmaker in St. Errol and have a couple of suitable travelling costumes made immediately. You will also need an advance of money. Pendower will attend to all that. I don't think there's anything else."

"Thank you, Mr. Dewaine," I whispered in a very small voice. Was he then dismissing me?

"Before you go, Miss Button," he said, "I must advise you that my aunt is something of an eccentric and a recluse. In fact, I am the only member of the family whom she is willing to receive with any show of grace at all. My father she cannot abide at any price. They haven't exchanged a line for over twenty years. She is a widow, Miss Button, and the latest news I have is that her sight is failing." He indicated the letter. "This was written by her housekeeper. Nevertheless, I hope, when I visit the Palazzo Dewaine in the late summer, as I intend, I shall find that you have settled down happily."

Mark would be in Venice in a very few months' time! I would see him again quite soon. This was not like leaving Landeric for good; more like taking some of Landeric to an alien land. Only one thing worried me. . . .

"What about Hester?" I asked. "You will have to find another governess for her, of course."

"Hester will commence at a boarding school for young ladies in Bath as soon as you have gone," he said. "I've discussed it with her and she is very content with the arrangement." He gave me a wintry smile. "I asked her not to mention anything of it till I had broached the subject with you."

I nodded meekly. Was it such a short while ago when the very thought of being so manipulated by the Dewaines would have made my hackles rise with a revolutionary fervour? So much does a woman relinquish of her heart and spirit's independence when she learns to love a man.

"I'll go and tell Hester that everything's settled," I said. "Will that be all, Mr. Dewaine?"

"We'll meet at luncheon," he said, crossing to open the door for me. "I'm glad you've taken my advice, Miss Button. Neither Hester nor I would have been happy to see you go out alone in the world—and you with so very little experience of that rather forbidding place."

I cast him a quick, sidelong glance, and was half-convinced that he was teasing me again.

"Thank you, Mr. Dewaine," I said quietly.

He paused, holding open the door for me to pass through.

"You will love Venice," he said. "I will tell you two things about her, and the first is this: Venice, Miss Button, is the one place on earth that truly separates the civilised person from the barbarian. I would say that anyone who rejected Venice is a barbarian; while the person who is truly civilised will take her to his heart at first sight and love her forever. My second observation is this: Venice, like Rome, is an Eternal City, for she has lasted through twelve hundred years against all odds, which means that she must last ten times longer, since all nature and all mankind must be so gently inclined towards her that no tempest would overwhelm her, no invading army burn her or navy bombard her; and no force of any kind would ever wittingly contribute to the downfall of a single stone of hers."

He was suddenly aware of the intentness of my gaze—and so was I. We both looked away from each other. The door shut quietly.

* * *

I came to Venice, from the last staging post at Padua, in a diligence that I shared with a taciturn priest who read his breviary all the way and never lifted his eyes, two market women, a pale student—all Italians. And a Norfolk country gentleman and his lady who were doing what they described as the Grand Tour. To escape my fellow-countryfolk, I feigned sleep. The scent of honeysuckle and new-cut grass came in through the open windows and I was soon nodding in earnest.

"You say you are going to reside in Venice, ma'am. Hey?"

I had learned, during the voyage to Genoa, that there is no way of escaping the ever-present, garrulous Englishman abroad. I opened my eyes.

"That is so," I confirmed.

"Venice, we are told," said the wife of the Norfolk squire, who was dressed, in the heat of Venetia, in a red velvet with at least five flounces, pagoda sleeves and undersleeves of heavy lace, "is a death-trap to the unwary. Cholera and the plague, you know."

"Armed insurrection is expected imminently," said her spouse. "The Austrians are in charge there, you see, and the locals don't like it one scrap. Wouldn't be surprised, from what we heard in Rome, if the locals . . ." he cast a rheumy eye at our fellow-travellers . . . "didn't rise up and start cutting Austrian throats one o' these days. What guarantee, I ask you, that there'll not be decent English throats cut in the bargain? How're *they* to know the difference in the dark, hey?"

"We must continue on our way to Rimini," declared his wife. "Just as soon as we have seen St. Mark's, the Palace of the Dukes and the house where that dreadful Lord Byron lived when he was here."

"Damned bounder," growled the Norfolk squire. "Versifying cad."

"I know," said his wife with complete conviction, "that I shall hate Venice as soon as I set eyes on the place."

"I'm sure you will, ma'am," I interposed—remembering Mark's observations upon people, both civilised and barbarian. "I'm quite prepared to believe that no sooner will you set eyes on Venice than you will hate it for the rest of your life. I have it from a friend—a very dear friend—of mine."

They both stared at me with affront, and the squire's wife took out a bottle of Oil of Lavender from her reticule and splashed some of the aromatic spirit over her. She had been doing this all the way from Padua, as a remedy against the mosquitoes.

At that moment, the student lowered the book that he had been reading. He smiled at me and, pointing out of the right-hand window, he spoke in perfectly-accented English.

"There is the lagoon, signorina," he said. "Everything that rises out of it belongs to Venice."

Beyond the stubbly grassland and the salt marshes was a line of blue-grey water studded with islands. The distance was hazed, but half out of the haze I could pick out the upper part of a noble city of golden stone shaded with mellow bronze and greeny copper. As we came closer, I saw tall bell-towers, domes and the many-windowed walls of great buildings. As I watched, a sunburst pierced the murky clouds and bathed the city in an ethereal light.

"Venice is beautiful," I breathed. "Beautiful!"

"To you, she will always be so, signorina," said the student. "Now you have decided it. That is how it always is with those who see her for the first time."

Through tears that suddenly prickled my eyes, I seemed to see Mark's face again as he took my hand and bowed over it, his lips touching my fingertips in farewell. I seemed to hear his voice. . . .

"A good journey, Miss Button. I think you will find Venice to your taste. Till we meet again, then . . ."

"Till we meet again"—the words had stayed with me, echoing in my heart, while the coach bore me away from the group of well-wishers on the white steps beneath the six tall columns: Mark raising his hat to me, Hester frantically waving her handkerchief, the small army of servants gathered to see me off. A curve in the drive —and they were shut from my sight.

"You have come a long way, signorina," said the student. "You are missing your home, perhaps?"

I gazed towards the lagoon, towards the dream city whose outlines were becoming more distinct with every passing minute. The past was behind me. Landeric was behind me. Some time in the late summer, I would see Mark again—in Venice.

"In a way, I feel as if I'm coming home," I said.

* * *

The diligence put us down on a quay at the end of what my student friend told me was the famous Grand Canal. There we were set upon by a horde of excited, gesticulating touts who seemed to be offering everything under the sun. The student— who introduced himself as Bruno—detached me from one of the more persistent of his compatriots and guided me to the edge of the quay, where a mass of sleek black gondolas bobbed in the limpid green water, poled by men in wide straw hats. More cries and excited gestures—then Bruno handed me down into one of the gondolas.

"This fellow will take you to the Palazzo Dewaine quite cheaply, signorina," he explained. "I will come with you and take the gondola on to San Marco."

I gratefully thanked him. Our gondolier bore his weight against his long pole, and we joined the press of craft of all kinds that were heading down the wide canal.

The first buildings we passed were fronted by wide streets edging the canal, but before we had progressed far, the houses rose straight out of the very waters, with steps leading up to their front doors. I glimpsed down narrow side-canals, shadowed from the sun, dark and remote.

We passed a handsome church, topped by a dome. Led by a smiling nun, a line of small, black-garbed children straggled into the darkness beyond its open door.

"That is the church of San Geremia," said Bruno. "I was baptised there. And ahead, signorina, you will see the Palazzo Corner-Contarini. Beyond that is San Marcuola, which is unfinished. A priest of that church once preached that ghosts do not exist, so all the people buried beneath San Marcuola rose up one night, dragged the priest from his bed and kicked and beat him. That is funny, don't you think? There is the Palazzo Vendramin Calergi, where the Duchesse de Berry lives in the style of the old French court. Coming in sight now, on your right at the bend of the canal, is the church of San Stae, and opposite that is the Palazzo Erizzo, where dwelt once a gentleman who disowned his son for wearing red socks. On the same side is the Palazzo Fontana, birthplace of a pope. The very stones of Venice have tales to tell."

Entranced by his lively descriptions, I feasted my eyes on everything that Bruno pointed out to me. The faded loveliness of the buildings touched at my heart. They were like tired, elegant old ladies, dreaming of their brilliant youth and beauty, yet cheerfully resigned to splendid old age.

I was reflecting on this when the gondolier made a sudden comment and steered our craft sharply to one side. I noticed that the boats ahead of us were doing the same, turning aside one way or another. Bruno growled something in Italian that sounded very like a curse, and this was echoed by our gondolier.

It was then I saw the object of their attentions: a long, low craft was speeding swiftly toward us from the direction in which we were going. It was propelled by four oarsmen. In the stern of the boat stood three men, two of them in dark-coloured uniforms and peaked hats. My attention was drawn to the third member of the party. He stood slightly apart from the rest, with his eyes fixed firmly in front. A youngish man in a broad-brimmed tall hat and a dark cloak, one end of which was tossed carelessly over his left shoulder. As the craft swept past us, I had an impression of faded blue eyes set in an impassive pale face that was framed by reddish locks. Next moment, he was gone.

Bruno and the gondolier exchanged another short comment. I looked questioningly at my guide, and he drew down the corners of his mouth in a grimace.

"Austrian police," he said. "They are the masters here, the accursed Austrians. They are everywhere. As a visiting foreigner, you will scarcely notice them, signorina. But to us Venetians, they are a constant affront."

With that, he relapsed into a brooding silence, and I had to content myself with enjoying the sights and sounds of the Grand Canal without the benefit of my highly-informative guide. Palaces and churches came and went, unnamed. We passed a teeming fish-market, then the riotous colours of a fruit and vegetable market. Just beyond the markets, the canal took a sharp bend and we were heading for the high arch of a bridge. I marvelled to see that there were actually shops built upon it. Bruno came out of his gloomy reverie and pointed.

"This is the Rialto Bridge," he said. "Just beyond, you will be able to see the Palazzo Dewaine."

We swept under the bridge, from which a row of grinning urchins waved and called down to us. Out in the sunshine again, we came to another long, straight stretch of canal. My long journey from Cornwall was all but over.

"The Palazzo Dewaine," said Bruno, pointing.

I caught my breath. . . .

If Landeric was sprawling magnificence, the Venetian seat of the lordly Dewaines was a jewelled miniature, importantly set at the junction of the Grand Canal and one of its lesser brethren, so that the palace was half-surrounded by water from which it rose in three grand tiers like an exotic wedding cake. Its richly-ornamented windows and balconies were of a pale stonework, contrasting with the ochre-coloured stucco of its walls. The Dewaine coat of arms was carved over a porch that was like the entrance to a cathedral, and shielded by double doors of latticed ironwork that gave a hint of a distant, sunlit courtyard beyond a recess of darkness and mystery.

I was enchanted from the first—as I had been enchanted by Landeric all those years before.

At a word from Bruno, the gondolier brought our craft gliding to a halt at the foot of the steps below the entrance, where a row of striped barber's poles stuck out of the water. He tied the gondola to a pole and helped Bruno lift out my trunks.

I thanked the young student for all his help.

"It has been a pleasure, signorina," he said, "to be of service to a new lover of Venice." He kissed my hand with the gallantry of one far beyond his years, and his dark eyes blazed with a strange intensity. "One day, signorina, one day not so far hence, our most serene city-state will be free of the accursed Austrian yoke. You may rely upon Venice's sons to see to that!"

He bowed to me and stepped back into the gondola. The rope was cast off, and one touch of the steering pole sent the slender black craft sliding away down the crowded canal. I never saw my young friend again.

There was a discreet cough behind me. I turned, to see two figures—a man and a woman—looking down at me from the open doors of the Palazzo Dewaine.

"Miss Button, is it?" The woman addressed me. She was in her late fifties, tall and grey-haired, with a lined and severe-looking face. Her eyes—dark, searching and strangely hostile—took in every detail of my appearance and did not seem greatly to approve of what they found.

"Yes," I replied.

"I am Adriana Ricci," she said, "and this is my husband, Alfredo, who does not speak much of the English." She turned to the man and addressed him in voluble Italian, pointing to my baggage. "Please to come this way."

The man flashed me a shy smile and stooped to pick up one of my trunks. He was shorter than his wife and rather frail-looking. It struck me that the task was beyond his strength. I was about to say as much to his wife, when a powerfully-built young man came down the steps and took hold of the other end of the trunk. He did not spare me so much as a glance.

"Please to follow me, Miss Button," called Adriana Ricci from the top of the steps. Responding to the note of impatience in her voice, I hastened to obey.

I followed her through the doorway and into the cool gloom of a covered courtyard that seemingly acted as an entrance hall to the palace. At the far end, a pillared opening let out on to a vista of sunlight, cascading water, white statuary and an abundance of trailing vines. This was the inner court around which the palace was built, in such a way that all the rooms in the building had windows looking out upon it. I followed the woman across the black-and-white flagged floor, past a fountain, where water gushed from the mouth of a marble dolphin held in the arms of a laughing cherub; on up a marble staircase leading to a gallery that surrounded the court and gave access to the next storey.

"How is Mrs. Newstead keeping?" I asked my guide, by way of breaking the oppressive silence that lay between us.

"Madame never leaves her suite," was the enigmatic response.

"I understand that her sight is failing," I persisted.

"Madame is ill in body and mind," replied Adriana Ricci. "In her life she has had to carry the burden of many sorrows. This way, please."

A pair of carved doors were open to admit us into a long room that, save for three vast gilt-and-crystal chandeliers suspended from a painted ceiling, was empty of furnishings. Long windows at the far end were unshuttered to reveal a line of distant rooftops and domes.

"Please to attend here while I go and enquire if Madame wishes to receive you at this time," said the woman.

She opened another set of double doors and went through, closing them quietly behind her. I heard the faint tap-tap of her footsteps fading away into what seemed a very far distance.

I gazed up at the ceiling, which reminded me of nothing so much as the painted ceiling in the ballroom at Landeric: the same pagan figures disporting themselves among fat clouds, with mischievous cherubs and prancing horses. I felt a sudden wave of nostalgia, and for what must have been the thousandth occasion since I came away, I tried to picture what he—Mark—might be doing at that very moment. And for the thousandth time, I was unable to conjure up even the memory of his face. Suddenly depressed, I turned and had another look about me. Noticing that the windows at the far end gave out on to a balcony, I went to investigate.

This balcony overlooked the small canal that ran along one side of the palazzo. It lay in deep shadow, though patches of reflected sunlight glanced from the wavelets below. Across the narrow strip of water, a clump of lime trees rose from behind a high-walled garden, and their leaves rustled in the light breeze.

I went to the edge of the balcony, rested my hands on the warm stonework of the balustrade and looked down at the dancing points of sunlight on the water. It was then that the sound of a slight movement—as of the scraping of a chair leg—told me I was not alone.

"Well, I'm damned! If it isn't little Miss Button, the young lady with the tremendous style!"

Turning with a start, I found myself looking into the disturbing blue eyes and lop-sided smile of the artist Durward le Lacey.

* * *

"What are *you* doing here?"

We both said it almost in unison, and laughed.

"I am still pursuing the elusive Dewaines, with a view to finishing that commission before I am too old and infirm to put brush to canvas," he said. "Mrs. Newstead, I am happy to add, is my last sitter. When I have made drawings of her—and I stress the word *when*—the family gathering will be complete. However, I have been cooling my heels in Venice for the last two weeks without getting any nearer to the chatelaine of the Palazzo Dewaine than her dragon of a housekeeper. But what brings *you* here, little Miss Button with the tremendous style?"

"I've come to be Mrs. Newstead's companion," I replied.

"You have?" he cried. "Capital! Now all my troubles are over. You shall whisper in the ear of Mrs. Newstead that your very old and dear friend, Mr. Durward de Lacey, Royal Academician, is languishing in her antechamber. You, my dear, my adorable Miss Button, will be the means of my performing my task and shaking the mud of this pestilential city from my boots."

"Oh, you don't like Venice, then?" I asked, disappointed.

"I love her," he said. "Venice is a beautiful woman, splendidly apparelled and sumptuously bejewelled—except that the rich clothes are shabby, their gold embroidery faded and torn, the jewellery probably stolen or due to be pawned tomorrow, and milady has not eaten for a week. Indeed, I love Venice dearly, Miss Button—but she is a lover who has become an embarrassment and would be better off in her grave. Sit down beside me, do, and tell me what you have been up to since that memorable first meeting of ours."

I sat in the chair next to him. He laid aside a sketch-book and I saw that he had been making a drawing of the view below the balcony.

"Since then," I said, "I have been governess to the youngest Dewaine daughter and assisting the housekeeper of Landeric. Nothing else has happened to me, except . . ." I had the wayward thought to add: "except that I have fallen in love with Mark Dewaine" . . . "no, all in all it has been a busy, but quite uneventful time," I concluded.

"And now the Dewaines have sent you to Venice," he said. "Well, I wish you well of your new mistress. In the cafés where I have been wasting my substance these last weeks, I have heard some very odd items of gossip concerning your Mrs. Newstead."

"Such as?" I asked, intrigued.

"They say she has the *mal occhio*, the Evil Eye. Nothing very remarkable about that. In most Mediterranean countries, ageing ladies of eccentric appearance and habits are invariably attributed with the ability to injure or kill at a glance. But that isn't all."

"What else?" I asked.

"There's something of a mystery about Mr. Newstead. He died some years ago, but there appears to be a veil of secrecy drawn across the manner of his departure. Then there is the rumour about the locked room, here in the Palazzo Dewaine."

"Locked room?" I felt a tingle of apprehension run down my spine. "What sort of locked room—and why is it locked?"

He gave me that mischievous, lop-sided smile again, and his blue eyes twinkled with pure pleasure at my fear.

"They say," he said in a hoarse, sepulchral voice, "that Mrs. Newstead keeps the embalmed body of her late spouse in a locked room that none but she is allowed to enter."

"How horrible!" I cried.

"And that she sits all day in that room, with only the light of a single candle, and contemplates the dead face of Mr. Newstead lying beneath the glass lid of his coffin."

"I don't believe a word of it," I declared. "It sounds like a horrid, malicious story put about by idle folk."

"I am sure you are right, Miss Button," he said contritely. "I have certainly been associating with some very undesirable folk these last weeks."

Further discussion was cut short by the return of Adriana Ricci. We heard her footfalls and the frou-frou of her skirts coming down the long room towards the balcony. When she saw the artist, her eyes narrowed with dislike.

"You are wasting your time, Mr. de Lacey," she hissed. "Madame will see no one today but Miss Button."

Durward de Lacey picked up his hat, cane and sketch-book. He smiled at me resignedly and hunched his shoulders.

"I look to you to intercede for me with your mistress, Miss Button," he said. "Or I shall be here for the rest of my life, or till this beautiful, ramshackle city falls into the sea—whichever is the shorter time."

"I'll do my best," I promised, giving him my hand. And I noticed the housekeeper throwing me a sharp glance of disapproval. "Good-bye, Mr. de Lacey."

"I shall call again tomorrow," he said. Perhaps, while I am here, I may have the pleasure of showing Venice to you—or you to Venice."

"That would be nice," I said.

Adriana Ricci gave a sniff. "Will you please be following me, Miss Button," she said. "Madame must not be kept waiting."

I followed her, passing Durward de Lacey, who grimaced mischievously after the housekeeper's retreating back.

* * *

"Miss Button, from England, madame."

"Hello, my dear. Do come and sit down. Come close to me first and let me see you." It was a deep and musical voice, curiously pleasing to the ear. I could see nothing of the speaker, for the room was in total darkness. "Thank you, Adriana. That will be all."

The door closed behind me.

"Come forward, my dear," said Mrs. Newstead.

Not quite darkness, I realised. My eyes, becoming accustomed to the gloom, began to pick out a thin shaft of diffused light coming through a heavily curtained window at the far end of the room. Presently, I was able to make out the shape of a figure seated in a straight-backed chair in front of the window. I walked towards it, hands stretched before me in case of impediments in the way.

When I reached Mrs. Newstead, she held out her hands and took hold of mine. Hers were dry, cool and delicate-feeling.

"Turn your head slightly sideways, my dear," she said. And I obeyed. "I can see so little nowadays, and even then I think I imagine it. No, I am afraid your appearance must remain a mystery to me. But let me hear your voice."

I moistened my dry lips. "I hope I find you well, Mrs. Newstead," I said.

"Capital!" cried Mrs. Newstead. "What a joy to hear a good West Country voice again. Takes me back to my girlhood days at Landeric. I was brought up there, you know. My father was the third baronet. If I had been a boy, it would be I—and not my cousin Tristan—who would be master of Landeric today."

My eyes, growing ever more accustomed to the faint light, picked out the shape of her head and shoulders. I saw full widow's weeds covering smooth white hair. Moving slightly sideways so that I could catch her profile, I saw a firm, proud chin and—to my amusement—the very straight Dewaine nose.

"Be seated, Miss Button," said Mrs. Newstead. "Tell me about yourself. Your people, I take it, are Cornish. Are they alive?"

"They have both passed away, ma'am," I said. "And both were Cornish. My father brought me to the Haven after Mother's death. It had been her last wish, that I should be brought up in the duchy."

"A splendid sentiment," said Mrs. Newstead. "Your dear mother was right. I would have wished the same for my own flesh."

"Yes, ma'am," I said.

"My own child," she said, with a catch in her fine voice, "my son, my own little boy, would have been brought up at Landeric, Cousin Tristan or no Cousin Tristan. Yes, I would have made my peace with Tristan, no matter what it cost me in pride and honour, in order to have given my Georgie something of his rightful heritage. Yes, if he had been spared, I would willingly have sent Georgie to be brought up at Landeric with young Mark. Of course, you know my nephew Mark?"

"Yes, ma'am," I said quietly.

"A capital young fellow, wouldn't you say, Miss Button?"

"Mr. Dewaine has many virtues," I murmured, fondly smiling in the gloom.

"Indeed he has, and you show good sense to have noticed them, my dear," declared Mrs. Newstead. "Mark has all the best qualities of the Dewaines. He is upright, steadfast, brave and true. A trifle deficient in sense of humour, perhaps—but none of us is perfect. My Georgie, if he had been spared, would also have shown the best of the Dewaine traits—indeed they were already very apparent, even in one so young. . . ." Her voice trailed away, and I saw a handkerchief flutter in the gloom as it was raised to her cheek.

I waited for a few moments, and then I said: "Shall I leave you, Mrs. Newstead? Perhaps you would like to rest."

"No, no, my dear," she replied. "I am perfectly composed now. Forgive me. I live somewhat in the past and the past has many sad memories. The moment has gone now. Let's speak of something else."

"Well," I said, "shall I ask you what my duties will be, here in the Palazzo Dewaine? As your companion, we shall no doubt meet every day?"

"Oh, yes," she said. "I shall wish you to call upon me every day. Every morning, I think, at about ten. For an hour. I never leave this suite of rooms. My eyes . . ."

"Do you like to be read to, Mrs. Newstead?"

"No, my dear," she replied firmly. "I was never one for books, even when I had all my faculties, and my deficiencies have not altered that. But I have always been a great letter-writer. From now on, I should like you to deal with all my English correspondence. Do you have any French?"

"I write and speak French quite competently," I said.

"Capital. I correspond with many French friends," she said. "Do you have Italian?"

"No, ma'am."

"Then Adriana will continue to handle my Italian letters. So much for that. In addition to acting as my private secretary, I should like you to be my eyes about Venice. I am passionately interested in the current modes of fashion, the up-to-date small-talk and the scandal. You must go out often. I will give instructions for the gondola to be refurbished and put in use again (I have never set foot outside for over twenty years). You must become a frequenter of Florian's, where the English congregate, but not

Quadri's, of course—that is for the Austrians. You must join in the daily promenade in St. Mark's Square. And every day, you must bring me back news of all you see and hear."

All these duties sounded very easy and agreeable, and I said as much to my new mistress.

"We shall get on well together," declared Mrs. Newstead. "I sense it already. And from now on, I will call you Susannah. Now, I have kept you long enough. After your long journey, you will wish to rest. Come back and see me again tomorrow."

Her white hand reached out in the gloom. I took it and marvelled at the nervous strength that lay within its wasted slenderness.

"I will summon Adriana to show you to your room," she said, and she pulled a bell cord.

It was then I remembered a promise I had made. . . .

"There is a Mr. de Lacey, ma'am," I began.

"The painter fellow," supplied Mrs. Newstead. "Yes, I have had him cooling his heels for a week or so. Do you know the gentleman?"

"I met him once before," I said. "At Landeric. He asked me to remind you . . ."

"I know all about it," said Mrs. Newstead tartly. "The picture that my cousin has commissioned Mr. de Lacey to paint. The family group outside Landeric. With the fourth baronet in the middle, of course. Lord of all he surveys—including the poor relation from Venice. I shall have to agree to have my likeness made, of course, for I live by my cousin's grace and favour—the roof over my head, every crust I eat. But not yet. Not for a while yet. Age and infirmity bring some consolations. One is not expected to do things in a hurry. Ah, here is Adriana."

The housekeeper entered the room, bringing a shaft of late afternoon sunlight with her through the open door. I saw Mrs. Newstead turn her face aside and shield her eyes.

"You rang, madame?"

"Convey Miss Button to her room, please, Adriana," said my mistress. "I wish you a good night's sleep, Susannah."

"Thank you, ma'am. And you also."

"Ah, one other thing occurs to me, Susannah."

"Ma'am?"

"Mr. de Lacey, who has had the temerity to try and use you as a go-between, will provide an excellent escort, to show you round

Venice. I am told he knows the city well." She laughed, with a hint of girlish mischief—and I was reminded of Hester. "Yes, Susannah, I think it will be quite a while before Mr. de Lacey gets the opportunity to make my likeness!"

* * *

My room was on the same side of the palazzo as the balcony where Durward de Lacey and I had met, and on the floor above. Its windows gave a view over the garden wall opposite and beyond, to the rooftops, towers and domes of the city. The furnishings were rich and almost oriental in character, with a delicious canopied bed of carved and inlaid wood, a comfortable button-back chair and day-bed to match, and a papier mâché dressing table. From the elaborate plasterwork ceiling hung a many-coloured glass chandelier that reflected tiny pinpoints of light round the white panelled walls. The whole effect was light, spacious and airy. I loved it on sight.

Night was falling and Adriana drew the shutters. The impression that the woman resented my arrival was deepened by the surly manner in which she asked me if I required any refreshment. I affected not to notice her manner and blandly said that I would like a tray of something light and simple before retiring early.

I had washed and changed into nightdress and peignoir when a young maid came in with my supper: a spiced omelette, a crusty roll of bread and a small carafe of a rosé wine. I settled myself down at the bedside table, to write a letter to Hester while I had my supper.

It was, of course, also by way of being a letter to Mark—for I had every hope that Hester would read out the interesting bits to her brother. So I made much of the fact that I was missing everyone at Landeric and to remember me affectionately to them. I particularly mentioned how Mrs. Newstead had spoken so warmly of her nephew and praised his manly qualities (Hester would certainly show him that). Nor could I resist telling that I had met again the handsome and charming Durward de Lacey and how he had offered to show me around Venice. Faint hope, indeed, that this piece of news would strike a chord of jealousy in the heart of a man who scarcely noticed I existed! I closed by asking Hester to tell Mr. Mark that I had fallen in love with Venice on sight, in consequence of which I hoped he would judge me to be one of the civilised people of this world.

Then I took a sip of the wine, and considered whether I would be going too far and reveal too much of my true intention in writing the letter, if I added a postscript reminding her again to convey my affection to everyone at Landeric.

The wine tasted unpleasantly bitter—so bitter that I nearly spat it out.

I decided against the postscript.

* * *

Though physically tired after my long journey, my mind seemed wide awake, and I lay with my eyes open for a long while, letting my thoughts drift where they would. They mostly stayed with Mark; but Mrs. Newstead came in for some attention. . . .

I had formed a very good impression of my new mistress. I liked her direct and friendly manner, and found it difficult to square with the reports that I had had from other people.

Mark had described his aunt as an eccentric and a recluse. This was certainly true as far as it went; but surely Mrs. Newstead's withdrawal from the world was on account of her infirmities and not through choice; she took a most lively interest in the bustling world beyond her curtained windows. Adriana Ricci had said she was ill in body and mind; apart from the long-continuing grief about her lost son (I presumed he died in infancy or early childhood—and was it after that loss that Mrs. Newstead became a recluse?), her mind had seemed as clear and normal as my own.

As for the rubbish that Durward de Lacey had repeated: the scandalous café gossip about the locked room in the Palazzo Dewaine—I refused to give it another moment's thought.

Sometime later, I dropped off to sleep.

When I woke up, it was like clawing my way out of a swampy ooze that threatened to drag me down again. I tried to cry out, but my throat was too dry to form the sound. My eyes strained the semi-darkness all round me—and fell upon a tall figure that was bent over something at the far side of the room. As I stared, the figure straightened up and turned round, as if looking to see if I was still asleep. Some sixth sense for self-preservation made me shut my eyes again.

I remember nothing else till I woke up with the morning sunlight streaming in through the cracks of the shutters. The glare assaulted my eyes and made me aware that I had a most terrible headache. A wave of nausea swept over me when I sat up, and I could hardly swallow for the dryness of my throat.

By the wall at the far side of the room stood one of my trunks.

The lid was flung open and some of the contents—my linens—hung over the edge of the trunk in considerable disarray. Instantly aware that something was wrong, I swung my legs out of bed and stood up. A wave of giddiness nearly made me fall over, and I had to cling to the bedpost for quite some moments before the feeling passed.

I examined my trunk. It had been violated. The evening before, I had unlocked it to take out my writing materials (it was the trunk that contained my stationery and books—including my Bible, with the silhouette portraits of Mark and me), and had left it with the lid down and unlocked.

Someone had been ferreting around inside the trunk. The linen at the top had been roughly dragged aside, and my writing case, diary and sewing box left lying in a heap on the top.

Someone . . . my midnight visitor?

He had not been a figment of a dream, but a real man of flesh and blood, who had come in with the intent of ransacking my belongings—for what?

Furthermore, he had either found what he wanted and departed without even bothering to tidy up the evidence of his intrusion or he had been disturbed in his task and had fled. The latter seemed more likely: he had heard me stir in my sleep and partly wake up.

Coldly angry, I summoned the maid and made her to understand that I wished to speak to Adriana. The housekeeper appeared with surprising haste—almost as if she had been waiting outside for my summons.

"Is everything correct, Miss Button?" she asked.

I had the impression that there was a slight change in the woman's attitude to me: the hostility was still there, but it was overlaid with something else—anxiety? Did she share the intruder's fears for having had to leave evidence of his visit?

"Everything is far from correct, Adriana," I said coldly, pointing to the open trunk. "As you can see."

I thought I detected an expression of relief flitting across the woman's harsh features. Her dark eyes narrowed and a ghost of a contemptuous smile touched the corners of her thin lips.

"I do not understand what you mean, miss," she said.

"Last night," I said, "someone—a man—came into my room while I was asleep and rifled this trunk. As you can see. When I went to bed, the lid was closed and the things inside arranged neatly."

Her eyes opened wide with shocked innocence. You are acting a part with me, woman, I said to myself. And you are not even troubling to do it very well.

"Who was this man, miss?" she asked. "Did you see his face?"

I shook my head. "I woke up for a few brief moments," I said. "It was more like a dream. No—I did not see his face."

She hunched her shoulders and spread her hands.

"*Mi scusi, signorina,*" she said. "But how can you be sure that it was not a dream, after all?"

"I've told you," I cried, and was instantly aware that I had done the wrong thing in losing my temper. "Because of the condition of the trunk and the things inside it!"

She hunched her shoulders again and said nothing. There was no need for her to say anything; all she had to do was to express silent disbelief.

I had gained nothing from the encounter—save the certain conviction that the housekeeper knew the intruder and had probably connived in the intrusion (that bitter-tasting wine—had it been drugged? Did that account for the way I felt?).

On the other hand Adriana had learned all she needed to know: that I was ignorant of the intruder's identity.

"That will be all, thank you," I said frostily. At least I was determined to salvage a few shreds of dignity from my defeat.

The housekeeper paused by the door and looked back.

"You will not be speaking of this . . . event . . . to Madame?" she asked. "It is a matter that would upset Madame's mind very greatly."

It was a crude attempt to blackmail me into silence by an assault on my conscience—and was, happily, quite unnecessary.

"I would not dream of doing such a thing," I snapped. "Nor shall I—even when I eventually find out who the man was who ran his filthy hands through my private possessions."

My shot struck the mark: the woman's eyes flared with a sudden hatred when she turned to go.

* * *

I was to present myself at Mrs. Newstead's apartments at ten, and I should be free at eleven. At eleven, I then decided, I would hire a gondola and make a tentative exploration of Venice. Or, perhaps, Durward de Lacey would arrive and escort me. . . .

To combine neatness with practicality, I chose to wear the second of the two travelling costumes on which the St. Errol dressmaker had burned so much midnight oil to complete in time for my journey: a tweed dress with a black silk coat over. I hoped that the tweed would not be too warm.

Shortly after half-past nine, my plans were thrown awry by a loud hammering on the door of the Palazzo Dewaine and demands for admission in a guttural-sounding language that echoed and re-echoed through the inner court.

The shouts were answered and counterpointed by excited cries in Italian from the staff of the palazzo. I went out on to the gallery and looked down into the court—in time to see a party of three men tramping in through the covered yard. They were led by Adriana's husband, Alfredo, who must have opened the door. The newcomers were in uniform.

Alfredo looked up and saw me. He excitedly addressed me in Italian mixed with broken English, gesturing to his companions. I caught one word: *polizia*.

"You are Fraulein Button?" One of the men called up.

"I am."

"You will accompany us to the Directorate of Police, fraulein."

"Now?" I asked, bewildered and somewhat alarmed.

"Immediately, fraulein."

"But—why? What for?"

The question seemed to puzzle the three policemen. They looked at each other, seemingly for guidance. Then the speaker shrugged and turned back to me.

"It is not correct for you to ask that, fraulein," he said severely. "You will come, please."

There seemed no alternative. I descended to the court and the three Austrian policemen grouped themselves about me, one before and two behind. In this way we progressed through the echoing covered court and out of the wide entrance arch of the palazzo, to where a long boat bobbed at the foot of the steps. And all the way, I drew an uneasy comparison between myself and some erring Tudor queen being led out to her execution.

At a sharp order, a rope was cast off, four oarsmen bent their backs against the current and we were swept out into the middle of the busy canal. Immediately, we were the object of all eyes.

From every passing craft, enquiring glances were turned to the group of us in the stern of the police boat. And I was uneasily aware that it was I—seated among the uniformed guardians of a hated, alien power—who was the true centre of attention, and that the looks which were directed towards me spoke of only one thing: pity.

Our progress was swift: all other craft kept well out of our way. Two sharp bends in the Grand Canal, and I saw the open waters of the lagoon ahead, with the glorious domes of what I now know to be the church of Santa Maria della Salute on the right hand and the bell-tower of St. Mark's rising grandly above the rooftops on the left; and, as we drew nearer the end of the canal, the splendour of San Giorgio Maggiore, rising from the very waters of the lagoon.

The wonders of the passing scene drove away all sense of time and even quietened my fears.

My fears returned again when the boat bumped gently against a landing stage, and a countless host of pigeons rose from the black-and-white marble flagstones of St. Mark's Square and swept over my head in a terrifying explosion of sound.

* * *

They brought me to the end of a narrow alleyway off the great Square, to a solid-looking house whose flaking walls were dappled with reflected sunlight from a small canal. I was escorted along a corridor, to a door at the far end. There was a knock, a brief exchange in German—and I was ushered in.

Sitting at a leather-topped desk, facing me, was the red-headed man I had seen in the police boat during my first journey on the Grand Canal to the Piazza Dewaine. He was smoking a large meerschaum pipe and regarding me through narrowed, pale-fringed eyelids. A moment's pause, and he lowered the pipe and got to his feet.

"Otto Beck. Inspector," he said, bowing stiffly. "Graciously take a seat, Miss Button. This matter will occupy only a short time."

I obeyed him; sat down and composed my skirts in what I hoped was a calm and unflustered manner. All the time, I was conscious of those almost colourless eyes upon me. I took off my gloves and folded them neatly on my lap. Then I looked at him.

"This matter of which you spoke . . ." I prompted.

His glance wavered, and he picked up a sheaf of papers lying on the desk before him.

"'It is nothing," he said. "A matter of formality. You arrived in Venice yesterday, is that not so?"

I nodded.

"Ah, yes. And you are staying with Mrs. Newstead at the Palazzo Dewaine. Are you perhaps related to Mrs. Newstead?"

"No."

He scribbled a word on the corner of the top sheet.

"A friend, perhaps?"

"A companion."

"Companion?" One pale eyebrow raised. "That is very interesting. Very interesting." Again, his pencil made a squiggle in the margin. "You are then employed by Mrs. Newstead?"

I could not see what business it was of his—or of Austria—but: "By Mrs. Newstead's family, the Dewaines," I said.

"Ah, the Dewaines." He sat back and regarded me with a quizzical expression. "They have had a long association with this city —ever since the old days of the Venetian Republic, have they not?"

"I am not familiar with local history, Inspector," I replied, with truth.

The pale eyes narrowed and crinkled at the corners. He was amused, or pretending to be amused.

"Oh, come, Miss Button," he chided. "You are not expecting me to believe that?"

"You may believe what you choose, Inspector," I replied. "I have not lied to you."

He raised a protesting hand. "I am not suggesting such a thing, my dear lady," he said soothingly. "Let us just say that you may have . . . forgotten . . . a few things. Will you graciously permit me to assist your memory?"

I shrugged. "As you will, Inspector."

He began: "You will know, of course, that, for the last thirty years, Venice and the whole of Lombardy-Venetia has been in the domain of His Imperial and Royal Majesty, Ferdinand the First of Austria?"

"I know Venice belongs to Austria," I admitted.

"Your memory improves, Miss Button. Let us continue. You will also know that there are those who object to this very excellent arrangement?"

"I imagine the Venetians themselves question the excellence of the arrangement," I said dryly.

"And others," he said. "As you are aware."

"Others? What others?" I asked.

"Foreigners," he said. "Foreign sympathisers. As you are aware."

I shook my head. "No."

"Conspirators!" he hissed. "Plotters. Planners of undertakings intended to endanger the safety of the sacred person of His Majesty, of the august imperial house, of the constitution of the state!"

"I—I don't know what you mean, Inspector," I cried.

"Foreigners who associate with known revolutionaries!" he continued, implacably. "Providing them with comfort and assistance in their doings. Offering them shelter, advice, money!"

"What has this to do with me?" I asked him, now thoroughly alarmed.

"Highly-placed foreigners," he continued. "Protected by wealth and rank. Sheltered by influence—or so they think!"

"Inspector Beck . . ." I began.

"The Dewaines! Your Mrs. Newstead!"

"Oh!"

"You feign surprise, Miss Button. I am not deceived." He picked up a paper and read out: " 'Marianne Newstead, formerly Dewaine. Husband deceased. Arrested fourth September, eighteen twenty-three, on charge of sheltering and assisting a wanted revolutionary. Charge quashed from lack of evidence and because British consul protested.' "

"But that was over twenty years ago," I cried. "And it says there was no evidence."

"Evidence!" the pale eyes blazed. "My predecessors had more than enough evidence to hang your Mrs. Newstead, but she was saved because of her position—because the consul protested. But times have changed, Miss Button. Otto Beck is now in charge, and your Mrs. Newstead is not too old to hang!"

"No!" I breathed. "You can't mean it!"

He rose to his feet. "I am suggesting, Miss Button, that you were aware of all this before you left England."

"No!"

"That the Dewaines sent you for a secret reason!"

"No!"

"That you came to Venice, bearing messages to Mrs. Newstead and other known sympathisers of the revolutionaries . . ."

"That's not true!"

"Bearing pamphlets, books, pictures of a political nature, to be distributed. . . ."

"I didn't!"

"Money! Gold coin, for the purchase of arms. . . ."

"No! No!" I covered my ears, to shut out his harsh, accusing voice. But there was no escape from the sound.

"I am suggesting, Miss Button, that you are working to endanger the safety of the sacred person of His Majesty and of the august royal house and the constitution of the state! I am suggesting that you are engaged in criminal activities!

"I am suggesting that you are . . . *a spy!*"

I screamed: *"It's not true!"*

He smiled and sat down. I fumbled in my reticule for a handkerchief and dabbed my streaming eyes. He had reduced me to a state of mortal terror and confusion—why was he now laughing at me?

"No, Miss Button," he said gently. "Of course it is not true. But I had to be sure of you."

I stared at him through my tears. "You mean? . . ."

"Simply that I have just confirmed my first impression of you, which was that you are a young lady of transparent honesty. A trifle stubborn and headstrong, perhaps, but entirely without guile. No, you are not a spy, Miss Button. And I would advise you not to attempt the occupation—for you would be a miserable failure. However . . ."

"Yes?"

"It would not be beyond your abilities to perform a small service for the state. In return, you might say, for being graciously permitted to stay as a guest in Venice."

"I don't know what you mean, Inspector Beck," I said. Nor did I.

He picked up his meerschaum and began to stroke its smooth bowl, watching me all the time with those inscrutable pale eyes.

"It was all true," he said, "about your Mrs. Newstead." He raised a hand to silence my immediate protest. "Oh, I am not suggesting that this old, blind lady is capable of overthrowing the state. But she has been actively engaged in revolutionary activities

in her time, and still corresponds with the state's known enemies.
. . ." He paused significantly.

I suddenly comprehended his meaning. And I felt a hot flush of furious indignation rise to my cheeks. I stood up.

"Inspector Beck," I said coldly. "If you are satisfied that I am not a spy, may I please be permitted to leave this place?"

"It is such a little thing to ask," he said. "Simply to inform me of the people with whom she corresponds. The names of her visitors."

"What you are suggesting is unspeakable!" I cried.

"Austria can be generous to her friends. I take it that you are not a young lady with a private fortune?"

"May I leave, Inspector?"

"Two names, particularly, interest me," he persisted. "One is Daniele Manin, the other is Nicollo Tommasseo."

"Please!" I cried.

He shrugged. Picked up a bell and rang it. I heard footfalls approaching down the corridor. When the door opened, Beck's red head was bent over his papers, ignoring me entirely.

"Escort the lady back to the Palazzo Dewaine."

I went out. His voice made me pause at the threshold, but only for an instant.

"Au revoir, Miss Button. I await to hear from you. Any time—day or night."

* * *

On my return, I went straight to see Mrs. Newstead. Naturally, she had been informed of the fact that the Austrian police had taken me away. To my surprise, she was not particularly put out.

"Stupid people," she said. "Their police and secret service have instructions to watch over every possible source of discontent in Venice. Which is why they censor our newspapers and spy on our laundry lists. They are particularly nervous about foreigners. I suppose they suspected you of being a revolutionary. You poor child, did it worry you very much? No work for you today. I believe that the excellent Mr. de Lacey is trailing his cloak somewhere round the palazzo. Tell him to take you out for luncheon."

Her contempt for the Austrians and ignorance of her own danger worried me. Inspector Otto Beck had seemed far from stupid, and I was prompted to tell her everything that had happened, but decided against it; since it would only upset her and there was scarcely anything she could do to allay Beck's suspicions. I would watch over her. The thought of acting as Mrs. Newstead's protector was curiously comforting.

I left her and went to look for Durward de Lacey.

He was sitting on the balcony overlooking the small canal, as before. And dressed in the same lemon-coloured suit—or similar to the one—that he had been wearing when we first met at Landeric. The recollection, and the train of memories that followed, brought a sudden lightness to my heart.

He stood up and put down his sketch-book when I approached.

"Good morning," he said. "I discern from your expression that you are the bearer of good news. Mrs. Newstead will see me now."

"Not now," I replied. "But she *will* see you, I promise. Today, she tells me, I must ask you to take me to luncheon."

He spread his hands and smiled his gay, lop-sided smile.

"There you are," he declared. "What did I tell you? Did I not say that you were the bearer of good news?"

* * *

We took a light luncheon in St. Mark's Square, at a café called Florian's: a charming little establishment with elegant ground-floor rooms scarcely bigger than railway compartments, done out with exotic wall paintings and dainty furniture. There was not a place to be had inside, so we were shown to a table in the arcade that surrounds the square. From where I sat, I could see the many-arched front of the great cathedral and three tall flagposts, from whose tops the black-and-white eagle banner of Austria curled lazily in the sunlight.

We ate typical Venetian food, chosen by my companion: a mixed fry of fish and crustaceans caught—so we were assured by our voluble waiter—in the lagoon that very morning. I was pleased to note that, in contradiction of his cynical and world-weary remarks about Venice, Durward de Lacey obviously both knew and liked the city very well indeed. He spoke the language, he was friendly with the people, and was a mine of information about even the most out-of-the-way trifles. As I speared my *fritto misto* and sipped the dry white wine of Verona, I watched and listened —and appraised him.

That I found him attractive was obvious. That he appeared to find me attractive was puzzling, since I would have thought that the artist's eye tended to appreciate beauty in its refined and classical form. How he could look with any pleasure upon my weather-beaten face was beyond all belief. (Since falling in love with Mark, I had been drinking a wine-glassful of vinegar nightly on retiring—a sovereign method of attaining a fashionable pallor that was failing dismally in my case.)

I told myself that I enjoyed his company because he reminded me of Landeric, and, in consequence, of Mark. Furthermore, he was the first man of any quality who had ever paid the slightest court to me (I preferred not to think about Sir Tristan Dewaine), and I was flattered and pleased to bathe in the warmth of his gallantry. And, on this occasion, there was a special reason for being grateful of his company.

"Mr. de Lacey," I said. "I have had a rather unpleasant experience, and I should like your advice."

He nodded. "I thought something was the matter. You've been like some beautiful Amazon queen contemplating the massacre of her captives, and letting me do all the talking. Please tell me about it."

"Well . . ." I began.

"And—please—let us set aside formalities. Do call me Durward, and allow me to call you Susannah, if you will."

"Of course, Durward," I said. Then I gave him a brief and unvarnished account of my summons to the Directorate of Police—omitting nothing, not even the fact that my mistress had been arrested for revolutionary activities twenty-odd years previously. When I came to that point, he gave a low whistle of surprise and concern.

"Not that I should be amazed at that," he said. "The Dewaines have had a place here since the days of the Doges, and it's hardly surprising that Mrs. Newstead identified herself with the Venetian cause. You say she's a strong-willed person—not the retiring invalid most people suppose her to be?"

"Aside from her almost total blindness and her personal grief, I would say she is a whole and complete person, and I have already come to admire her greatly. I can well imagine her, twenty years ago, being a martyr for the cause of freedom."

"And now—in eighteen forty-six?"

"That is what worries me, Durward. I think that Inspector Beck may be right, and that she still continues to identify herself with the Venetian cause." And I told him about her copious letter-writing, her wish to hear all the latest gossip of the promenades. I then continued the account of my interview with Beck.

At the end of it, Durward said: "That fellow Beck is notorious in Venice for his persistence and unscrupulousness. I shouldn't wonder if he doesn't have hundreds of informants in the city. Some people will do anything for money—or from blackmail or fear, poor wretches. And now he's trying to get you to spy on Mrs. Newstead, eh?"

"I left him in no doubt about my reaction to his suggestion."

"Mmmm. That's all very fine and large. But, my dear, I'm afraid you will have to face up to the possibility of being threatened with deportation from Lombardy-Venetia if you don't cooperate."

I stared at Durward, appalled. "They wouldn't do that, surely?"

"I'm afraid they would, Susannah—and frequently do, at the slightest provocation and on the slenderest pretext. Speaking of provocation, look over there, where we are about to witness the Venetians quietly expressing their disapproval of being the subjects of His Imperial and Royal Majesty."

Immediately opposite, at the other side of the great square, was a similar café, named Quadri's. Durward had already pointed out to me what I had already learned from Mrs. Newstead—that Quadri's was frequented by Austrians and, in consequence, shunned by all Venetians. There was a bandstand in front of both cafés, and a party of gaudily-uniformed players were now taking their places upon the one at Quadri's and tuning up their instruments.

"The Imperial Guards' Band," supplied Durward. "You will hear the very latest Viennese valses by the Strausses, father and son. But first there will be a little light entertainment. Watch carefully. Watch the *clientele* in Quadri's and the people over here."

The bandmaster raised his baton and brought it down. Immediately, the band struck up with a ponderous, four-square tune, and, with a scraping of chairs that could be heard right across the *piazza*, the people at Quadri's rose to their feet.

"You are listening to the Austrian national anthem," said Durward. "In Venice, it is always played three times through."

"Shouldn't we stand up, out of respect?" I whispered.

"Not yet. Watch."

I watched. The Austrians at Quadri's—most of the menfolk

were in uniform—stood stiffly to attention. Likewise, among the people who thronged the square, several were betraying their nationality by standing still. The men removed their hats, while the soldiers and sailors turned to salute the flags on the high poles before the cathedral.

The rest of Venice, and his wife and child, went on their way, all unconcerned. The crowds continued to stroll, the people seated all round us continued to chatter.

The anthem rolled to a close—and began again.

Durward took my hand. "As foreign visitors," he murmured, "this is where *we* pay our respects."

I stood up with him. "What happens at the third verse?" I whispered.

"Then—and only then—do the Venetians stand up!"

* * *

"There's something else," I said. "Last night, a man came into my room and rifled my trunk."

We were sipping coffee. The band was playing a lilting valse and, notwithstanding the warmth of the afternoon (my tweed dress had proved, after all, to be too heavy), I would have loved to have danced in the great square.

"Was anything taken?" asked Durward.

"No. It must have been connected with the Beck business, don't you think?"

"Oh, yes," he said. "And, since places like the Palazzo Dewaine were built to be proof against intruders, your visitor must have been someone inside."

I told him of my encounter with Adriana.

"Your man was either her husband or that oafish son of theirs," said Durward firmly. "Sullen-looking brute. I should think they're all in Beck's pay. Just the types. They are probably doing it in return for the son's freedom. He looks like a petty criminal to me."

"What was he looking for, I wonder?"

"The things Beck mentioned to you," said Durward. "Compromising letters, pamphlets and so forth. Large sums of money."

I shuddered. Once more, the thought that alien hands had been rifling among my possessions made me feel physically sick. I had a mental picture of Adriana's hulking son thumbing through the pages of my Bible and finding Mark's and my silhouette portraits. And I clenched my fist till the knuckles were white.

"Terrible people!" I cried. "They shan't learn anything from me, and I will help and protect Mrs. Newstead all I can."

"Bravo!" he said. "But be careful, Susannah. As you yourself have pointed out to me, Beck's no fool. Best to make sure that your mistress is kept well out of trouble. She's too old to survive imprisonment in that grim building across the Bridge of Sighs."

"Beck mentioned Manin," I said thoughtfully. "Daniele Manin and another man called something Tommasseo. He said he was particularly interested to know if either of them visited or communicated with her."

"Tommasseo I have never heard of," declared Durward. "But Manin's no revolutionary. He's a lawyer and a moderate patriot, whose main interest is to see a railway built from here to Milan. Are you quite sure he said Manin?"

"Quite sure."

"Very strange. Really, these confounded Austrians see revolution everywhere. I tell you, my dear Susannah, there'll be no revolution in Venice—or anywhere else in Italy—while the present Pope is alive. You mark my words. Now. We have had a protracted and entirely delightful luncheon. I have listened to your troubles and given you what advice I can—which is to keep your beautiful Amazon queen's head out of trouble. What would you like to do for the rest of your afternoon? Would you like to look round St. Mark's, or climb the Campanile, or visit one of the islands of the lagoon?"

I hesitated. "Well . . ."

"What then? What cultural feast do you have in mind, Susannah? Do you hanker after the paintings of Tintoretto? There are acres of them in the Scuola di San Rocco. San Giorgio Maggiore is very fine. There may be a matinée performance at the Fenice theatre. I am at your service to cater to your every whim."

"I think I should like to visit a dressmaker," I blurted out.

"Capital! Capital!" Durward smote the table and laughed heartily. "How like a woman. Oh, how I love the delicious practicality of the fair sex."

"I don't have the right sort of clothes for Venice," I explained.

"Then you shall, my dear," he cried. "You shall! There are dressmakers in Venice who rival the best of the Rue de la Paix. Put yourself entirely in my hands, and I will see you well fixed."

He paid the bill with a flourish and gave the waiter what appeared to be an extremely generous tip. It occurred to me that my friend must have drunk all but one glassful of the two empty bottles of wine that stood on the table.

He offered me his arm. "Come, my dear Susannah."

We set off along the arcade, and had not gone more than a dozen paces before a figure stepped out from a doorway: a figure in a dramatic cloak and broad-brimmed hat.

Inspector Beck!

"Good afternoon, Miss Button. Mr. de Lacey, is it not? A pleasure, sir." He bowed stiffly from the waist, removing his hat.

I knew, with an absolute certainty that this was no chance encounter; but that he had been watching us—spying on us—all the time we had been at luncheon.

He gestured towards the band, across the square.

"You greatly enjoy the valse, I think, Miss Button."

I nodded. "Yes."

"I thought so," he said. "While you sat there, you tapped your feet to the music of Herr Strauss. And in perfect time. Good day to you, dear lady. Sir."

Replacing his hat, he walked swiftly away from us, his cloak billowing.

"Confounded cheek of the fellow!" growled Durward. "Made not the slightest attempt to hide the fact that he was spying."

"More than that," I said. "He made a special point of letting me know that he was watching me very closely."

The thought disturbed me.

* * *

Perceiving my unease, Durward bent every effort to soothe my mind. This ability to catch a person's mood was, I was soon to discover, very characteristic of him. I put it down to the heightened sensibility of the artistic temperament, and it was certainly very strongly developed in my new friend.

By the time we came to the dressmaker's, he had joked and quipped me into a much happier frame of mind. The shop was in a narrow street overlooking a small canal beyond St. Mark's Square and was kept by a tall and elegant lady who spoke excellent English. I made my wants known (two day costumes suitable for the coming Venetian summer and a gown for formal evening wear), and she produced pattern books and samples of materials.

Durward settled himself in an armchair. Hat tipped forward over one eye and one hand perched atop his silver-knobbed cane, he began a conversation—in Italian—with the signora's extremely pretty young assistant.

My eye was swiftly taken with an illustration of a day dress with the fashionable tight pointed bodice and overlapping, flounced skirt. It occurred to me that the dressmaker's suggestion, to make it up in a light woollen material of dusky pink, was a good one.

My next choice was a silk skirt with a short, skirted jacket in a velvet of a contrasting colour. After some consideration, I plumped for brilliant blue and white stripes for the skirt and deep mauve for the jacket. It was about this time I noticed that Durward was flirting outrageously with the assistant. The poor girl's delicately-olive cheeks were quite pink, and the signora looked up from the pattern book and clucked with disapproval.

We came to the choice of an evening dress. This was my special concern, for, when Mark arrived in Venice in the late summer, I was determined to make a better showing at the dinner table than I had made at Landeric, in my dowdy old dark brown. Leafing through the pattern book, the dressmaker showed me several creations of the sort I had in mind: all exquisite—and all dreadfully expensive, so that I was grateful that Mark had given me a very generous clothing allowance for my Venetian appointment.

The silly little goose of an assistant was giggling at the other side of the showroom by the time I had made my final choice: of off-the-shoulder gown with five deep flounces at the skirt—to be made up in white silk edged with maroon tassels. It was everything I had hoped for. In a gown such as that, I knew, I would be able to shine with an unaccustomed confidence in Mark's presence. With the candlelight falling softly on my bare arms and shoulders, and on my fashionably pallid cheeks (my nightly dose of vinegar would be increased to two glasses immediately), I could hold my own with anyone—even with Amelie de Quatrefois.

The assistant was prised reluctantly away from Durward and made to write down my measurements. In the fitting room, while the signora plied me with her measuring tape, my thoughts were gnawing jealously at the girl whose name had just sprung to my mind.

What would I do—how could I carry on living—if Mark married Amelie de Quatrefois?

I decided that I would simply die. Food and drink—all forms of sustenance—would cease to have any meaning or temptation. Bereft of any desire for nourishment, I would quietly slip into a decline and fade out of life. They would bury me somewhere, and perhaps Mark would come to see me. Alone, of course; not with his hateful new bride. He would lay flowers on my grave. Rosemary . . .

"The signorina will look ravishing in her new costumes," cried the dressmaker. "Such a figure. Like a pagan goddess." She cast a contemptuous glance at the poor little assistant. "Not straight up and down like a stick of spaghetti!"

I would look ravishing. I clung to the thought. Mark would be coming to Venice in August or September, and he would encounter the new and ravishing Susannah Button. And be swept off his feet.

This would be my last, my only, chance. As soon as we met again—as soon as his eyes lit upon me after the months between—I would know where my future lay.

My woman's intuition would tell me, at one look into his sea-green eyes, if I had any hope.

Just as I would immediately recognize the familiar, disinterested glance; the cool, flat appraisal of a piece of furniture—human furniture, but no more interesting for that—which was the only way he had ever looked at me.

"Quite ravishing!" repeated the signora.

Chapter 5

It rained on our way back to the Palazzo Dewaine; drumming on the roof of our little cabin, and drenching our gondolier and his colleagues who swung past us, driving their craft through the green-grey waters of the Grand Canal. I thanked Durward for giving me luncheon and escorting me around. When I chided him for flirting with the poor little assistant, he laughed and said that it was incumbent upon the rich and successful to spread happiness among the needy—a piece of typical arrogant male rubbish that, for some reason or other, annoyed me greatly. I also recalled those two empty bottles of wine and ruefully came to the conclusion that my new friend had his fair share of imperfections. Nevertheless, we parted on good terms: he kissed my cheek and handed me out of the gondola and up the steps of the Palazzo Dewaine.

I dined alone that night, served by one of the young maids of the palazzo who spoke no English. The day's excitements brought me a night of tranquil and dreamless slumber that made waking a sheer delight—so that I flung open the shutters of my windows and leaned out, to see small boats being poled along the little canal below; all laden down with fruits and vegetables; with cheerful market people who waved up to me; with their children, babies, with their dogs, cats and coloured birds in wicker cages.

At ten o'clock, I presented myself at Mrs. Newstead's apartment. The sitting room was in near-darkness, as ever. She greeted me kindly, making no reference to the events we had discussed the previous day, but asking me to take my place by the window curtain in such a way that I should be able—by means of the thin shaft of light coming through the chink—to write letters to her dictation.

In fact, she directed me to write three. The first—to my utter delight—was to Mark. In it she spoke of her great pleasure at receiving me at the Palazzo Dewaine and how she was greatly looking forward to his projected visit in the late summer. She closed with repeated expressions of her continuing love and esteem —sentiments that I wholeheartedly echoed.

The second letter was to her bankers in London and merely requested them to sell certain securities and arrange the transfer of the resultant moneys to a banking house in Venice.

The name of the third letter's addressee sent a sudden shock of alarm through my body, so that my pen dropped a blot of ink upon the page.

Signor Daniele Manin . . .

Mrs. Newstead's voice was quite calm and matter-of-fact as she dictated the lines to Signor Manin, residing at an address in nearby Verona, to the effect that she had greatly missed his company in the last few months and would he be so kind as to call upon her? She gave a date and a time: late in the evening a week hence.

It was on the tip of my tongue, there and then, to warn my mistress of the danger she was in. Then I remembered Durward's comment on Manin: that he was not in any way a revolutionary, whatever Inspector Beck's interest in him, and I again decided to keep my own counsel and watch developments.

On the evening of Manin's visit, I took care to be standing in the shadows of the gallery overlooking the inner court at the appointed time. The summoning knock on the outer door sent Alfredo to open it. He came back into the court, followed by a figure in a slouch hat and dark cloak. I had the impression of a man in his early forties; a man of considerable force and energy— but I never caught sight of the face below the wide brim of the hat. Moments later, he was out of sight.

The incident worried me greatly, since, if the Riccis were indeed in the pay of the Austrian police, news of Manin's visit would certainly have been brought to Inspector Beck without delay. For days, I lived in dread of knocking on the door and the sound of guttural orders—but none came. I searched Adriana Ricci's face for some indication of the woman's feelings; but met up with only a blank wall of indifference and resentment. Her husband, Alfredo, seemed positively to avoid me at every turn; darting away whenever I approached and lowering his face to avoid my eye when we passed. The son—Aldo—appeared to share his mother's feelings for me, treating me always with the minimal courtesy that bordered on insolence; the Riccis were giving nothing away.

And so the days passed. I went out most afternoons, sometimes alone, sometimes with Durward, who continued to wait with remarkable patience for Mrs. Newstead to grant him a sitting. By then it was quite obvious to me that my mistress's earlier, petulant reason for keeping him cooling his heels had been replaced by the sounder motive of ensuring me an agreeable escort in Venice. And she was well repaid for her action: I brought back to her all the tidbits of social and political gossip that Durward picked up around the cafés that he frequented.

Touching on Durward's life in Venice: apart from his outings with me, I gleaned from certain remarks he let drop that his time was spent between work and play—with the latter activity predominating. I know that he did many drawings around the canals and narrow streets of the city, for I saw his sketch-book; I also know that he spent a very great deal of time in the cafés and at the card tables. It soon became very clear to me that he was a man with a very mixed share of the vices and virtues to which mankind is heir. I can only add that, with me, he was at all times the model companion: courteous, charming, amusing—and impeccably correct.

He took me to the Fenice, a delightful theatre in the Baroque manner—all pink plush and gilded cherubs disporting themselves across the ceiling—that had only recently been rebuilt after a disastrous fire. We went by boat to the islands of the lagoon: to San Michele, Murano and Torcello, to Chioggia and San Lazzaro degli Armeni, Burano, San Francesco del Deserto, the Lido. I have the names before me still, in my diary of that unforgettable year of 1846. They bring back memories of wide skies and calm waters; of noble domes and towers rising out of the illimitable blueness; velvety evening light and the sound of mandolines; the laughter of happy children.

There were shadows. Sometimes, on a crowded public boat or in a restaurant, I sensed that I was being watched. We saw Beck on one other occasion when we were out together, but I think the encounter was accidental: he rose from a table outside Quadri's and gave us his stiff-from-the-waist bow as we strolled past.

Though she never confided in me about her Venetian sympathies (because, I supposed, she did not want me to become involved in any more trouble with the police), I came to know Mrs. Newstead much better, and I liked what I saw. She bore the affliction of her almost total blindness with great fortitude, and was mostly forthright and cheerful. Occasionally, however, an inner darkness seemed to fall across her life. She turned silent, brooding and depressed. At these times, there was nothing to be done with her. No amount of encouragement would lift the burden that seemed to oppress her mind. I connected it with the recurring memories of the child she had lost—her little boy, Georgie, who had been so much like Mark, and whose going had seemingly destroyed a part of her. At these times, it puzzled me that she was still able—with her increasing age and afflictions—to interest herself in the Venetian cause, if this indeed was the reason behind her connection with the patriot Daniele Manin. It did not seem to be of a piece with the inner grief and the darkened room. The more I thought of it, the more I became convinced that there was some central secret connected to my mistress. Others must have sensed it too—hence the rumour about her possessing the Evil Eye and the wild tale of the locked room.

Every morning, at ten o'clock, I went to her sitting room and—unless the dark mood was upon her, in which case she sat in silence—she would ply me with questions about my perambulations of the preceding afternoon: whether I had gone with Durward or alone, where we went, what restaurants and cafés we had entered, whom we saw, what they said, what they were wearing—nothing was too trivial to escape her attention. When I had finished, she would draw comparisons between my experiences and similar Venetian promenades she had taken in the past, as a child, as a young woman and with her late husband. It was when she touched upon the latter that the black mood sometimes came upon her. These daily meetings, which began as an hour's duration, gradually expanded to fill up the whole morning.

We fell into the habit of dealing with her correspondence twice a week, on Wednesdays and Saturdays. It was mostly composed of letters to friends and distant relations in England and France, with an occasional short note to Daniele Manin in Verona. It struck me as strange that she always wrote to him in English—till

I realised that it was for secrecy's sake. Not that the contents of her letters to him were anything but commonplace: enquiries as to his health, reminding him to give her best wishes to mutual friends, and so forth.

I read her the correspondence that came in return. Red letter days were those when I recognised Mark's familiar handwriting on the packet. My heart leapt, and I could scarcely hide the delight in my voice when I read aloud of his doings. And always in the end— blessedly—he conveyed his "sincerest good wishes to Miss Button." Did ever a woman in love make do, and with such delight, with such slender tokens from the loved one?

I had other news from Landeric: Hester wrote to me that she was home from school because she had fallen from a pony and sprained her ankle. Everyone was well, she said, but her father was not able to get about without a Bath chair. Then—something that saddened me very much—she told me that Mrs. Horabin had passed away, peacefully in her sleep. My sorrow in losing a good friend was softened by the thought that she had died as she would have wished: still housekeeper of Landeric and breathing her last within its beloved walls.

In the evenings, I often sat on the balcony below my room and worked on the quilt that I had brought from Landeric. It had started as a pattern of interlocking hexagons, but rapidly deteriorated (so haphazard and impatient am I by nature) into a crazy patchwork of coloured silks and velvets, with the patches edged by herringbone stitchery in filoselle. At any event, it kept my fingers busy—and allowed my mind to go wandering into forbidden fields of speculation and imagery.

And who should be in the centre of my imaginings, but—Mark?

I saw him arriving at the steps of the Palazzo Dewaine in the family gondola, with Aldo Ricci in his gondolier's livery at the long oar. He was all in dark brown, that set off his dark handsomeness; hatless, his black hair gleaming like a raven's wing in the dying light of a Venetian evening.

I was alone to greet him. Dismissing Aldo, I extended my hand and he took it in his. His head stooped and bent over my fingers. I felt his lips warmly brushing my fingertips.

How many times did I prick myself with my needle, when it came to that moment!

The anticipation of Mark's arrival filled a great part of my waking thoughts. Between daydreams, I made practical arrangements:

the new costumes were soon finished, and I put away my lovely dinner gown, wrapped in a sheath of muslin, to await the occasion; I attended to my complexion and was delighted to see that it was getting noticeably paler—though I am sure it was due more to my new habit of never setting foot outdoors without a parasol, rather than to the effects of the vinegar.

According to my diary, it was the twentieth of May—and Venice was almost unpleasantly hot and sultry—when Mrs. Dewaine gave Durward a sitting, at last. He drew her by the thin chink of light coming through the curtain, and the pencil portrait showed her seated stiffly in her chair, pale hands on lap, eyes closed.

That night we went to see a new opera about Joan of Arc, by the Italian composer Verdi. The nature of the subject gave rise to noisy expressions of patriotic sentiment from the mainly Venetian audience, so that one could scarcely hear the music. Afterwards, we had supper in a restaurant near to the Fenice.

There—to my utter surprise and quite sincere pleasure—Durward asked me to be his wife.

I thanked him very much for the honour, but told him that I could not accept. It was quite impossible to explain why. He begged that we should always remain friends—to which I, of course, agreed—and urged me to get in touch with him if ever I was in need or trouble, writing out his London address on the back of the restaurant menu and putting it into my reticule.

Next day, he left for England.

* * *

The sultry heat of late May had its climax in a night of storm that broke over the city just after sunset. I watched the spectacle from my bedroom window, in my peignoir, with my hair unbound, ready for bed. Jagged forks of lightning played above the rim of rooftops, and the thunder echoed along the cavern of the canal below me in long drum rolls. It was frightening, yet strangely exhilarating, to stand there and see Venice as the plaything of the elements: one moment dark, the next moment whitened like bone in the pitiless glare of the lightning flashes. And the rain sheeted down.

I watched for some little time and was just in the act of closing the shutters when I heard a scream. And then another.

They came from within the *palazzo*, from the direction of the inner court. My first thought was for Mrs. Newstead. Heart pounding, I rushed to fling open my door and went out into the covered gallery beyond that looked out into the rain-drenched inner court. It was there, peering over the edge, that I saw a group of three figures struggling to climb the staircase below.

Barefoot, I ran down to join them. Two pairs of frightened eyes flared wide to see me: the eyes of Adriana Ricci and her husband. They were supporting the bulky figure of their son Aldo, and half-lifting, half-dragging him up the stairs. His head was bowed on his chest, and his dark hair hung in matted rats' tails.

"What's the matter? What is it?" I cried.

"He is hurt!" wailed Adriana. And I saw that she was near to hysteria. It was obviously she who had screamed.

Coming closer, I saw that the young man's right hand was clutching a tight wad of his coat, pressed against his side. And as he stood there, swaying in his parents' grasp, a tell-tale splatter of bright blood fell onto the tiled steps.

"He is dying. My *bambino* is dying!" cried the woman.

"Bring him to my room," I said, and took hold of his left arm myself. Alfredo seemed gratefully to relinquish his own part in assisting his son to climb the stairs; the poor wretch seemed half-stunned with shock and fright.

"Alfredo, go and fetch hot water," I ordered him. "Hot water, you understand? As much as you can carry and as hot as you can make it. Bring it up to my room as quickly as you can."

"*Si, signorina,*" he said. "*Acqua calda. Si, si.*" And he flashed me a look of dog-like devotion before running off down the steps in the direction of the kitchens.

Adriana and I managed to get the stricken Aldo, by easy stages, to the threshold of my room and inside, where I brought a straight-backed chair. He sat down heavily and uttered a low groan of pain and weariness.

"He is dying!" wailed Adriana.

"Nonsense!" I said briskly. "Now, Adriana, tell him to take his hand away from his side, so that we can see what damage has been done."

The woman spoke to her son in low, coaxing tones, and together we managed to prise his clenched hand away from his side. This immediately brought forth a fresh splashing of blood. Adriana moaned like a wounded animal all the time we were peeling off his

138

jacket. She screamed when his shirt proved to be wet and red-
dened all down the right side from shoulder to waist.

"Let me see it, Aldo," I murmured encouragingly, lifting up his
arm. Another scream from Adriana. With a sudden twinge of
nausea, I saw the deep and ragged furrow that scored his side. The
flesh was laid wide open for the length of a hand's span, and when
he breathed, I could see the white bone of a rib moving in the red
mouth of the wound.

"*Mio bambino!*" cried Adriana.

"It's a nasty gash," I said, "but, bad as it looks, it's only a graze.
He won't die of it, Adriana."

It was then that Alfredo arrived with a steaming kettle of water,
which I poured into a hand-basin. Tearing one of my shifts into
rags, I proceeded to clean the wound. The mother and father
stood as mute and helpless as sheep, watching me, huge-eyed. Aldo
made no murmur, though I must have been hurting him and was
going to hurt him very much more; but sat with his head bowed
against his chest, eyes tightly closed and mouth hanging limply
open.

Closer inspection of the wound revealed that it was indeed a
clean, but ragged, gash—such as might have been caused by being
struck a glancing blow from a heavy pointed object. Something
like a sharpened stake . . .

Or . . . *a bullet!*

I went to my workbox and took out one of my sewing needles
and a length of floss silk with which I stitched my patchwork
quilt. The operation I was about to perform was one I had
witnessed many times during the old days in the Haven, when
men were brought in from the boats with cruel wounds—from
fish-hooks, gaffs and other sharp tools of their trade—which were
treated by Jesse, who had a natural talent as a surgeon.

To the accompaniment of anguished keening from Adriana, but
a stoic silence from my patient, I drew together the raw edges of
the wound and joined them with a swift line of oversewing.
Alfredo shivered—but gave no other sign of feeling—when I band-
aged him up with a length of torn shift and secured it firmly.

"What he needs now," I said, straightening up, "is a good
night's sleep."

It was then that Aldo fainted clean away: I managed to catch
hold of him round the shoulders as he slipped off the seat. The

three of us carried him, head lolling, to my bed, where we laid him out on the counterpane.

"He can stay here tonight," I told them. "I'll sleep in another room."

"Signorina is very kind," muttered Alfredo brokenly.

I met Adriana's eyes. Dark and impassive as ever, there was, nevertheless, something there that I had never seen before. It was almost as if that gaunt, grim woman was reaching out in the darkness and trying to make some contact with me.

"Signorina . . ." she began.

"What has happened tonight, Adriana?" I demanded. "Where has your son been—what has he been doing, . . . to?"

I was interrupted by a loud hammering on the great doors below. A harsh shout for admission echoed up the open court. A peal of thunder followed immediately after.

"*Polizia!*" wailed Alfredo.

Adriana's face was suddenly stricken with a mortal terror. Her gaze flashed to the unconscious figure on the bed, and she gave an agonised moan.

"Adriana!" I cried. "You've got to tell me what's going on. Have they . . . are they looking for . . . *him?*"

She nodded.

"*Si!*"

"Adriana!" I demanded. "You've got to tell me. Is he—is your son . . . a *revolutionary?*"

Again the nod.

"*Si.*"

"Oh, my God, Adriana!" The full import of the peril came teeming into my mind. "What has he done out there tonight, Adriana? And how could he come back here in that state?"

The knock was repeated. And again. There were more shouts.

"If he's found here," I cried, "do you realise what will happen to Mrs. Newstead? She'll be imprisoned with the rest of us, for harbouring him!"

The woman buried her face in her hands.

They were knocking continuously now, and the shouts were getting louder and more insistent. Something had to be done. And quickly—before the Austrians broke down the doors and we stood convicted of our guilt.

"Let them in, Alfredo," I commanded. And when the man

stared at me, slack-mouthed and only half-comprehending, I gave him a shove towards the door. "Hurry! Hurry!"

Sobbing, Adriana made a move towards the figure on the bed: holding out her arms, as if to gather up her son and try to carry him away.

"Leave him there, Adriana," I cried. "There's nowhere to hide him."

"The attic," she wailed. "We carry him up together. . . ."

"No time, Adriana," I told her. "And the attic is one of the first places they'll look." I reached out and drew the curtains of the bed, hiding him from view. "Our only hope is that they'll never look here."

"Oh, signorina . . ." the woman's gaunt frame was racked by a fresh outburst of sobbing.

"Compose yourself," I said. "Adriana, your son's safety—Mrs. Newstead's safety—depend on you. Dry your eyes and go downstairs. Be standing in the court, near the foot of the stairs, when the police come in. Go now—and leave Aldo to me."

Gathering up her skirts, the woman fled from the room. Below, I heard the rattle of bolts and the voice of Alfredo calling out reassurances to the waiting Austrians.

I took a swift look round my room. The bloodstained water still lay in the hand basin: I tipped it back into the kettle. Next, I wiped the spots of drying blood from the tiled floor around the chair; bundled up the remaining scraps of torn shift and crammed them into a drawer. There was nothing else I could do: nothing further to hide the unconscious figure lying behind the flimsy drapes of curtain.

Casting a quick glance at my reflection in the mirror, I shook my head and ran my fingers through my hair, tousling it.

Then I forced myself to walk out into the gallery and look down into the inner court—in time to see Alfredo emerge from under the archway with a group of armed police at his heels. . . .

And Inspector Otto Beck!

Beck snapped an order, and two of his men seized the terrified Alfredo and began to question him in Italian, pushing him and shaking him roughly as they did so. This brought a cry of protest from Adriana, who had stationed herself at the foot of the stairs, as I had told her. I breathed the hope that Beck would think that the manhandling of her husband would account for her tear-streaked face.

The moment had come for me to intervene. I took a deep breath.

"Inspector Beck. What is going on down there, please?" I called out in a loud, calm voice.

His head snapped up, and his pale eyes met mine across the open space that lay between us. He took off his hat and smiled thinly.

"So sorry to disturb you, Miss Button," he said.

"I have been awakened by this terrible noise," I said. "And I should be grateful if you could explain what it all means."

He nodded. "Certainly, Miss Button," he said. "If you would be graciously pleased to descend, I will explain all."

"Down there?" I cried. "Are you blind, Inspector? Can you not see that I am *en déshabillé?*"

He hunched his shoulders. "Indeed I can, dear lady."

I saw the uniformed policemen exchange amused glances.

"Then, Inspector, you must come up here," I said flatly. "For I am not parading in the rain in my night attire." By now, the rain had slackened to a thin drizzle, and the thunder was rumbling distantly over the Adriatic.

After a brief pause, Beck snapped a guttural order to his subordinates that wiped the grins from their faces. They sprang to attention and saluted in concert. I turned towards my open door when I saw him begin to mount the staircase from the inner court.

My heart was beating so loudly that it must surely have betrayed me. I took stock again of the room. The floor, the chair in which Aldo had sat, the chest of drawers concealing the tell-tale bloody linen, the kettle sitting by the fireplace—all might pass muster; but nothing on earth could detract from the veiled bed at the end of the room: my guilty eyes were dragged towards it against my will.

Beck's step was light on the threshold outside the door: I had not realised that he would move so quickly, and gave a start to turn and see him there. I wondered how long he had been watching me.

He bowed. "You will graciously permit me to enter, dear lady?"

I nodded. He walked over the threshold, and his pale eyes never left me as he turned and, with a studied gesture, pushed the door close with the toe of his Hessian boot.

"Such a pity to have disturbed your slumbers, Miss Button," he said smoothly. "But it is always a great delight to resume our so friendly acquaintance. If I may be permitted to remove my wet cloak?"

My back was turned to the bed. And my racing mind was coming to terms with the fact that a single sound or movement from Aldo—however slight—would destroy us all. For the moment, I was safe—we were all safe, but it was safety poised on a knife-edge.

By deliberately inviting Beck up to my room—to the very place where the man he sought was hidden (and so imperfectly hidden!), I had, I hoped, allayed any suspicions he might have concerning me. My next problem was to make sure that he left—and quickly.

"Now, tell me, Inspector," I said briskly. "What is all this about?"

He cocked his head on one side and eyed me quizzically.

"You have not been to see me, Miss Button," he said. "And that has been a matter of great disappointment, for I had great hopes of you."

A vein was ticking in my right temple, ticking in time to the frantic beating of my heart: surely he must notice it.

"I have had nothing to tell you, Inspector," I said.

"You disappoint me, dear lady," he said. "Both of us would need to be very naive to believe that. This house, the Palazzo Dewaine . . ." he gestured about him ". . . is a hotbed of revolution, and you are trying to suggest to me that you are unaware of it: that your mistress and the family Ricci have not aroused your suspicions? Tonight, for instance?"

I licked my dry lips. "What happened tonight?" I demanded, with the last of the coolness at my command.

He frowned. "Tonight," he said, "a group of fanatical revolutionaries—the very scum of the cut-throat breed who are seeking the overthrow of the constitution of the state of Lombardy-Venetia, to the dismay of His Imperial and Royal Majesty—infiltrated the sentries guarding the Arsenale. Their object—to make off with arms and ammunition, to use in the furtherance of their abominable plans. Happily, they were detected in the act and fired upon. Two of them were killed. The others escaped by jumping into the lagoon and swimming to a waiting boat. It is likely that at least one of these was wounded."

"And?" I asked. "How does this concern me—or the Palazzo Dewaine?"

"One of those who escaped was clearly seen and recognised," he said, "on account of the fact that he was already a known suspect under surveillance. His name—Aldo Ricci!"

He spoke the name loudly. I had the thought that the sound of it would arouse the unconscious man on the curtained bed and cause him to sit up with a start. And my skin crawled.

"I see . . ." I breathed.

"He will hang, Miss Button," hissed Beck. "And if my officers find him sheltering within these walls, the Riccis and Mrs. Newstead will be arrested also. Your mistress, dear lady, will discharge the long-standing debt that she owes to the state. Twenty years is a long time, but the state is patient."

"You mean—you would imprison her?"

He nodded. "She will be incarcerated during His Imperial and Royal Majesty's pleasure," he said. "And that could be for the duration of her natural life. High treason, Miss Button, is normally a capital offence, but in view of her age and infirmities, the state will wish to be lenient."

"It would kill her!" I cried. "She couldn't exist any time at all outside her own darkened room. Her mind would collapse under the strain. You don't understand . . ."

He raised a hand, soothingly. "Please do not fret yourself, dear lady," he said. "We are a civilised and cultured people. The lady in question will receive every medical care and attention. And, of course, I am only speaking of what will happen *if* we find Aldo Ricci hiding in the palazzo. It is quite likely that he fled elsewhere. In which case, the state will have to bide itself with patience for a little longer—before Mrs. Newstead is called upon to discharge her debt."

(*If* they found Aldo! I must get rid of Beck immediately!)

He was smiling, now, and coming towards me. My instinct was to back away.

"In any event, my dear Miss Button," he said smoothly. "Whether the scum is found here or not, it will not concern you and our . . . relationship."

How could I back away? That would take me nearer to the bed and to Aldo!

"I—I am glad to hear that," I whispered, through dry lips.

"Our very special relationship," he said. He was so close, now, that I could smell the stale odour of tobacco that lay on his person and clothing. "For you see, my dear lady, I am quite convinced that you are well disposed to the state of Lombardy-Venetia and to the person of his Imperial and Royal Majesty. So convinced am I, in fact, that I have reported as much to Vienna. That pleases you, *hein?*"

"Yes," I said in a very small voice that sounded quite unlike my own.

He moved even closer. "You are pleased to have found favour with the state," he said softly. "You are, perhaps, also pleased to have found favour with one of the state's devoted servants. I refer, of course to yours sincerely."

I would have given my all to have been able to retreat before him, but every step would have taken me nearer to the curtained bed. Much nearer, and Beck would surely hear the unconscious man's breathing. I fixed my thoughts firmly on the things that mattered: Mrs. Newstead's safety . . . Mark's adored profile . Landeric in the sunshine . . .

"You are pleased?" he repeated.

"Yes. I am pleased," I whispered.

"That is . . . nice."

His face swam before me, with its pale, regarding eyes and thin, smiling lips. I saw his hand come up: saw his fingertips take hold of the end of one of the ribbons that tied the corsage of my peignoir. He raised it up, smiling quizzically. I had an uncontrollable urge to scream into his face. My body began to tremble all over.

There was a double knock on the door, and it was flung open. One of the policemen stood on the threshold. He saluted Beck and addressed him in their own language.

Beck scowled and replied. Then he turned to me.

"My men have searched the *palazzo* from top to bottom, and the criminal is not here," he said. "A pity. We must now depart and look elsewhere. Fortunately for your Mrs. Newstead, the state will have to bear itself with patience a little while longer."

My relief was cut short by the sudden awareness that Aldo was stirring slightly behind the curtain: a wispy ghost of a sound—the mere movement of fingertips, no doubt—that only I, with my senses tuned in that direction, could hear. But it could herald his awakening. Beck must go.

I drew myself up with all the dignity at my command; held out my hand to him as if I had been a queen terminating an audience.

"I must not detain you any longer from your duties, Inspector," I said. "So kind of you to keep me informed of what is going on. Good night to you."

He took my hand and kissed it.

"Good night, gracious lady," he murmured, with meaning. "Such a pity. We must continue our so—interesting—discourse on another occasion."

"That will be nice," I replied primly.

I was trembling again by the time the door closed behind them; when I heard their footfalls crossing the open court below and fading away under the archway, my legs would no longer bear my weight, and I sank slowly to my knees on the tiled floor and buried my face in my shaking hands.

* * *

Later, Adriana and I went together to Mrs. Dewaine's apartments, to make sure that she had settled down comfortably—for she had been rudely aroused by the police when they came in to search her rooms.

Our mistress slept on a *chaise-longue* that was kept made up in the corner of her sitting room. By the light of a solitary candle, we crept in and inspected her. She lay on her back, hands crossed on her breast, face white and mask-like in the frame of the muslin night cap that she wore tied under her chin.

"The Austrian devils!" breathed Adriana. "I thought they would hurt Madame when she refused to give them the key."

"The key?" I asked, puzzled.

"The key of her special room," said Adriana. "Has Madame not spoken to you of her special room—the one that is always kept locked?"

The locked room! My thoughts returned to what Durward had told me, and I felt the hair of my scalp prickle with a nameless dread.

"No, she has not," I said.

"Then I will say no more of it," said Adriana. "Madame will tell you of it in her own time."

"The Austrians—they took the key from her and opened it?" I asked.

"I persuaded Madame to give it to me," she said. "And I opened the door. There was nothing inside to interest those animals, who were only concerned with finding my Aldo."

I smoothed the silk shawl that covered Mrs. Newstead. She stirred slightly in her sleep and gave a soft moan. Adriana shielded the candle with her hand, so that it should not fall upon the near-blind eyes of the sleeper.

"She's quite peaceful now," I said. "I only hope tonight's upset doesn't send her into one of her black moods of depression tomorrow."

"I shall pray for her tonight," said Adriana. "No child of God should suffer what Madame suffers in her mind."

We tip-toed out of the room together and shut the door. Adriana, who slept in a small bedroom nearby, within earshot of Mrs. Newstead's bell, parted company from me in the corridor. In doing so, she seized my arm. Her ravaged face was dramatically lit by the flickering candle flame. The dark eyes fixed me with a brooding intensity.

"You saved my Aldo tonight," she said. It was the first allusion she had made to the night's events since the departure of the police.

"I did it for Mrs. Newstead's sake," I replied. "I wouldn't like you to think that I did it for any other reason, Adriana."

She nodded. "I know that, Miss Button," she said. "My Aldo is nothing to you. The freedom of Venezia is nothing to you. But the thing has been done. You gave my son his life—and the debt will be repaid. One day."

She gave my arm a convulsive squeeze, and was gone.

* * *

May went out, taking with it the unseasonably oppressive heat; and the city and lagoon lay under limpid blue skies and a tangy freshness. June also brought the news of the death of the reigning Pope, and all Venice speculated upon who his successor would be. Mrs. Newstead and Adriana were closeted together for hours in the curtained sitting room, and Daniele Manin became a frequent visitor—but always late at night.

I was severely excluded from all political discussion in the Palazzo Dewaine, at the orders, I believe, of Mrs. Newstead, who was anxious that I should run no further risks with the police. Adriana was the sole member of the household to share her confidences on this subject. Of course, it was now clear that, far from being in the pay of the Austrians, the Riccis (mother and son at any rate; I could not see poor old Alfredo in the role!) were dedicated revolutionaries, and that Aldo had searched my baggage immediately on my arrival—after his mother had given me the drugged wine—in order to make sure that the newcomer from England was not a police spy.

I never saw Aldo again after the fateful night of his wounding and never enquired after his whereabouts, assuming that his compatriots had smuggled him out of the city and the province. Adriana never alluded again to the matter of my saving her son from Beck and his men; but her attitude to me underwent a change. I would not say that we became friends, that would be putting it too high. Rather, that stern and unbending woman condescended to notice my presence and even to indulge me in small things.

She discovered, for instance, that I was interested in culinary and household matters, so she volunteered to instruct me in the secrets of Venetian and Italian cookery. Under her able tuition, in the vast, spotless kitchen of the *palazzo*, I learned to fresh-boil *spaghetti* so that it was correctly *al dente*, that is, neither too hard nor too soft; I was tutored in the art of turning the humble codfish, with the aid of milk, parsley, onion and anchovies, into the delicious local dish known as *baccalà*. I became familiar with the favourites of the common people: with *risi e bisi*, a risotto of peas and ham; and I learned not to look down my nose at the humble *poleta*, a corn flour cake mixture, rather heavy to the English taste, which is the staple diet of the teeming poor of the city.

Adriana introduced me to the markets of Venice. With her to guide me, I came to know the Rialto Bridge and maze of colourful streets leading from it, where housewives, rich and poor, make their daily purchases: of cheeses from Asiago and Gorgonzola; seafood from the lagoon and the Adriatic beyond—sardines and octopus, shrimps, prawns and minute crabs, mussels, oysters and John Dorys; exotic meats; game birds of all kinds; and the vegetables and fruits—such a richness of choice—oranges and tangerines from far-off Sicily, great red apples and suave pears, mountains of cherries, strawberries, peaches, melons of all colours. Everything in abundance.

We would move slowly from stall to stall, with Adriana choosing every purchase, however small, by feel or taste; haggling with the vendors and beating them down if she decided that the quality of their goods did not measure up to the prices; while poor Alfredo ambled stolidly behind us, his arms laden down with our purchases. Then it was back to the palazzo by gondola, to the great kitchen.

The act of cooking always seemed to mellow the normally taciturn Adriana, and she became quite garrulous. She told me of her childhood on the nearby island of Murano, centre of the Venetian glass industry since the Middle Ages. Her own father had been a master glass-blower till the consumption had taken him off—this being a disease that frequently strikes the men who exercise this ancient and demanding craft. She had worked at the Palazzo Dewaine, she told me, since the age of eleven, and had married Alfredo when he had been the Venetian valet to Mrs. Newstead's father, the third baronet.

She would never speak of the Newsteads, husband and wife; for some reason the subject of our mistress's earlier life was always ignored whenever I broached it. In time, I came to accept that Adriana had absorbed something of the sorrow that surrounded Mrs. Newstead's bereavement of husband and child—and felt it to be an act of irreverence to share it with an outsider, a stranger.

Once she asked me about my own childhood, and I told her about my life in the Haven, and how Father and I had come there, after Mama passed away, because it had been her last wish for me to be brought up in her native Cornwall.

Adriana was, naturally, curious about Landeric—which she had never seen, but which was the almost legendary abode of the rich and powerful foreigners who had been masters of her and her kin for so many years. I explained how it was bigger and more imposing than even the greatest *palazzo* on the Grand Canal—dwarfing in size and splendour the Palazzo Rezzonico or the Querini, and comparable only with the Palace of the Doges. She marvelled at this and demanded to know how many servants were kept to maintain such an establishment. Her eyes widened when I was able to tell her—with perfect truth—of an occasion when Mrs. Horabin and I, determined to answer this selfsame question, had each taken an independent tally of the indoor staff, and had come up with two widely different totals.

Later in the month of June—my diary tells me it was Monday the eighteenth—came news that the new Pope had been elected a few days previously in Rome. He took the name of Pius IX. Adriana called him *Pio Nono*, and was so delighted with the result of the election that she forgot discretion and confided to me that *Pio Nono* was a man of a very different colour from his predecessor: that he was a liberal and a patriot, who would never bow the knee to the Austrian oppressors. Mrs. Newstead, also, was greatly cheered by the news. Fully a week passed without her suffering from one of her terrible fits of depression. I was happy for her; but concerned that she might associate herself with some hare-brained revolutionary *coup*, and give Beck the opportunity he was seeking to arrest her.

Then I remembered Mark: how he would be arriving in Venice in the late summer. I would tell him all, and his broad shoulders would lift the responsibility of his aunt's safety from me. Yes, Mark would cope with the situation—he might even persuade Mrs. Newstead to leave Venice for a while, till the disturbances following the papal election were over (every day came news of riots and demonstrations, and there had been a fight between the respective patrons of Florian's and Quadri's).

Greatly daring, I even toyed for a while with the notion of writing to Mark and begging him to come at once to Venice and take Mrs. Newstead under his care; nor could I conceal from myself that the arrangement would delight me for entirely different reasons. . . .

As it turned out, events overtook my plans for the immediate future—in the shape of a letter from Mark himself, addressed to me, that provided another of the great turning points of my life.

Landeric
June 27th, 1846

Dear Miss Button,

I have to inform you that my father passed away peacefully in his sleep last night. I am glad to be able to add that, since his return to Landeric, the two of us had grown closer together and had settled more of our differences than I would have believed possible. But no more of that.

There is now no impediment to your return here, and I urge you to do so with all speed. The funeral is three days hence, and Hester has been summoned from Bath; it is, of course, impossible for my sisters Alicia and Jessica to be here in time for the obsequies. If it were not for the funeral and for the many duties that have befallen me on Father's demise (I have to go to London on family business immediately after the ceremony), I should come straight out to Venice to see you. . . .

It was at that point of the letter that my heart turned over and the whole world moved beneath my feet. I closed my eyes and opened them again. I had not been mistaken. It was true—the precious, lovely words were there before me. . . .

. . . I should come straight out to Venice to see you, for the matter that is uppermost in my mind at this time can scarcely wait.

Impossible to begin to explain in a letter. Make all haste, I beg you, to return to England and to Landeric by the quickest route open to you. Then you will hear, from my own lips, what you should have been told a very long while ago.

I will close now. Please convey my dearest love to my Aunt Marianne, and tell her that nothing that has happened—or will happen—will prevent me from keeping my promise to see her in the late summer.

Farewell for the present.
Believe me I remain,
Yours sincerely,
Mark Dewaine.

By chance, another packet had arrived for me by the same delivery. This also bore the St. Errol impression and was addressed in a spidery, scholarly hand that I knew of old. I opened it and skimmed through the contents almost without taking them in. My whole mind was on the wonderful, wonderful communication from Mark.

St. Agnes's Rectory,
Pennan,
Cornwall.
Sunday, June 28th, 1846.

My Dear Susannah,

Truly "the priests, the Lord's ministers, mourn" (Joel 1.9.). You will have learned of the passing of Sir Tristan and also grieve at the loss of one who was your benefactor (1 Cor.13.13.).

Sir Mark Dewaine has apprised me that he has summoned you to return to Landeric forthwith. I am greatly concerned that you should call upon me, on your way through the village and before you reach Landeric, because I have some news of great import to divulge to you.

I beg you not to neglect the urgent request of your devoted old teacher, my dear Susannah. It is vitally important, for: "I will instruct thee and teach thee in the way which thou shalt go: I will counsel thee with mine eye upon thee." (Ps. 32. 8 & 9.)

> May the Lord bless you,
> my dear Susannah,
> Your old friend and mentor,
> Cyrus Mawhinney.

Tossing the rector's curious epistle into the top of my workbox, I rushed to bear the news to Mrs. Newstead.

* * *

She said no word till I had read Mark's letter right through to her, then she fussed in her reticule and produced a handkerchief, with which she dabbed her eyes.

"Upon my word, I don't know why I should cry for that dreadful man," she said. "He has treated me abominably in the past. When I think of how I stood in need of him when my beloved Georgie passed away. . . ." Her voice broke, and I feared that she was about to progress into one of her terrible attacks of melancholy . . . "not to mention his total lack of understanding when I was widowed. But here I am weeping for him. And why? Because I remember the time when we were children together, my cousin Tristan and I. At Landeric. And he was sometimes kind to me."

I waited for a while, and then I said: "You won't mind if I leave for England at once, Mrs. Newstead? I'm sure Adriana will fill my place very well. She is so devoted to you. But, of course, if you would prefer me to stay for a while . . ."

"Go, my dear," said Mrs. Newstead. "Go now. Immediately. Fly to him, or you will be sorry for the rest of your life."

"But—Mrs. Newstead," I faltered, shocked and bewildered.

"I have known it all the time," she said. "I knew it from the first. The tone of your voice when you first mentioned Mark's name to me. I knew then—for the blind have special powers of catching truth and falsehood from the very whisper of wind in leafy trees. You love my nephew, my dear. And you have chosen well."

152

Not only the blind have powers: I recalled the woman who saw through to my heart at the St. Errol Fair.

"Yes, I love him," I admitted.

"Come over here to me and hold my hand, Susannah," she said.

I obeyed. One hand holding mine, she reached up with the other and touched my cheek, describing the shape of it to herself, or so it seemed.

"You are beautiful, Susannah," she said. "And it is right and proper that you should be so, for like calls to like. It is the way of nature. And he loves you in return."

My heart was lifted up. "Oh, if that were so, indeed," I breathed.

"It is so," she affirmed. "That is why he is sending for you, now that my cousin is dead—he who would have opposed, tooth and nail, any suggestion that his son and heir should marry a girl of the lower classes. Why, if Mark had had the chance, he would have brought you the news himself. And his heart, to lay at your feet. You read it in his letter, Susannah dear."

"I had . . . hoped it might mean that," I admitted. "But, as you say, I am a little nobody. And I only dared to dream that one day he might come to notice me as a living and breathing woman, instead of a servant—a piece of living furniture."

She took my face in both her hands. Her blind eyes were trying to search and find me in the curtained gloom.

"We have not known each other for long, my dear," she said. "But this I know: my nephew Mark is very dear to me, dearer than any person on this earth. But I could not be more happy, Susannah, if Mark had been my own child—my own lost Georgie —and he wanted to make you his wife and the mistress of Landeric."

"Oh, Mrs. Newstead," I cried. "Dear Mrs. Newstead, you have made me so happy."

All the barriers between me and the recluse of the Palazzo Dewaine, the restraints that resulted from the disparity in our ages, our totally different upbringings, her illness and my buoyant health—were swept aside by her declaration. I flung myself at her feet and she embraced me, pressing my face closely to her breast and stroking my hair.

"My child," she murmured. "It will provide the last great pleasure of my life, to see you happily married to dear Mark. There must be no delay. Be wed in Landeric chapel—oh, how I wish I had, but it was not to be—and come to see me straight after. Come and spend your honeymoon time in Venice."

"But that's exactly what Mark intends!" I exclaimed. "Don't you see, Mrs. Newstead? He says in his letter that I am to tell you that nothing that has happened—by this he must mean Sir Tristan's death—or will happen . . ."

"By which he means your wedding," she supplied.

"Nothing will prevent him from keeping his promise to see you in the late summer," I cried.

She hugged me closer to her. "You must now learn to call me Aunt Marianne, my dear," she said. "As Mark does. How lovely, to think that I have won myself a niece after all these years—for I scarcely count that little baggage Alicia, who takes after her father if you ask me. And I have never even met Jessica and Hester."

"I shall try to be a good and dutiful niece to you, Aunt Marianne," I said gravely. And we both laughed and hugged again.

It was then I saw a shadow pass across her face, and a tear started at the corner of a sightless eye. I knew the signs—they were visible in every line of her face and in the suddenly tired sag of her thin shoulders. A wave of her terrible depression had come over her.

"What is it, Aunt Marianne?" I asked, squeezing her hand encouragingly. "What has suddenly saddened you so?"

She signed. "Help me to my feet, Susannah," she said. "There is something I must show you. And then you will know the true depth of my grief."

I did as I was bidden. She rose painfully from the chair and leaned heavily on my arm.

"The key," she said. "There is a drawer in the little table by the window, Susannah. In it you will find the key to my special room."

The special room! The time had then come when I was to be admitted to the secret of the locked room. I reached out in the gloom and, opening the drawer, I took out a small key with a piece of silk braid tied to it.

"This way, Susannah," she said, guiding my arm. "It is only fitting, now that you are so soon to be a member of the family, that you witness the souvenirs of my sorrow."

We progressed across the room and out of the door to the corridor beyond, at the end of which was a small door set in the panelling. It was to this door that my sightless guide directed me.

The key turned easily in the lock, and the door creaked open.

The room within was long and narrow and lit by the daylight coming through the chinks in the window shutters. The furnishings told me immediately what manner of room it was—or had been.

"Why!" I cried. "It's a nursery!"

"My darling Georgie's nursery," she whispered. "Where my darling passed his few happy months upon this earth—before he fell asleep forever. Nothing has been moved since that terrible day. Come . . ."

She guided me down the length of the room, to where stood a carved wooden crib with a blue-trimmed canopy. Lying across the tiny counterpane was an embroidered christening dress in white silk. Mrs. Newstead touched the crib, and it moved gently on its rockers. In the faint light, I saw a ghostly cloud of dust rise from it, each particle gleaming in a thin shaft of daylight.

"He was christened in the Anglican church," she said. "And my darling was asleep when Adriana laid him back in the crib. I shall never forget his sweet expression. Now you will see the little bed he moved into when he was older."

Numb with a sorrow and sympathy I did not have the words to express, I let her guide me to a small brasswork bed. It, too, was hung with blue and covered with a patchwork quilt made up of sprigged flower shapes. A small nightdress that might have fitted a child of eighteen months or so lay across it.

Mrs. Newstead's hand reached out, questingly, for the small garment; found it and raised it up to her lips. Her tears were coming unchecked, and she seemed to have forgotten my presence. Looking about me, I saw that there was a small table by the bed. On it, covered by a thick rim of dust, stood a child's feeding bottle, inside which were the darkened remains of what must once have been milk. There, also, was a half-empty medicine bottle and a spoon. A wooden soldier doll was propped forlornly against a leg of the table. I felt an intruder.

"He was so happy," said Mrs. Newstead brokenly. "The happiest baby you ever saw. If he had not been taken from me, he could have lessened the grief of my widowhood—but it was not to be. He passed away in this bed you see here."

I reached out to touch her. "Mrs. Newstead," I began. "Aunt Marianne, you mustn't upset yourself so. It was lovely of you to show me your dear Georgie's nursery, but . . ."

She was not listening to me. She clutched the nightdress to her breast, and, throwing back her head, gave a sound the like of which I had never heard issue from the throat of a human being, nor hope ever to hear again: it was like the despairing cry of some creature of the wilds calling for her lost young—knowing all the while, in her primitive heart, that the little thing will never again nuzzle itself against her.

"Aunt Marianne," I cried. "Come away."

She shook off my hand and buried her face in her hands.

"We could have been so happy together," she moaned. "Why did you have to go away, my darling? I could have made you happy, you know that."

"Let me take you back to your sitting room," I pleaded.

But she was too far gone in her wild grief to heed me; I doubt if she was even aware of my presence by then.

"No one ever loved you as your Marianne loved you, my darling heart," she said. "So how could you desert me? How? . . . *How?*"

Helpless to do anything to reach across the wide gulf that now separated us, I could only stand and stare—as she slipped slowly to her knees and grovelled, like a frightened child, up against the wall, with her face pressed against the dusty panelling.

"Monday," she moaned. And again, "Monday . . . Monday the nineteenth of April."

I touched her shoulder, but it was no use. She was far away in a world of her own and I had simply ceased to exist. She crouched there, keening quietly and mumbling to herself, over and over again, the same date . . .

"Monday the nineteenth of April."

How long I watched over her, I have no way of telling. After what seemed like an age, I heard footsteps approaching down the corridor, and a moment later Adriana appeared in the doorway. She gave a gasp of horror and her hand went to her cheek when she saw her mistress grovelling by the wall.

"Oh, madame, you should not have come in here again," she cried.

"I had no idea, Adriana," I said. "If I had known the effect it was going to have . . ."

"No blame is on you, Miss Button," said Adriana quietly, as she stooped and took Mrs. Newstead firmly round the waist. "Come now, madame," she said in a loud and matter-of-fact voice. "It is time for Madame's chocolate, which Adriana has prepared."

"Chocolate?" The poor creature turned her blind face towards the housekeeper and smiled vacantly. "Chocolate for Marianne?"

Adriana's eyes met mine and she gave me a tight-lipped smile and a nod of reassurance.

"You can leave her with me now, Miss Button," she said. "She is better with me alone."

I left them. The last I saw of Mrs. Newstead—Aunt Marianne —she was submissively allowing Adriana to raise her up.

*　*　*

Two days later, a public gondola took me and my luggage away from the front step of the *palazzo*, on the first stage of my journey home to Landeric. At Adriana's suggestion (she had been watching over her mistress, day and night, since the awful incident in the old nursery), I went in to say good-bye to the recluse of the Palazzo Dewaine. Not entirely to my surprise—for I had seen her quickly recover from her dark moods before, though I had never known her to suffer such a severe attack—she was sitting up in her chair as sprightly as you please, full of excitement about my hoped-for marriage with Mark and begging me to write as soon as the nuptial day was decided. She kissed me over and over again, calling me her dearest niece and telling me how she would look forward to seeing Mark and me on our forthcoming honeymoon in Venice. We parted in a mood of gaiety and high hope; it was as if that dreadful scene in the dead child's nursery had never taken place.

All across the north Italian plain to Genoa, I thought of what I had seen and heard in the pathetic room. Over and over again, in time to the rattling hoofbeats and the swaying of the diligence, the same phrase dinned out in my mind: *"Monday the nineteenth of April . . . Monday the nineteenth of April."*

What was the significance of that date?

Was it the date of her child Georgie's death? Most likely. Either that, or the day on which she became a widow.

Later, strolling the decks of the packet that took me to Southampton, and staring up at the myriad of stars in the black velvet of the Mediterranean night, I pieced together the things that Mrs. Newstead had babbled in her strange delirium.

As I recalled, she had first seemed to have cried for the loss of little Georgie; but later on—when the excess of her grief clouded her brain—her invocations had seemed, rather, to have been addressed to her dead husband.

Had she not said: "No one ever loved you as your Marianne

loved you?" That, surely, must have been addressed to the dead husband. And, from what she had said afterwards, Mr. Newstead must have deserted her.

Was it then desertion, and not widowhood, that was the root cause of her grief—grief that had been deepened and widened by the death of her infant son?

Did Mr. Newstead still live?

It was all very puzzling.

* * *

I came, at last, to the wild Western Land. A hired carriage from St. Errol railway station brought me jouncing down the long, winding lane leading to the coast. Craning my neck, I presently saw a flash of blueness between the horses' heads. A slight ascent in the lane, and the wide panorama of sea and headland came into view, with Ramas rising over all.

Following instructions, my driver took a side turning for Pennan village, avoiding the Haven—for I could not bear one extra moment's delay in seeing Landeric again. There remained the tedious necessity of calling on the rector, as he had so urgently requested in his curious letter (surely the old gentleman was in his dotage: what news of great import could he possibly have to divulge to me of all people?).

The village green was deserted on that languid afternoon of high summer, and I guessed that the whole population would be out haymaking. We rounded the church, and the rectory came in sight between the screen of cedars. We rattled up the drive and I told myself that the coming interview would be as brief as I could decently make it.

Mr. Mawhinney's ancient housekeeper answered the door. I doubt if she even recognised me in the finery of my Venetian costume and millinery, but made a stiff curtsy and, showing me into the library, went off to inform the rector of my presence.

I sat in that room that smelt of wax polish and old leather, while the long-cased clock ticked away, remembering the patient hours of my childhood that had been spent there, bowed over the table in the corner by the little window that looked out over the churchyard. To give him his due, Mr. Mawhinney had been an able tutor. Under his guidance, I was soon able to read and write tolerably well, and to add, multiply and divide by both simple and long methods. I could also recite large parts of the Old and New Testaments by heart (and still can), also the names of the principal countries of the world and their capital cities. A pity I had never learned to like the rector.

I heard his halting tread and was not prepared for the change in his appearance. In the few months I had been away, Mr. Mawhinney seemed to have aged a decade; though, on closer inspection, the unhealthy tinge of his cheeks and the dark pigmentation about the pouched eyes revealed that it was not increased age, but the onset of illness that accounted for the way he looked.

I rose and gave him my hand.

"My dear Susannah," he wheezed. "I trust I see you well. Alas, it is not so with me. In the last few weeks, I have scarcely been able to get about, let alone attend to the multifarious demands of my flock. Be seated, do. I have much to say, and, to tell you the truth, I hardly know where to begin."

My gaze flickered impatiently towards the window that looked out on to the drive, where my carriage waited. The driver had taken out nosebags and was feeding the horses, who stood flicking flies with their long tails.

"So—ah—you have returned from Venice," said the rector. And he cracked his knuckles.

I nodded assent. It occurred to me to wonder if Mark might still be in London and not waiting for me at Landeric.

"You have done well in your position," continued my companion. "Remarkably well. I was of the opinion that it was entirely suitable that you took employment at Landeric. Entirely suitable. Hum."

Silence.

I shifted impatiently in my seat. "In your letter—your very kind letter," I said tactfully, "you told me that you had important news for me, Mr. Mawhinney."

"Ah yes," he said. "Quite so. But, as I have told you already, Susannah, I scarcely know where to begin."

"The beginning would be as good a place as any, sir," I rejoined tartly.

The faintest flush appeared in his unhealthy cheeks, and he cracked his knuckles again.

"Have you received any communication—as I believe you should have—from Sir Mark?" he asked.

It was the first time I had heard Mark referred to by his newly-inherited title, and I was confused for a moment.

"Why, yes, I have," I replied. "It came by the same delivery as your own."

"Quite so," he said. "Would it be impertinent to ask what was the main theme of his letter? I hasten to assure you, lest you think I am prying on your private affairs, that your answer concerns the matter about which I asked you to come here."

"It concerns the important news you have for me?" I asked.

"Indeed, yes."

"Well, he told me that his father had passed away," I said.

"Naturally, naturally," the rector waved his pale, bony hand impatiently. "I would expect that. What else did he say?"

I took a deep breath. What did it matter if the Reverend Mr. Mawhinney had wind of my wonderful, wonderful news? What matter if all the world knew?

"He said that, but for the funeral, he would have come straight out to Venice to see me," I said proudly.

The rector nodded. "And?"

"That there was a matter uppermost in his mind that could scarcely wait."

"Yes. And? . . ."

"That I should return to Landeric as quickly as possible, so that I could hear something from his own lips—something that I should have been told a very long while ago."

The rector's face fell. To my astonishment—and sudden unease —he buried his face in his hands and emitted a low groan.

"What's the matter?" I cried.

He lowered his hands, and his pouched eyes regarded me sadly.

"What do you deduce from the contents of that letter?" he asked.

"Why—what should I deduce?" I replied. "It's plain enough."

"Tell me, though."

"Well . . . I . . ." I felt my cheeks flame redly. He surely must see my answer in my expression.

"Oh, dear Lord!" he cried, burying his face in his hands again. "It is worse—far worse—than I thought!"

"Mr. Mawhinney! What do you mean?" I demanded.

The question that followed came hardly as a surprise.

"Am I to suppose, Susannah, that you greatly esteem Sir Mark Dewaine?"

"Why, yes," I replied primly. "I—I think he is a very fine gentleman, and worthy of the greatest esteem."

"Do not prevaricate with me, my child!" shouted the rector. And now he was my old schoolmaster again. "I am not speaking of the commonplace likes and dislikes that inform the normal, day to day relationships between human beings. . . ." He leaned forward in his chair and pointed a bony forefinger at me. "I am speaking of . . . affection!"

"Affection?" Why was he badgering me so?

"Call it what you will. Call it . . . *carnal love!*" He spat out the words.

I felt a sudden and overwhelming sense of hostility towards him. What right had this old man to rant and rave at me? And why should he think I was prevaricating? I was not ashamed of my feelings: there was only the normal delicacy one felt about revealing them to a person whom one basically disliked.

"If you mean, do I love Mark Dewaine? Well then, I do, Mr. Mawhinney," I said. And the words: "Not that it is any business of yours" hung in the air—clear, if unspoken.

He groaned. "I blame myself," he said. "I thought it was entirely suitable, but I never should have permitted you to go to Landeric. I should have seen the danger. Mark is a fine upstanding gentleman—fit to turn the head of any impressionable young person of the female persuasion."

"Mr. Mawhinney!" I began. But he silenced me with a gesture.

"My dear—my poor Susannah," he said. "Do I have it correctly? Am I to suppose that—how shall I put it?—you believe your sentiments to be returned by the gentleman in question; and that, Sir Tristan now having been gathered to the bosom of Abraham, there can be no one who could possibly have any objection to your joining yourself in Holy wedlock with Sir Mark Dewaine, or of your becoming Lady Dewaine and the chatelaine of Landeric? Tell me, do I have it correctly?"

I replied angrily: "If that is Mark's wish, and if it is my wish, I cannot see how anyone could possibly object, sir!"

The Reverend Mr. Mawhinney rose unsteadily to his feet. Though ill and bent, he loomed above me like an avenging angel, and his voice echoed sonorously round the book-lined room.

"I will tell you who would object!" he boomed. "The Holy Church would object! I—in the person of the Almighty's humble and obedient servant—would object! The laws of both God and man cry out that you could never marry Mark Dewaine!"

I sprang to my feet.

"Why?" I screamed into his face. "Why?"

"Because," he said, "you offend the laws of consanguity. *You are his half-sister in bastardy!*"

* * *

He had the compassion to summon his housekeeper, who was suspiciously close at hand with *sal volatile*. I lay back in the chair and stared up at him, trying to convince myself that it was some waking nightmare from which I would soon emerge to true reality.

"As I said, I blame myself," he cried. "I should have forseen that such a thing could happen: that you would persuade yourself into a romantic attachment with him. But it seemed so entirely suitable, at the time, for you to take up genteel employment at Landeric."

I found my voice. "Tell me, Mr. Mawhinney," I asked. "Tell me how this thing you have said about me can possibly be true. That I am . . . that I am . . ." I pressed my hands to my face.

"Joe Button," he said. "He whom you called Father—a worthy, but totally unschooled and ignorant fellow—confided in me the secret of your birth. It came about this way: shortly after his arrival at the Haven and his taking over the tenancy of the Frigate tavern, Button called upon me and asked me if I would undertake to attend to the rudiments of your education, so that you could—in his words—'rise in the world to be a lady.'

"Naturally, I had to inform him that my parochial duties precluded my taking on a full-time pupil. It was then he produced a purse of money, there must have been at least fifty sovereigns in gold—and laid them on the table over there. That was my fee, he told me, and implied that there was plenty more where that came from: enough to take you on to a school for young ladies when the time was due.

"What could I do, my dear Susannah? Not for myself, of course, but for the sake of the poor people of my parish with whom I share my every crust, I could not refuse such a handsome fee. I agreed to attend to your primary education. It was then that I had the—ha—temerity to enquire how he, a poor seaman turned innkeeper, had managed to lay hands on a quite considerable fortune. And out of the simplicity of his heart and respect for the discretion of my cloth, he then confided in me. . . .

"I can see him now, Susannah, standing over yonder, by the table. 'Rector, sir,' he said. 'I will tell you this, and may you never breathe it to a living soul. I am not the child's father—she is a Dewaine!'"

"He told you that?" I cried.

"As God is my judge, Susannah," replied the rector.

"Then—who *is* my father?"

Mr. Mawhinney spread his bony hands.

"Why, Sir Tristan sired you, Susannah," he said.

"*Sir Tristan?*"

"Who else? He was a man, God rest his soul, given to certain— ah—tendencies. But none of that. It is not for us to sit in judgment upon the dead."

"It isn't true!" I cried. "That man my father? It can't be true!"

"I tell you, Susannah," he said tetchily, with an old man's peevishness, "that I had the story from Button's own lips, in this very room. What would it profit him to lie to me—or I to you? He told me how your mother was given a handsome endowment by Sir Tristan, to take their unwanted child far away from Landeric; but how, on her death-bed, she prevailed upon the simple fellow who had married her—in his Christian charity, to give the child a name—to bring the child back here."

The scales were falling from my eyes. I remembered that far-off autumn evening; Father and I walking, hand-in-hand, to see Landeric for the first time. . . .

"He took me there," I said. "Almost the first thing he made sure to do was to show me Landeric. Now I know why."

"Your mother had instructed Button to reveal to you the secret of your birth," said Mr. Mawhinney. "This he was to do, he told me, on your twenty-first birthday. But, as we know, the Grim Reaper intervened and he passed away shortly before that event."

Once more, I was crouched on the narrow strip of beach, listening to the final utterances of a dying man, above the crash of breakers. . . .

"Almost the last word he spoke to me," I said, "and it was as if he was trying to tell me something—almost his last word was 'Landeric.'"

The rector made a gesture of irritation. "I remember well," he said. "Button had some thought of the child—in his own phrase— 'taking up her rightful inheritance when the time came.' Poor ignorant fellow. He had no knowledge, of course, of the laws of inheritance. He was not to know that you have no rights. No rights at all."

I felt the righteous anger rise in my gorge.

"I would not wish any rights in the matter," I cried. "And I would not accept any inheritance from the man who so wronged Mama."

The rector nodded approvingly and looked relieved.

"Your sentiments do justice both to yourself and—hum—your mentors," he said smugly. "But, while I sympathise—indeed, share —your censure of Sir Tristan's treatment of your mother—who was a young woman under his care and protection, a field worker on the Landeric estate, so Button informed me—I have to remind you that, when he took you into his household and treated you almost as one of the family, your benefactor had no idea of his— hum—relationship to you."

I thought of the true motives behind my "benefactor's" action —but I said nothing.

The rector was racked with a fit of coughing. When he had composed himself, he said: "You see now why I summoned you here before you went to Landeric," he said. "For, of course, now you know the truth, your natural delicacy of feeling—which does you great credit—will not permit you to accept any further favours from the Dewaine family. Sir Mark is at present in London, as it happens, so there is no danger of your meeting him. You can depart quietly and with dignity."

The old man's mumbled phrases washed over me unheeded. A terrible realisation was dawning upon me: not only was it totally impossible for Mark and I to marry under any circumstances whatever, but I had been completely misled by his letter into supposing that he felt about me as I felt about him.

The thing he wanted me to hear from his own lips was not that he loved me, but that I was his illegitimate half-sister; the reason why, but for the funeral, he would have come out to Venice was not because he wanted to ask me to marry him, but to make some sort of financial arrangement for me.

That wretched, interfering old man had broken the news to him —no doubt immediately after his father's death. Mark—upright and honourable—had immediately acted the way his conscience demanded.

But there was only one thing I wanted from Mark. Neither his money nor his friendship would do. In truth, not even his title, a position at his side as his lawful wife, not all the wide lands he owned, nor Landeric itself, would have been enough, if they had been given to me without the only thing I really wanted—his love.

But not only was I forbidden the true fulfilment of love; I had not even been loved in the first place!

It was that realisation which broke me. And then the tears came, and all that mattered was to get away from that old man and his mumbling. I stood up, fumbling in my reticule for my handkerchief.

"Thank you for everything, Mr. Mawhinney," I blurted. "But I must go now."

He gazed at me and spread his hands.

"My dear Susannah, what can I say? You know that I am always your friend. If there is any assistance I can offer, you have only to write to me. I do not speak of financial assistance, of course, for, as you are aware, I am not a man of substance."

"You are very kind, Mr. Mawhinney," I said. "Good-bye."

* * *

Somewhere to be alone. To think. And what better place than within sight of Landeric, where it had all begun.

I gave my driver his instructions, and soon we were passing between the lion-topped gateposts. The gatekeeper and his wife came out and, recognising me, waved and called out. I returned their greetings. Mark was in London, and it did not matter who else saw me.

On up the steep drive and into the green gloom of the avenue of tall trees; I held my breath for the moment when the familiar white stonework would appear through the trees, and wept fresh tears when it did.

We stopped near the spot where I had first met Durward de Lacey, with all Landeric laid out before me. I asked the driver to lift down my trunk, and I opened it and took out my Bible. He then drove off, leaving me alone under the plane tree with my thoughts and memories.

Wayward memories . . .

The afternoon I had set in that spot and mourned because I felt that I must leave Landeric after the tragic end of the girl Annie and Mark's revelations about the man who—unbelievably—I was from henceforth obliged to regard as my father.

Shut out the thought . . .

The dinner party on Christmas Eve, when Mark had actually smiled at me briefly. It had pleased me then, though I had been unawakened in my love at that time. He, on the other hand, had never loved me—nor ever would.

No! Turn to other memories . . .

The day of St. Errol Fair, and the strange insight of the old woman at the silhouette stall: she who had turned my gaze upon the wonderful thing that had happened to my heart.

I opened the Bible and our two silhouettes lay facing each other. It had become my hope to have them both mounted in one frame and hung where all could see them and know us for what we were; I had planned, on the packet coming through the Bay of Biscay, that they should hang together in my sitting room at Landeric. Now they were doomed to remain hidden between the leaves of my Bible, to grow old and yellowed. Perhaps, one day, long ahead, when I was dead and gone, someone would open the pages to find them. And then truth would blend into romance—as in all the best novels—and it would be supposed that Mark and I were young lovers in that bygone age of the mid-nineteenth century, and a kind heart would have us framed together. So, in the end, through the magic of romance, my dream would come true.

One of my tears fell upon the corner of Mark's silhouette.

Not lover; but brother. Was it possible? Had there not, after all, been a terrible mistake? Somewhere, between poor Joe Button's illiteracy and the rector's dotage, had the tale been twisted out of shape? Did we really share the same father?

Something directed my hand—for I had no clear notion of what I intended to do—when I took my silhouette and laid it, face down, upon Mark's. That done, I lifted the two sheets and held them up towards the sun.

And saw the truth.

Two profiles looking in the same direction, both overlapping; but not overlapping by more than a tiny margin here and there: allowing for his masculine jawline and his slightly more pronounced Dewaine nose; taking into consideration my feminine softness at the mouth and slenderness at the neck—I was looking at the death-knell of my last, wild hope.

Joe Button had been right. The rector had been right.

I was a Dewaine, and Mark my own brother.

* * *

The afternoon shadows were lengthening across the downward sweep of parkland when I left the plane tree and walked along the terrace, past where my carriage was waiting, beyond the west wing, to the chapel.

One thing more had to be done before I made my last departure from Landeric; one formal acknowledgement to be made.

The tap-tap of mallet on steel sounded loud in the stillness of the chapel as I walked down the aisle. A workman was crouched by the wall beyond the family pew. He turned when he heard my approach, and, no doubt recognising me from the Christmas Tenants and Staff Ball, got to his feet and touched his forelock.

They had buried him—my father—next to the black slate monument that graced the remains of his wife, in a marble catafalque that was still uncompleted. The man was carving the inscription, and I had interrupted him in the act of telling future generations of onlookers the name and quality of the man who lay there.

> *Tristan Hugo Dewaine*
> *Fourth Baronet*
> *Departed this life*
> *June 27th, 1846*
> *"I am the resurrection and the . . .*

I should have prayed, but I could think of no prayer to fit the occasion. This man had never known me for whom I was. If he had, his first thought would likely have been to stop my mouth with gold and send me packing, as he had done to Mama.

I should have hated him, but you cannot hate a dead person whom you have discovered to have possessed a different face from the one he briefly showed to you in life.

I contented myself with the simple acknowledgement that the stone before me guarded the remains of my natural father, and the father of the man I had loved, but now must learn to love no longer. That done, I nodded to the stone-mason and took my leave. The tapping of the mallet on the head of the chisel recommenced before I stepped out of the shadowed nave and into the dying sunlight of the summer's afternoon.

News of my arrival had reached the staff, and they were grouped to see me on the steps. They had smiles and homecoming greetings for me, and Strawson hurried forward to take my hand. He wished me a happy return and was puzzled and dismayed to hear that I was immediately leaving again. At my request, he sent footmen to fetch the few things of mine that still remained in my old room. They came down with my hamper and Joe Button's battered sea chest, and loaded them on to the coach. It was hello and good-bye.

I could not bring myself to look round when we drove away, but I heard the good wishes that they shouted after me. Nor did I dare to turn, till Landeric had vanished from sight behind the trees.

Chapter 6

It had to be London. There was no other place in the land big enough or remote enough from Landeric to provide me with both the refuge and the hiding place I needed.

By its very contrast with rural Cornwall, London would save me from going out of my mind with the weight of memories. How long, in those crowded thoroughfares, would I be able to trust my recollection of the way—the special green and splendid way—that the long glade of parkland stretched down from Landeric to the lake? How, in that smoke-laden air, could I retain the memory of the wine-fresh wind that forever blows over Ramas Head? And, surely, with all those myriads of faces, it should be possible—even for a little time—to blot out the vision of that one face which haunted me.

So I came to London, and an advertisement in *The Times* newspaper brought me to a modest furnished apartment in Great Queen-street, Lincoln's-inn-fields, consisting of what was described —optimistically—as a spacious sitting room and bedroom communicating. I took it for a month, and paid in advance. A month, I reckoned, would give me ample opportunity to look round for a position with living accommodation.

I took stock of my situation. Financially, I was quite well-secure, having spent little or nothing of the money from the sale of the Frigate stocks or of my year's wages from Landeric: in all, about thirty-two pounds.

Determined to run no more risk of involvement in the lives of another family, I set my face against being a governess again, or even of working in a private establishment. It seemed to me that the position of an under-housekeeper in one of the new, large metropolitan hotels would suit me well. I had been learned much about the management of a big establishment from Mrs. Horabin, and I thought Adriana's cookery lessons in the kitchen of the Palazzo Dewaine would stand me in good stead.

My very first application to an advertisement was for an assistant housekeeper at the railway hotel at Euston Station—and it brought a letter inviting me to attend for an interview. This I did, wearing one of the day dresses I had bought in Venice. Throughout the interview, which was conducted by the housekeeper herself and two gentlemen of the board of management, I was conscious that my manner, dress and appearance were all contributing to a good impression, and that my accomplishments were more than equal to the requirements of the position.

It was only when my interviewers touched upon the matter of my previous employment that I felt my confidence begin to falter. I had carefully prepared my line of approach and delivered it as well as I was able: I told them that I had assisted my father in running a tavern in Pennan Haven till his death (which was true), after which I had served for nearly a year as governess and occasional assistant to the housekeeper at one of the largest mansions in Cornwall, till the recent demise of the owner. This led neatly to my answer to their next question: what references could I produce? Sir Tristan having passed away, I said (under no circumstances did I want any application to be made to Mark!), I could offer the names of the rector of Pennan, my old tutor—and that of a gentleman who had known me during my employment, Mr. Durward de Lacey, R.A. My interviewers exchanged most approving glances at the mention of Durward's name, and I knew from that instant that the position was mine. They took note of the addresses of my two references and bade me a most cordial good day, telling me that I should hear from the management in due course. I went out into the bustle of Euston Road, walking on air.

My new life had begun.

The old life ended on July 30th, the day I learned who I was and turned my back on Landeric for the last time. On that day, I drew a line across the final entry in my diary and closed it forever, consigning it to Joe Button's old sea chest. It was while doing this that I turned out his things, hoping to find anything that might add to what I had already learned about my background. Of course, there was nothing. Neither he nor Mama had been able to read or write; Joe had learned my secret from her lips and had carried it in his head. I turned over the coarse, slop-shop clothing; a stick of plug tobacco; a battered tin box containing his sailor's knife, marlinspikes, sailmaker's needle and palm; a lock of hair in a pinchbeck locket (a baby curl—probably mine); a cheap coloured print of the Infant Jesus. The very feel and smell of his few possessions brought back the image of the stolid and simple-hearted man who had reared me as his own, and—after his fashion—with love and devotion. I cried when I remembered how I had used to scold him for his slowness to learn his alphabet: if I had been more understanding, he might not have turned to drink and bad company, perhaps.

One other thing remained to be done before the account of my old life was properly closed. I had to make some explanation to Mrs. Newstead: she who would be waiting for the arrival of a happy honeymooning couple with the late summer.

The letter gave me more difficulty than I had bargained for. Remembering that it had to be read aloud to her by Adriana, I did not feel inclined to name names or to go into any great detail; nor did I want to embarrass us both by starkly pointing out how grossly wrong we had been in the interpretation of Mark's letter. I compromised by glossing over the unhappiness and softening the edges of the drama in such a way as to suggest to her that it had been a simple misunderstanding and that everything had turned out for the best, now that I had left Landeric. The whole communication was no more than twenty lines long and I closed it with the words: *"I am sorry that the matter we discussed is not to be, but I sincerely hope that we may, nevertheless, meet again."* I did not put my London address in the letter: it was a total severance, and it hurt me more than I could have believed possible. I had felt a real bond between "Aunt Marianne" and me.

London in high summer was dust-laden and dry, so that walking the main thoroughfares was far from pleasant. While waiting my expected summons from Euston, I passed my days with reading and with needlework. I could not allow myself the luxury of idleness; no sooner was my mind at rest than there sprang the vision of a face and the recollection of a voice that I must learn to forget.

In the cool of the evenings, when the dust had settled in the quieter streets, I would walk from Lincoln's-inn-fields and down to the river embankment, past the ancient Temple. London astounded me as a place of dramatic contrasts: massive wealth rubbing shoulders with the most abject poverty; mellow antiquity cheek-by-jowl with brash and garish newness. I marvelled at the traffic in the streets and the quality of the horses and carriages of the rich: dashing phaetons, gigs, victorias, barouches and broughams; it distressed me to see crippled children begging, barefoot in the gutters. The noble old buildings were very fine; but glimpses down side-turnings leading off even some of the smartest main streets gave hint of unspeakable filth and decrepitude. All in all, I liked the best of the new in London: I liked the smart omnibuses in their bright red livery; I liked the imposing Houses of Parliament—still unfinished—whose towers hovered in the heat haze of the summer evenings; I delighted in the big shops—mouth-watering emporiums of delight to a person whose early shopping had been bounded by the Pennan village store—that had recently gone up in Piccadilly, Knightsbridge and Oxford Street.

Returning home after a typical evening's walk (I remember well that I had ventured as far as Buckingham Palace, but the Royal Standard was not flying there, and a friendly policeman informed me that the Royal Family had gone to Osborne on the Isle of Wight: Parliament had granted £20,000 for alterations to the palace, said my informant, and not a moment too soon), I was surprised to find that the door of my apartment was ajar. At first, I could only suppose that my landlady, who lived on the lower floor, had used her key to go in and clean up for me—as she used to do on alternate mornings. I scarcely had the opportunity to realise that the time was all wrong for this explanation to fit, before my nostrils were assailed by a heavenly scent of fresh flowers.

The reason was soon made plain to me: the whole, or so it seemed, of my not-so-spacious sitting room was aflame with roses; red roses, varying in shade and hue from the most delicate of pale cerise, through hot crimsons, to sumptuous cardinals and carmines; all of them displayed in woven baskets of cunning and elaborate shapes; a whole rose garden crammed into four walls, all on one unexpected afternoon.

"How beautiful!" I exclaimed. "But—who could have? . . ."

A voice answered me from over by the window, just beyond a screen of limpid carmine.

> *"Her beauty made*
> *The bright world dim, and everything beside*
> *Seemed like the fleeting image of a shade."*

"Durward!" I cried.

"It took the pen of poor Shelley to tell how you look at this moment, dear Susannah. How are you? Not so ravishingly bucolic as when we last were together. The Dresden shepherdess has fined-down somewhat. Are you pining for unrequited love, my dear?"

He had not changed: still the same, elegant, flippant and world-weary Durward. And how glad I was to see him.

"Durward, how nice! What a lovely surprise."

We embraced and kissed cheeks. Not only was I glad to see him, but I realised, for the first time since I came back to England, how completely bereft and lonely I had been. And here was the one friend in my life who gave to me totally and never asked for anything in return, but to be listened to and admired—and who could resist either listening to or admiring dear, brilliant Durward?

"How did you find me?" I demanded.

"I received a most curious communication," he said, "from a gentleman with the unlikely name of Choppins, posing as a director of the hotel at Euston Road station, who requested me to comment upon the character and aptitudes of Miss Susannah Button, of Number 17a Great Queen-street in Lincoln's-inn-fields. Knowing that the said Miss Button had never set foot within eight score miles of Lincoln's-inn-fields in her life, I resolved that this Choppins was clearly a lunatic, and I prepared to reply to him in similar vein. . . ."

"Oh, Durward!" I cried. "You haven't cost me my position at the hotel? Please tell me that you are teasing."

He gently silenced me with a flicker of his pale, immaculately-manicured hands.

"However," he continued, "on reflection, I decided to call upon Number 17a, Great Queen-street, to see if—against all likelihood—the insane Choppins had access to information of Miss Susannah Button's whereabouts that she, as a friend of moderately long standing and deepest affection, had not thought to communicate to me herself. . . ."

"I'm sorry, Durward," I said. "But I had truly intended to get in touch with you, just as soon as I had got myself settled down and independent."

He gave a bow of acknowledgement and went on: "So I

repaired to the address in question and I find that my friend Miss Button is indeed living there. But why are you wishing to take up employment in a London hotel, my dear? What happened to the Palazzo Dewaine, not to mention Landeric?"

"It's a long story," I said. "I will tell you one day, perhaps, Durward. But don't quiz me too closely now, please."

He hunched his elegant shoulders. "Tell me what you will, when you will, Susannah," he said. "Landeric's loss is Euston Road's gain. Mr. Choppins is to be congratulated."

I smiled at him. "Oh, Durward, you *did* reply nicely to the hotel. How silly of me to have thought otherwise for a single moment."

"I informed Mr. Choppins," said Durward, "that my valued friend Miss Susannah Button is a lady of exemplary character and excellent domestic talents—modest assertions, you will notice, not attempting to strain credulity. I could have added, of course, that my friend Miss Susannah Button is also, without doubt, the most exquisite creature to have blessed the metropolis with her presence this summer season—but that might have registered to your demerit with Mrs. Choppins, supposing that Mrs. Choppins has access to her spouse's correspondence, as seems to be the custom among married ladies of my acquaintance. But, my dear, you are looking rather interestingly pale. Have you been enjoying some harmless and romantic malady, like a heroine in one of the better novels?"

"It's only the hot weather, Durward," I lied. "That and all the travelling I've done since we parted company. Oh, the roses are so lovely. How can I thank you enough for turning my poor room into a garden? You are extravagant."

At all costs I had to prevent him from speculating on my appearance and repeating what had probably only been a light remark about my "pining for unrequited love." This was too near the mark for comfort; and I was too vulnerable, and Durward too shrewd, for him not to realise this next time it was said.

"The flowers are a modest token of my esteem," he said, "inexpensively purchased in the height of the rose-growing season, from a merchant in Covent Garden with whom I have an arrangement. I am so very glad to see you again, Susannah."

"And I you, Durward," I replied, with great sincerity.

"Tonight, we will dine at a discreet and elegant café-restaurant of my acquaintance," said Durward. "It is a double celebration, and there will be champagne."

"A double celebration?"

"Not only have I found you here in London, Susannah," he said, "but today, I have received wind of a portrait commission which—if it comes off—will almost certainly set the seal on the De Lacey fame."

"How exciting," I said. "Who is the sitter, Durward?"

"Sitters," he whispered, mock-conspiratorially, "and the highest in the land!"

"Oh, Durward! Not? . . ."

He nodded. "The Royal Family," he said. "Her Majesty wishes a group portrait of herself, Prince Albert, and the Royal children. I'm pretty sure to get the commission, for I have the backing of the President of the Royal Academy, who put my name forward." He frowned irritably. "The only other contender is the German fellow Winterhalter, who did an absurd and syrupy head-and-shoulders of Her Majesty, which she gave to the Prince for his twenty-fifth birthday. On that account, the fellow fancies his chances for the big group commission—but I have it from the P.R.A. that Winterhalter hasn't a hope. Yes, my dear, I think I may count my chickens and make it a double celebration this evening. I will call for you at eight—will that suit?"

"Eight o'clock?" I felt like Cinderella summoned to attend the ball: frightened and elated all at the same time. "Yes, of course, Durward. I'll be ready then."

(But what to wear? The white silk evening gown that I had had made in Venice for the purpose of dining with . . . no! Shut out the name!)

"Capital, then, Susannah. See you at eight."

"Durward!" I cried.

"What is it, my dear?" he asked.

I gestured about me: at the banks of roses that stood on every available piece of furniture and empty space in the room.

"What shall I do with all these, Durward?" I cried. "I don't think I could turn round in this room in my dinner gown—the skirt is too wide!"

"Persevere, my dear," he said gravely. "It may not come easy, but you will get used to it in time."

* * *

So I wore my gorgeous off-the-shoulder white silk with its great, bell-shaped skirt held out by an army of petticoats: the first one of flannel, the next of horsehair padding, then cotton stiffened with braid, then one with horsehair flounces, all topped by three of starched muslin. And I felt—and looked—like a duchess.

Durward handed me into a victoria that he had thoughtfully provided for our transportation (a hansom would never have accommodated my mountain of petticoats!), and we drove through the lamplit streets in a smart shower of rain that drummed on the roof and sweetened the night air of the teeming metropolis.

I forget at which café-restaurant we dined: it was either Fenton's or Ellis's, or it may have been the Clarendon. Durward took me to all of them in time. He had ordered a table for two in an alcove off the main dining room, where we had the personal attention of the *maître d'hotel* and three waiters. It was: "So delightful to see you, Mr. de Lacey, sir" and "Sincerely hope that you will find everything to your satisfaction, Mr. de Lacey, sir." I suppose it had never before occurred to me that, as a fashionable portrait painter and Academician, Durward was a quite considerable public figure. I quizzed him about this, and he gave his lop-sided, cynical smile.

"I am not the greatest painter since Raphael," he said. "But I am good enough to pass. Half a dozen well-chosen commissions in the next five years, and I shall be well on the way to achieving my aim."

"Which is?" I asked.

"My knighthood and my first half-million by the time I am forty," he said. "Now, my dear Susannah, let us raise our glasses to a toast. I give you: 'to the happy reunion of two devoted friends.'"

"To us, Durward," I said, and we touched our glasses together.

He was, as ever, the perfect host that evening: witty, attentive, considerate and recklessly extravagant of his charm and his talents as a mimic and raconteur. He had me in fits over his reconstruction of a certain Royal Academy dinner, where—as he demonstrated, playing both parts—a prominent Liberal statesman and elderly Academician of pronounced High Tory views ended a bitter altercation by throwing trifle across the table at each other. Our waiters and the *maître d'hotel* joined in the mirth, mopping up the trifle with excellent good grace.

Durward, I told myself—and not for the first time—was good for me. It was good to be liked and admired for oneself alone, and with no strings attached. His attentions flattered me; soothed the rough edges of my bruised spirit and gently led me to accept that my new life need not necessarily be all shadows and greyness. That night, I laughed for the first time since I had arrived in Pennan and heard my fate. Durward held out promises that there could be laughter in my future.

"When you have gained your position as assistant housekeeper at the Euston station hotel," he said, "I shall begin a campaign to speed your promotion to the ranks of management. To all my rich and influential friends and clients who wish to travel by the railway in a northerly direction (or whichever way is served by Euston —I can never remember), I shall give instructions to stay at the station hotel, and afterwards to write most effusive letters in praise of Miss Susannah Button to the board of directors."

"Durward, I believe you capable of it," I laughed.

"At that rate, you will be lady chairman of the board at about the same time that you come and witness me being knighted by Her Majesty," he said. "Afterwards, we will dine at your own hotel. We shall both be tremendously distinguished, slightly grey and dreadful snobs."

"It all sounds lovely," I said, following his mood, "apart from the greyness. With the help of henna, I don't intend to go grey till I'm at least fifty."

"Seriously, Susannah," he said. And he looked serious. "Is it absolutely necessary that you take this position at the hotel?"

"Of course, Durward," I said. "I'm a working girl. I was educated beyond my station in life—true. But I am just as dependent upon my own labour to provide me with food and shelter as the meanest fishwife in Pennan Haven. I have no fortune, Durward. No, that's not quite true; my fortune is the education with which I was lucky to be provided."

"Marry me, Susannah," he said.

"Durward . . ."

"No, give me a hearing, my dear," he said. "Before you repeat the outright dismissal of the previous occasion in Venice, please listen to what I have to say. I am not the best catch in all London. I am not the most virtuous, the most abstemious, fellow around. Add to that, though I am far from achieving my first half-million, I already spend with a millionaire's airy disregard for the grey morrow." He grinned his disarming grin. "Are you impressed so far?"

"Oh, Durward, you are a dear, dear fool," I said. "And now you're making me cry." This was true: and why was I crying, I asked myself—was it the relief and the delight of being wanted and admired, the way a woman needs?

"Dab your eyes, and I will continue," he said. "Notwithstanding my many shortcomings, of which those I have mentioned constitute but a shame-faced and shifty display intended to mask even worse revelations, I have one or two saving graces. Firstly, I am about the third best portrait painter in Europe (I estimate Winterhalter to be something like the tenth best).

"My other virtue, dear Susannah, is that I am quite extraordinarily fond of you."

"Durward, I . . ."

"Continue dabbing your large and beautiful eyes, and I will elaborate on my last statement. You will notice that I do not say I love you. Indeed, I think I should find it quite impossible for me wholeheartedly to love anyone—and I do not exclude loving myself. But, of all the women I have ever met, you are the most pleasing to the eye and to the intellect. When I look at you, I know that those Ancient Greek fellows were not lying—as often in my student days at the Royal Academy Schools, when drawing from antique casts, I swore they must have been lying. Because I have seen you, I can now believe that, somewhere in bygone Hellas, there could have been women with that nose and that brow; women who walked like goddesses, straight and tall. Susannah, will you marry me?"

"You are unfair," I said. "First you make me cry, then you turn my head with flattery of the most blatant kind, that would win you a slap from one of the fisher-girls of Pennan Haven."

"I will make you happy," he persisted. "No, that isn't right. I will try to make you happy."

"Durward," I said. "There's something you must know . . ."

"You don't love me," he said. "Yes, I have taken that into account. I'm sorry, and I don't deny it; the flaw in my character which makes it impossible for me to love is no bar to my delight in being loved. But you are tremendously fond of me. I should be a blind fool not to know it. We are both tremendously fond of each other. There have been deliriously happy marriages built on far less promising foundations."

"What you say is true," I said. "But that was not what I meant." I looked down at my hands, then hid them beneath the table when I saw that they were trembling. "What I have to tell you concerns the reason why I left Landeric and came to London."

"I don't need to hear it, Susannah," he said. "If the Dewaines saw imperfections in you and dismissed you, that is their misfortune and my gain. I shall not look to your imperfections, but to your virtues . . . in the hope that you will treat me the same."

It had to be explained, though I was tempted to keep my secrets locked away forever. This wise, witty and essentially good man must not be deceived.

"In the first place," I said, "Button is not my true name. I was— I was born out of wedlock."

"Wha-a-a-at?" he cried.

I flinched before his stare, dropped my gaze.

"My—my father and Mama were not married," I whispered.

Next moment, his laughter was echoing through the dining room. I stared at him in horror; anger and shame fighting for their places in my mind. Then I looked about me for my shawl, but a waiter had taken it away. I got to my feet, deciding that a swift retreat into the night, shawl or no shawl—and before he recovered from his paroxysm of cruel mirth—was the only course left open to me.

Through streaming tears, he saw me get up, and gestured to me to take my place again.

"It does not please me to be mocked, sir," I said. "I wish you a good night."

"Susannah, Susannah," he said, rising. "Your pardon for giving way before the delicious irony of this moment." He gestured to the maitre d'hotel, who had been summoned by the commotion. "Another bottle of champagne, Gaston! Madame and I have yet another cause for mutual celebration!"

"At once, sir. Madame." The man bowed and hastily departed on his errand.

I stared at Durward. The wild mirth had gone; only the lopsided, self-mocking smile remained.

"You mean?" I breathed, "you mean that you, also? . . ."

"Yes, my dear," he said. "We are two of us in the same boat, you and I. Delightful people, both—but, from Society's point of view in this year of grace eighteen hundred and forty-six, not quite nice to know!

"Damn those confounded Dewaines for throwing you out on

that account, Susannah. Ha! We won't invite 'em to the wedding!"

* * *

It was a betrothal that was founded on a lie. Or, at best, a half-truth. A sin of omission. Driven to it, I could not have it any other way. I was totally unable to say to Durward: "I am a Dewaine, and I love—have loved—used to love—my own brother. And it was carnal love—to quote the Reverend Mawhinney." In my heart, I knew that what I felt—had felt—for Mark was clean and pure and fine. But, somehow, it would seem soiled in the telling.

And so, on a rainy summer's night in London, I became the fiancée of England's most promising young portrait painter, whom I did not love and who did not love me; but to whom I was bound by a mutual admiration, and because he made me laugh when I had thought that I would never laugh again.

Next day, I took a hansom and visited Durward's studio in Cheyne Walk. The day was very fine, and the view across the river to Battersea Fields provided a rural background to the gracious terraces of Chelsea.

I was admitted by Durward's daily woman, Mrs. Hoskins, a merry butter-ball of a person with fly-away hair piled high under a monster lace cap, and a face of a very high colour. Durward had told me all about Mrs. Hoskins. I liked her on first sight.

"Miss Button, hain't it?" she cried. "Come alonger me, lovey. Mr. de Lacey axe me ter keep an eye out for you, an' I wuz peerin' frew the curtins when you step' out o' the cab. Mind 'ow you put yer feet. Fings is all sixes an' sevens 'smornin'.."

I knew Durward lived all alone in bachelor state, and that he refused to have living-in servants, relying on the daily ministrations of Mrs. Hoskins and the fetch-and-carry meal service from a Chelsea chop house—but nothing he had said quite prepared me for the chaos of untidiness that met my eyes. The studio was an elegant narrow-fronted terrace house of the last century, with a long hallway and a spiral staircase at the end. The whole of the floor space from door to stair was cluttered with the bric-a-brac of my betrothed's working life: picture frames and canvases were stacked against the walls; there were open packing-cases issuing forth festoons of straw; hideous Hottentot masks; a life-sized plaster statue of—I think—Venus; and, unbelievably, a stuffed bear. I followed my guide through it all and up the stair, making a private resolve in my woman's mind that before many days had passed, I should be along with a dustpan and broom, to make good the shortcomings of merry Mrs. Hoskins.

The studio proper was on the top floor of the building, and was lit by skylights and a long window at the end which looked out over the rooftops of Chelsea and Kensington as far as the green smudge of Hyde Park. Durward was working at a large easel with his back to the window. He put down his palette and brushes and advanced to greet me, hands outstretched.

"My dear," he cried. "Considering I delivered you home well past midnight, how can you dare look so radiant? Doesn't she look radiant, Mrs. Hoskins?"

"Loverly, she looks," said that worthy woman. "Reely loverly."

I took off my bonnet.

"I expect you would like some coffee, Susannah," said Durward. "Bring a pot of coffee please, Mrs. H."

When the sound of Mrs. Hoskins's slippered footfalls had faded away down the stairs, I said to Durward: "How can you bear to live in such untidiness when you are so fastidious about your own person?" He was dressed for work in a light-coloured frock-coat; neither it, nor his white shirt cuffs, showed the slightest trace of paint, and his fingers were immaculate as ever.

"It is a question that has frequently been asked of me," said Durward, "and I have never been able to answer it—for reasons that you will appreciate. The answer lies in my upbringing."

"Then you mustn't speak of it, Durward," I said hastily. "Remember what we decided last evening: that we both foreswore the past and all its associations. We are tomorrow's people."

"You put the question," he said. "And you, above all, as the person who had decided to share my life, must know why I am such an enigma in my personal habits."

"Very well, Durward," I conceded. "Tell me by all means, if you think it important."

"I was reared in a parish orphanage," he said. "A stark building with high ceilings that were lost to view when the fog swirled in through the unglazed windows. That place was empty. Empty of everything: of life, of joy and laughter, of hope—and, most particularly, it was empty of furnishings and belongings. We wretched orphan brats were not permitted to possess anything. Nothing at all. I once found a rag doll on a scrap heap, and treasured it for a while as a friend till it was taken off me and burned. All we had were the clothes we stood up in, and even those poor rags were the property of the parish."

"Durward," I murmured. "Don't go on. Please. I can see that it's hurting you. I never knew—never realised."

Again the lop-sided grin. "At a very early age, Susannah," he said, "I made a resolution: I swore that, if I survived the life of the orphanage (and many did not), and grew to manhood and riches, I would wear only the finest of linen—and never more than once. And I would wear suits only of the lightest-coloured and least serviceable of materials, and discard them as soon as they showed the slightest signs of use. In that way, I have compensated for the one ragged shirt and pair of breeches that saw me through most of my boyhood."

"Poor Durward," I said. "Who would have guessed that, behind your bright charm, is a man who has suffered and can still remember suffering?"

"As to the untidiness about the place," he said, "this is caused by my fierce reluctance to part with any possession, however mean and trivial. If someone—Mrs. Hoskins, for instance, though she would know better—were to get rid of a mere shoe-box, it would be like having my rag doll burned all over again."

"But—what about your clothes?" I cried. "What about the linen that you wear only once?"

"At first," said Durward, "I hung the garments up when I had discarded them, but finally I ran out of wardrobe-space. Now I have set aside part of the cellar for old clothes."

"But, my dear!" I cried. "In years to come, we will need to move out of here and into another house, leaving this one to once-worn linen and boot-boxes!"

He laid a hand on my shoulder and looked down at me.

"When I have you to share my life," he said, "I shall not need the reassurance of possessions to convince me that the days of the parish orphanage are over and can never return. As soon as we are married, you may begin to clear the place out. How's that?"

"Nothing will be thrown away," I said. "I will not have you unhappy for my sake. But I shall take the liberty of rearranging things in some sort of order and making sure the place is spotless."

He moved closer to me, and I had the impression that he was about to kiss me—a prospect which I did not find unpleasing—but our *tête-à-tête* was disturbed by the return of Mrs. Hoskins with a tray of coffee and biscuits. By the time she had poured us two cups and departed, the atmosphere had changed between us and the moment was past.

"What are you working on today, Durward?" I asked him.

He crossed over to the easel by the window and turned it round on its castors.

"You will need more than a little imagination to identify the sitters," he said. "This is only a preliminary sketch in oils, full-sized, to establish the main masses of the design, but . . ."

"Why, I recognise them at once," I cried. "They are the Royal Family! Oh, Durward! Have you got the commission then?"

"I had a note from the P.R.A. this morning," he said. "Apparently, the final say on the picture will be from Prince Albert, who is something of a designer and draughtsman in his own right. It is the Prince's command that the two artists under consideration—Winterhalter and me—should submit full-sized sketches, and the Prince will choose from them. As you see, I have wasted no time in getting started."

I gazed at the sketch, which showed the Royal Family grouped in a rich green landscape. I could make out the seated figure of the Queen, in white gown with a blue sash over her left shoulder. Beside her stood a martial figure in scarlet who could only be Prince Albert. The little Princes and Princesses were grouped about their mother, who had the newest baby on her knee. The effect was crude and sketchy-looking, but undeniably vigorous.

"I'm sure it's very fine, Durward," I said hopefully.

"I'm satisfied with my design," he replied. "You see how the masses are grouped in a pyramid form in the centre; its base established by the Prince's right foot and the line of the Queen's skirt? That's how the old masters built their pictures—like bridges, to last forever. You may be sure that that German fellow's sketch will show up all his fumbling incompetence when it comes to handling the essentials. His design will have no more solidarity and coherence than a child's scribble. Oh, yes, I'm well satisfied that His Highness has decided to judge between us. If he has the knowledge I think he has, he cannot help but choose me."

I hoped so, for his sake, because it was quite clear that he had completely set his heart on this important commission—representing, as it did, the highest accolade of Royal patronage that a painter could receive. What would happen if, after all, the despised Winterhalter was chosen, I did not care to dwell upon.

"Ah! I've something else to show you, my dear," said Durward.

"That is, if you can bear to gaze upon it without losing your temper."

He brought forward another easel, bearing a large canvas draped with a cloth. Before his hand reached up, I had a premonition of what I was about to see, and an involuntary cry of protest was rising in my throat—when it stood revealed.

The long months—a whole eternity of time—were swept aside in the instant, and I was standing before Landeric as it had been on that very first occasion. If Durward's rough sketch of the Royal Family had given me any misgivings about his competence, I lost them in the instant of coming face to face, once more, with the Landeric picture—which was not merely a picture, but a window through which I was once more gazing upon those beloved walls and shaded lawns.

And not only Landeric itself . . .

"How do you like them, your former employers?" asked Durward flippantly. "Do you think I have them well? Have I overdone the arrogance, perhaps?"

They stood grouped on the lawn. The man whom I now knew to have been my father—the dead Sir Tristan—was in the centre of the group, his elbow resting negligently on the plinth of a statue. Alicia and Jessica were next to him in their walking costumes, bonneted and be-muffed. Before the plinth, Mrs. Newstead —"Aunt Marianne"—gazed blindly out of the picture from her chair. Hester was slightly in the background, in riding-out habit, holding the reins of her pony.

And Mark . . .

"I thank heaven it's finished," said Durward. "The confounded thing has been hung round my neck too long by far, thanks largely to Mrs. Newstead. I shall dispatch it to Dewaine as soon as I've done some retouching and varnishing. Do you think I have him well, Susannah? Mark Dewaine, I mean."

Durward had hardly changed the pose of the pencil sketch from which he had made the finished portrait. Mark was lounging up against the opposite side of the plinth from his father, arms folded, head held rather high, gazing at me down the side of his Dewaine nose . . . our Dewaine nose . . .

"I shall exhibit it at next year's Academy," said Durward. "Together with the Royal Family group. They'll make a fine pair, side by side. My dear, is anything the matter? You're as pale as a ghost."

"I'm all right." I said. "Just a little dizzy, that's all."

He guided me back to my chair. I was glad to turn my back on the picture; but nothing could shut out the memory of the scene through that imaginary window into my past.

"I kept you out too late last evening," said Durward. "But I shall now call a cab and send you straight home to rest. And I'll not take no for an answer, my dear."

I made the merest show of protesting, for fear that he would change his mind: for fear that I would have to spend a moment longer in that studio, with that almost living and breathing reminder of an unholy and unhallowed love that I had to learn to forget. Durward fussed round me, taking my arm to escort me down the stairs, lifting aside the rubbish in the hallway to let me pass more easily, handing me solicitously into the waiting hansom.

"I will call upon you tomorrow about noon," he said, "and take you out to luncheon. Till then, you are to take things very gently. Have a light meal sent in to you and mind you retire early." He kissed my cheek. "Bless me, you're crying," he added.

"Because you are so kind to me, and I really don't deserve it," I told him.

Indeed, this was half of the truth. I was overwhelmed with a sense of guilt concerning Durward: the guilt of deception, of having promised myself to a man whom—no matter how much I admired and esteemed him—I could never grow to love.

As my hansom carried me along Cheyne Walk and away from Durward, I came to terms with the truth about myself: that nothing had changed in my heart, and that the dark and forbidden love I bore for Mark Dewaine would forever prevent me from truly giving myself to any other man.

* * *

I should have ended my engagement there and then. All that day, I toyed with the idea of writing to Durward and telling him all. I made several attempts to write such a letter—but they all ended up in my fireplace. In the end, I set light to them and watched them burn away to ash.

Durward's roses looked down on me from all sides (I had made the room more habitable by giving some of them away to my landlady), reminding me of his wit, his cheerful devotion. He had never, from first to last, made any demands upon my emotions. All he had asked for was my companionship.

We were two of a kind, he and I, as Durward had truly said; condemned by the circumstances of our births to be social outcasts. I had always thought that he was invulnerable to the world's troubles; that he sailed through the stormy seas of life, serene and untouched by the batterings of fate. I knew differently now. Durward's manner—his flippancy and world-weariness—was only an armour against hurt, and a thin and insubstantial armour at that. A man who can laugh at fate is not frightened to wear a shirt more than once.

So it was that Durward's roses became his silent advocates, soundlessly pleading his case at the bar of Susannah's conscience.

I had thought that it was I who was greatly in need, that Durward's attentions were a boon that I should never be able to repay; it was now quite clear that he needed me as much as, if not more than, I needed him.

So there could be no question of my deserting him by ending the engagement.

* * *

In the weeks that followed, I saw ample evidence of Durward's inner loneliness. As always, he was the perfect companion and host. He dined me in every smart hotel and restaurant in London, and introduced me to people of distinction and title: Academicians, politicians, generals and admirals, members of high Society—people who were fellow-members of his clubs, colleagues in the arts, or sitters to his brush. They all treated him with extreme courtesy and obvious respect. But none of them appeared as a friend.

Those who might have been called his friends—the people who appeared to like him for himself—were men and women of the lower orders: waiters and cab-drivers, crossing-sweepers, shopkeepers, the common folk of the great city with whom he came into regular and easy contact. To them he was always, "'ello, Mister de Lacey, sir," and "how is it with you today, then Mister de Lacey, sir?" With these people, he always seemed at ease—though recklessly over-generous with his presents of money. I have seen him press a whole sovereign into the hand of a barefoot urchin of a crossing-sweeper in the Strand.

The solitariness of his existence stood revealed when it came to making plans for the wedding. It had already been agreed between us that we should avail ourselves of the provisions of the 1836 Marriage Act and be joined in matrimony at an office of a registrar. Durward had mooted the idea, declaring himself to be a Liberal in politics and a free-thinking atheist by religion: an attitude which I sensed to be a token protest against a society that would certainly have cold-shouldered him if he had paraded the truth about his birth and upbringing (which he was sensibly careful not to do). I readily agreed to the arrangement, not wishing to be part of an elaborate spectacle.

It was when the matter of wedding invitations arose that Durward hummed and haahed. First, he decided, he must have the president and two or three of his fellow-Academicians. This seemed to suggest that several of his more important sitters should also be invited, including a noble duke, a former Lord Mayor of London, and an Admiral of the Fleet. The absurdity of such a distinguished company of gentlemen—and their wives—crowding into the poky confines of a registrar's office reduced us both to helpless laughter. Afterwards, I wiped my eyes and seriously asked Durward if he did, indeed, have any true friends whom he wished to invite, and he ruefully admitted that he had none. Since I was similarly placed, and there being no other alternative but to invite a host of waiters, crossing-sweepers and shopgirls, we settled for simply asking Mrs. Hoskins and her husband to act as witnesses. The licence was obtained, and we were bidden to present ourselves at the superintendent-registrar's office, close by Chelsea Town Hall, at eleven o'clock on Saturday the twelfth of September.

There can scarcely ever have existed a woman who approached her forthcoming marriage with such a total lack of purpose. It was certainly Susannah Button who searched the big stores of Knightsbridge and Oxford Street for a wedding outfit, and finally decided to wear one of her costumes from Venice; it was assuredly she who moved into the assault on the studio in Cheyne Walk and did battle with the doughty Mrs. Hoskins on the question of what did and did not constitute cleanliness in the home; who chose new curtains for the living rooms and new wall-papers for the bedrooms and kitchen. Susannah Button may have done all those things with an end in view: to become Mrs. Durward de Lacey and the châtelaine of a smart studio-house in artistic Chelsea —but never with conscious intent. Looking back on those few days leading up to the wedding, I cannot truly remember my giving a moment's thought to Saturday the twelfth of September and all it was going to bring. I suppose that, in some way that only nature can devise, my mind was sparing itself the trouble of picking over the threads of a decision that already had been irrevocably settled for good or ill. Instead of thinking, I made myself busy, and the days flew past.

I have two very clear recollections of that time: I can remember the elaborate precautions that I took against going into Durward's studio and running the risk of coming face to-face once more with the Dewaine family group painting; and I shall never forget waking on my wedding morning with the sudden and shocking realisation that I was about to bind myself to a man who was not Mark Dewaine.

* * *

We had arranged to arrive at the registrar's office independently, with Durward preceding me, in imitation of a church ceremony, where the groom waits for his bride at the altar.

My hansom made a good journey through the Saturday morning shopping crowds, arriving at the office as the Town Hall clock struck a quarter to eleven. Mr. and Mrs. Hoskins were waiting outside: she in an enormous floral bonnet, and her spouse, a stout man, in a dusty tall hat of such antique shape that it must have seen service for generations.

"Cor, you're lookin' loverly, Miss Button," cried Mrs. Hoskins, and she nudged her life partner vigorously. "Ain'tcher got any manners, 'Oskins? Wotcher fink yer abaht? Take yer 'at orf t'the lidy!"

Mr. Hoskins fumbled for his hat. I caught a whiff of beer on his breath and realised that he had spent some part of the morning in a public house, with no improvement to his sense of balance.

"Did you see Mr. de Lacey go in?" I asked.

Mrs. Hoskins shook her head firmly.

"'E ain't come yet," she said. "We bin 'ere since a quarter past, an' we ain't seen 'air nor 'ide of 'im."

"Not come yet? That's very strange. He said he would be here soon after half past, and be waiting for me inside."

"Well, he ain't been frew that door while we been 'ere," declared Mrs. Hoskins.

I was immediately worried, for Durward's promptness and punctuality was all of a piece with his immaculate habits of dress, and he had often teased me about my own tendency never to be ready when he called at an appointed time to take me out. The reason for his not being there could only be something beyond his control. Perhaps, I thought, looking down the milling traffic of the King's Road, his cab has been held up.

When the Town Hall clock told five to the hour, I grew really uneasy. Also, the three of us were being eyed with some interest by curious passers-by: me in my wedding finery, Mrs. Hoskins and her outlandish bonnet and her spouse, who was producing a quart bottle of beer from his capacious coat pocket, from time to time, and taking long and noisy draughts.

"I think it would be a good idea to go in and let them know we're here," I said, leading the way through the door.

There was a bare waiting room with an alcove in the wall that looked like the window of a railway ticket office. This bore a notice: *KNOCK*. I knocked—and a shutter flew up to reveal a wizened little man who peered at me keenly over the top of steel-rimmed spectacles.

"The De Lacey ceremony, was it?" he demanded.

"Yes," I said.

"You've cut it very fine," he said. "The registrar likes to have you in your places punctually." He craned his neck through the aperture and peered round the waiting room. "Is everyone here?"

"My . . . the groom hasn't arrived yet," I faltered.

"Not here?" cried the little man, affronted. "But it's nearly the hour, and the registrar won't be kept waiting. There's another ceremony to follow punctually at the half hour."

"I'm quite sure he will be here in time for the ceremony to begin," I told him, with an assurance I certainly did not feel.

He shook his head disapprovingly and tut-tutted. "You must take your places now," he said. "I will summon the registrar at the hour. If the groom be not here then, I'm afraid that will be the end of it. This way . . ." he vanished from sight and reappeared a moment later at a door by the side of the aperture. "Come in and take your seats. Bride on the left, and witnesses to the rear."

I sat down in a stiff-backed chair, one of a pair that faced a table, on which stood a pen-and-ink set, a decanter of water and a glass, and a vase containing a sheaf of arum lillies. On the wall opposite, hung side by side, were framed engravings of the Queen and Prince Albert. Through the discreetly curtained windows came the clip-clop of horses' hooves and the trundle of iron tyres on the cobbles of King's Road. I breathed a prayer that Durward was near at hand and coming on quickly; and took consolation from that fact that, when it was all over, we should derive a lot of amusement from the situation. How well, with his great talent for pantomime, would Durward re-enact the scene, playing all the parts himself: the fussy little assistant registrar; Mrs. Hoskins, Cockney accent and all; Mr. Hoskins with his bottle of beer. I smiled to myself and immediately quenched the smile when I met the little man's affronted stare.

"It is eleven o'clock," he said severely. "And I must now advise the registrar that all parties are not present to enable him to commence the ceremony."

The clock began to strike outside. A door banged. There were footfalls, and Durward came into the room.

Immediately I saw him, I sensed that something was wrong; urgently, dreadfully wrong. There would be no light-hearted pantomime in memory of our wedding day; the man who stood before me was not recognisable as the witty, gay, urbane Durward who had courted me.

"I'm sorry, my dear Susannah," he said huskily. "But I appear to have kept you waiting."

I summoned up a smile and murmured something incoherent.

"Well," said the little man. "If all are here, I will inform the registrar that we are ready for commencement. Be seated, Mr.—er—de Lacey."

Durward sat down on my right. When the little man had left the room, I stole a sidelong glance, and saw that, at close quarters, he was in an even worse state that I had believed.

He was hatless. His light-coloured hair, usually so sleek and smooth, had clearly not been brushed that morning; nor, from the fair stubble on his lips and chin, had his face seen the razor. He was wearing one of his light-coloured suits, which was quite impeccable; but his shirt and necktie—both originally white—bore, on this Saturday of all days, traces of Friday's London soot. My groom had not only neglected to wash and shave, but he had broken a long-standing habit by not changing his linen. And on his wedding morning.

Nor was that all. His face was pallid, and there was a bluish, leaden colour in his lips and about the tips of his ears. A rime of sweat bedewed his whole face, from brow to chin. And his eyes were closed.

"Durward," I whispered, "are you ill?"

He gave a start, like one wakened from a deep sleep, and his eyelids flickered open.

"Susannah, is that you?" he said.

It was at that moment that the door swung open and a tall man in a dark coat swept across the room, with the little assistant registrar trotting after him.

"Good morning, ladies and gentlemen," boomed the newcomer, laying a sheaf of papers on the table before him and eyeing us all encouragingly from under bushy eyebrows. "Pray do not rise. This preliminary part of the proceedings I prefer to keep as informal as the solemn nature of the occasion permits. You, sir," he said, addressing Durward, "are Mr. Durward de Lacey, presently residing at number 32a, Cheyne Walk in the Borough of Chelsea. A bachelor by estate and an artist by profession. Do I have these details correctly?"

There was a protracted silence. The registrar cleared his throat and looked at me questioningly. I turned my head and saw that Durward's eyes were closed again and that he was breathing heavily, like a man asleep.

I took his hand and shook it hard.

"Durward!" I cried. "Are you all right? For pity's sake, speak to me."

"If the gentleman has an—hem!—indisposition," said the registrar, "it were better that these solemn proceedings be postponed till another occasion."

Durward's eyelids snapped open. In a dramatic change of attitude, from complete stupor to steely vivacity, he thrust his head forward and glared at the dumbfounded registrar, his pale eyes gleaming.

"Correct, as you say, in every detail!" he cried. "An artist by profession, and, let it be said, the youngest Royal Academician so far of this century, and by common consent of all whose opinion matters a damn, the finest portrait painter in England and one of the finest in Europe. Do you hear that, hey?" His voice rose to a pitch of frenzied excitement.

"Er . . . quite, quite," stammered the registrar. He went on hastily: "And now, to proceed. You, ma'am, are Miss Susannah Button, presently residing at Great Queen-street in the Borough of Holborn. A spinster by estate and . . ."

"What is *that* doing there?" A sudden interruption from Durward.

"Of what are you speaking, sir?" cried the registrar.

Durward was pointing across the room, to the framed engravings of the Royal couple.

"That German fellow!" he cried. "It is an affront, to parade that fellow's likeness before me. It is a conspiracy. Under the circumstances, it is a studied insult." He turned his pointing finger upon the wide-eyed registrar. "What does he know of design?—answer me that. The solid, weighty matters of sound construction, as comprehended by the old masters, by Raphael, by Michelangelo, by the sublime Rembrandt—what does he know of these things, hey?—this dilettante sprig of a minor German princeling, who fancies himself as a designer and draughtsman in his own right."

I was beginning to comprehend the reason for Durward's astounding behaviour. I laid my hand on his arm.

"My dear," I said. "It doesn't matter. Nothing matters today, and tomorrow you will get other commissions. Important commissions that will make you even more famous. . . ."

His pale eyes stared into mine. They were unnervingly expressionless, but with an inner wildness—as if the fire of an all-consuming passion was raging within his brain.

"Winterhalter!" he grated. "That syrupy scribbler! That pretty enameller! Preferred before . . . *me!*"

I looked appealingly at the registrar, whose expression had changed from angry indignation to total bafflement during Durward's outburst.

"I fancy that Mr. de Lacey has had some bad news this morning," I explained. "But I am sure he is well enough to continue with the ceremony."

The registrar looked doubtful; but, muttering something about the need to make allowances for such a distinguished gentleman of artistic temperament, he bade us both rise, and, taking up a printed card, he proceeded to read the form of civil marriage, at a brisk rate.

Durward had relapsed into a stupor again, and the sweat was gathering heavily around his mouth and dripping from his chin. But he answered readily enough to the responses; produced the ring when asked, and slipped it on my finger.

"So, by virtue of the authority vested in me," concluded the registrar, "I now pronounce you man and wife."

I kissed Durward on his chill, dank cheek; the registrar shook hands with both of us; Mrs. Hoskins burst into a flood of tears; her spouse pronounced a loud "Amen," followed by a hiccup.

I was Mrs. Durward de Lacey.

It was outside, while waiting for a hansom, that Durward collapsed in the street. It took the combined efforts of the three of us to lift him into the cab, where he lay with his head lolling and eyes turned upwards in their sockets. I held him steady all the way back, down the King's Road and the lime tree-shaded quiet streets leading to the river, till we reached Cheyne Walk. The Hoskinses, who had followed in another hansom, helped me to lift him out and carry him indoors, to a sofa in the ground floor drawing room. Then Mr. Hoskins went off to fetch a physician—and I begged him to hurry, for Durward was obviously getting worse. He lay like a rag doll, mouth open and eyes rolling. I loosened his neckcloth and found it and his shirt to be soaked with sweat. This prompted me to slip a hand inside his coat and feel for his heartbeat: it was feeble and fluttering.

"What can be the matter with him?" I cried.

"Well it ain't for me to say," declared Mrs. Hoskins. "But I reckon as 'ow 'e's been at the bottle agin."

Drink? Yes, of course. I had sensed immediately Durward arrived at the registry office that he was intoxicated, and it was not difficult to see why he had sought the consolation of alcohol that morning. He had never made a secret of his weakness in that direction. But, surely, he would have had to consume an enormous quantity to reduce himself to such a state. He looked—and the thought sent me back to another occasion, on a wave-lashed beach, with another limp figure lying before me—he looked as if he was dying!

"Yus, 'e's been at it agin, right nuff," said Mrs. Hoskins.

The doctor was not long in arriving. He bustled in through the door: a cadaverous-looking man with heavy Dundreary whiskers and an impatient manner.

"What's amiss here, ma'am?" he demanded.

"My husband," I said—and the unfamiliar appellation sounded strange to my ears—"My husband suddenly collapsed in the street. He was acting . . . strangely . . . before then. He had an unpleasant shock this morning, and I think he may have been drink . . ."

I stared at the physician, as, brushing past me, he bent to one knee beside the figure on the sofa. With one thumb, he turned up one of Durward's eyelids to reveal the upward-staring, pale blue iris. Next, he bent his head and brought his nostrils close to the open mouth.

He gave a harsh exclamation.

"Doctor, what is it?" I cried.

He ignored my question. Still kneeling, he turned to Mrs. Hoskins, who was standing behind me, and snapped: "You, woman, make coffee. Hot and strong. And hurry about it, do you hear?"

"Yessir!" cried Mrs. Hoskins, hastening to obey.

"And after that," said the doctor, "make mustard poultice. Plenty of it and piping hot!"

"Mustard poultice! Right away, sir," cried the woman. "Come alonger me, 'Oskins. You can be a-doin' of the poultice." The two of them departed swiftly to the kitchen.

"Doctor, will you please tell me what's amiss with him?" I pleaded.

He looked up at me, treating me to a glance that was half-angry, half-incredulous.

"Oh, come now, ma'am!" he snapped. "You must know—or be in the position to make a very good guess—as to the reason for your husband's condition!"

I felt suddenly dizzy; swayed and nearly fainted. He reached up a hand and steadied me.

"I—we were only married this morning," I cried.

His harsh face softened slightly, and he got to his feet.

"Then, ma'am," he said gravely, "are you not aware that the man you have married is an opium-eater?"

"An opium-eater?" I stared at him uncomprehendingly. "Do you mean that he? . . ."

"He is an addict," said the doctor. "And he must be an addict of long standing, accustomed, from continual use, to taking the drug in extraordinarily large quantities. It must be so, for such a quantity as he has taken today would kill a normal person!

"And may well kill him yet, ma'am, unless we keep him on his feet and conscious!"

* * *

We dragged Durward from the brink of the grave that afternoon —the afternoon of our wedding day; with me supporting him at one side, and the doctor at the other; marching him to and fro down the length of the drawing room; eleven paces one way—turn —eleven paces back; plying him, every so often, with draughts of strong and scalding coffee; with Mr. Hoskins flicking his legs and ankles with a knotted towel to wake him whenever his eyelids faltered. This we did for three hours, while the world went about its September Saturday afternoon outside the drawing room window, and boats passed to and fro on the sunlit river. When he was out of the coma's grip, we stripped him and laid him down on the sofa again, where we applied mustard poultices to the soles of his feet and the insides of his thighs and legs.

At four o'clock, he fell into a light sleep, and the terrible livid colour had gone from his face. The doctor said he could safely be left alone provided he was kept warm, so we piled him high with blankets and a quilted eiderdown. Mrs. Hoskins drew the curtains, and I quietly closed the door—with one last look towards the sleeping figure on the sofa.

I gave the doctor my hand and thanked him.

"Is there nothing that can be done to help my husband?" I asked.

"You have taken on a terrible burden, ma'am," he replied. "And one that I would not wish upon any daughter of mine. You ask me if there is anything to be done? I cannot answer that, for I do not know the patient. But this I do know: while ever it is possible to purchase alcoholic tincture of opium—or laudanum, as it is popularly called—at any street corner chemist's shop, we shall have people who will buy it in small quantities to soothe the agony of a rotten tooth, or—a hideous practice—to quieten a restless babe. There will be others who will buy it to supplement the effects of alcohol, and there will be those who—like your husband —have so addicted themselves to the drug that they are compelled to take near-lethal doses in order to satisfy their cravings."

"But surely," I cried, "with my support and encouragement, he could learn to exist without laudanum?"

He pursed his lips and shook his head.

"You are young, ma'am," he said. "With your whole life of promise before you. I have had some experience of opium-eaters. I also have a daughter in the flower of her youth. Knowing what I know, can you guess what advice I would give my daughter, were she in a like situation to yours?"

"No, doctor," I said. "Please tell me."

We were standing by the front door. He opened it and pointed down Cheyne Walk, towards Westminster and the teeming City.

"I would say to her: 'There is no profit for you here, my dear, and no prospect of happiness. All life is out there. Go to it. Run from here. And never come back!' That is what I would say, ma'am. I wish you a good day."

He put on his tall hat, picked up his bag, and, without another word to me, he walked off into the throng of afternoon strollers.

I closed the door and met my reflection in a mirror on the wall. My eyes looked haunted and my mouth was slack with fatigue. I pinned back a straying strand of hair, squared my shoulders, and went off to find Mrs. Hoskins in the kitchen. There were still things that remained to be asked.

She was making a pot of tea, and her husband was asleep in a basket chair by the kitchen stove. I went straight to the point.

"You knew about Mr. de Lacey's habit of taking laudanum," I said. It was not a question.

She had taken off the ridiculous bonnet, and her fly-away hair was like a hayrick after a gale. She looked at me pityingly, her head on one side.

"I din't fink for one minute as you din't know too, mum," she said with sincerity. "Blimey, 'e's allus at it. 'Nip rahnd the corner and fetch me a shillin's worth o' the Milk o' Paradise, Mrs. 'Oskins,' he'll say. Or: 'Can't git started wiv the work s'mornin', Mrs. 'Oskins. Best 'ave a drop o' the naughty stuff.' 'E's allus at the laudanum bottle, mum. Mind you, 'e 'olds it very well, does Mr. de Lacey. Ain't never seen 'im before like 'e was s'mornin'.'"

I took a deep, shuddering breath.

"Where does he keep it, Mrs. Hoskins?" I asked. "The laudanum?"

"Up in the studio, mum. In a decanter, it is."

We went together up to the studio. There was a cut glass decanter and a wine glass on a table by the big north-facing window. Both were empty. I picked up the glass and took a tentative sniff of it. My nostrils were assailed by a heavy, pungent odour that I had met before, during the long afternoon, when I had helped to march my bridegroom of a few hours up and down the drawing room, for his life's sake—and he with his head lolling on my shoulder.

There was a crumpled ball of paper lying by the decanter. I picked it up and, opening it out, read enough to piece together the scene that must have taken place there—when?—quite soon before Durward was due to leave for his wedding ceremony, perhaps. It had been written that morning and delivered by hand.

Royal Academy of Arts,
Trafalgar Square
12th September, 1846

My dear De Lacey,
I am greatly put out of countenance to have to inform you that I have received a communication from His Royal Highness's secretary, to the effect that, following upon an examination of the oil sketches submitted by yr-self and Herr Winterhalter, His Royal Highness regretfully . . .

"Bit o' bad news what 'e 'ad, eh, mum?" asked Mrs. Hoskins.

"A bit of bad news indeed," I replied. "Tell me now, Mrs. Hoskins, does Mr. de Lacey keep any more laudanum in the house, do you know?"

The good woman gestured about her—at the untidy turmoil that surrounded Durward's working life: the piles of books, picture frames, canvases, chests and cupboards, all covered with dust and debris. I had not ventured into the room since the day he had showed me the Landeric painting.

"I arsk you, mum," she declared. "In all this 'ere mess, 'ow would I know? 'E could 'ide enough o' the naughty stuff in 'ere to sink the Marines, an' you'd never find it. Them as takes to the laudanum, they gits wery cunnin' wiv it, mum!"

I only half-heard her. A prompting of my memory had directed my eyes to a large canvas that stood in a corner of the studio by the north window. The face of it was covered by a dust sheet; but I knew, from its size and shape—and I knew because my treacherous heart told me so—that it was the Landeric picture.

"Can I getcher a nice cupper tea, mum? You look fair wore aht."

"No, thank you, Mrs. Hoskins," I replied. "Please feel free to go as soon as you wish. It's been a long day, and you have both been very kind and helpful, you and Mr. Hoskins."

"Are you sure there's nuffink else?"

I turned away, so that she should not see my tears.

"No, I shall be all right now, Mrs. Hoskins. Please leave me now."

"Well if you say so, mum. Arternoon, mum."

"Good afternoon, Mrs. Hoskins."

Whatever happened, I was determined not to break down till I was alone. And break down I did, as soon as I heard the front door close behind the Hoskinses.

In the end, it was not the strain of my wedding day, the hideous embarrassment of the ceremony, Durward's collapse, and my horrific discovery of his addiction that laid me low; it was the sudden remembrance of Landeric and all the might-have-beens.

* * *

I sat at the long window of the studio, till the dying sun cast deep shadows over the Chelsea rooftops and the dust haze of the great city merged with the gathering darkness. And one by one, I took out some of the strands of my life, as from a tangled skein of wool, and laid them out to look at and to reflect on.

That strand concerning Landeric and all it implied had been severed in one slash of fate's shears, and was an object only for tears and regrets. The strand could never be mended. My only hope was that the wound would grow less with the passing of the years, and the remembrances fade.

Gently, probingly, I drew out the strand representing my association with Durward. In the light of what I now knew about him, I re-examined the early images of that complex and stimulating personality which had insinuated itself in and about the skein of my life.

Durward on the occasion of our first meeting, when he had mistaken me for yet another Dewaine (strange that the significance had never struck me before: his artist's eye must have lit for an instant upon the family likeness—and then lost it again). I had been fascinated by him then, because of his lively manner and the way his eyes lit up when he smiled. He was drinking champagne that sunny afternoon, under the plane tree. Had he also been taking alcoholic tincture of opium?

Durward in Venice. The gay luncheons and the amusing gondola trips along the shaded backwaters; his bubbling wit and stimulating conversation; the impression of a strange, inner excitement that had coloured all our golden days together in the city of the Doges—had it all been counterfeit? Can you buy brilliance by the shilling bottle at a street corner chemist's shop? Can the quality of fascination be drunk down by the wineglassful?

I had married a man for whom I had not love, but admiration. Where was that admiration now?

Was it not possible that—setting aside his brilliance as a painter, which was considerable—the man whom the world knew as Durward de Lacey was only an empty shell of a human being? Destroyed, perhaps, by the terrible experiences of his upbringing in the orphanage; and only brought to life under the influence of laudanum?

It was nearly dark in the studio when I heard a soft footfall on the spiral staircase, and I turned with a start of alarm. Surely, Mrs. Hoskins could not have come back at such a late hour. And Durward was fast asleep. . . .

The door opened. Durward stood on the threshold, swaying

slightly. He was wearing a dressing gown, and his fair hair hung all awry.

"Is that you, Susannah?" he croaked. "Why is there no damned light in here?"

I found a candle. The Lucifer match ignited with a shower of bright sparks that illuminated the pale and dissolute face of my bridegroom. He scowled and shielded his eyes.

"Gad, what time is it?" he asked. "Why have you let me sleep the whole day through?"

"It is gone eight o'clock," I told him. "And you have been ill. Very, very ill. Durward, I must speak with you . . ."

"Don't preach at me, for heaven's sake," he said. "I feel nigh to death, and in no mood for preaching." He swayed away from me, his hand pressed to his head. "Now . . . where did I put that? . . . ah! . . ."

The candlelight glinted from the decanter and wineglass still standing on the table by the window. He crossed over to it, picked up the decanter, turned it over, and grunted in disgust.

"You drank it all, Durward," I said coldly. "This morning, before our wedding—if you remember."

"Wedding?" he said muzzily, passing his hand across his eyes. "Ah, yes I remember. I drained the lot. But there's some more. Now, where did I put that bottle?" He staggered across the studio floor again, colliding with an easel and cursing it roundly.

"Durward!" I cried. "If you take any more laudanum today, you will kill yourself, sure as fate!"

"What do you know about it?" he growled morosely, rummaging among a pile of books and papers. "Curse it! Where did I put that confounded bottle?" He hurled a drawerful of papers to the floor and kicked them across the room. "For pity's sake, woman, can't you help me?"

"Help you?" I breathed. "Can you think that I would lift a finger to? . . ."

"Ha!" he gave a shout of triumph and produced a dark wine bottle from a drawer. "I knew I had it here somewhere."

I rushed across to him and lay a restraining hand on his arm, just as he was about to raise the neck of the bottle to his lips. Our eyes met: his were pale, cold and totally without human feeling: the eyes of a complete stranger.

"Durward," I pleaded. "You must not—you shall not—have any more!"

"Shall I not?" he said flatly. "Observe me closely!"

That said, he removed the cork with his teeth, and, blowing it across the room, he put the bottle to his lips and took a draught of the contents. And all the time, his eyes never left mine.

"You must be insane, to do that," I said. "If you had seen yourself this afternoon . . ."

He lowered the bottle and smiled: his familiar, lop-sided smile that had once so enchanted me. It had not changed; only I had changed.

"You are totally mistaken about me, my dear Susannah," he said. "And, in this, you are one of a piece with the rest of the well-meaning but totally ignorant army of respectable people who condemn the habit that I share with some of the finest creative minds of our century." He walked across and laid the bottle carefully down upon the table beside the carafe. When he turned to face me again, his eyes were shining with candour, and tolerant good humour was written on his lips.

"How am I mistaken?" I asked dully. This was the Durward I knew; but it was as if I was seeing him for the very first time.

"Your admirable perceptiveness was led astray, my dear Susannah, by this morning's . . . regrettable contretemps," he said. "But for that unfortunate incident—of which more later—you would have gone through life in serene ignorance of my little weakness. Come now, my dear. You have known me quite intimately for what is admittedly a short while. Have you ever suspected that I am the monster of depravity you now imagine me to be? Of course not—for what you now imagine is just not true." He tapped the bottle on the table, and it tinkled against the decanter. "I have my appetite well under control. As you have seen, I take a little nip now and again, to quench the evil humours and raise the spirits. Just a drop, now and again . . . observe . . ."

He picked up the bottle and the wine glass. His fingers were steady as he poured a modest measure into the glass. And his pale eyes twinkled at me over the rim of the glass as he took a small sip.

"All very restrained and civilised," he said. "We could be sitting at table outside Florian's, watching the *beau monde* of Venice parading past. Come, my dear. Heighten your enjoyment of the occasion—take a sip."

I backed away from him in horror when he held out the glass to me.

"Durward! No—how could you suggest it?" I cried.

"As you please," he said with continuing good humour. He tossed back the dregs of the glass, and poured himself another, larger, measure. "For one of your background and upbringing, you really have the most incredibly *bourgeois* attitudes. If you had been reared in the parish orphanage, you would have learned at a very early stage the advantages of being able to carry contentment around in your pocket, and of enjoying oblivion at will.

"Only the very poor and wretched on the one hand, and the creative and sophisticated on the other, truly understand the uses of this divine tincture, this Milk of Paradise. It has many supporters among the most distinguished of us. Poets, authors, painters, musicians. Byron used it, well-laced with brandy. Shelley, too. De Quincey wrote a book condemning it when he was younger—said he had escaped from its baleful influence. Ha! I am able to inform you, because I am well acquainted with him, that Tom de Quincey, now a hale and hearty sexagenarian, is still quenching his thirst, daily, at the fountain of many delights!"

He took another pull at the glass.

"Durward, you nearly killed yourself this morning," I said evenly. "If you want to see the dawn, you must stop what you are doing—now."

"This morning," he mused, looking down into the glass. "Yes, I grieve for this morning. That was a conjunction of events and circumstances adding up to a disaster of such magnitude as could scarcely be expected to happen twice in a lifetime. That the occasion of my nuptials should coincide with the most resounding blow ever struck at my professional pride and reputation. . . ."

A tear was starting in the corner of his eye. My heart softened to him.

"Durward . . ." I began.

"I had hoped that the good news would come in time for me to tell you before the ceremony. I had asked the P.R.A. to send me the verdict as soon as he received it. It was to have been my wedding present to you: that tremendous commission which would have insured that you would, quite soon, become Lady de Lacey."

"And when it didn't happen, you despaired and sought oblivion!" I said. "Oh, Durward, why did you do it? It isn't that important. Let Winterhalter have this commission—there'll be many more. You're young, Durward, with all your professional life ahead of you. You have it in you to prove to Prince Albert, to the whole world, that you are a hundred times the better painter than Winterhalter. If you really want to, there is nothing you can't do —nothing!"

"Yes! Yes!" he cried, his eyes flashing with a wild and ungovernable enthusiasm. "By heaven, you're right, Susannah. I was a fool to forget it, and I am indebted to you for reminding me. I am De Lacey, youngest Academician of this century. Destined to be the Academy's youngest president. Not a trumpery knighthood, but a peerage, shall crown my efforts. Did Michelangelo crawl to popes and princelings? Did Leonardo da Vinci bow the knee? No! In future, I shall direct my own destiny. This right hand shall paint what my will commands. . . ." His voice trailed away into incoherence.

I took his arm. He still held the glass of laudanum. Somehow, I had to get it from him.

"Tomorrow, Durward," I said soothingly. "All that begins tomorrow—the bright, brave future. And now, you must rest. Tomorrow, you will take up your brushes again and show the world; but now . . ."

My hand slipped over his wrist, past his fingertips, and on to the glass. I watched him all the time; his eyes were staring out into the shadow gloom beyond the loom of the candlelight, fixed upon some vision of his drugged imaginings. Gently, I began to detach the glass.

"Come, my dear," I whispered. "Time for rest . . ."

Next instant, his unresisting fingers became like steel. His eyes flashed round to meet mine, suddenly and frighteningly full of malevolence and suspicion. And his lips parted in a slow, hellish grin.

"I don't trust you, my dear Susannah," he hissed through bared teeth. "I do believe you are trying to deceive me."

"No," I whispered. "No, Durward. I promise . . ."

Still grinning, he took a pace towards me. I backed away.

"Come here," he said. "Come here, my bride. My beautiful Amazon queen, my Dresden shepherdess. Circe. Deceiver."

"Durward. Please . . ."

I looked around me for some means of escape, but he was between me and the door. Two more steps back, and my skirts came into contact with the wall.

The hellish grin remained, and he was close enough for me to see a trail of spittle coming from a corner of his mouth. I closed my eyes and clenched my hands behind me, bowing my head.

A long time passed by in complete silence, and I had a thin hope that he might have gone away. I strained my ears, but could detect no sound above my own laboured breathing.

When I opened my eyes he was still there. Grinning down at me—with the glass of laudanum held towards me.

"Drink!" he commanded.

"No!"

"Drink, I say!"

The glass was advanced towards my trembling lips. When I moved to one side, to try to avoid its contact, his other hand came up and took me by the shoulder. He held me there, and then the rim of glass was against my lips, and the laudanum was spilling into my mouth, pungent and sweet.

"The Milk of Paradise!" he cried. "You will see such dreams, this night, that your soul will cry out for joy. From this night forth, my Susannah, you will turn your back upon the world of mere mortals, the world of the commonplace. You will come with me, Susannah. We will travel together, through dreams and noonday visions, to a grander and more shadowy world . . ."

I screamed and spat out the disgusting draught. When I opened my mouth to scream again, his steely fingers slid from my shoulder to my throat, choking me to silence.

"Escape!" he cried. "Escape with me to the unbelievable ecstasies that lie just beyond the raised curtain!"

My senses were slipping away from me. A great roaring filled my ears. I was beginning to fall down a long, dark tunnel. From somewhere far off, a voice was telling me that I was dying. There was only one escape. Opening my mouth wide, I strained against the choking grip and mouthed the words . . .

"Let . . . me . . . drink! . . please."

Instantly, the killing grip relaxed. I took a sobbing breath. My vision cleared. His face was still before me. That—and the proffered glass.

"Drink, then!" he cried.

I lifted my hands and took the glass from him, raising it to my parted lips. An instant's pause. Over the rim of the glass, I saw his pale eyes wide with triumph and expectation.

He screamed when I tossed the glass and its contents into his face; clawed for me when I swiftly edged my way along the wall. Not swiftly enough: his fingers hooked in the neck of my dress; as I pulled away, I felt the back of the bodice rip from neck to waist.

I reached the door and the staircase beyond, and I heard him behind me as I hurled myself down the steps. The landing below was lit by a hanging lamp, and the door of the second floor sitting room was ajar. I rushed in and slammed it in his face, my fingers fumbling for the key in the lock, and every nerve in my body screaming a prayer for deliverance.

Blessedly, the key was in place. Sobbing with relief, I turned it, and felt the handle move at the same time. Thwarted, he bore his weight against the door, but it held. With only a shaft of moonlight to guide me, I dragged a heavy armchair across the room and thrust it against the door, following that with a side table and another armchair. I heard him call out, reviling me and threatening what he would do to me unless I opened for him; but his frenzied cries only spurred me to greater efforts. Not till every portable item of furniture in the room was piled up against the door did I lean against my defences and hang there, fighting for breath.

His muffled voice was still assaulting me, as the strength left my legs, my brain swam, and I felt myself slipping to the floor.

* * *

I opened my eyes, in the early dawn light, to an unfamiliar sweep of carpet stretching from within an inch of my nose and across an empty room. There was the memory of a sound that had roused me, and it was repeated a few moments later, coming from down in the street outside.

"Any knives to grind? . . . bring your knives to grind"—the cry of a street trader summoning pale-faced Chelsea maids-of-all-work from their dark basements.

I sat up and touched my throbbing temples. My throat was sore, and there was a sour and unfamiliar taste in my mouth: the laudanum.

I got unsteadily to my feet. My bodice hung in rags, so I slipped it off, shivering in the morning's chill. There was not a sound in the house as I slowly and carefully began to take down my barrier of furniture, fearful least I should make the slightest noise. That done, I put my ear to the door and listened for a very long time.

I held my breath, and my heart doubled its beat, as I turned the key in the lock—and eased the door open for a hairsbreadth.

The lamp still burned on the landing. It revealed nothing but shadows and emptiness.

Slipping off my shoes, I tiptoed across and silently opened the door of the room opposite. The counterpane of the double bed—that which was to have been my marriage bed—was smooth and undisturbed. Beyond was a dressing room, where Durward himself had deposited my luggage on our wedding eve. A makeshift plan had already suggested itself to me: to cram a few of my most treasured belongings into a case, dress myself decently—and leave that accursed house forever.

Durward had been there before me: I recoiled with shock on the threshold. . . .

My clothes were strewn across the floor of the dressing room, ripped and defiled. My old wicker hamper and Joe Button's chest —neither of which possessed locks—had been wrenched open and upturned and the contents scattered and trampled. A small case and another trunk—both still locked—had escaped his ministrations.

Something impeded my stocking foot. Looking down, I saw that it was my Bible. In his drugged frenzy, Durward had taken it and ripped it apart; but the precious silhouettes had not been disturbed; they had remained safely in their place, face to face, between the pages of the Song of Solomon. I breathed a sigh of relief.

Then I remembered my unfinished diary for 1846, which had been lying in the sea chest next to the Bible. Where was it? I looked about me, probing and turning over the scattered clothing.

I saw the diary . . .

It lay on the dressing table where he had left it, opened at last entry: the entry for July 30th . . .

> There are two secrets in my life which condemn me to leave Landeric forever. The first is that I am the bastard daughter of Sir Tristan Dewaine. The second secret— which I must keep forever locked in my heart—is that I love Mark Dewaine, my half brother, with a love that is sinful before God and man. . . .

Some time in the dark hours of the night that had just passed, my bridegroom had learned what I had never dared to tell him.

What had been his reaction? Had he begun his frenzied orgy of destruction before or after his discovery and reading of the diary? And where was he now—and in what sort of state? My conscience struck at me, driving away my terrors. If he had persisted in continuing to take the laudanum, I might, indeed, be alone in the house with a dead or dying man.

I resolved to look for him, starting with the studio. Pausing only to throw a shawl over my bare shoulders, I rushed out and up the spiral staircase.

Durward was lying on the studio floor, over by the long window, face uppermost, mouth open, and arms spread wide. The bottle of laudanum lay by his head—empty.

He was alive—that much was certain. What was more, there was no hint of the livid colouration about the mouth and ears that had been so noticeable on the previous afternoon. He was in a profound sleep and breathing heavily.

I had plenty of time to effect my escape. Time to repack my things and summon a carriage to take them all away. Time, even, to have one last look round.

Time for a last, yearning look at Durward de Lacey's masterpiece—the Landeric group portrait . . .

It was turned to face the window, with the back of the canvas towards me, and the dust cover—to my surprise—had been taken off and was lying on the floor beside it.

I walked round the easel; not till I was facing the picture did I raise my eyes and gaze upon its surface; probing through its imaginary window to the scene beyond.

"No . . . oh, no!"

I cried out in horror of what I saw there.

Durward had completed his masterpiece during the night: the new paint was still glistening wet and smelling of linseed oil.

He had painted a new figure in the centre of the group, between Jessica and Mrs. Newstead: the figure of a woman, ashen-faced and emaciated, and with her arms folded on her breast. Signs of decay were already upon her brow and in the hollow sockets of her closed eyes. She was clad in a dusty shroud—the grim cerements of the grave—and lay stiffly within an open coffin that stood propped upright against the plinth of the statue.

There were no longer six Dewaines in the picture, but seven. And the thing in the coffin was me.

Chapter 7

I next saw the sea—the first time since I left Cornwall—between the green shoulders of the South Downs and above the rooftops of Brighton in the rain.

"Brighton . . . this is Brighton!"

We steamed into the station, and a voluble array of urchins descended upon the passengers, offering to carry baggage at a farthing a piece and as far as you liked. I entrusted my trunks and cases to one of these, who, upon hearing my needs, said that he knew the very lodging house for me; and he set my things upon a barrow and led the way to a small terraced house in a turning off the main road from the station; clean and neat, and charging only one-and-sixpence for bed and breakfast.

That night—the second of my disastrous marriage—I had a horrendous dream, in which I was pursued through the alleyways of an empty town by a muffled figure who forever called after me that, run though I might, he would sooner or later catch up with me. I awoke with the sound of my own scream echoing in my ears, and got up and dressed—being too frightened to risk returning to the same nightmare.

While the dawn sky lighted the houses opposite, I sat by my window and examined my fears. Was it likely that Durward would pursue me? I thought so. The bond that had drawn us together—the mutual liking that was surely based on the fascination of opposite temperaments—had been shattered by the events that culminated in the wedding night; but it had been replaced by other things: in my case—revulsion; in Durward's case—what? Bitterness, I thought. Hatred, too. The bitterness that would come from the revelation that, unlike him, I was not a piece of human flotsam from the parish orphanage; but the offspring—however despised and unwanted—of one of the most distinguished families in the land. Yes, that would be gall and wormwood to Durward. That was the bitterness which had directed his hand to paint the hideous caricature of me—the rotting corpse among the Dewaines. He would hate me, also, because I had been the witness to his shame: I had the marks on my throat that proved him to be self-deceived; he was not the master of the drug that he called the Milk of Paradise—he was its victim, and it was destroying him.

These thoughts—as well as simple fear—had coloured my actions after leaving Cheyne Walk in a carriage with all my baggage. To get out of London had been my first impulse; Brighton simply a matter of convenience—the proximity of the railway station, the town at the end of the line. Surely, I told myself in the mirror that grey dawning of my third day as a married woman, Durward could never find me here.

How wrong I was. . . .

The task of finding some employment was, as always, bedevilled by my lack of references. There was no longer Durward de Lacey, R.A., to dangle before prospective employers, and I decided not to use the Reverend Mr. Mawhinney again for fear that he and Durward were in contact. With no one to vouch for my character and industry, I was poorly placed in the labour market. Nevertheless, I put on a bold face, my most serviceable costume, and ventured forth to seek my fortune in the famous resort of the South coast, lately favoured by the last of the royal Georges and recently by our present monarch.

On a clear morning, in a brisk breeze that set the masts of the fishing smacks heeling out at sea and white water to break over the Chain Pier, I called at every hotel and lodging house on the seafront, fruitlessly asking for work. In the mid-afternoon, despondent, I was more lucky. Just off the Old Steine, I found a second-class establishment called The Regent, where a gimlet-eyed housekeeper looked me over and said I might suit as a chambermaid at eighteen pounds a year—references permitting.

I had introduced myself as Mrs. Susannah Lacey and implied that I was a widow. This would be my first employment since before my marriage, I told her, and I could produce no references.

She looked me up and down again, and said I might still be considered for the post—and would I come back at the same time on the following day? With no suspicion in my mind, I readily agreed, supposing that the woman merely wished to clear the matter of my lack of references with her superior.

I spent the next morning shopping for a few necessities—not covered by my wedding trousseau—for my coming life as a chambermaid in an inferior hotel: a pair of stout button boots, heavy woollen stockings that would stand up to plenty of hard kneeling, a warm dressing gown for early rising in the chilly winter dawns; three items that ate into my lean capital to the tune of twenty-five shillings.

It was three-fifteen by the clock when I turned off Old Steine and walked up the steps to the plate glass doors of The Regent hotel. Before my hand could touch the door handle, however, I had a sudden sense of malaise: and, almost as if a cloud had passed overhead, shielding the sun, a slight chill passed through my frame.

One swift glance through the glass was enough.

Standing at the foot of the main staircase, and deep in conversation with the housekeeper, were two men. One of them was a police constable. The other had his back to me—but I knew, by the fall of his light hair below the slouch hat, by the set of his shoulders, by the unserviceable shade of his pale grey suit, by every shrinking fibre in my body, that it was the man I had married only two days previously.

And they were waiting for me: even as I stood there, the woman consulted the fob watch that hung from her belt and frowned with slight impatience. Stifling a cry of alarm, I turned on my heels and ran—past strollers who cursed me when I brushed against them, or called coarse endearments after me—till I reached my lodgings.

The next train that set off for London took me with it, baggage and all: nor did I take my seat and relax till I had assured myself that the tall and dandified figure in pale grey had not come into the station at the last moment and joined the train.

It was clear what must have happened: the hotel management had applied to the police, to find it a certain Mrs. Susannah Lacey was known to them as a thief, vagrant, or other person of bad character. The Brighton constabulary had already been informed —no doubt by the new electric telegraph—that a Mrs. Susannah de Lacey, bride of the eminent Academician, was missing from her home and wanted by her husband.

"Wanted by her husband"—the chance phrase springing, ready-assembled in my over-heated mind, had the potency to make me shudder with dread. And I recalled that I had sacrificed more than my maiden name at the Chelsea Register Office: I had given over my freedom into the hands of a man.

I was a person without rights: a wife, a piece of chattel. Durward could pursue me, like a hunted animal, through the length and breadth of the kingdom—and the force of the Law would gladly offer him every help and encouragement. I had no rights in the matter: I was only a married woman.

* * *

I came to Cambridge. Again, this was arrived at more by chance than by choice: my instinct for flight sent me in an opposite direction from Brighton, and Cambridge was simply a name somewhere along the line that was familiar to me.

It was nightfall when I arrived there, and I had no heart to venture out into a strange city in search of lodgings. A kindly station master let me into a waiting room, where a pot-bellied stove glowed brightly, and gave me a mug of strongly flavoured coffee. I had no appetite for food, but a great weariness fell upon me, and I was glad to fall into a basket chair that my new friend provided for me from his own office. I fell asleep before the stove—and was awakened by the shrill whistle of the first train that steamed into Cambridge just after dawn.

My friend provided me with more coffee, and invited me to leave my baggage with him while I found myself somewhere to stay. I was grateful to be unencumbered, and set out into the morning air. At the end of every street, I could not resist a fearful glance backwards, to see if I was being followed by . . . *him.*

I reached the centre of the city, with its turreted colleges and dark archways leading to secret lawns. It would have been about ten o'clock. Suddenly the church bells began to ring, and from every gateway and arch there poured hosts of chattering men—young men and old men—in academic dress: dour clergymen in bands or twice-about neckcloths; fresh-faced boys scarcely out of school, puffing on important-looking pipes and declaiming loudly to their fellows. Suddenly, I felt as if I had become the only woman in Cambridge, and, indeed, I was uncomfortably aware that every eye was upon me. Confused, I turned sharply up a narrow street, and all but fell into the arms of a stout young man in a mortar board hat and shabby gown, who removed his hat and made a great fuss of enquiring as to whether he had trodden upon my foot and could he call a cab and escort me home? Gently disentangling myself from his supporting arm, I escaped by pushing open the glass-fronted door of a nearby shop. There was a tinkle of a bell. I shut the door behind me, and smiled through the glass into the disappointed face of my late admirer.

"You will be safe from the attentions of young Mr. Anstruther," came a voice behind me. "Mr. Anstruther's account remains firmly unpaid for the third month running, and I hear that he has already spent his October allowance. He will not come in here, ma'am. You are safe."

I turned, to see a white-whiskered old man looking at me from behind a counter that was set with lacquered jars all labelled *tobacco*. He wore a rusty tall hat, a seedy black coat to match, and his gnarled fingers emerged from woollen mittens. The blue eyes in the pippin-cheeked face held all the mischief of boyhood.

"Unless you have indeed come in to purchase tobacco," he continued. "As you can see, ma'am, I have a collection of most varieties of the noble leaf. I have the finely-cured Oriental tobaccos from Greece and Turkey; subtle blends from Santo Domingo, Cuba and Brazil; and the lighter leaf of Virginia, favoured by Indian savages and the master of a Cambridge college who shall be nameless. But, as I perceive from your bemused expression, you have not come in for tobacco—it was, as I had thought, to rid yourself of the tender importunities of young Mr. Anstruther."

I smiled. "Yes," I said. "And I think he's gone on his way now."

"Then I will bid you good day, ma'am," said the old man.

"Good day to you, sir," I replied, opening the door to the musical tinkle of the bell. It was then I saw, for the first time, a piece of lettered card that had been attached to the inside of the glass.

> WANTED—young person of honest disposition & sober habits, to assist in this emporium. Emoluments: £20 per annum, plus full board and accommodation with fmly. Apply in person.

I read it through, and turned back to him, heart beating, hardly able to keep the anxiety out of my voice.

"This position . . ." I began.

"Yes, my dear young lady? This position, you say."

"It . . . it isn't yet taken?"

"The card has been in the window so short a while," he said, "that the flour-and-water paste with which I affixed it has scarce had time to dry."

"Then . . . the position is not taken!" I cried.

He pursed his lips. "Ah, but I have to tell you, my dear young lady, that the position *is* taken—in my estimation, at least."

"Oh, dear," I said, disappointed beyond belief.

His face broke into a merry smile that crazed the rosy skin into a thousand wrinkles of good humour, and the blue eyes danced with mischief.

"But perhaps I am being presumptuous," he said. "More presumptuous, even, than the excellent Mr. Anstruther. Perhaps you are the daughter of an earl or of a London alderman. Perhaps, even, you are a peeress in your own right. Or a very young millionairess. You have the looks and the manner, my dear young lady, to be any, or all, of these. On the other hand, your easy and assured manner may not spring from high birth and affluence, but from an inner honesty and integrity, which is a horse of a vastly different colour. And, perhaps, you are seeking employment—in which case the position is yours for the asking, without further ado, as a mark of my esteem, or *honoris causa*—as we say up at the 'varsity."

"But," I protested, "you know nothing about me. You haven't even asked my name, let alone enquired about my experience and references."

"What's in a name?" he cried. "And mine, by the way, is Mr. Joel Gathercole. As to experience in the retail tobacco trade—why, you have already had your first, invaluable lesson from my own lips, concerning the varieties of leaf that we carry in stock. As to references . . ." he went to the back of the counter and called through a doorway "Henrietta, my dear, would you please be so good as to step this way and give me the benefit of your valued judgement?"

"At once, my dear," came a reply. "Coming at once."

Footsteps on the stair beyond, and an exceedingly plump old lady in a mob cap descended with surprising lightness and stood behind the counter. So tiny of stature was she that her smiling face barely reached above the counter. Her eyes were all kindness behind steel-rimmed spectacles.

Mr. Gathercole indicated me. "You see the young lady before you, my dear," he said. "Now, tell me quickly—what would you think if I straightway informed you that I have just now offered this young lady the position of assistant, the details of which you so recently limned in your own elegant hand for display at our door?"

"Why!" cried little Mrs. Gathercole. "I would think that you have made a very good choice. A very good choice, indeed."

"Thank you, ma'am," I murmured gratefully.

Mr. Gathercole tapped the side of his nose and seemed to attempt—with conspicuous lack of success—an expression of cunning and shrewdness.

"But what of character, my dear?" he demanded. "What of the young lady's honesty and sobriety, not to mention her probity and so forth? Do you not wish to see her references, heh?"

Mrs. Gathercole gave me a closer inspection over the top of her spectacles, and what she found seemed to allay a momentary doubt that her spouse's last words had implanted in her mind.

"Why, no, Joel dear," she replied mildly. "Just as Cain carried the mark of evil on his brow, so does this young lady—Miss, er . . ."

"*Mrs.* Button," I supplied. "I am married, but I am parted from my husband and have decided to revert to my maiden name."

"I was going to say," continued Mrs. Gathercole, "that Mrs. Button's virtues are as plain to see as her face is pretty."

Mr. Gathercole spread his hands and appealed to me.

"Are you satisfied yet, my dear young lady?" he asked. "Or must I provide even further evidence to support that which your mirror must quite adequately supply every time you gaze into it?"

"Sir, I don't know what to say," I cried. "Your kindness overwhelms me."

"Best inform Mr. Oswestery, my dear," pronounced Mrs. Gathercole. "He will be interested to hear that we have been fortunate in so quickly filling the position."

"And he, too, is an excellent judge of character," said her spouse. "Mr. Oswestery will be able to provide Mrs. Button with further reassurance that I have not chosen too hastily." So saying, the old tobacconist took a stout cudgel from an umbrella stand near the counter and hammered upon a part of the wall that bore marks of many such hammerings. This drew a muffled cry of response from the far side of the wall.

A few moments later, a tall young man in a brown frock coat bobbed into view through the panes of the shop window, and entered the door. I had an impression of shyness in a pair of soft, brown eyes that were turned upon me. Mr. Oswestery was about five and twenty; untidy of appearance and endearing of manner.

"Mrs. Button, may I present my colleague from the next door shop," said the tobacconist. "Mr. Oswestery is a bookseller. Also, I may add, a poet and *litterateur* of considerable promise."

Mr. Oswestery blushed and smoothed back a straying lock of thick yellow hair.

"Mrs. Button, we hope, is going to accept the vacant position of assistant," supplied Mrs. Gathercole.

"But she is a little concerned that she is unable to offer any references," added Mr. Gathercole.

All eyes—mine included—were upon the young bookseller. And his were upon me. To my alarm, he seemed to hesitate, as if unwilling to express an adverse judgment. Mr. and Mrs. Gathercole waited with a smiling patience that I could not share.

Presently, he got it out, stammeringly.

"Wha-wha . . ." he began.

"Yes, dear?" prompted Mrs. Gathercole.

"Wha- what need of references?" demanded the young bookseller. "Any fu-further judgment upon Mrs. Button would be tu-totally superfluous."

He stooped to kiss my hand.

"There! What did I tell you?" asked Mr. Gathercole of no one in particular.

Mr. Oswestery looked up into my face. "I hu-hope that you will su-soon learn to be at home here," he said.

I gazed at the three of them through my tears.

"I think I am at home already," I said.

* * *

There followed the most tranquil and contented period of my life, at Gathercole's Select Tobacconist's in Petty Cury, Cambridge, next to Stanley Oswestery—Bookseller to the University and the Public.

They gave me a delicious, pink-walled room under the steeply-pitched roof, with a view out of a dormer window to the roof of

King's College Chapel and the spires, towers and battlemented walls fading away into the hazy blueness.

There was no one to deny my right to hang the silhouettes of Mark and me over the little fireplace. Mark's likeness was the last thing I saw before I snuffed my candle and the first to greet me with every new dawn. The circumstances following the Reverend Mr. Mawhinney's fateful revelation—my flight to London, the disaster of my marriage, and my subsequent journeyings—had served to remove any traces of guilt I might have felt about my love for Mark. Though in the eyes of God and man I might be clinging to the memory of a sin, I no longer had any shame about it. And I was stronger on that account: the weakness of spirit that had driven me to accepting Durward's proposal would never return to trap me again. I was married; yet not married. In that state of natural celibacy, I was determined to remain for the rest of my life.

Only one thing clouded my days: the fear that Durward would once more run me to earth. To this end, I never entered the shop to serve a customer without first spying the reflection of its interior in a mirror hung by the door at the bottom of the stairs; and I never walked abroad in Cambridge without a well-concealing bonnet. There was little else I could do by way of precaution.

One day, in the following summer of 1847, I chanced to notice an item in the newspaper to the effect that the foreign secretary, Mr. Palmerston, had given it as his opinion that Herr Winterhalter's new portrait of Her Majesty and her family was the best modern painting he had ever seen. This—clearly a reference to the fateful commission that Durward had lost to the successful German artist—reminded me quite forcefully that many of the people who had played such a big part in my former life must frequently be reported on in the press. Accordingly, from that day forth, I became an avid newspaper reader and collector of press cuttings.

Mr. Palmerston's declaration produced no further comment (how the foreign secretary's extravagant praise of "that pretty enameller" must have humiliated Durward), but I did notice that the name of Durward de Lacey was not among those Academicians whose pictures were shown in the R.A. exhibition of 1847.

The newspaper was delivered to the shop in the mid-afternoon, when trade was quiet. It was then that Mrs. Gathercole brought me a cup of tea and a biscuit, and I went through the paper, beginning with the announcements of Births, Marriages, and Deaths. Every day, throughout my years in Petty Cury, I died with dreadful anticipation, and was reborn again when I did not see the fateful linking of the names Dewaine and De Quatrefois in Holy Wedlock. Only one familiar name met my eyes in those particular columns: when, in July of 1848, I read that the Reverend Mr. Cyrus Theodore Mawhinney, Rector of the Parish of Pennan in the Duchy of Cornwall, had departed this life, aged eighty-three.

It was in the same year of 1848 that I read of the stirring events in Venice. Following a riot in the city, in which the people turned against the Austrian garrison, none other than Daniele Manin—the same patriot who had been secretly received so many times at the Palazzo Dewaine—proclaimed the restoration of the Venetian Republic with himself as President. I quietly rejoiced for Mrs. Newstead—Aunt Marianne, as I had come to think of her in my memories—and hoped that she was alive and well, to enjoy her beloved city in its newly-won freedom. My rejoicing turned to alarm when some months later, Austrian forces beseiged Venice and bombarded her from the sea. An outbreak of cholera further added to the city's misfortunes, and I thought of the inhabitants of the Palazzo Dewaine, and wondered how they were faring. It was almost a relief to read of the Venetians capitulating on honourable terms in August; but my relief was short-lived when it was later announced that the leaders of the revolt were not to be included in the general pardon. In the days that followed, I searched for the mention of Mrs. Newstead's name among those who were punished, with exile or imprisonment, for their part in Manin's short-lived republic—but was relieved not to see it there. The kindly, tragic recluse of the Palazzo Dewaine—if she still lived—was not fated to join Manin in his bitter exile.

The summers came and went, the years waxed and waned. Nothing changed in Petty Cury. Mr. and Mrs. Gathercole became like a father and mother to me, and I the beloved child they never had. Similarly, dear Stanley Oswestery took on the role of a brother, confiding in me all the problems of his life, as the older and more experienced sister (though I was younger than he): how he hoped to publish a slim volume of his verse that was to be bound in red suede leather, embossed with gold lettering on the front, and dedicated to "my friend and constant supporter, S.B., without whose patient attention and constructive criticism this work would never have been published." Alas, poor Stanley—the years went by, and the collection of poems remained firmly unpublished. Every summer, he would take me punting on the River Cam, drifting in the scented warmth of the long afternoons, among the weeping willows and the trailing osiers, with the gaily-blazered undergraduates and their elegant ladies; and there he would read me his verses, over and over again, till I could recite them with him. They were very like dear Stanley: very simple, very sincere; but lacking the vital spark.

Handling a mountain of petticoats in the narrow confines of a Cambridge punt presented problems that were not entirely overcome by the introduction of the crinoline which—as I see from my press cuttings—first appeared in 1850. The modern crinoline, with its framework of hoops which dispensed with the need for voluminous petticoats, was a blessing that I was glad to embrace: I bought a crinoline dress for my fateful visit to London.

The occasion was the Great Exhibition of 1851. It provided the setting for the last major turning point in my life, that set in train a pattern of events so far-reaching that I still do not see their end.

* * *

It seemed as if all the world was preparing to flock to London for the Great Exhibition. For months past, everyone had been talking of the wondrous palace of glass that was going up in Hyde Park; and the newspapers were full of boundless enthusiasm for this, the first international event of its kind in all history. Long before the opening, there was not a bed to be had in the metropolis; in foreign parts, it was said, tickets for sea passages to England changed hands for unheard-of sums. No one, to tell the truth, seemed to know exactly what it was all to be about; there was talk of vast displays of machinery and mechanical inventions, of manufactures, sculptures and the plastic arts, of raw materials; one heard that a fully-rigged frigate was to sail on the Serpentine lake; one read of enormous temporary lodging houses that would be able to accommodate a thousand people every night for one shilling and three pence a head. Of one thing everyone was certain: the fairytale palace that Mr. Paxton was putting up to house all the exhibits was destined to be one of the wonders of the world. Not to be going to see the Crystal Palace was not to be alive in 1851.

Mr. Gathercole sprang his surprise upon us over the supper table one February evening. We were all going to the Exhibition, he told us: the two of them, Stanley Oswestery and myself. What was more, he had bought season tickets (three guineas for gentlemen, two guineas for ladies) that entitled us to attend the opening ceremony, which was to be performed, on May Day, by Her Majesty. We were going down to London for three days, he told us—and staying at a hotel at his expense. It was to be his present to all of us, and he would brook no protest or argument.

Stanley, who was supping with us, choked with emotion on his lamb chop. My first feelings of excitement at the prospect of seeing the Crystal Palace and the Queen were quickly replaced by terror at the possibility of my meeting Durward in London; but the others' enthusiasm was so infectious that I quenched my fears. London, after all, was a very big place; it was to be packed to suffocation with people from all over the globe, and the chances of encountering my husband were negligible. I might—and the thought gave me a brief, delicious tremor—I might just as easily see Mark. Indeed, if in the years between he had regained his commission in the Household Brigade, he could very well be part of Her Majesty's escort of cavalry at the great state event. The remote possibility of being able to view—secretly, safely and from afar—the object of all my desires, my forbidden but not forgotten desires, gave an added touch of splendour to the whole thrilling enterprise. I rejoiced at the opportunity and kissed dear Mr. Gathercole for his generosity in making it possible.

We travelled down to London in a crowded excursion train from Cambridge in the early hours of the Wednesday morning. The capital was teeming with activity; the main thoroughfares a solid mass of slowly-moving vehicles; the pavements a sea of bobbing, tall hats. Our carriage took over an hour and a half to reach our hotel in Pimlico, where the hallway was stacked high with luggage and jammed with people—pleading, cajoling, wheedling, weeping, blustering, threatening people—all desperately looking for somewhere to lay their heads. When our menfolk fought their way through to the reception counter, and it became clear that we were in the privileged state of actually having bookings in the establishment, Mr. Gathercole was overwhelmed with offers of money—waved under his nose in the currencies of half the world —in return for our accommodation. Of course, he ignored all blandishments; not so the management, who had obviously accepted a higher offer for part of our booking: Mrs. Gathercole and I still retained our double room, but poor Mr. Gathercole and Stanley were reduced to sharing a makeshift attic dormitory with twenty other unfortunate males. Nor was this considered a great hardship in the frenzied emotional climate of the Great Exhibition: I saw a prosperous-looking Latin gentleman weep with relief at being permitted to sleep in a bath.

We passed the rest of the day quietly, resisting the temptation to go and spy upon the wonder palace of glass from afar (there was no question of seeing it at close quarters, since all the roads leading to Hyde Park were sealed by police and troops), and retiring early so as to be well rested for the hectic morrow.

* * *

May Day dawned brightly, but with scattered clouds that threatened the possibility of rain. In the early light, the street below our bedroom window was thronged with people and carriages—all going in the same direction: towards Hyde Park.

Printed upon our tickets was the instruction to be in our places in the Crystal Palace before eleven o'clock, or admission would be refused. The Queen was due to arrive at midday. Mr. Gathercole had ordered a carriage to be ready for us in the mews behind the hotel at nine o'clock; and we had decided to abandon the carriage and proceed on foot, if the traffic on the streets came to a standstill, as it had done so many times during our journey from the station the previous day.

In the event, we made good progress. The police had made excellent arrangements to channel the traffic towards its destination —the main entrance of the Palace—and to disperse the empty vehicles northwards through the park. In less than ten minutes from leaving the hotel, we were passing the great archway surmounted by the equestrian statue of the Duke of Wellington that stands at Hyde Park Corner, and turning down the wide, rutted expanse of Knightsbridge. Almost immediately, we saw a long parade of flags rising above the tree-lined limits of Hyde Park on our right.

"My dears," declared Mr. Gathercole. "This is the moment we shall treasure for the rest of our lives. We are here! Yonder stands the Eighth Wonder of the World!"

"By jove!" In his excitement, Stanley overcame his stammer. "The Crystal Palace!"

"It's lovely!" I cried. "Utterly beautiful!"

As we drew closer, I could see that the palace of glass had all the noble simplicity of the main central block of Landeric—the comparison sprang immediately to my mind. But it was Landeric bedazzled by a million diamond panes that reflected every delicate shade of shifting sunlight and scudding cloud; a Landeric that seemed to stretch out of sight in both directions, as our carriage swept through the Park gate and joined the long line being marshalled before the entrance porch under the great semi-circle of the looming centre arch.

Stanley handed me down, and I took his arm when we entered. Inside was all space, air and sound; muted sunlight and awestruck murmurings from the throats of assembled thousands. I was shocked to see, before me, within the vast, crystal walls of the Palace itself, a giant elm tree in all the glory of its springtime greenery. And another. They had imprisoned the very trees of the Park within the high vault of shimmering glass.

"Tickets, please. Show your tickets here! One at a time! Do not crowd us!" A group of scarlet-coated Beefeaters stood just within the doors, passing tickets from one to the other and calling out which way everyone should go.

"Second tier, south-west of the transept," we were told and were directed across an open expanse of newly-laid wooden flooring, to the foot of a sweeping curve of staircase.

The hum of voices was constant, like the sound from a hive of bees; from somewhere far off, the silvery sound of a trumpet trilled a scale along the echoing vault of glass.

"They'll be getting ready to play the Royal fanfare," said Mr. Gathercole.

"They'll not be playing that for a while yet," replied his spouse. "'Tis barely nine-thirty and we have two and a half hours to wait for Her Majesty."

"Thank heaven that we have brought ample provender," cried Mr. Gathercole. "You still have it with you, I hope, Stanley?"

"It is hu-here," said Stanley, lifting up the hamper that he carried. "Su-sandwiches, bottled soda water, lemonade and ginger beer."

"A blessing that we brought no strong drink with us," laughed

219

Mr. Gathercole, and he pointed to a notice at the head of the staircase.

> *Drinking of alcohol, smoking of*
> *tobacco, and the company of dogs*
> *is prohibited within this building,*
> *and there is no Sunday opening.*

We reached the first gallery, and the staircase continued. The second gallery—the uppermost—lay immediately under the glass roof and gave us a view down to the vast, open space formed—as in some mighty cathedral—by the crossing of the longest stretch of the building with the high, arched central transept.

The wide open space in the middle of the crossing was laid with a scarlet carpet, in the centre of which was a stepped dais and a throne that stood beneath a suspended canopy all hung with tassels and surmounted by blue-and-white plumes.

"That's where the Queen will perform the inauguration ceremony," whispered Mrs. Gathercole awesomely.

"I am hungry," declared her husband. "Dispense the victuals, Stanley. And I will read you all about the delights that await us."

White marble statues lined the great central space. The dais was flanked by giant equestrian figures representing the Queen and the Prince, and beyond the dais a tall fountain of bright crystal sent a million diamond points of water half-way to the high vault of glass. I stared in wonder. Stanley nudged my elbow.

"Susannah, will you have gu-gentleman's relish or tu-tongue sandwiches?" he asked.

Mr. Gathercole was reading aloud from a catalogue of the exhibits that he had obtained at the door:

" 'Some one hundred thousand objects are gathered under this roof,' " he intoned. " 'Along a frontage of ten miles, sent by over fifteen thousand contributors.' Now what do you think of that?"

"We are living in a Gu-golden Age," declared Stanley. "Nu-nineteenth century England has tu-taken over the torch of enlightened progress from Periclean Athens."

" 'Included in the Exhibition,' " read Mr. Gathercole, " 'are French tapestries from the Gobelins and Beauvais; a steel gun from Krupp of Essen; a pharmaceutical product obtained from the livers of cod fish; a collapsible piano suitable for gentlemen's yachts; a fine collection of fruit stones, carved in minute detail by Prince Albert's brother, the Duke of Saxe-Colbourg-Gotha; a three hundredweight block of gold from Chile; false teeth on an improved principle; a window cleaner for the protection of female servants from fatal accidents and public exposure . . .'"

"A little more gentleman's relish, Su-Susannah?" asked Stanley.

* * *

People were still filing through the transept below us; upturned faces awestruck at the first sight of the vast interior and the towering, captive elm trees.

Shortly before eleven—and we had finished our sandwiches—gorgeously apparelled figures began to mass about the dais, bringing forth a hubbub of excitement from the watching thousands.

"There we have the Officers of State," said Mr. Gathercole. "And all the Ambassadors of all the nations. See the Turkoman in his fez and mark the Egyptian fellows. And there is a Chinee. And there, if I be not mistaken, is the Iron Duke himself."

A great roar of applause greeted the ancient victor of the Battle of Waterloo, scarlet coated, white haired and cruelly bent, as he limped across the open space below us and took his place in the front rank of the brightly uniformed throng.

"I fear it is going to rain," said Mrs. Gathercole. And indeed a sudden darkness had fallen over the crystal roof above us; a sable shadow across the glittering splendour below. Almost at once there came the sound of rain, drumming and thrumming on the arched vault.

It was still raining at half-past eleven. At this time, the Royal party would just be leaving from Buckingham Palace, and the last of the ticket-holders were still not yet in place. Our gallery was nearly full. We were half a dozen rows from the front. Only a few more seats around us remained unoccupied, and attendants were fussily ushering the last of the line of latecomers to their places. When these were all seated, Mrs. Gathercole clicked her tongue fussily.

"Dear me," she said. "I hope that gentleman in the second row takes off his hat before the Queen arrives, for it is quite blocking my view of the throne."

The object of little Mrs. Gathercole's remark was in front of both her and me, though, with my added stature, I could see over the top of the shabby, tall hat that the newcomer—alone of all the menfolk in sight—continued to retain on his head.

"I'm sure he will, my dear," said her husband. "But if he does not do so within a short time, I will call out to him and ask him to show some consideration for others."

"The rain has stopped," I said, and indeed the whole of the interior was suddenly suffused with radiant sunlight as a pall of cloud had been drawn away, like an enveloping curtain.

There came a distant roll that sounded like thunder.

"The guns in St. James's Park!" cried Mr. Gathercole. "They're firing a salute to Her Majesty. The Royal procession must be passing Hyde Park Corner. Oh, how happy she must be feeling, with all the sunshine and the salutations."

An atmosphere of expectancy swept through the gathering, as tangible as a brushwood fire. I was caught up in the sudden wave of excitement. From the carriage drive outside came the sharp cries of officers calling their troops to order. Looking down, I saw the Duke of Wellington produce a very large watch from the breast of his uniform coat, put it to his ear, examine it, and nod approvingly. The great moment was nearly upon us.

"That gentleman has still not removed his hat," complained Mrs. Gathercole.

"He shall do so immediately," cried Mr. Gathercole. "Such discourtesy and lack of consideration is not to be borne an instant longer" . . . he raised his voice, and for all his age the tobacconist of Petty Cury could summon up a quite loud voice . . . "You there, sir! Be so kind as to remove your hat, so that the ladies may have an uninterrupted view of the proceedings!"

"Hu-he didn't hear you, Mu-Mr. Gathercole," said Stanley.

"Nor it seems," said Mrs. Gathercole. "But those immediately behind him have, and are remonstrating with him."

At that moment, the whole of the interior of the Crystal Palace resounded with a flourish of trumpets; echoing and re-echoing from the vaulted roof all round us; a triumphant blast of silvery sound that set the very nerve ends a-tingle.

"The Queen has arrived!" cried someone.

"Make him take his hat off!" shouted Mr. Gathercole.

Those behind the offending wearer of the tall hat were leaning over and addressing him—seemingly to no avail. Instead of complying with their requests—requests that were quickly taking on the appearance of demands—he stared steadfastly to his front and hunched his head and shoulders further into the high collar of the cloak that he was wearing.

The Royal fanfare swelled to a noble wavecrest of sublime harmony.

"Take it off him, the saucy fellow!" shouted someone above the trumpets.

This was done. A hand came out and snatched the hat from the man's head, revealing an unhealthy white pate, bald as a skull, save for a ragged fringe of grey locks in the nape.

The fanfare stopped on a high, loud note. The sudden silence had the power to shock.

My gaze was fixed upon the bald-headed man, as he turned in fury, to see who had removed his head covering. For my part, there was no instant recognition: the pale, emaciated face and the staring, red-rimmed eyes had no meaning in the life and recollections of Susannah Button. Even when he looked beyond those immediately behind him and caught sight of my face, so that his mouth fell open with the shock of encounter, I experienced no emotion more particular than a vague distaste that the creature should make me the object of his attention.

Only when he rose to his feet, and, still staring over the rows of heads that separated us, shouted one word—one name—through the open cavern of his toothless mouth, did I know the truth of it.

"Susannah!" The cry was like the screech of the seabirds circling the windswept headland of Ramas.

It was Durward de Lacey—my husband!

The awful mouth gaped open again; but its next shout was drowned by the opening of another fanfare and a burst of cheering that began outside the building and spread within, till the whole gathering was crying out for the Queen. Everyone was standing, but, because I was higher than he, I was not hidden from the gaze of the wreck of the human being whom I had wed five long years before.

He was still shouting; but not for the Queen. And the loyal acclaims and the shrilling of the trumpets mercifully drowned the unspeakable words he was hurling at me.

I stood, frozen with shocked horror; till I saw that he was roughly elbowing his way past those surrounding him, and his eyes never left mine.

He was coming to me!

I caught sight of Mrs. Gathercole's astonished face close to mine, as I brushed in front of her and clawed my way, past the applauding line of people, to the aisle.

At the top of the aisle was the head of the staircase. A glance over my shoulder showed me that *he* had also gained the aisle and was beginning to mount the steps after me.

A uniformed attendant stood by the staircase: he barred my way with his outstretched arm.

"Everyone to remain in their place!" he mouthed above the fanfare and the shouting. "The Royal party's just entered the building."

I ducked under the man's arm and threw myself down the long, curving sweep of steps, stumbling over my skirt and only saving myself from disaster by clinging to the handrail. In this manner, I reached the lower tier. Sobbing with terror and exertion, and not daring to look behind me again for fear of what I should see, I descended the second flight. Both staircases were empty of people, but I saw a line of scarlet-clad gentlemen-at-arms immediately below. Plumed and helmeted, they stood to attention, tall halberds raised aloft, their backs towards me, barring my path.

The cheering increased. Beyond it all, an organ had taken over from the chorus of trumpets. When I reached the lower floor, someone reached out from behind a line of red cord and plucked at my sleeve, to hold me back. Brushing off the restraining grasp, I edged my way along the backs of the gentlemen-at-arms. One of them turned: his monocled face was red with fury and astonishment. Babbling some soundless excuse to him, I looked this way and that for some avenue of escape. Somewhere else to go, to elude my pursuer.

To my right were a pair of high, bronze gates, overtopped by crowns and rampant lions, and guarded by two Beefeaters. Immediately in front, across a sweep of red carpet, I saw, at the end of a short corridor, a small door that was open to the sunlight.

My way of escape.

As I moved forward, the vast audience fell silent before a single trumpet blast. Half-way across the red carpet, I glanced to one side and received a blurred impression of two persons entering through the bronze gates. One was tall and dressed in military scarlet; the other was a dumpy figure in a pink crinoline gown that sparkled with diamonds and silver. They were looking at each other and smiling: I think they did not see me crossing their path. A few instants later, I was blinking in the sudden sunlight outside.

I was met by a dazzle of colour and movement, the clatter of horses' hooves and the jingle of harness and accoutrements. Life

Guards, plumed and gleaming, moved past me. Their officer's moustached mouth was open in a shout. I saw a gap in their ranks, the gates leading to Knightsbridge, and the secret anonymity of all London beyond. I raced to embrace it, whispering the desperate prayer that I had left my pursuer far behind; that someone had arrested him within the Palace.

I all but stumbled and fell in the middle of the carriage drive. People were shouting to me, from ahead, from behind, and from above. The upper branches of the trees were thick with humanity: urchin children hung from them in clusters, like grapes. They were shouting warnings to me. With a sound like a rushing wind, something passed close behind me. There was a scream; the sound of carriage brakes, hastily applied, shrill whinnies of terrified horses. I stumbled again, and fell into the arms of a blue-clad figure who moved forward from the crowd to seize me.

"By heaven, I thought you were done for! Steady now! You're not clear yet!"

The constable dragged me forward. Turning, I saw a pair of rearing horses with their hooves lashing. A liveried coachman was hauling frantically on his reins to control them.

There was something else—something lying in the dust and confusion beneath the plunging hooves.

"Your friend was not so lucky!" cried my rescuer.

Then I was screaming. I was still screaming when they dragged Durward from under the carriage, his bloodied, pale skull lolling like the head of a broken wooden-top dolly. Then someone had the presence of mind to smack me smartly across the cheek, and I was shocked to silence.

Silent, I watched them lay him at the edge of the carriage drive and cover him with his own cloak. From inside the Crystal Palace came the sound of the mighty organ and massed bands leading the people in the tremendous, sweeping cadences of the national anthem.

* * *

It was the police who took me home, back to the hotel. The Gathercoles and Stanley found me there, in bed, when they returned; they had made frantic enquiries about their missing friend at the Crystal Palace and had been told of the tragedy.

As to be expected, they were kindness itself. Mr. Gathercole insisted on a physician being summoned. The latter having come, having examined me and pronounced me to be in a state of hysteria—which, by that time, I most certainly was not—forced me to swallow myrrh and aloes pills, and was only prevented, by my flat refusal, from bleeding me.

Later that afternoon, a pleasant police inspector called upon me and questioned me about Durward. Of course, I was not able to tell him much, save that he had been living at Cheyne Walk when I had left him five years before. It seems strange, but I was able to speak of the tragedy with perfect calmness and rationality. When the inspector enquired of my husband's financial means at the time of his death, I was, of course, not able to help. Two things he was able to tell me however: that Durward had not been living in the house in Cheyne Walk, and, more surprisingly, that the state of his clothing and linen suggested that he was either greatly impoverished or that he had long since ceased to care about his personal appearance.

I thought back to the Durward of old: the elegant and fastidious Durward who could not bring himself to wear any other but a newly-made shirt and neckcloth. On his change in appearance from the disconcertingly handsome man with the lop-sided smile, to the toothless wreck who had confronted me that nightmare midday, I could not bring myself to contemplate.

The inspector left, telling me that there would have to be an inquest into the accidental death, and that he would keep me informed.

My first day of widowhood—the irony of it!—ended on a quiet note. Dear Mrs. Gathercole sat with me (somehow or other, they had persuaded the hotel management to provide her with a separate room, so that my sleep would not be disturbed) until the effect of the sleeping draught that the physician had left took its effect, and I passed a peaceful night—uninterrupted by ghosts, real or imagined.

But, already while I slept, the mills of fate were grinding out a future pattern of events that had been set in motion, for she whom the world knew as Susannah Button, by the happenings of that fateful May Day of 1851, which will evermore be remembered as the opening day of the Great International Exhibition.

* * *

The morning's newspapers, as was to be expected, devoted themselves almost totally to the reports of the inauguration ceremony and the first day of the Exhibition, which they unanimously declared to have been a sensational success, unmarred by the slightest hitch.

Naturally, the accidental death of Mr. Durward de Lacey, R.A., was heavily overshadowed by what was regarded as the outstanding event of the nineteenth century thus far. Poor Durward received only slender reports in the back pages. One paper pointed out that Mr. de Lacey had not exhibited his paintings for five years. Some mentioned that the wife of the deceased, the former Miss Susannah Button, had been present at the time of the tragedy—a gobbet of news which they must have gathered from the police report. All, without exception and probably by deliberate intent, so as not to mar the glories of the previous day's occasion, refrained from pointing out that the accident had occurred within the shadow of the Crystal Palace at the time of the Queen's arrival there.

The reports, brief as they were, sufficed to alter the whole course of my life.

They brought me two visitors.

The first announced himself, by a visiting card that a hotel chambermaid brought in, as Mr. Arthur Salomon—Print Dealer & Artists' Agent, upon which he had scrawled the words: *"requests to see Mrs. de Lacey ref. the affairs of the late Mr. de Lacey."*

I received Mr. Salomon in my room, sitting in the armchair by the window. He was revealed as a slender man in his mid-thirties, wearing a rusty dark suit. The eyes that looked out on the world from behind thick pince-nez were meek as a fawn's. I had the impression—soon to be confirmed—that he had been crying. He took my proffered hand, after wiping his own on the skirt of his coat.

"I came as soon as I read the dreadful news in the paper, ma'am," he said. "Oh, it is terrible. Terrible. Poor Mr. de Lacey. Such a loss."

"Please sit down, Mr. Salomon," I said. "You knew my . . . you knew Mr. de Lacey well?"

"Three years," said Mr. Salomon. "Three years going on four, I have known Mr. de Lacey. Right from the time when he was dropped by the nobs. Right from the time when the President gave word to the doormen at the Royal Academy School that they were not errand boys, to be sent out for Mr. de Lacey's laudanum in the mid-mornings when he was taking the life class there. He never went near the Academy again. And after that he was dropped by the nobs, as I have said."

"What exactly do you mean by that, Mr. Salomon?" I enquired.

"Why, ma'am, he had no more commissions," said Mr. Salomon. "And that meant no more money. Plenty of past fame, still, but no money. A gentleman may rejoice that his portraits hang in the great town houses of London and in the stately homes of the shires—but when it's all in the past, done and paid for, ma'am, there's little profit. You can't sup off past fame, ma'am. And laudanum's cheap—that's the pity of it."

Mr. Salomon took out a red spotted handkerchief and blew his nose loudly.

"I—I saw my husband yesterday," I said. "Before he was . . . before the tragedy. Tell me, Mr. Salomon, how long had he been —like that?"

Mr. Salomon sniffed. "It didn't take long, ma'am," he said. "Once he wasn't working, the laudanum took a complete hold on him It was in—let me see—the winter of 'forty-eight that the landlord turned him out of Cheyne Walk and I found him lodgings in Whitechapel. By that time, he was scarcely eating anything, and there's precious little nourishment in laudanum. It was after his hair fell out that he took to wearing his hat all the time, both indoors and out. There was still the touch of conceit about the way he looked, you see. Even the laudanum couldn't quite kill that."

I remembered the incident of the hat in the Crystal Palace: the fateful—and, for him, fatal—incident, but for which we might never have set eyes on each other again.

"Why did he go to the inauguration ceremony, Mr. Salomon?" I asked. "Surely, after the unjust way he considered that he had been treated over that commission to paint the Royal family? . . ."

"Ah, Herr Winterhalter and all that," said my companion. "Yes, he never did forgive Prince Albert for giving the work to the German fellow. But, for all that—despite Winterhalter, the Royal Academy cold-shouldering him, the nobs dropping him—he always had a sneaking longing for the old days. 'Arthur, old fellow', he'd say to me, 'I came within an ace of a knighthood and the presidency. One day, I shall go back and see how they're all faring.' Which was why he went to the opening ceremony, you see, ma'am? He tried to borrow the three guineas from me on account, but, fearing that he would spend the money on more laudanum, I purchased the ticket for him myself. 'Think of it, Arthur,' he said to me. 'Tomorrow, I shall see them all dolled up in their finery: the dukes and statesmen and admirals and such— those who were once glad to sit as still as mice for my brush.' That was the last time I saw him, ma'am. On . . . Wednesday evening."

Mr. Salomon took off his pince-nez and ran his fingers across his streaming eyes.

I waited till he had composed himself somewhat, and then I said: "You spoke of money on account, and you mentioned on your card about my late husband's affairs. Is there . . . am I to suppose that my husband died owing you money?"

The effect of my question upon my visitor was instantly to check his tears, and his dark, liquid eyes regarded me with something approaching resentment.

"Can you think that of me, ma'am?" he demanded. "That I should come to see you for no other reason than to demand money?"

"I am sorry, Mr. Salomon," I said. "But I am confused about your relationship with my late husband. Supposing you enlighten me?"

He nodded, and his face softened again.

"Chance brought Mr. de Lacey and me together, ma'am," he said. "I came upon a small, signed portrait by him in an East End picture dealer's—a thing of his student days, but already showing promise of the mastery that he later achieved. Remembering that De Lacey had not exhibited for a couple of years and hearing a rumour that he had fallen upon hard times, I went to see him at Cheyne Walk with a certain business proposition."

"And what was this proposition, Mr. Salomon?"

"Mrs. de Lacey, I am a dealer in prints. Not your fine prints, of the sort that your connoisseur will keep in a portfolio of tooled morocco leather, to proudly display to his friends; but the sort of cheaply produced prints that hang on the walls of working people's front rooms, the saloon bars of public houses, hotel bedrooms . . ." here his liquid brown eyes swam around the walls about him . . . "and so forth. On the evidence of Mr. de Lacey's student effort—which was of a young child weeping over her broken doll—I was able to assure him that he could make a decent living by painting such subjects to be turned into prints, with twenty-five percent commission for me. And I was proved to be correct."

So Durward had ended by doing hack work for an East End print dealer. He who had been the youngest Academician of the century. It was too hard. A taste for laudanum should not have destroyed a man so completely.

"I see, Mr. Salomon," I said. "And what do you require of me?"

"There is the question of the moneys outstanding," he replied. "I had thought Mr. de Lacey to have been alone in the world. But, ma'am, when I saw your name in the newspaper, my conscience drove me to come and tell you of the outstanding moneys."

I smiled. "Your scruples do you credit, Mr. Salomon," I said. "But I have no need of the money, for I am far from destitute. It will serve to save my late husband from a pauper's grave. As to what is left over—if there is any left over—I should be most happy for you to have it, since you have been a kind friend to Mr. de Lacey."

The gentle dark eyes clouded with puzzlement.

"Ma'am, I think you don't understand," he said.

"Understand what, Mr. Salomon?" I asked.

"Why, ma'am," he said, "I am not speaking of ha'pennies and pennies when I speak of the moneys that I hold to Mr. de Lacey's credit. Nor am I speaking of a few guineas, ma'am. Why, his first print, entitled: *The Goodbye Kiss* was a raving success and has been widely reproduced on the Continent and in the Americas— all on a solid royalty basis, I can assure you. Then there was: *Remember me to Mother* which outsold all other lines in the market till this year's record sales with: *Will I go to Heaven, Papa?* Then there was . . ."

"Mr. Salomon!" I cried. "What are you trying to tell me?"

"Why, ma'am, that you are a rich—I may say a *very* rich lady."

"I?"

"Who else, ma'am? You are his legal wife, I take it. And I know for certain that Mr. de Lacey had no blood relations, for he admitted me to the secret of his birth—a thing he did not tell to many."

"How much was my husband worth, Mr. Salomon?" I asked quietly.

"There is all of thirty thousand pounds in hand, ma'am," he

replied. "With royalties mounting up every day. As I said, you are a very rich lady, ma'am."

* * *

It was another hour before I shook hands with Mr. Salomon. By that time, my heart had warmed towards him, and I had come to have more understanding of the enigma who had been Durward de Lacey.

"I never dared to give him more than a few coppers," he told me, "for every penny went on his 'Milk of Paradise,' as he called it. Everything he needed, I bought it for him—and it wasn't much. He lost interest in what he wore and scarcely ate. Whenever I could persuade him, I'd take him round to my mother's for a meal."

"And he never spoke of me?" I asked—guessing at the answer.

"Not as his wife, ma'am," replied Mr. Salomon. "But he often spoke of a lady to whom, as he said, he had done a great wrong. He said to me once that he would give what was left of his life, to see this lady again and tell her . . . now, what was it he wanted to tell her?"

"Please remember, Mr. Salomon!" I pleaded. *"Please!"*

"I remember the gist of it, ma'am, though I may not have the words quite as he delivered them. It went somehow thus: *'I would go after her and tell her that love is everything,'* he said. *'And that she should defy God and man and take her love.'* Yes, that was the gist of it."

I closed my eyes. It was for this moment that Durward had given—as he had offered to give—the rest of his life.

"I'll say good-bye, Mrs. de Lacey," said the print dealer. "And I will be in touch with you, on matters of business, at your Cambridge address." He paused at the door. "We were very fond of Mr. de Lacey, Mother and I. And sorry for him. He had nothing and no one. He was so poor. So alone. Good day, ma'am."

* * *

The wheels of fortune that chance had set in motion had not finished shaping my future. Durward's brief obituaries brought another visitor to my hotel room that day, hard on the heels of Mr. Salomon. He introduced himself as Mr. Aubrey Swayle, of Swayle, Jarvis, Coombe and Fox, solicitors of Bedford Row.

Mr. Swayle was young, pinch-faced, and greatly on the defensive. He declined a seat and remained standing during our brief interview.

"You are Mrs. Susannah de Lacey, née Button, ma'am?" he asked stiffly.

"Yes, sir. I am," I replied primly.

"Formerly of Pennan Haven, in the duchy of Cornwall, ma'am?"

I nodded, and a bead of perspiration appeared on the upper lip of the young lawyer. He coughed nervously.

"Only daughter—as you understand—of Joseph Button, a seaman, and Elizabeth Button, both deceased?" he asked.

After a moment's hesitation, I nodded again.

"And the date of your birth, ma'am—as you understand—was the twenty-seventh day of April, eighteen hundred and twenty-four?"

"That is correct, Mr. Swayle," I said. "But why are you asking me these things?"

Mr. Swayle grew very red, and it was some time before he ventured to reply.

"Madam," he said. "The matter upon which I have come to see you relates to a time before I joined the partnership. In fact, it was handled by my father, now deceased. The clients in question were Mr. and Mrs. Joseph Button, who called on my father in the year of eighteen hundred and thirty-four to execute an affidavit under oath. I should say that it was Mrs. Button who executed the affidavit. She was at that time seriously ill with the consumption and likely to die."

"An affidavit, Mr. Swayle?" I stared at him, puzzled. "I don't understand . . ."

"An affidavit, ma'am, is a written statement of fact, signed before an officer who is empowered to administer oaths. In this case, the affidavit contained certain facts relating to the birth of a child."

I bowed by head. "And that child was me?"

"Yes, ma'am. Before she died, Mrs. Button wished to put these facts on record. She then gave verbal instruction to her husband—who was totally illiterate, like herself—to bring this child, on her attaining the age of twenty-one, to the offices of Swayle, Jarvis, Coombe and Fox, to have the affidavit read before her."

I exhaled a deep breath. "So *that* was Mama's intention," I said. "But poor Joe Button was killed only a few days before my twenty-first birthday."

Mr. Swayle cleared his throat. "I must tell you that, anticipating such a contingency, my father urged that if you did not present yourself on your twenty-first birthday, we should get in touch with you. Unfortunately, my father had also passed away, and we were sadly in error. Not till late in 'forty-six was it realised that you had not been informed of the contents of the affidavit."

"Then you tried to contact me," I supplied, "but I had disappeared without trace!"

"That is so, ma'am. Not till we read the account of Mr. de Lacey's tragic death—and I offer, on behalf of the partnership, our sincere condolences in your hour of grief—were we able to trace you. And I have come straight to you, with a true copy of Mrs. Button's affidavit."

He opened the briefcase that he carried, took out a long fold of paper tied with pink string, and laid it on the table beside me.

"I will leave you, ma'am," he said. "You will wish to peruse the contents at your leisure. Alone."

My name is Elizabeth Button, formerly Penworthy, and I was born near St. Errol in the duchy of Cornwall, in the year 1802, or it might have been 1801. I did not know my parents.

This affidavit is given before Henry Tudor Swayle, a Commissioner for Oaths, of 24a Bedford Row, London, on the 18th day of July in the year of Our Lord 1834.

I have been duly sworn, and I depose and say the following . . .

It was in the spring of the year 1824, and I lately having lost a child at birth, that my employer, Sir Tristan Dewaine, Baronet (who had fathered the said child), relieved me of my work as field-hand and sent me to Venice, to be wet-nurse to a child that had lately been born to his cousin, Mrs. Marianne Newstead, of the Dewaine palace in that city. It appeared that Mrs. Newstead, who had lately received news of her husband's death in another foreign country, had taken ill of a brain fever and was thought to be out of her mind.

I nursed the child. All the time I was at the Dewaine

palace, I never saw Mrs. Newstead, nor, to my knowledge, was she ever well enough to see her child.

In late August of that same year, Sir Tristan came to Venice and gave me the following instructions: that I was to take the child back to England and rear it for my own. For this I was to receive the consideration of five hundred pounds. There were two conditions: that I must not take the child into the duchy of Cornwall, and I must not tell the child, nor anyone, of its true mother.

To this day, I have kept these conditions. Now an infirmity of body ordains that I shall soon be gathered to my Maker, and it is my wish to set things to rights, in view of the love that I bear for the child Susannah, who has become like my own. . . .

There was not much more: through my tears, I read of Mama's wish that Joe Button should take me, after her death, to live near to Landeric, so that I should at least be close to what she considered to be my birthright. The document ended with her mark: a small, neat cross.

The following morning I was on my way—to Venice.

Chapter 8

The diligence lost a wheel beyond Padua, which delayed our arrival in Venice till nearly dusk. The city of the Doges lay under a pall of streaming rain in the half light, and I had the greatest difficulty in persuading a sullen gondolier to take me to the Palazzo Dewaine—but money makes straight many paths, and I had plenty of money.

The Grand Canal was ghostlike and deserted, its surface rippled with raindrops, the stately buildings shadowed in the falling night with no hint of life within their tight shutterings. We passed under the Rialto Bridge without meeting another craft, and the Venetian seat of the Dewaines slid into view, dark and silent like all the rest.

My gondolier made fast to a striped pole and, at my instruction, unloaded my valise and rang the bell under the dark portico. Presently, I saw a lantern's light appear behind the latticed ironwork of the doors. Someone was approaching down the covered courtyard.

A rattle of bolts. The door creaked open. By the light of her lamp, I saw the worn face of Adriana Ricci. When she met my eyes, she cried out as if in pain.

I busied myself in paying off the gondolier, and the simple act helped to calm my racing mind. It was with a fair degree of composure that I picked up my valise and joined the woman in the entrance to the courtyard.

Adriana still leaned against the open door, head back, eyes staring at me as if I had been an apparition.

"You have come back," she breathed. "Always I have known you would come back, and always I have prayed that this would not happen till Madame was no more. My prayers have been answered."

I had expected it, but the sudden sense of loss was like a knife thrust to the side. I found myself trembling.

"When did she die?" I whispered.

"During the siege," said Adriana brokenly. "The fever took her. It was swift and merciful. She died a holy death, rejoicing in the freedom that she believed had come to Venice."

She stooped and picked up my valise, setting off down the courtyard, with the lamplight making wavering, great shadows of our figures on the arched ceiling.

I followed her, as I had followed her that first time, through the inner court—the dead vines dripping with rain and the fountain silent—and up the marble staircase to the gallery. She led me through the carved double doors and into the long room with the painted ceiling, and beyond that to Mrs. Newstead's apartments . . . Aunt Marianne's apartments.

My mother's apartments . . .

Her sitting room had not changed. Adriana laid the lamp on the table and turned to regard me.

"You know!" she said. It was not a question. She was watching my face as I looked about me; saw my gaze light upon the empty chair in front of the curtained window.

"You knew also," I said challengingly. "You could have told me. You could have told her—my mother."

She closed her eyes wearily.

"I guessed from the first," she said. "And if Madame had had the eyes to see, she would have known as soon as she looked upon you. The face of your father shines through your face. I saw it at once. Afterwards, I made you speak of the one you called Mama, and I knew she was the girl who came here from England: the wet-nurse who took away the *bambina*."

"But why, Adriana—*why?*" I cried. "Why did you let my mother live in a world of dreams, a world of make-believe? She even pretended that I—that the child—was a little boy, who was christened 'Georgie' and who died in the nursery. But she never even set eyes on the child. How could you have allowed the fantasy to go on for all those years?"

"When she receive news that the child's father is dead . . ." began Adriana. But I interrupted her.

"He died on Monday the nineteenth of April," I said. "Only a week before I was born."

"She receive the news just after she had given birth," replied Adriana, "in a letter sent by a friend. That date—the nineteenth of April—haunted her forever after. Straight away, Madame's mind was clouded with a terrible melancholy. Many times have I seen it happen to other women after childbirth—often without a reason that could be spoken of. But Madame had plenty of reason for her melancholy. It nearly drove her to kill herself. Once I fought with her, to take a knife from her hand. When it was done, she wept on my breast. After that, she became herself again —most of the time."

I remembered the terrible depressions from which the recluse of the Palazzo Dewaine had suffered so cruelly, and I knew what Adriana meant.

"I could have told her," continued Adriana. "At any time in all those years, I could have told her that her baby lived. But I feared for her mind. No child of God should have suffered as she suffered, and that which she had—what you call the fantasy—kept her mind balanced between despair and death." The woman stared appealingly at me. "I could not risk it, Miss Button. To have heard that there had been no Georgie, and that he had not died in her arms as she believed—the shock would have driven her mind into the eternal darkness."

"But why did her cousin, Sir Tristan, send away her child?" I asked. "Surely, newly-widowed, the child would have given her something to live for—when she had recovered from the shock of Mr. Newstead's . . . my father's death." I had deliberately to bring myself to the realisation that it was me—my own life— that was under discussion.

Adriana gave me a sharp glance. She seemed to take measure of a new and unexpected situation; to decide how she should react to it—and in the end, she decided that the stark truth was all she had to give.

"There was no husband, Miss Button," she said softly. "Did you not know that?"

"No husband?" I faltered.

"Mrs. Newstead was a name only," said Adriana. "He who was your father was not married to Madame. They were . . . lovers. Sir Tristan—ah!—how he raved when he came here. It was he who drove Madame into the darkness of the mind with his violent and wicked words. No cousin of his would flaunt a bastard in Society—those were his words."

The double standard of morality: one law for the buck and another law for the doe! I blessed the fate that had freed me of the belief that that evil man had fathered me!

"Who was Mr. Newstead, Adriana?" I asked.

"Are you so strong?" she replied. "There are many who would not wish to know the thing you ask."

"Who was my father, Adriana?" I persisted calmly.

She shrugged her gaunt shoulders, picked up the lamp again and motioned me to follow her. We left the room by the nursery corridor and came to a carved and gilded door that the woman opened with silent, slow reverence.

"This was the bedchamber of Madame," she said. "Before the coming blindness made it easier to remain in the sitting room always. It has not been used since then. Madame passed away on her couch in the sitting room."

The bedchamber was decorated in the ornate Venetian manner, with swags of carved woodwork, ceiling paintings and a great bed all hung with looped silks.

Adriana crossed to an elegant bedside table that was cluttered with small picture frames, books, letters and knick-knacks of all kinds. Pausing, she chose one of the frames and held it out to me.

"Look upon the face of he who was your father," she said.

It was an engraving of the head and shoulders of a man in his early thirties. Head held high, with more than a touch of arrogance; darkish hair worn in the Roman manner and inclined to curl; a strong throat rising from a loose collar; a firm jaw and a sensuous mouth. And the nose and eyes—give or take the Dewaine additions—were all mine.

It was an engraving I had seen a hundred times. In print shops, lovingly framed and hung, in the frontispieces of books. There were few men in England, and surely not one woman, who could not have put the name to the face.

"It's unbelievable! Unbelievable!" I breathed.

"It is all here," said Adriana. "His letters, the things that he wrote to Madame. Books he gave her. See . . ."

238

She handed me a calf-bound volume that fell open at the flyleaf, upon which was written, in a wild and dashing script that went with the face in the picture, the dedication: *For cara Marianne, from her devoted husband Newstead. 16.VII.23.*

I turned over to the title page:

DON JUAN
(cantos I and II)
by
George Gordon Noel,
Lord Byron
MDCCCXIX

"Newstead!" I exclaimed. "That was the name of his . . . of Lord Byron's estate in Nottinghamshire."

"Milord gave her the name," said Adriana. "When they were together it was always 'Mr. and Mrs. Newstead.' They met during the carnival all those years ago, at a masked ball at the Fenice. The morning after, they rode together at the Lido, along the sea shore. I shall never forget the expression in Madame's eyes when she come back to the palazzo."

I picked up another framed engraving from the table. It showed the famous poet wearing a military helmet of a flamboyant, antique style.

"He had many other loves," I said.

"Others?—Pah!" Adriana spat out a venomous-sounding epithet in Italian. "The others were nothing! There was only Madame, I tell you. It was a love that outlasted all the others. Milord kept her . . . apart. Secret. It was not the same for her. When he left and went to Genoa, she followed after him. Hers was a love that knew no shame. . . ."

"No shame." I seemed to hear Durward's words: "Love is everything. You should defy God and man and take your love." That was the way it had been with my mother.

"She was with Milord to the last," said Adriana. "She saw him leave Genoa and go to fight and die in Greece."

I looked at the picture again: the fighter in the helmet.

"Milord was all revolutionary," said Adriana proudly. "Here in Venice, when he first came, the Austrians suspected him. And in the end, it was for Greek freedom that he gave his life."

Facts were falling into place, like pieces of a mosaic, and the answers were coming fast. . . .

"That was another bond between them, between my mother and my father," I said. "Their fervour for the cause of freedom!"

"Madame gave her all for the movement to free Venice," said Adriana. "When Milord departed for Greece, she felt that she was carrying on his work here—and it was the same, in spite of her grief and ill-health, till the end of her days."

"And she was once actually arrested by the Austrians," I said.

"That was soon after Milord departed for Greece," replied Adriana. "She was caught sheltering one of our people and taken away."

"And released through lack of evidence," I said, remembering.

"Not so," declared Adriana. "Madame was saved only because she was three months gone with child. The British consul here—Mr. Hoppner, who was a great friend to Milord—made a great protest to the accursed Austrians about her condition and secured her release."

So I had been of some service, after all, to the woman I had never known alive as my mother. In the act of carrying me, she had been saved from imprisonment or worse.

"How Milord rejoiced when he learned of the coming child!" cried Adriana. "He wrote to Madame from Greece. It was to be a boy, he said. Nothing else would do. And the boy was to be named after him. When he had done what had to be done, he said, and Greece was free, he and Madame would marry, and the boy would be his heir."

"She—my mother—also wanted a boy?" I asked.

"Passionately!" cried Adriana. "And none of us had the courage to tell Madame that she had been delivered of a girl-child."

"You mean," I said, "you mean that . . . *she never knew?*"

Adriana drew her breath sharply. "Oh, Miss Button. I have said a bad thing. There are many things you should not have heard!"

I turned my back on her and busied myself in arranging the knick-knacks on the table. The treacherous tears were coming unbidden.

"That's all right, Adriana," I said. "I asked you to tell me all of the truth, and I must accept it. And, when that has been said, I must tell you that I agree that it was best that my mother never knew about me. She . . . needed the baby boy Georgie. She never needed me. And now, Adriana, would you leave me, please? I should like to sit and think for a while."

The woman spread her work-worn hands.

"Miss Button," she said, "you must stay in the Palazzo, and where better than here, in Madame your mother's own room? I will fetch linen . . ." she moved towards the door, and paused there. "I do not think I should have told the truth to Madame," she said, "but my conscience has given me much trouble when I think that I might have told you the secret, Miss Button. You saved my son, my Aldo, and I promised to repay that debt."

"Adriana," I assured her. "It doesn't matter. You owe me nothing."

"I have been punished," she replied brokenly. "My Aldo was killed in the uprising, and my husband died of the fever during the siege, like Madame. Oh, yes, Miss Button, I have suffered for my sins!

"And my debt to you still remains unpaid, Miss Button. But I will repay it. Oh yes, I will repay!"

* * *

So I slept in my mother's bed in the Venetian palace of the Dewaines—my family. And I turned over, in my mind, the answers to all the questions that had clouded my life. Being half a Dewaine was not the only legacy with which I had to contend: there was the dark inheritance that had descended upon me from my father. Small wonder that my life had been such a turmoil, when I compared it with his own: a social outcast driven from his own country; all the violence and the misunderstanding; the restless searching for love and affection that had led him down so many dark and unsavoury paths—I could find some parallels with my own stormy career. He had even stood accused of the carnal love of his own sister. That legacy, at least, I had been spared; Mark was not my half-brother, but my half-cousin.

Not that it made any difference—nor would ever have made any difference. I was nothing to Mark.

I felt asleep with that bitter thought, and woke to see the sunlight streaming in through the windows. Adriana was drawing back the shutters to the new day that burst in upon the room in a glory of blueness reflected from the illimitable Adriatic sky and the shimmering waters of the Grand Canal below. It—the sudden light, the colour and the very feel of it—was curiously not unexpected. It was . . . *familiar*.

Adriana had the answer.

"It was in this room that you first saw the light of day, Miss

Button," she said. "I took you from your mother and laid you in your cot. Here—by the window."

* * *

It was some two weeks later, and I went to visit my mother's grave on the cemetery isle of S. Michele, as I had visited it, rain or shine, on all the days between. This time, I told myself, it would be good-bye. There had been nothing to take me back to England in a hurry; everything to keep me in Venice for a short while. Adriana had begged me to remain at the palazzo, but I had not wished to continue to avail myself of Dewaine hospitality uninvited. I also told myself that they were nothing to me—and knew that I lied.

That morning, two letters from England had arrived for me at the modest *pensione* where I was staying. The first was from dear Mr. Gathercole, sending all love from everyone, and assuring me that I must continue to regard the little shop in Petty Cury as my home. The second was from Mr. Salomon. The gentle-hearted print dealer hastened to tell me—in answer to a communication which I had sent him—that he could perfectly easily arrange for the publication of a slim volume of verse, and that the poet would not be informed that it was being done at my expense. So Stanley's dearest dream was to come true after all—my fortune had done some good to someone. Mr. Salomon went on to say that he was anxious to settle Durward's affairs and to pass over the remainder of the very large sum of money that lay to my credit, and to arrange for further large royalties to be paid to me half-yearly. I had no idea what I was going to do with all that money; it seemed wrong that a person of my modest tastes should be in such a position when so many in the prosperous England of the Great Exhibition year were starving.

I had replied to Mr. Salomon immediately, telling him I would return at once. And now I was on my way to pay my last respects at the grave of the recluse of the Palazzo Dewaine.

A black-plumed funeral gondola was preceding me towards S. Michele; shaping a crabwise course, against the tide, the gondoliers bowing their heads before the wind, towards the isle of the dark cypresses.

The storm that had threatened all morning was closing down upon the lagoon. Low clouds were piling in from the Adriatic, shutting out the sight of the low-lying Lido and the smaller islands between. I told myself that I should be in for a wetting before I arrived back at my *pensione*.

Would I ever return to Venice again? I decided that I would. My memories of this place—though flawed—were all good. The golden days with Durward were pleasant to reflect upon. The warmth of feeling that had grown up between me and the woman who was now revealed as my dead mother—that had been good. And Venice was free of any unhappy association with Mark. He had never come to Venice after all. Throughout the time of my first visit, I had known the delight of serene and untrammelled love for him.

The funeral gondola came close to the cemetery wall, past a lantern raised on a post sticking out of the water. Moments later, it swept alongside a flight of steps that led up to an iron-studded gate. The coffin was brought out and carried, swaying, up the steps and into the silence of S. Michele. Presently, I followed after.

The enclosing walls kept out the blustery wind, but the rain began to fall. I put up my umbrella and set off down the path that led to my mother's grave, down a long avenue of whispering cypresses.

It was a simple headstone of white Carrara marble that had been put there, so Adriana had told me, at Mark's instructions. It carried the dates of her birth and death, and her true name: Marianne Dewaine.

I stood before it for a very long time, scarcely noticing that the wind slackened and thin sunlight had taken the place of rain. The sound of approaching footfalls brought me out of my melancholy reverie, and I turned to see who it might be, since my mother's grave lay at the end of the path, and there were no other graves nearby.

Coming towards me was the slight figure of a young woman in a brown costume and bonnet. Her eyes were upon me with a look of recognition, but it was not till she gave a shy smile that I knew her.

Jessica Dewaine!

"They told me at the *pensione* that you would be here," she said, holding out her hand. "How are you, Susannah, after all these years?"

I took her hand, and she gave mine a small, comforting squeeze. It came back to me then—how, as a sixteen year-old girl in those far-off days at Landeric, she had always given me the impression that she wanted us to be friends.

"I am—well, thank you," I replied guardedly. "And you—and the family?"

"Hester is well and thriving," she replied. "She is growing exceedingly beautiful and turns all heads in Bath, where she is still at school."

"Hester was a pretty and engaging child when I knew her," I said.

Jessica gave a small cough and avoided my eyes.

"My sister Alicia passed away two years ago," she said quietly. "After a long illness, bravely borne. She was always delicate, you know, and I think it sometimes turned her into a very unhappy person."

"I'm sorry," I said.

There was a long silence between us.

At length, she said brightly: "Mark has regained his commission in the Blues. The business of supervising the estates has always bored him. Besides, he says, we are going to have trouble with the Russkies before we are much older, and my gallant brother would count his life wasted if he were not leading the first charge against the Russian Imperial Guards."

"He . . . he must look very fine in his uniform," I said in a small voice.

Jessica smiled. "He does," she said. "But it is a new uniform, for my darling brother has put on a little weight while playing the country squire, and his old tunic did not quite meet across the middle. We are all growing older. You have not changed a great deal, Susannah. Still as striking as ever. Your complexion must be the despair of every woman who sets eyes on you."

I ignored the compliment. A thousand questions were cascading around in my mind. Jessica had been to the *pensione*, to enquire after me. Why? How long had she been in Venice? Was she here on her own?

"I came to see your aunt's grave," I said. It was a pointless and superfluous remark, but it filled the aching gap of silence that suddenly rose between us again.

Jessica paused for a moment, and then she said: "You mean, you came to see *your mother's* grave."

"You know!" I cried. "Of course, you must have known all

244

along. All of you. All the Dewaines!" A great anger and resentment suddenly swept through me.

"No!" cried Jessica. "You are wrong, Susannah. I had no idea that we were cousins—not until Adriana wrote to me about two weeks ago and told me everything. Everything, do you understand? And she said that you were here, in Venice."

I looked at her, and shook my head.

"No. I'm sorry, Jessica," I said. "I'm afraid I don't understand at all. Let me put it this way: immediately after your father's death, your brother, Mark, wrote to me here in Venice, telling me to return to England immediately because he had something that I should hear from his own lips; something, he said, that I should have been told a very long while ago. If you didn't know the secret of my birth, your brother certainly did."

She shook her head. "Mark knew nothing of it," she said firmly.

"Oh come, Jessica!" I cried. "He had heard either one story or the other. If he heard it from the rector, he heard the garbled tale which was the result of the Reverend Mawhinney's misunderstanding: my stepfather told him I was a Dewaine, and he leapt to the conclusion that I was the illegitimate offspring of your father. If, on the other hand, your brother heard the story from Sir Tristan's lips—as a deathbed confession, perhaps—he heard the true account."

I was angry, and I knew it. And, in a perverse way, I was enjoying it. I waited for her to comment. When she did, my stupid anger evaporated like a raindrop before the glory of the noontide sun of high summer.

She began, "My brother wrote to you, asking you to come home . . ."

"Yes?"

"To offer you his hand in marriage."

I felt my face collapse. The tears came. All strength and resolve, all fury and indignation gone, I became like a frightened child that seeks comfort and reassurance.

"Jessica," I pleaded. "I have never knowingly done you any harm in my life. How can you mock me so?"

Her shy eyes were unwavering; her smile all sincerity and compassion.

"Mark loved you from the first moment, Susannah," she said. "I remember it well, all those years ago. You in your rough apron and carrying a tray of drinks, demanding ready money from poor

Mark. He was completely bowled over. When we arrived home, Alicia, he and I went into the drawing room—Hester was not with us, she never knew anything of it. Alicia was storming with fury about you—well, you know how poor Alicia used to go on so. Mark was very quiet and pensive, making no comment. Presently, Alicia rounded on him and said: 'Well, what are you going to do about that insolent baggage, Mark?'

"Mark made no reply for a while, and then he got to his feet and said—I have never forgotten it: 'I am going to watch over her, from afar, and see to it that she comes to no harm. When the time is ripe, and she is grown to womanhood, I am going to try to break through that barrier of resentment and win my way to her heart. And then, my dear sisters, if she will have me, I will marry her and make her mistress of Landeric!' With that, he smiled at the two of us and stalked out of the room, leaving poor Alicia and me gasping after him."

There came a sharp cry from above. A seagull was hovering over the cypressed isle, high above us, balancing in the high wind with tiny movements of its tail and wingtips. To my mind sprang the old Cornish belief that seagulls are inhabited by spirits of drowned sailors.

"Mark really sent for me, to ask me to marry him?" I breathed.

"He gave prior news to the rector," said Jessica. "Called upon him, to inform him that he might well be reading the banns of marriage before long. Mr. Mawhinney, so Mark said, showed a distinct lack of enthusiasm. Mark attributed this to the old man's snobbishness and took his leave somewhat curtly."

Carnal love! The rector had raved to me about carnal love—that had been his great fear. To prevent Mark and me from committing the sin of incest, he had never revealed to either of us the true feelings of the other; but had told me what he believed to be the secret of my birth, in order that I would fall in with his suggestion of leaving the vicinity of Landeric. Quietly, as he had put it, and with dignity. Forever.

To think that my whole life, my whole happiness, had been destroyed by one old man's foolish misunderstanding!

Not to speak of Mark's life and happiness . . .

Jessica continued: "Mark made me his confidante, for we had always been close, the two of us. He informed me every time he saw you, telling me how splendid you always looked; how proud and distant. He tactfully probed the rector about you, and learned to his great satisfaction (for he is a very practical person, for a man) that, despite your humble background, you had been educated as a lady. Imagine his horror, when he returned to Landeric one day to find you established there—all unknowing—as our father's new fancy woman-elect."

"Mark was very cold and horrid to me," I said. "I can scarcely imagine that he could have had much esteem for me then. Looking back, it was almost as if he thought I was a party to the arrangement."

"Men are strange creatures, my dear," said Jessica. "Mark is not one to wear his heart on his sleeve—save on carefully calculated occasions—and he has more than his fair share of the human vice of jealousy. And I can tell you he protected you—oh, how he protected you!—from Father's advances."

"He offered me money to leave there and then," I said.

"When that failed," said Jessica, "he tackled Father direct: told him that you were not to be dishonoured. Father was furious. Threw a footstool at Mark and broke a mirror. Mark even went so far as to tell Father about his feelings for you—but, of course, Father being Father, he simply did not believe Mark."

"I remember that quarrel," I said. "I watched it take place from the staircase window."

"After that," continued Jessica, "Father simply bided his time till Mark returned to his regiment. Only, as we know, Mark not only did not return to his regiment, but he resigned his commission. For your sake." She laid her hand on my arm appealingly. "Oh, my dear. Believe me, he would have asked you to marry him then; but after Father's attack, the physician confided in him that there was no hope—that it would only be a matter of a year, or less, before another seizure would carry Father off. For your sake, and for everyone's sake, he thought it best that you should remain safely in Venice till he could send for you."

The high wind was doing its best to drive away the rain clouds. Against all likelihood, a few patches of cerulean blue were beginning to appear above the domes and towers of the city across the water. The day was changing.

Everything was changing. . . .

"You came to Venice," I said, "to see me and to tell me all this?"

"I set off as soon as I received Adriana's letter," she replied. "I had been meaning to get in touch with you, after I read of your husband's tragic death. I don't know what I hoped to achieve. I scarcely know now. Discovering that we are cousins made things so much easier for me to approach you. So I came, to ask you—to ask you . . ."

"Jessica," I pleaded. "What are you trying to say?"

"He has never forgotten you, Susannah," she said. "After you disappeared and married Mr. de Lacey, he never spoke of you again. But I know my brother—I know nothing has changed for him. He has loved you in all the years between, and he will love you all his life."

The clouds were scattering before the conquering sun. A bird was singing among the cypresses. I thought that Jessica must surely hear my heart beating out for joy.

"If you could find it in you to be kind to him, Susannah . . ."

Her gentle eyes were anxious. I stared at her, a million words of reassurance springing to my lips; but too bewildered and bemused to find utterance. Surely she must guess—surely my answer was written in my face.

"He has never looked at another," she pleaded. "Poor Amelie de Quatrefois was so furious that she went off and married a man ten years older than herself. Surely faithfulness is worth something. . . ."

"Jessica," I cried. "Where is he—where? Is he in London with his regiment? Or is he in Landeric? And did you tell him that I was in Venice?"

"Oh, no!" she replied. "I would never have dreamed of telling him that you were here. I simply said that I felt the need of a vacation and persuaded him to act as escort. He was quite reluctant . . ."

"You are not saying that Mark is here—*in Venice?*"

"Why yes," she said. "This afternoon, I made an excuse to come out on my own, and called in at the *pensione* where you are staying. . . ." Her voice trailed away. She came closer to me, her eyes staring into mine, her lips parted. "Oh, Susannah! Do you really mean? Is it true?"

"Where will I find him, dear Jessica?" I said, taking her hands in mine. "Where is he now, at this moment? Tell me quickly, or I shall go out of my mind!"

"He is to meet me," faltered Jessica, her eyes brimming with happy tears. "At four o'clock. For tea."

"Where, darling cousin Jessica? . . . where?"

"Why, in St. Mark's Square. By the *campanile*."

* * *

The four strokes of St. Mark's great bell of the hours sent the pigeons flying—which was strange, for they must have heard the bell innumerable times. They soared over my head and all about me; circling up and up into the new sunlight of the Venetian Maytime; up past the ancient marble and mosaics, the golden horses and the gesticulating Apostles; then came swooping down again, gliding close past and settling down in front of me; carrying on as if nothing had happened, with their strutting little walk.

The square was crowded, for it was approaching the hour of promenade for the Venetians and it was tea-time for the English.

I began to count, and told myself that I should see Mark before I had reached number fifty. I quickly lost count, and then it became important to walk on the light-coloured flagstones and not on the dark. So intent was I upon this new task that I bumped into a handsome young Austrian officer, who saluted me and apologised most gallantly. I smiled back at him and went on my way.

There was a knot of people waiting at the foot of the *campanile*. None of them was Mark. I walked on, looking to left and right. The important thing—or so it seemed to me—was that I should see him first. A sudden panic, as I decided that I could no longer recall what he looked like.

(Calm yourself, Susannah. He is tall and dark. Hair as dark as a raven's wing and the bronzed skin of a countryman and soldier; green eyes; the Dewaine nose. There, you see! You went into a panic for nothing.)

If he were to see me first, he would have the opportunity of studying me, unseen, from afar. My bonnet—the bonnet that I had bought in rather a hurry, in London—was surely a disaster, and my costume was not the one I would have chosen for a surprise meeting with the man who was the one love of my life. If he saw me first, and decided that, after five years, I did not measure up to his fond memories, might he not go on his way (with or without regret) without making himself known to me? It had all been too hasty, too unconsidered. I should have asked Jessica to arrange a more formal occasion for our meeting again: a tea-party, perhaps, where I should be able to shine in a pretty gown, with the right words and phrases already assembled on the tip of my tongue. Cool, collected Susannah . . .

"No!" I said the word aloud, and an elderly gentleman turned and, after treating me to a sharp stare, raised his hat and went on his way.

No subterfuge. Come what may, there must be honesty. If he still loves me, as I love him, nothing will change it.

"Love is everything," as Durward had said.

I heard a child's cry, and a coloured ball bounced past me and went off across the square. A small boy in a sailor suit broke from his nanny and came running towards me, calling out to me in English.

"Oh please don't let my ball go into the water!"

I picked up my skirts and ran after the still merrily bouncing ball that certainly had sufficient momentum to carry it off the end of the quay and into the lagoon. I was aware that there were several people ahead of me, but they were all with their backs turned towards the bouncing ball.

But not all of them. A tall figure in a broad-brimmed hat moved quickly forward and trapped the ball with his foot. I panted to a halt as he stooped and picked it up; stood there, tossing it gently in his hand, looking left and right for the owner.

He saw me.

I was present at the birth of recognition. I saw it in the green eyes that looked quizzically at me, down the length of his nose—his very straight Dewaine nose.

After recognition came the thought that illuminated his whole expression. It was all I had ever dreamed of and hoped for; all I had ever wanted to see there. It promised a serene joy that stretched out, beyond the limits of hand and eye, for ever and ever.

I was loved.